SILVER OR LEAD

A PALLAS GROUP SOLUTIONS THRILLER

Peter Nealen

CHAPTER
1

"Not again."

The flashing blue and red lights outside the expansive McMansion, where we were supposed to meet Rodney Carr for our first shift as his close protection detail, weren't exactly the same as the cartel shooters' cars outside Camarena's house, but it still didn't bode well. That we should have gone to meet someone only to find that the bad guys had beaten us to the punch *again* was bringing up a bad taste in my mouth. There were two police cruisers, an ambulance, and fire engine parked out front, with yellow police tape around the sides of the driveway.

It didn't help that I was with Ken this time. It had been a few months since Drew had taken a bullet in that hellish fight outside Mazatlán, but it still hurt. He and I had been close as brothers, even as we'd moved from unit, to unit, and finally to contract, since we'd gone through the Basic Reconnaissance Course together, almost twenty years before.

You'd think that I'd maybe start to get used to it, given all the brothers who'd gone into the ground ahead of me, from combat, accidents, sickness, or their own hand. You don't get used to it, though. Never.

"I don't think they're going to let us past the police line." Ken, wiry, half a head shorter than me, and with slightly more gray in his hair and beard than I, was leaning on his elbow in the right seat as I pulled the truck over to the curb. "Still, we'd probably better ask. We haven't exactly been released yet."

I nodded. A contract is a contract, and we didn't know what had happened, so we were still under obligation to meet up with Mr. Carr and assume our duties as his security. I parked the truck, checked that my Glock 19 was still concealed—I had the paperwork, just in case, though Tennessee was now a permitless carry state—and got out. Business was business.

We approached the police line out front of Carr's house, careful not to appear too aggressive or anything other than concerned. We'd had enough dealings with law enforcement over the last year, not all of them friendly, that we were going to step very gingerly until we knew what was up.

A young policeman, his hair cut in a screaming high-and-tight, saw us coming and stepped up to the line of yellow caution tape, holding up a hand. "I'm sorry gentlemen, but I can't let anyone else on the premises at the moment without authorization."

I looked up at the front of the house. Only two stories tall, it still sprawled over six thousand square feet, though at least it had been built in a sort of colonial brick style. "We're with Pallas Group Solutions. We were supposed to meet with Mr. Carr to start work as his security detail at ten." I checked my watch. It was 0945. Fifteen minutes prior. Some habits don't ever go away.

The young man looked us over. Both of us were probably old enough to be his father, though Ken had a good five years on me. We were both still in pretty good shape, though, and neither one of us got so fixated on any particular person or object to stop scanning the street and the rest of the neighborhood.

2

Both of us had been carrying a gun in dangerous places for a living for over two decades and, try as we might to be at least somewhat nonchalant and inoffensive, it showed.

"Well, then, I'm sorry, gentlemen, but I'm afraid I have some bad news." The cop ran a hand over his jaw and looked down at the ground for a moment, his face creasing as he tried to think of a simple and innocuous way to put this. "It appears that Mr. Carr took his own life this morning." He jerked a thumb toward the house. "The coroner's in there right now."

I traded a glance with Ken. Neither one of us was buying it. Not that I thought the cop was lying. As young as he was, I knew enough about law enforcement work that I knew he'd seen some pretty gruesome stuff. Whatever had happened inside, he was apparently convinced that Rodney Carr had, indeed, committed suicide.

We just didn't believe it. Not when he and his company had been looking for a security detail only two weeks before, and especially not after the reasons they'd given Goblin for it.

Pallas Group Solutions wasn't some rent-a-cop agency you went to when you needed some rando in a pseudo-police uniform who'd passed a bottom of the barrel online certification. PGS was the sort of company you went to when you had some serious threats to deal with—war zone level threats.

The odds that the man who'd hired PGS would *coincidentally* end his own life the very day that his security detail was supposed to link up with him were pretty damned long.

"What happened?" I was fishing for information more than anything else, and fortunately, since it was an apparent suicide, the cop didn't think that it was necessarily "part of an ongoing investigation."

"It looks like he used a shotgun." He put two fingers under his chin. "It's pretty messy in there."

I didn't doubt it. I sighed, and it wasn't a put on. "What the hell are we supposed to do now?"

Almost on cue, a Mercedes pulled up outside, and a slightly pudgy, middle aged man got out, dressed in shirt and slacks. He walked quickly toward the police line, pulling his wallet out. "I'm Gage Romero." He offered his ID to the cop. "I just got the call."

The cop started to step aside. "I was instructed to let you in, Mr. Romero."

Romero looked at us with a faint frown. "We're the Pallas Group Solutions contractors, Mr. Romero." We had Romero's contact information, since he was the second in precedence in Carr & Sons Chemical, the company that PGS was formally contracted with. "We just got here. We were supposed to meet Mr. Carr at ten."

Romero glanced at the cop, and I could see the wheels turning behind his eyes. This guy was a thinker, and he was putting pieces together. "You need to come in with us, too." He met the cop's gaze. "These men were hired by Carr & Sons, and I'm now the acting president, so they work for me."

For a moment, it looked like the police officer was about to object, or at least hold us up long enough to get instructions from his higher. But he gave us one more appraising look, then nodded. Either Nashville PD was a lot more professional and willing to give their officers considerable leeway in judgement than some police departments I'd been around, or else Officer Corley's attitude was something along the lines of "better to beg forgiveness than ask permission."

"Just don't touch anything yet." He sounded almost apologetic. "Procedure."

Romero waved a hand dismissively, and we walked past the police line toward the big, oak double front doors, which currently stood open, propped wide so that the emergency services people could get in and out easily.

Our new client slowed as we got close to the steps, turning to face us. "Call me Gage." He stuck out his hand. His grip was firm, his palm more calloused than I would have

4

expected. Romero must have worked his way up the ladder. Either that, or he had some serious hobbies in his workshop.

"Chris."

"Ken."

"Well, Chris and Ken, I'm glad that you got here promptly. Unfortunately, it wasn't in time to do anything about this, but that was the contract. We should have hired you sooner." He lowered his voice. "One of the reasons we came to your company is because you offered more than just close protection. We'll talk more later, but please keep your eyes open in there."

He didn't need to say any more than that. Hell, under the circumstances, he didn't need to say even that much. This was already suspicious as hell to me, and Ken was on the same page.

We'd been at war with some very powerful, very dangerous people since the company's very first contract, with Merritt Strand. It didn't look like that was going to change, and I found myself wondering if we'd taken another contract with another high-profile target, or if our taking the contract had *made* him a target.

Granted, we'd done a pretty good job of covering our tracks on both sides of the border, but there's only so secret you can keep a war, no matter how good you get at misdirection.

Romero led the way inside the house. The entryway was big enough to be a ballroom, almost, and had been decorated in that antebellum South style, chandelier, grand staircase, and everything. It looked like the set of *Gone with the Wind*. Yeah, I'm that old.

There were a couple of cops in the entryway, as well as a couple firefighters, mostly just chatting as they looked around at the extravagant interior. I didn't see any family members, but that fit our initial brief. Carr had lived alone, his estranged ex-wife two states away, and he'd liked it that way.

If it were me, I would have probably moved somewhere a little smaller, but Carr wasn't me.

Now, he wasn't anybody.

Romero looked around as Ken and I stood behind him, then started up the stairs. The only noise in the mansion seemed to be coming from up there.

Carr's study was at the top of the stairs. A couple of EMTs stood outside, their gloves still on but with nothing to do, while a couple more cops and a woman I presumed was the coroner moved around the study, snapping pictures.

As the cop downstairs had said, it was a mess. The ceiling, vaulted and framed with moldings as it was, had been painted with gore, though it had mostly congealed and dried, still sticking hair and bits of bone to the plaster.

The body was on the other side of the huge, antique desk. As we came around, we could see Carr's corpse sprawled on the rug, a dark puddle dried and staining the woven fibers beneath the ruin of his skull. Just enough of his face was still intact that I could identify him, though what a shotgun blast under the chin does to a human skull isn't pretty.

At first glance, it did look like he'd fallen about as naturally as you might expect from someone who had just blown the top of his own skull off while standing at his desk. The shotgun, a Mossberg Shockwave, lay on the rug next to the body.

I looked over not only the corpse but the rest of the room. Something was bugging me about this, and I didn't think that it was just my already existing suspicions.

The coroner looked up. "Nobody's supposed to be in here."

"I'm his business partner and the closest he has to family." Romero stepped around the desk, tilting his head to look at Carr's body. The pain on his face was palpable, and as near as I could tell, entirely real. If he really had been as close to Carr as he'd said, he was feeling it.

There was anger there, too. And I didn't think it was the sort of anger that I'd felt almost every time one of my brothers in arms had taken his own life.

Romero didn't believe this was a suicide, either. Still, he held his peace and waited as the cops and the other emergency personnel finished their work, bagged up the body, wheeled it into an ambulance, and took it away to the morgue. The cops and the investigators spoke with Romero, who seemed to have a power of attorney for Carr, gave him contact info for where he could get more information, and then, though a few of them seemed reluctant to leave a crime scene—even if the crime's only victim was its perpetrator—they cleared out. Romero had a right to be there, and since we worked for him, so did we.

As soon as the cops had left, Romero turned to us. "Okay, here's the deal. I don't believe that Rod killed himself, and I don't think you do, either. This isn't the time or the place to get into why not, but do I understand correctly that Pallas Group trains its contractors as investigators and intelligence officers as well as protective agents?"

Romero had done his homework. "Mr. Walker thought that it would enhance our ability to keep our clients safe if we could build a complete threat intelligence picture of the environment around them. That requires skillsets beyond what are generally characterized as protective measures." I was getting good at the boilerplate.

Romero nodded. "I don't have a whole lot of time, as there are a lot of balls in the air at the moment, but I can stay here for a little bit. Can you take a look around, see if there is anything that would point to foul play?"

Ken looked around at the leftovers of the investigation and the removal of the body. "We can look, but there might not be much of anything left." The crime scene investigation would have either picked up anything or trampled it.

"Just check, if you would." Romero wasn't looking at us, but at the desk and the bloodstain on the rug.

I met Ken's eyes, and we both nodded. We'd split the house between us, and even then, we probably wouldn't have time to look for anything but the most obvious telltales.

Not that those were nearly as easy to spot as you might think or hope. I'd picked enough locks to know that you had to be one hell of an amateur to leave the scratches that some writers describe. If someone had snuck in, murdered Carr and made it look like a suicide, without security camera footage, it was going to be damned hard to prove.

I didn't think that the cops had bothered looking for fingerprints aside from Carr's, given how obvious the setup was.

I went downstairs to check the doors. As I'd suspected, there was nothing that I could point to as slam-dunk evidence of forced entry. More than likely, anyone who *had* forced their way in would probably have posed as delivery drivers or utility workers. There's more than one way to do social engineering.

A sweep of the house didn't turn anything else up, except for the fact that Carr *did* have a security camera system hooked up. Unfortunately, I didn't have the login information, but maybe Romero did.

The two of us met up with the client back in Carr's bloodied study. Ken shook his head first. "Nothing jumps out at me, sir. If they knew what they were doing, even a little, there's nothing we could find on a cursory inspection. Not short of a full forensic investigation is going to turn that up. Fingerprints, hair that doesn't belong, that sort of thing."

Romero was listening, though he wasn't looking at us, his eyes still fixed on Carr's desk and the carnage soaked into the rug behind it. "Maybe I can get the forensics people to take a closer look at the body. If this was done by force, there should be signs, I'd think." He finally glanced at the two of us.

I shrugged. "You'd think." I suspected, even then, that it would be a wild goose chase, quickly shut down by someone higher up in the local government. Not that I was saying Nashville or the State of Tennessee were necessarily corrupt, but I'd seen enough to know that all it takes is one greedy, amoral bastard in the wrong place to turn everything sideways.

"We should probably go." Ken was looking outside. It wasn't noon yet, but if someone *had* bumped Carr off, that probably made Romero the next target on the list.

It took a moment for our new principal to shake himself out of his reverie and nod. "Ken will go with you, sir, and I'll follow." I wasn't going to leave our truck there—it was a company truck, outfitted just about the way that most of us had run our vehicles overseas, back in the day when we'd been working for various three letter agencies around the world—and I doubted that Romero wanted to leave his vehicle behind, either.

With a deep sigh, Romero turned away from the scene of carnage. "You're right. Let's go."

I led the way down the stairs. If Romero was our principal, now—and if he was genuinely concerned that someone wanted him dead—we had a few more precautions to take. I didn't draw my weapon, since there wasn't a need yet, but I pushed ahead, clearing the entryway from a position where I would have my back covered and would have just the right angle to buy myself a second or so to draw my Glock and get to work.

No one had followed us in. Not that I expected it in the middle of the morning, that soon after the cops had left, but I was being paid to be paranoid, so paranoid I would be.

From there, it was a quick movement to the front doors, an equally quick check from inside before I stepped out, and then a sweep of the surrounding neighborhood. The rubberneckers who had been watching the flashing lights had gone back inside, and all was quiet, as you might expect from an expensive suburb of Nashville in the middle of the morning.

I still loitered near the truck, where I could get inside to my Recce 16 carbine and go bag if need be, until Ken had retrieved his own go bag and carbine—the Recce 16 shrouded under a jacket that might or might not conceal it enough that people wouldn't see a long gun in a rich residential neighborhood—and gotten into Romero's vehicle. Romero himself was driving. He apparently didn't want someone else behind the wheel of what had to be at least an eighty-thousand-dollar car. Not that I blamed him, but we'd probably driven more expensive vehicles in our day.

With one more look around the still, quiet neighborhood, I swung into the truck, started it up, and followed.

What new front in the seemingly endless shadow wars of money, drugs, and violence had we just stepped into?

CHAPTER
2

Nick lay in the rocks and the sagebrush, propped up on his elbows with his rifle by his side, scanning the desert and the low bits of fencing running through the cactus, creosote, and sage in the broken, rugged hills along the border. It was getting hot, despite the time of year, and he was glad that the creosote bushes, at least, provided a little shade.

Doug Chen lay beside him, taking his break from observation, resting his eyes. None of them were getting any younger, and time on glass got more taxing with age. That didn't mean Doug was sleeping, though. Nick was starting to doubt that the former Delta operator ever slept more than about four hours a night.

Besides, they were on the border, less than five miles south of Ruby, Arizona. This wasn't a place to sleep.

After the raid on the conclave of cartel bosses, Chinese agents, and Mexican government officials in the hills above Mazatlán, some of the Pallas Group Solutions contractors had stayed in place, keeping an eye on the involved factions of the Sinaloa Cartel to see what would happen next. They'd finished their contract with DFL Shipping in Mazatlán, all without any further incidents, but Goblin, the company's founder and CEO, a former special operations contractor and staffer with at least one three letter agency, hadn't been convinced that everything was over. So, he'd sent Nick and the rest of the B Team to Arizona.

They weren't there as a team, not per se. Arizona Border Recon was a volunteer non-governmental organization dedicated to supporting Border Patrol and law enforcement with recon and intelligence along the border. Goblin hadn't flat-out ordered the B Team to Arizona, but he had put out a call for volunteers, as well as an almost casual comment that anyone who did volunteer might get a bonus. Totally unconnected with taking up with Arizona Border Recon, of course.

Since they were all independent contractors, it was pretty easy to work out. Each man took care of his own application, background check, transportation, gear, and weapons. They weren't carrying PGS Recce 16s. In fact, Nick was running the Frankengun AR-15 he'd built in his garage while he'd still been in 10th Group. He'd lost track of the number of companies' worth of parts in that rifle, and some of them didn't exist anymore. Doug had a Noveske SPR lying beside him. For as expensive as that rifle was, Doug had rattle-canned it, and it had clearly seen some hard use, the paint scarred and rubbed away in a lot of places.

Most of the team was down there, though he didn't know for sure who was on watch at the moment. It felt a little strange, after all this time, not to be working with an all PGS team, but it was necessary for security reasons.

It bothered him that there was one who hadn't come down with them. Maybe it was because Frank Moretti was technically a PGS employee, not a contractor, but there had been an increasing degree of friction between Frank and the other contractors over the last few months. As a man who'd counted Frank a friend for years, Nick wasn't comfortable with the way things were heading.

He blinked and brought his attention back to the scan. It had been too long since he'd been in a long-term OP. His mind was wandering. It was easy to do, once you'd been in place for a while, with nothing going on in the target area. It didn't get any better when he checked his watch. They'd only been in place for about three hours, and they had another six to go before they were relieved.

At which point, they'd go down the hill and rack out in the bush before their turn on observation came up again.

The whole point of having PGS contractors as Arizona Border Recon volunteers was to keep tabs on the cartels and their activities along the border. The C Team was still in Juarez, still running security for Morales Logistics, and simultaneously keeping an eye on the ever-shifting snake pit of narco traffic and violence in that major border plaza. Nick hadn't gotten any solid word, but he suspected that the company had personnel in San Diego and possibly across the line in Tijuana, too.

Going to war with a cartel, which they'd effectively done in the course of defending Strand and the Bowman Ranch, wasn't something you could just dust your hands of, declaring victory after you smoked a few of them. Pallas Group Solutions would have to be forever vigilant going forward, and that was costing the company a lot. The fact that Goblin had put the money and foresight into preparing for just such an eventuality, and was taking lucrative contracts that were mostly going back into company resources for these sorts of operations instead of shareholders' pockets, just told the contractors just how much their boss had been planning this and for how long.

"Still got a long time in place, brother." Doug hadn't turned from where he was leaning back against his ruck, watching their back trail and their flank. He'd sensed more than seen Nick checking his watch.

The two of them had been partners long enough that Nick was starting to get used to Doug's seemingly preternatural powers of observation. It wasn't that the man was a mutant—though sometimes Nick suspected that he was, since he *had* been Delta, had done the Long Walk a *lot* of years ago,

13

and was still capable of running most of the other contractors into the ground—but just that he'd gotten so practiced at observation that his situational awareness just *seemed* superhuman.

Of course, there had been that assault on the line of technicals outside Mazatlán. Doug had almost single-handedly massacred the entire cartel react force, and Nick had only been able to cover his flank and stare in awe.

With a sigh, Nick returned to watching their sector. They were there for a reason.

Time passed slowly. The wind whispered across the desert as he watched the Mexican side of the border. The sun began to dip toward the horizon to the west, and Nick and Doug switched out twice more before anything but the lizards, coyotes, and buzzards stirred out there in the tumbled, wrinkled desert hills.

Nick had just gotten back on the binoculars, doing his first scan, when he saw movement. It was still a good mile on the Mexican side of the line, but it was definitely there. He adjusted his position, steadying the binoculars and cupping his hands around the ocular lenses to shut out as much light as possible.

It took a few seconds to find the source of the movement again. Whoever was down there, they were trying hard not to be seen. Nick and Doug had the advantage of elevation, though, and movement stands out, even if it's camouflaged.

There. A figure in drab, earth-toned clothing climbed out of another gulch, looking around under a dark ballcap for a moment before beckoning to someone behind him and continuing up the hill, toward the border.

Nick kept watching, but he murmured, "Contact."

Doug rolled over to join him, his radio already in his hand. "Talk to me."

"Got six military age males. Two might be coyotes. They seem to be guiding the rest, and they're keeping a lookout. Seem more familiar with the terrain. Dressed in plain clothing that blends in, dark ballcaps. The others are all in civvies. Nothing too bright, but it doesn't look like they dressed for camouflage, either." He paused while Doug passed the information along to the Border Recon command post. "No weapons that I can see."

"Any big backpacks?" The question was sort of the obvious one. If they were moving drugs, then the illegals or mules would be loaded down.

"No. Looks like about three kids and two women, too." Nick kept the binoculars to his eyes, doing his best to keep his emotional reaction tamped down. He was getting a better picture the closer they got. The binoculars weren't quite high powered enough for a whole lot of detail, but he could still read a lot just from body language and the way that the group bunched up. "Looks to me like more migrants."

"Illegals, you mean." Doug's voice was light, but serious. "Don't fall for the redefinition of terms. They're coming across the border illegally, and probably paying a pretty penny to the cartels for the privilege. They're illegals."

Nick let it go. He hadn't intended to get all politically correct. It had just been a term. Doug got touchy about very few things, but stuff like politically-motivated screwing with words was one of them.

After watching the group cross another gully and continue toward the border, Nick was pretty well convinced. "More illegals. Probably going to be indentured servants for the cartel for an indeterminate amount of time, if they make it."

He realized as the words left his mouth that Doug might object to calling it "indentured servitude" instead of "slavery," which really was what it was, but his partner just passed the information along.

"Might have to keep tabs on them for a little while before Border Patrol can pick them up." Doug kept the radio out, having moved to a position where he could sort of look over Nick's shoulder. He had his own binoculars—they were a

Border Recon requirement—and he picked up the little caravan pretty easily. "Far cry from what you boys stopped on the Bowman Ranch, from what I heard."

Nick grunted. A nod wouldn't have worked, not when he was still watching through his binos, and Doug probably wouldn't have seen it, anyway. "Yeah, this doesn't look like the raid force we caught coming across the border over there."

They continued to watch the caravan for the next hour, sending updates periodically as they tracked the illegals toward the nearest road. They were probably expecting a pickup there. They were going to be disappointed.

The sun was just going down when the red and blue lights started flashing on that road. The Border Patrol was on the case. Hopefully with overwatch, though that wasn't a Border Recon task. The rifles at their sides were only for self-defense. Arizona Border Recon gathered and disseminated intelligence. They weren't enforcers.

Nick watched the roundup for a moment. The coyotes had run for it, and some of the illegals, too, but for once there weren't just the two Border Patrol trucks assigned to the interception. Half a dozen agents on horseback were spreading out through the gullies and the hills, forming a pincer that would hopefully round up all of them. Most especially, to Nick's way of thinking, the coyotes.

He'd been a Special Forces soldier. He'd always taken the Special Forces motto, "De Oppresso Liber," "To Liberate the Oppressed," seriously, even when he'd suspected that a lot of his brothers in arms—not to mention his commanders—didn't really. He knew a few people who would think that letting these people in unmolested would count as "liberating" them from "oppression." He'd also been around long enough to know better.

Human trafficking rarely liberated anyone. Those coyotes were getting well paid to deliver underpaid labor at best, outright slaves at worst.

16

He'd seen one of the "rape trees" on the border. He knew what these people were probably in for if the Border Patrol *didn't* take them down.

He finally turned back to their sector. There probably wouldn't be any more traffic that night, not with Border Patrol lights right there on the line. Granted, it was still *possible*. It just didn't seem *probable*, not after what they'd seen over the last few days.

It was shaping up to look like the cartels weren't pushing the war much farther. Not yet, anyway. Between how quiet it had gotten in Mazatlán, and the lack of extraordinary activity on the border, maybe they had bought some breathing room. Not that he thought they'd put more than a small dent in the drug traffic to begin with. That was going to take a lot more than one rogue PMC, no matter how competent and ruthless they might be.

Which only begged the question.

What was next?

Because Nick was damned good and sure that they hadn't won the war yet, and that Goblin wasn't going to sit back and assume they'd done their part.

CHAPTER
3

Romero didn't waste time. The meeting with the entire A Team, Goblin, and a good chunk of the staff of Carr & Sons Chemical went down the next morning, in the main conference room at the headquarters building just across the street from the Tennessee Army National Guard Headquarters.

I'd been in a few corporate meeting rooms before, and this one didn't bring any surprises. Blank, upholstered walls to dampen sound, a big plasma screen at one end, complete with an extensive videoconferencing setup, a long, fake mahogany table—that was probably particle board underneath—and about a dozen cheap but fairly comfortable office chairs.

Ken and I had come in with Romero, to find one of the company execs, Jacob Carr, waiting along with Goblin, KG, Phil, Marcos, Rob, and Custus. The rest of the team wouldn't be there for this meeting, since they were either getting tasked out or were off duty. This was already shaping up to be a large-scale contract, even though we really didn't know for sure what the threat was.

I wondered about that. Was this somehow connected to our secret war with the Chinese and their cartel allies, a war we'd practically stumbled into when we'd taken the contract to protect Strand and defend the Bowmans, against what seemed at the time like just another shady, corrupt leveraged buyout? Or was this something else?

In a way, I realized, as I took a seat and Romero went to speak to Rodney Carr's nephew, it didn't actually matter that much. Not that I was discounting the seriousness of the situation we'd found ourselves in only a few months before. It was a war, and while we'd eliminated some of the coordinators who might be able to bring that war to us and our families, none of us were under any illusions that we'd finished it.

But there's more to any war than just the front line fighting. When the war is a "fifth gradient" war, mostly fought with money, information, subversion, and the occasional outburst of violence that straddled the dividing line between guerilla warfare and crime, sometimes it takes on weird aspects you didn't see coming.

Money being one of the biggest weapons any side in this war could wield, making more of it was a strategic move in and of itself. If this contract was lucrative enough, Goblin was still fighting the war just by putting us on it.

That could go downhill fast. I'd seen it with more than one contract company. Once the higher ups started seeing dollar signs first, things tended to unravel, starting with our pay, leading to lower standards, lower expectations, and finally, a near-complete disregard for the actual mission. Just so long as a few more nickels could get squeezed out for the shareholders.

I didn't think Goblin was going to go that way. Not after what we'd already been through. It was a concern, though. You can know a guy well, until you go your separate ways for a while, and then you find that you don't.

I should have had a bit more faith in him. He'd been setting this game up for a long time. In fact, I was beginning to suspect that he spent what little time he had when he wasn't coordinating paperwork, logistics, intel, and money for our operations in the field looking for the next contract that might put us within striking distance of another target. In a battlespace that was as shadowy and fluid as the 5GW conflict we found ourselves in, that was a hell of a trick.

"Okay, gentlemen, let's get down to it." Goblin was actually the one kicking this off, not Romero. That was interesting. "Yesterday, our client appeared to commit suicide by suck-starting a shotgun barely half an hour before Backwoods and Rip were supposed to meet up with him and start our coverage. Now, that might seem like just another tragic occurrence, no matter what our hard-wired paranoia says. Lots of people are fighting battles nobody sees, and the time they pick to check out doesn't always make sense.

"*However.*" He lifted his spitter to his lips. Years in government service and corporate boardrooms hadn't led him to kick the dip habit. In fact, I thought he'd become even more of a dip fiend since the Bowman Ranch than I'd ever seen him, even back when we'd been contractors in the same car, driving around Baghdad. "While his obituary has already hit the news, and the coroner has officially pronounced it a suicide—not that that speed's suspicious or anything—there are quite a few indicators to make us think that it was nothing of the kind."

"We won't get hard medical evidence that he was held in place and the shotgun put under his chin." Romero's voice was hoarse, and there were deep bags under his eyes. I could attest that he hadn't slept much that night, because Ken and I had been rotating through personal protection for him in his home the entire time. We'd gotten more sleep than Romero had, and that was because one or the other of us was crashing on his couch for a couple hours at a time. "The fact that the coroner already declared it a suicide tells me that much and tells me exactly how far we can trust law enforcement. The line cops are probably good dudes, but somebody's already got the city government by the balls."

He stood and leaned on the end of the table, his back to the plasma screen, which remained dark. I eyeballed the videoconferencing setup, hoping that Romero was sure it was off. "For some further context, I need to tell you about everything that's been going on with the company for the last few months.

"It was decided, about two years ago, that we needed to start 'inshoring' our operations. Carr & Sons started as an all American company, but when the offshoring trend started in the '90s, Byron Carr was advised to shift a lot of the processing operation to China. That was the new market, and the labor was enormously cheaper. It allowed for financial streamlining and kept us competitive.

"The cost has been too high, however. We've lost multiple patents to Chinese intellectual property theft, the quality of the product has slipped... and..." He sighed heavily. "The fact is, we've become a pawn in what Rodney recognized as a low-level war being waged against the United States. We're one more operation effectively dependent on the Chinese Communist Party, an operation providing vital chemicals for American industry and national security. As long as the bulk of our processing—meaning about ninety percent of it—is done in mainland China, Beijing has us over a barrel.

"So, over the last two years, we've started working on bringing that operation out of China. We still can't afford to bring it all the way back into the US yet. That's a hope for the future, but Honduras is a lot closer, a lot less expensive, and not necessarily subject to Chinese interference." I wondered about that, given how extensive we'd heard the Belt and Road initiative was in Central and South America, but I was starting to suspect I knew just why Goblin had gotten us this contract.

"That would be the whole story, except that we know it's not." Romero looked down at the table for a second before lifting his eyes to scan the stony faces around it. None of the PGS contractors were showing our thoughts. We'd all gotten good at that, working for various clients and commands over the years that might just turn around and stab us in the back if they knew just what we were thinking. "Carr & Sons Chemical has always been a private company. We've never gone public, have no stockholders. That's been family tradition since the company was founded, and the Carr family has held to it. We've had to take out loans from time to time, but going

22

public hasn't been on the table." I thought that was a little strange, given the outsourcing to China, but one thing I had learned over the years was that people don't always act consistently.

"Between that fact, and the fact that there hasn't been any public announcement of our inshoring to Honduras, it's a little suspicious that we were approached by representatives of a hedge fund that wanted to buy into the company about six weeks ago."

Goblin was watching the rest of us for a reaction, but again, we were in briefing mode, faces blank as we took in what was being said. A couple used their spitters, but that was it.

"I wasn't there for the meeting, but apparently, they approached Rodney in private and were quite aggressive. He told me that he turned them down flat, said that there was no stock to sell, and that there was nothing to talk about. They got angry and insisted that a partnership was in the company's best interest, but he still told them to get lost.

"After that, the harassment started. Phone calls, attempted break-ins here and at his house. There was a concerted effort to block our purchase of the new facility outside San Pedro Sula, though we got through it, and setup has begun. However, the facility appears to be under threat, which is the main reason why we decided to hire your company. San Pedro Sula has a lot of gang activity, and some of that violence has spilled over into the area of our property. There have been threats and at least one attempt at arson."

Jacob Carr stepped forward. "As Mr. Romero said, we're not convinced that my uncle killed himself. It's even more suspicious that I got a call from some of those same hedge fund people only six hours ago. Almost as if they knew he was dead, and they wanted to get to me while I was still dealing with it."

I glanced at Goblin, who was just watching and listening. He'd probably heard all this already.

The picture was getting clearer, though the mission was going to be anything but. We'd already seen the ChiComs use proxies on top of proxies, but if this was what it looked like, we were going to be shadow boxing with them on a level we hadn't before. This wasn't going to be like hunting Sinaloa narcos in Mexico.

"That's the basic picture, gents." Goblin stepped forward, squirting another blob of dip juice into his spitter. He clearly had few fucks left to give, if he was dipping that hard in a corporate meeting with the client. "I'm pulling the B Team from Arizona here in another day and getting them on a plane down to Honduras. They're going to have some handicaps down there, operating publicly. The violence has, predictably, coupled with government corruption, and since they are so tangled with the problems, they've started cracking down on firearms ownership. So, to start with anyway, those guys are going to have to run with the weapons and ammo they can get from the government."

There was a chorus of groans and muttered curses at that idea. Not only were the options probably going to suck, but every single one was going to be on some government ledger somewhere, subjecting the team to surveillance and harassment.

"Yeah. Not ideal. We're going to work on getting some more hardware down to them, but it's going to be unserialized, throwaway stuff. Doesn't mean it's going to be crap, but it will be stuff that can't be traced back to the company."

I thought it was interesting that he was saying all of this in front of the client. He and Romero must have had one hell of a meeting of the minds over the last few hours. I knew that they'd been on the phone a lot.

"You boys are going to be up here for the time being. We won't do the client a whole lot of good if we secure the plant down in Honduras, but the bad guys get to the company headquarters anyway. So, settle in for a close protection gig." He smiled coldly. "And get ready to put some of that intel

24

collection skillset to good use. I want to know who murdered our original client, and then I want to nail them to the wall."

CHAPTER
4

With the big picture briefing out of the way, we got down to work.

"So, there's been some more information." We weren't at the office anymore. Romero was still suspicious about how the unknown hedge funders had found out about the inshoring to Honduras, and there appeared to be a relatively small circle inside the company that he really trusted. So, we were in the current team house we'd gotten set up in a rental on Wingate Avenue. We weren't all staying there—that would have been a bit suspicious, having eleven grown men in a small house in the middle of a residential neighborhood—but it was a good hub for planning and staging, away from the office.

"Rodney did have security cameras in his house." Romero was leaning against the little mini bar in the dining room, off the kitchen counter. "However, we don't have the recordings. Any of them." He was speaking through gritted teeth. "If they'd just wiped them, we might have been able to reconstruct some of the data, but they didn't just wipe them. They pulled the drives and replaced them with blank ones. The cops didn't even notice, but nobody's going back and investigating."

I raised an eyebrow, glancing at KG. Thickset, balding, and with a placid, almost sad face, Kevin Gates had been around the block. I hadn't been sure about him to start with, but he was strong as an ox and as steady as they came. There was no corporate bullshit with KG. He was concerned with the mission.

It was always good to work with professionals.

"Nobody?" KG sounded about as skeptical as I felt. We all had gotten plenty of experience recently with corrupt government and law enforcement—as far as I knew, the FBI investigation into Merritt Strand was still ongoing, despite the fact that they wouldn't find much of anything—but there wasn't a truly monolithic organization to be found *anywhere*, let alone in the United States. There had to be *somebody* on Nashville PD who smelled a rat.

"Nobody that I know of." Romero was a little annoyed at having to walk back his outrage, even a little. "The case is closed. The DA's said as much. Suicide. Neat, clean, tied up with a bow, done."

I could understand his frustration, but that was also why we were there. "Cold cases have been reopened with sufficient evidence." Moping about what the bad guys had done wasn't going to get us anywhere, unless we really were just supposed to protect Romero and the other staff. "If there's no security footage, what's the new information?"

Romero just looked at me for a second, then sort of shook himself. Almost as if he'd gone down a mental rabbit hole over the security footage and had forgotten where he was going with the conversation. "Right. Okay. So, Rodney had a young protégé, an aide and secretary named Anna Edmonds. She went over to his place first thing that morning, before sunrise." At the raised eyebrows around the table, he shook his head. "I have no reason to believe that their relationship was anything but professional. She is young enough to have been his daughter, and I've known Rodney Carr long enough to be damned good and certain he wouldn't dip his pen in company ink, even if he had a thing for the younger women. Which he didn't. If anything, it was the opposite, even at his age."

"Okay, so, what about this aide makes her of interest to the investigation?" KG was trying to get things back on track.

Romero looked at him with a frown, as if he'd just completely missed the point. "She's probably the last one who saw Rodney alive, aside from his murderers. She's probably the closest thing we have to a witness. She also didn't come to work this morning, and apparently, she isn't answering her phone."

That didn't sound good. "Anything on the police reports to suggest her body's been found?"

"Not yet. And believe me, I've been checking." Romero looked down at his hands. "I've thought about having her declared missing. It might get things moving. On the other hand, I don't know who I can trust."

"Doesn't it take forty-eight hours before the cops will declare someone missing?" Brian asked.

"That's an urban legend." KG shook his head. "Anyone with any experience will tell you to call the cops as soon as you realize you can't locate someone." He turned back to Romero. "I take it you want to keep this quiet, though, just so the wrong people don't figure out that we're looking for her?"

Romero nodded. "If she's alive, anyone who would have murdered Rodney and tried to make it look like a suicide won't have any qualms about silencing her permanently. If she's not, then letting the wrong people know that we're looking for her might give them too much warning."

I didn't say what I was thinking. Nashville was a city of almost seven hundred thousand people. Finding one missing girl was tantamount to finding a needle in a haystack. It wasn't impossible, but it wasn't going to be easy, either. "What do we know about her? Where does she live, any known friends or associates, hangouts, that sort of thing?" May as well get busy.

Romero dug out his phone—less than ideal for the security of the team house, but it couldn't be helped—and started pulling up notes.

***

29

The Avery Apartments looked like a dozen other such apartment complexes I'd seen over the years. A cluster of two-story, beige buildings grouped around the attached parking lots and common yard areas in a sort of distorted L-shape, with a small pool in the larger leg.

Ken and I parked near the managerial office and started across the parking lot toward Edmonds' apartment. We were both dressed similarly, in jeans and untucked shirts that wouldn't look out of place in most major cities in the US, or most minor ones, for that matter. The shirts covered our Glock 19s, but both of us could get them out of the way quickly enough.

The parking space out front of the apartment, with its matching number, was currently empty, suggesting that Edmonds wasn't at home, but we still had to check. With a glance around, just in case someone else was casing her apartment, I moved up to the door while Ken stayed at the base of the steps, watching our surroundings. It looked a little like we were either missionaries or cops, but with one body on the ground already, we weren't going to take too many chances.

I knocked on the door and waited. A part of me rebelled at the fact I was standing right in front of the door, in full view of the peephole, right in the middle of the fatal funnel. After the last few months, getting back on the war zone train, even while most of the work had been Stateside, all the old habits were coming back with a vengeance, and I found that I had to often make a concerted effort to overcome them, if only for tactical reasons. Like blending in when out in public and possibly being observed by the opposition, whoever they were.

It was the middle of the day, and the clouds had rolled in. The complex was quiet, except for the sound of a crying baby coming from one of the nearby apartments. I glanced out at the parking lot as I waited, scanning the parked cars and SUVs, watching for the surveillance that *had* to be there.

Turning back to the door, I knocked again. Still no answer.

"Well, it was a long shot." Ken hadn't moved. "If she's not answering her phone, the odds that she'd be at home were pretty long."

"It's a start, though." I passed him as I came down the steps.

He grinned in that salt-and-pepper beard of his. "I ain't criticizing, brother. Just observing."

I shook my head. "Let's go find the manager."

***

The manager wasn't much help. She didn't keep track of tenants' whereabouts, and she was almighty suspicious of the two men asking about one of them in the first place. Even after we explained that Edmonds hadn't shown up for work and wasn't answering her phone.

I wasn't sure if the manager was trying to be protective of her tenants, or just was annoyed that we were taking up her time. Either way, we weren't getting anywhere, and so we left.

The next few stops weren't much more fruitful. Edmonds seemed to have led a fairly reclusive life outside of work, and we'd only been able to identify a few hangouts and a small circle of friends and relatives from her limited social media. I didn't know what she did in her spare time, but it wasn't spending all her time on the internet. That was good for her from a certain point of view, but for gathering intelligence that might help us find her, it sucked.

Two of those friends we were able to reach out to. Neither one was any help. They didn't really know her all that well and hadn't seen her in days.

The last option we had appeared to be a relative. Maybe a sister? It was hard to tell.

We had to reach out through social media. Noah Radford, our team intel weenie—and he was an intel geek's intel geek—could fairly easily gotten us a phone number, address, anything we wanted. That might become necessary, but it would probably be better to avoid appearing creepy to start. We had to win this woman's trust, first. Sometimes that means holding back from what you *can* do.

She hadn't answered the message immediately. When she had, though, I thought I saw what had happened. Her reply was short and to the point. *Meet me at Cumberland Park in one hour.*

"That was quick." Radford was frowning at the screen as he sipped from his barrel of energy drink. The kid drank so much caffeinated sugar water that I was still astonished his heart hadn't exploded. And that's coming from a guy who'd washed down Hydroxycuts with a Red Bull in Iraq.

"My guess is she tried calling Edmonds and got no answer." I straightened from where I'd been looking over his shoulder at the screen. "She's smart, though. She wants the meet in a public place with long sightlines."

"You think we should both go?" Ken was already looking at the map on his phone. Our work phones were as bulletproofed as we could get them, though no security is flawless. Still, they provided a much more unobtrusive way to handle some of the stuff we needed to do, like take photos and use maps and GPS, than most other devices.

I shook my head. "She's going to be nervous enough as it is. Better if I meet her alone."

"It's a risk." Ken wasn't comfortable with this. If there really were murderers involved who were capable of suiciding a man in his own home and taking the evidence, they might not balk at a hit in a city park.

"Maybe." I was, frankly, kind of ambivalent about the whole thing. It did *seem* like there was some skullduggery going on, but so far, we had only circumstantial evidence.

There's only so far you can carry paranoia, even for a guy like me. There comes a point where you have to take a step back and realize that even the most competent and nefarious of antagonists can't be everywhere and see everything. And acting like we were waiting for the hammer to drop all the time would only stand out and attract attention, some of which was probably hostile.

"Let's go. It's going to take most of that hour to get to Cumberland Park and get set up."

***

Cumberland Park was essentially a couple of big, circular grass lawns, surrounded by walkways, on either side of a big, industrial style pavilion, under the shadow of the Korean Veterans Memorial Bridge on one side and the John Seigenthaler Pedestrian Bridge on the other. It felt kind of hemmed in and in the low ground to me, but it was where Sarah Kellerman wanted to meet, so that was where we were meeting.

I had my back to the river, leaning against one of the shiny steel pillars that held up the oval pavilion roof, watching the handful of pedestrians making their way through the park. So far, I'd seen a woman with a stroller, two younger women jogging, and an older gent walking his dog.

None of them were obvious threats or surveillance assets. Didn't mean they weren't less-than-obvious threats or surveillance assets. But if they were, they were uncommonly good at hiding it.

While a good surveillance operative can hide what he's looking at, nobody's perfect, and everyone has a tell. Any poker player can tell you that. Someone on surveillance, who's serious about it, isn't going to be so focused on avoiding detection that they're never going to look up and around. None of the people I'd seen so far had paid the least bit of attention to their surroundings. The women hadn't even looked at me, which wasn't particularly wise on their part, but still made it seem a lot less likely that they were there to spy.

Now, if they came back through more than once, *then* I'd sit up and take some more notice. A lot of surveillance detection boils down to checking correlation over time and distance. I wasn't moving, so I had to keep track of who went by.

My phone vibrated. *Anything?* Ken wasn't in the park, but he was close enough to intercept if something went sideways. So were Phil and Marcos, another block over on the other side of the park.

Not yet.

I looked up as a figure approached. *Stand by.*

Sarah Kellerman didn't *quite* look like her photos on Edmonds' social media posts, but that wasn't surprising. Most of those photos had been taken at some party or another, so both women had been dressed up and made up, and there's usually some distortion introduced by the camera that doesn't transfer to real life. Still, she was easy enough to recognize. Late twenties, early thirties, brown hair, reasonably fit, pretty enough, though she was now wearing a look of worry that added years to her face.

"Are you Chris?" Radford might have done most of the legwork, but I'd been the one to make contact, since I was sort of spearheading the investigation element. The four of us—Ken, Phil, Marcos, and me—had gotten that job, since the other six on the team needed to work protection for Romero, the junior Carr, and some of the rest of the staff. We were getting spread a little thin again, though most of us had gotten used to that a *long* time ago.

"That's me." I levered myself off the pillar. I didn't bother to extend my hand. Under different circumstances, it might be a good idea to put her at ease, but she was nervous enough, and this meeting was irregular enough, that I didn't want to spook her. "Have you heard from Anna?"

She shook her head, folding her arms around her. "I haven't, and I tried three more times on the way here. It's not like her not to answer the phone. We're really close, and she always calls me back if she can't get to the phone right away."

"Have you seen her since yesterday?" I had to be quick, though the issue of getting Sarah to trust me was also foremost on my mind. I couldn't come out and tell her that if we didn't find her in another twenty-four hours, she was probably dead, but it was starting to look that way.

"I haven't. That's not all that strange." She was studying me, while I kept my eyes on her but still glanced away to check our surroundings from time to time. That was another calculated risk. I didn't know this woman from Eve, and if I spooked her, this could easily fall apart, all without the presumed bad guys even knowing about this meeting. "She's very dedicated to her work and she's pretty introverted. She doesn't hang out a lot. The phone thing, though…" She trailed off, studying me. She was worried, all right, and not just about where Anna was. She was wondering about me.

I stand about six foot one, still in good shape, though with more gray in my hair and beard than was there a few years ago. I sure wouldn't pass for a social worker. Maybe an undercover cop, though most cops I'd known lacked some of the edge that guys in my line of work carry around with us. I was a threat, and she sensed it.

I wasn't a threat to her or her sister, but she didn't know that. All she knew was what her instincts were telling her.

Which way she'd jump was going to depend on what she thought about those instincts. No one is entirely beholden to their emotional reactions. That's a choice we make. And she was about to have to make that choice, whether or not she'd ever really thought about it.

"You're a private investigator?" I'd told her that much over messenger.

"Among other things." I nodded, hopefully reassuringly. "I've got some experience in hostage rescue, too."

"You think she was kidnapped?" The fear was getting more tangible in her expression and her voice.

I thought about it. "It's possible. I don't know that for sure, though. She may be a witness to a crime, and she might be in hiding. If she is, then…" I had to think of how to frame this. "It's good if she's in hiding. Much better than if she's been kidnapped. If the criminals involved know or suspect that she saw or heard something, though, she could still be in danger. And unless we know for sure that she's hiding out, we have to assume that she's a target."

She looked out past me toward the river, chewing her lower lip, thinking it over. That was a good thing, I thought. She wasn't watching me intently anymore, which suggested that I'd won at least a bit of her trust. I wasn't sure how, since all I'd been able to give her were suppositions and speculation, but it seemed to be working.

I hoped I wasn't overstating the case, either. If I was, that could backfire in a whole other set of ways.

Finally, though, she turned back to me, searching my face as if looking for some reassurance that she was about to make the right decision. Then she reached into her purse, pulled out a small notepad, and wrote an address on it before ripping out the page and handing it to me. "I'm trusting you. If anything bad happens, I'm calling the cops and giving them your description, you understand?" She held onto the note for a moment before letting me take it, fixing me with her eyes. "She's my sister. She's the only immediate family I have left."

"I understand." I looked at the address in my hand.

"It's a family cabin, up by the Natchez Trace. If she was going to go hide out somewhere, it's the first place I'd think of." She had folded her arms again and was still searching my face.

I felt like I needed to give her some reassurance. It meant telling her more than I probably should, but if Sheriff Hernandez hadn't made an issue of it, she probably wouldn't. "Just a few months ago, I went into a cartel kill house and got a young girl out, probably half your sister's age. Trust me, ma'am. This is what I do."

It took a long moment before she nodded. "I'm counting on you."

"Thank you." I pocketed the note. "But keep the cops on speed-dial, just in case." I turned and walked away, feeling her eyes on the back of my head the whole way.

CHAPTER
5

Nick gripped the front of his shirt with two fingers and flapped it away from his chest. "Feels worse than Mazatlán."

"It is." Doug, for his part, seemed unfazed by the heat or the humidity. "We're farther south and almost as close to the ocean. It's gonna be hotter and muggier."

Nick glanced at his partner. Doug was Doug. Clean shaven, since his genes seemed to preclude much in the way of facial hair, he watched the city go by from behind glorified hipster sunglasses. Nick had never asked just how many countries Doug Chen had operated in, since he was pretty sure the older man couldn't tell him. They all had things that still fell under the NDAs they'd signed when they'd been working for the US government. Somehow, Nick still suspected that Honduras wasn't nearly as new to Doug as it was to most of the team.

There'd been a time when it would have been almost a second home. The guys who had trained him, the generation of SOF troops from before the GWOT had kicked off and given most of these men their combat experience, had done most of its work in Central and South America.

After Mexico, Nick wasn't sure if that had been the relative paradise that he'd always believed it had been while he'd been deployed to Afghanistan, Iraq, and a few other equally shitty desert countries in Africa. The narcos could give the jihadis a run for their money in the savagery department.

He didn't know for sure what kind of cartel activity they could expect in Honduras, but he'd read the briefing materials. Not only was it on the cocaine route from Colombia and Venezuela, this was a battleground between *Mara Salvatrucha* and *Barrio 18*.

He suspected that he was going to miss the sectarian fights between Sunni and Shi'a soon.

The trip from the airport to the hotel didn't last that long. It wasn't that far. They passed between an industrial complex and a residential neighborhood before turning off the main highway. Nick watched both sides of the four-lane highway as best he could, taking in the environment, trying to get some feel for the atmospherics.

San Pedro Sula wasn't as much like the Middle East as even Mazatlán had been, though there were still some similarities. The houses were mostly cinderblock, plastered over, and while they were generally more colorful than any Middle Eastern buildings Nick had seen outside of Iraqi Kurdistan, and had peaked roofs to let the rain run off, there was a certain dinginess that he'd now seen across the Third World. The curbs were more overgrown than they would be in the desert, but since there was jungle all around San Pedro Sula, that shouldn't be any surprise.

Rounding a tall, green hill, they moved through a warehouse district and turned into the Hotel K-Lisma, the three SUVs pulling into the parking lot, sheltered from the rest of the city by the elaborately landscaped, impeccably painted, green, red, and yellow stone and brick buildings. Nick's eyes narrowed a little as he saw that they were the only vehicles in the lot. Were the PGS contractors the only guests in the hotel?

A vaguely familiar figure stepped out of the office and lit a cigarette. He looked like he was almost Doug's height, if slightly lighter, and he had long hair, walking with a bit of a bowlegged swagger. He leaned back, letting his hair fall over his shoulders as he blew smoke into the blue sky.

"I'll be damned. Figaro's here." Doug shook his head as he pushed the door open. Nick joined him, coming around behind the SUV as the others climbed out of their own vehicles.

"Howdy, boys." Nick knew now why he'd thought he'd recognized the man. It had been a long time since Kandahar. Vern Vargas had been kicking around the contracting world so long that Nick honestly couldn't remember which service he'd been in before. "Sorry for the sudden appearance, but there was a lot to do, so I had to get down here with a quickness." Vern spoke with a drawl that Nick had never quite been able to place. It wasn't Texan, it wasn't Southern, and it wasn't Plains. It was…Vern. "There's been a little bit of a shakeup. Casper's gone on to a different tasking, so I'm taking his place."

Nick was simultaneously relieved and disappointed. Relieved, because he no longer had to worry about the growing friction between Frank Moretti and the rest of the team. Disappointed because it meant that the man hadn't been able to get over his own ego check, at least not fast enough for Goblin's tastes.

Vern beckoned inside. "Come on. We've got some things to figure out, then you boys have some errands to run."

Nick stifled a groan. He'd been worried that this had gotten laid on so fast that they'd have to set things up on the fly once they got on the ground, and it looked like he'd been right.

Doug just shrugged. He'd been all over, seen it all. He'd probably had to set up more than one operation from scratch. Nick forced his own disappointment down, recognizing it for what it was. This was the job. This was the work. It wasn't all being high speed and snooping around with a gun. That was part of it, but there was always a lot of legwork and foundation building that had to happen first, and in PGS, they rarely had the support network established to take care of it without the operators needing to go do all the tedious, dirty, boring stuff themselves.

It was like being back on an ODA, setting up a FOB from dirt. Not that he'd actually had to do that in the real world when he'd been in 10th Group, since they'd just been rotating in on already established FOBs in a counterinsurgency environment that had been in place for years ahead of time. Still, he'd had the training, and even if he hadn't, some of this stuff was just common sense.

They followed Vern into the conference room on the first floor. It was smaller than most that Nick was used to Stateside, but still clean and comfortable. More so than most of what he'd seen in Mazatlán.

There was no projector, no plasma screen with briefing slides set up. Not even a briefing packet. Vern just went to the head of the meeting table and leaned on it, looking around at the men with duffels and backpacks.

"I don't know all of you, but I know a fair few. What's up, Salt? Frog." He squinted at Nick for a second before he snapped his fingers. "Croak! Been a long time. Okay. Down to business." He looked around the room again. "We'll go out to the plant here in a bit. We'll be staying here indefinitely; rooms are paid for by the month. The hotel staff's happy to have the clientele. Things have not been good lately. The gang wars haven't slowed down, and this hotel doesn't exactly cater to the people desperately trying to get out ahead of those gang wars.

"Once we get everybody checked in, we'll drive to the plant in single vehicles. A motorcade will be a target, at least in a couple of the neighborhoods we're going to pass by. Especially once they figure out where we're going. A low profile is going to be the best way to go here.

"Most of the paperwork is done, of both the licit and illicit varieties, so weapons should be available in the next week. Trust me, that's fast as hell here. Everyone's going to have to go get their own. I tried to see if I could get a mass shipment, but the government's being ornery. Pallas Group can't purchase weapons locally as a company, at least according to the Honduran bureaucrats I've had to deal with, but each contractor can purchase one for self-defense." He pointed to a box on the table. "It's all going to be with company funds, though depending on how conciliatory the folks at La Armeria are feeling, we may end up having to reimburse for them.

"Weapons will be limited to pistols for the time being. If you can, get Glocks. La Armeria has a lot of them, so we can maintain commonality of magazines and ammunition. Watch what you're picking up, make sure they're all 9mm. I know, I know. I'm a 10mm guy, myself, but the nines are the most common, so we're sticking with them for ammo compatibility.

"We do have comms, though they're not the greatest. So, we're working on getting mesh network nodes moved in. That's going to take a few days. Same with the drones. Drones are a little tricky here; whether or not they're legal unregistered seems to depend on which bureaucrat you're talking to, and how much money he wants. We'll have to feel that out.

"There are cameras on the plant, though coverage is still limited, and the command post is a glorified mop closet." He sighed. "We're going to be roughing it for a while, fellas. The facility is really new, and there isn't even a decent perimeter fence. Some of the posts are up, but the wire's late."

"I've got a question." Saul Drake stood probably a head taller than Vern and was not only the biggest man in the team, but carried the most authority by sheer weight of his presence. Casey Moore would have contested that, but Casey still hadn't quite gotten over the fact that he wasn't a Sergeant Major anymore. Yet even Casey would back down when Saul turned that heavy-lidded, cold as the Arctic Circle stare on him. Nobody wanted to cross Saul. "What are we supposed to do if we take contact, and weapons are still a week out?"

Vern smiled bleakly. "We've got some good lengths of pipe."

Nick almost flinched, waiting for Saul's acerbic reply, but Vern looked so tired and resigned that the big man held his peace. "I know, man. I know. Like I said, we're roughing it for a bit, which means we're going to have to get MacGuyver inventive for a while."

Saul looked around the team with that look that was simultaneously annoyed and ready to come to Vern's defense if anyone started bitching too loudly. Generally speaking, despite the odds they'd found themselves up against over the last few months, the Pallas Group Solutions contractors had found their situations fairly well set up. This was the first time they'd ended up on the end of a long supply line, without a government backing it up, this far from home. "Well, let's get checked in and then get over there and take a look around."

***

The plant might still be incomplete, but it already sprawled across what had been a farmer's field until recently, a maze of pipes and tanks that looked like an industrial nightmare, surrounding the blocky central building, constructed of concrete and corrugated sheet metal. Just looking at it gave Nick the willies, especially as he considered all the ways that someone could cause a catastrophic failure if they got too close. And without a fence, that was going to be interesting.

His initial impression from the briefing in the states had been that the plant was closer to the city itself. He'd been a bit worried about the location, as there was an irrigation ditch along the back side in that position, and only one way in or out. Now that he was actually on site, looking at the overall position and the neighborhoods to southwest and north, with some standoff through the fields but not that much, he was starting to think that maybe the cul-de-sac, hemmed in by an irrigation ditch, wouldn't have been more defensible.

"This sucks." Casey couldn't keep it in anymore. "We need at least another team and a whole container's worth of gear."

"Well, we don't have it." Saul beat Vern to the punch. "So, as our Marine brethren would say, we have to adapt, improvise, and overcome."

"We'll have to set up regular patrols, in some force." Vern was looking at the scene along with them. "None of us present the sort of target that either MS-13 or Barrio 18 tend to go after, and in enough numbers, even with improvised weapons, we should present at least some deterrent." He pointed to the cyclone fence posts that had already been installed. "If we do some digging out there after dark, we might get some obstacles in while we wait for the wire."

"Do we have any floodlights?" Carl was one of the newer guys on the team, though he'd proved himself in LA and Mexico, and he'd had a decent amount of experience under his belt before he'd even come to PGS. That was kind of expected, but there was still a tendency to view a newcomer as an FNG until he proved himself in *this* team.

He also didn't sound like he expected floodlights to deter *mareros* all that much. But every little bit helps.

"There is lighting on the plant, but we've also got a few generators with lights." Vern seemed to have been expecting the question. "We've got enough illumination to keep anyone from getting inside the perimeter without being spotted. How useful that's going to be…" He spread his hands.

"Well, let's get the full tour, so we can figure out where we need to cover and where we can fall back to." Doug rubbed his hands together. "Provided we don't all go up in a fireball…"

CHAPTER
6

It was a long drive to the Edmonds family's cabin. The place was up in the hills, on a backroad leading off the Natchez Trace Parkway, way back in the woods. The deeper we got into the trees, rattling and bouncing on a dirt road that steadily got less and less "improved," the less I thought we really had that much to worry about. Who could know that Edmonds had a family cabin back this far, and even if they knew it existed, how would they find it?

I reminded myself, as the truck rocked over another bump, where someone had tried to repair a pothole and gotten a little too enthusiastic about it, that if we could find it, so could they.

Whoever "they" were. This didn't feel like the hits on Strand. Archer and his cronies had hired *Mara Salvatrucha* hitters to murder Merritt Strand and get him out of the way for their land and mineral grab on the Bowman Ranch. The *mareros* were vicious, but not particularly subtle, and we suspected that they'd relied on Archer's government contacts for intel. Whoever had offed Carr—presuming that it had been a murder and not just a suspiciously timed suicide—was considerably lighter in their touch.

Ken was holding onto the "Oh Shit" handle as we bounced our way along the road, the undercarriage creaking and groaning as we rattled down the road. We weren't alone.

Phil and Marcos were about a quarter mile behind us, and they were only that far out because we were being very careful, in case someone was watching our movements. I could almost hear Phil cussing the road from there.

I don't know what made me stop, probably another quarter mile from the cabin itself. Maybe I'd seen tire tracks. Maybe I just had a hunch. I know it wasn't what I told Ken by way of justification next, though that didn't mean it was wrong. "If she's scared, and armed, just rolling up in front might not be a good idea."

Ken didn't seem to doubt my reasoning. Either that, or he was getting the same sort of weird heebie-jeebies I was.

I'd experienced this sort of thing before. No reasonable explanation I can come up with for it. Just a hunch, a feeling that things were about to go pear-shaped, even though I couldn't see or hear anything that might have triggered it. Hell, it had happened on one op in the Marine Corps, before we'd even left the wire. I never entirely relied on it, but when I had the option to approach the objective more carefully, I was going to take it.

Pulling over to the side of the road, I parked the truck and got out, pulling my bag out of the back. The company's Recce 16s didn't have the folding stock adapters that some of us had started using on our personal rifles, so I'd had to break the weapon down to fit it in the pack, but if I needed it, at least I'd have it, and it wouldn't be as obvious as walking through the woods with a chest rig and weapon. There was still some subtlety needed here.

After all, I didn't *know* that there were bad guys in those woods. And if we came out of the trees looking like a redneck infantry patrol, then *we*'d probably turn into the bad guys to Edmonds.

Sometimes it sucks, dealing with people who really aren't read into reality.

We waited at the side of the road until Phil and Marcos pulled up in an equally dusty Ford Explorer. Phil stuck his head out of the driver's side window, looking around the woods for a second. "What's up?"

"Heebie-jeebies." I didn't need to say anything more than that. Phil just nodded, killed the Explorer's engine, and rolled out with his own rifle bag. We were all rolling low profile at the moment. Nashville was far from perfect, but it wasn't a war zone, either, and we'd had to keep our profile as nonthreatening as possible most of the time in Juarez, too.

"'Heebie-jeebies?'" Marcos wasn't as tuned in. "Is that what we're basing operational decisions on?"

"Don't discount the heebie-jeebies." Phil slung his rifle bag on his back and checked his Glock. "My platoon dodged an ambush because the gunner in the lead vic got spooked."

Marcos just shook his head, but he didn't say anything as he grabbed his own gear. Once they were ready, I led the way into the woods.

It was tough going. Not so much because there was a huge amount of undergrowth, though there was. It was more because the woods were so thick that I couldn't see more than about ten to fifteen yards, and I really didn't know the terrain that well. Without a map—that was an oversight—there wasn't a good way to terrain associate, and I could pretty easily get turned around.

The only alternative was to handrail the road, so that was what I did, keeping about ten to fifteen yards off and moving through the woods parallel to it as best I could.

It was still almost impossible to stay quiet, especially since we could only afford to move so slowly. If Edmonds really was in danger—and I was fully aware of just how ephemeral my suspicions were—then she might not have a lot of time.

Presuming she was still alive.

I ducked under another low-hanging branch and almost got stopped cold as it snagged my rifle bag. I had to back up and drop lower to get under it and keep going. Staying quiet was almost a lost cause, between the thick carpet of dead leaves and the branches we had to get through and past. Fortunately, I hadn't heard anything yet that might make me think that we'd been heard.

About ten minutes after we'd left the vehicles, I looked up and saw the cabin through the trees ahead. It wasn't where I'd assumed it was; if I hadn't handrailed the road, we really *would* have gotten lost. *Need to practice the old land nav some more, Chris.* Slowing down, I moved up to the edge of the trees and got low, dropping to a knee behind one of the bushier trees. There weren't that many of the gnarled old behemoths in those woods that might provide some cover. The forest was just too thick for that kind of growth. So, concealment was going to have to do.

And I could already see that I'd need it. That formless, sourceless sense of unease hadn't steered me wrong.

There were two SUVs parked out front, in addition to an ancient, rusty Scout. The Scout had to be Edmonds' vehicle. The other two were an Explorer and a Nissan Pathfinder, both considerably newer, if dusty from the drive. They had out of state plates, too, one from Kentucky, another from Arkansas. Probably rentals.

If Edmonds was hiding out, I doubted these were friends. Unless she was a lot dumber than I thought—and not answering her phone when even her sister called didn't fit that profile—she wouldn't have told anyone where she'd gone. Which meant that either there was a tracker on her, or they'd done a deep dive and put some pieces together.

Movement. Someone was coming around the back of the cabin. I stayed completely still, careful to only breathe through my mouth. I was less than twenty yards away. Nose breathing can whistle and make more noise.

The man was medium height and slender, wearing a black polo shirt and jeans. The butt of a SIG P320X stuck out of his waistband, next to a reload in an inside the waistband holster. The way he carried himself was vaguely familiar, but probably because I'd known guys who would have taken a hitman contract without a second thought. In fact, I'd known one who'd gotten rolled up for attempted murder for hire in Nashville, itself, only a couple years before.

Not everyone of the highest integrity or morals gets into this business.

I didn't recognize this guy, but that wasn't a huge surprise. As small as the contract world can be, it's still big enough that you can't know *everybody*. There are too many vets out there, too many contracts, too many unstable, shithole countries where security is needed.

The man came around to the Explorer, dug around in the back, pulled out a tacticool black backpack covered in MOLLE weave, and headed back toward the rear of the cabin.

I didn't know what he was up to, but I didn't like it.

A glance at Phil, who had come up next to me, confirmed that I wasn't the only one. His hawkish face was hard, his eyes watching the man in the black polo with unblinking intensity.

If this guy was up to what we thought he was up to, we were going to end him. With a quickness.

As soon as he'd disappeared around the corner, I was easing my rifle bag off my shoulders. I still had to move slowly, since we were so close that if I made too much noise, we could end up being compromised before we were ready to move.

Then I heard a high-pitched yell, suddenly cut off, and decided that this was going to have to happen the quick way. I lowered the bag the rest of the way to the leaves—the weight and bulk were just going to get in the way—drew my Glock, and started to get up.

Phil cursed under his breath but did the same. There wasn't time.

"Marcos, you stay here on overwatch." Phil clearly wasn't comfortable with going into that without *someone* having a long gun. Since we didn't know what kind of hardware the bad guys might have inside—or even how many there were—that was reasonable, but we were out of breathing room. Or, rather, Edmonds was. I just hoped they hadn't killed her just then, though it had sounded more like a hand put over a mouth instead of a killing.

While Marcos practically ripped his go bag open and dragged out the upper and lower of his Recce 16, Phil, Ken, and I pushed out of the trees, our Glocks up and searching for targets.

We moved fast to the corner of the cabin, pausing just long enough to check our surroundings and make sure we weren't about to get walked on by some hitman coming out of a door or around a corner. I could hear voices around back, but there were two windows to get past first.

One thing at a time.

I pied off the first window, peering in over my pistol's sights to see what looked like a rustic bedroom, the only light inside apparently coming from that very window and an open door onto a short hallway beyond. There was no one in the room. I kept going as Ken took up security on the window behind me.

Just before I reached the second window, I heard a voice raised. "These fucking mosquitos are driving me nuts. Why don't we just do it inside? How many people go outside to do themselves, anyway? Are *you* planning on coming back to use this place as a vacation spot, Cooter?"

"Don't fucking call me that."

"Oh, that's right, I forgot. Sorry, 'Peaches.'"

"You motherfucker…"

"I'm gonna bury both of you sorry cocksuckers if you don't shut the fuck up." The voice was deep and commanding, but with an edge of something else in it. It kind of reminded me of Casey, only worse. "Jock's right, though. It makes more sense to go inside. We don't want her to just disappear. Then there's a search, and questions get asked. She slits her wrists in the bathtub, and it's real sad, close the book and get on with life." There was a grunt. "Let's go, honey. Too bad for you, but we'll make it as painless as we can."

We had a little time, but we still had to move fast. Instead of bothering to pie off the second window, I just ducked low and moved quickly to the corner.

They'd been closer to the back porch than I'd thought. By the time I eased my Glock and one eye around the corner, they were already going through the door and inside. None of them were holding security. They thought they were all alone and in the clear.

That was probably going to be our one advantage.

The back porch was looking out over a clearing in the woods. Not a big one, but picturesque enough, opening on the slope of the hills behind. The porch itself was covered, with a couple of old lawn chairs set on the planks, facing a fire pit in the grass just beyond.

Two windows and the back door faced the same clearing. Which meant we were just going to have to move fast, get across the opening and through the door as quickly as possible. Speed, surprise, and violence of action were about to be the only thing keeping Anna Edmonds alive.

Especially as I put a boot up on the porch, and the plank creaked like a door in a haunted house.

In training, I might have frozen, as every cuss word I knew went through my head. Fortunately, I'd trained enough that I didn't freeze, but launched myself onto the porch as the guy in the black polo turned to look, locking eyes with me through the window, which looked in on the living room.

He was the rearmost, with a big, barrel-chested man going to fat hauling Anna Edmonds, gagged and zip-tied, by her wrist toward the bedrooms in front, and a red-haired, pencil-necked dude off to the left.

Black Polo's eyes widened as he registered not just me, but the weapon that was currently indexed on his T-box.

Now, if I'd been on my own, I might have been in trouble, and Anna Edmonds in even more trouble. But Ken and Phil were right there with me, weapons leveled.

I was on the outside, so I started moving, taking the risk as I broke contact just long enough to get to the door. That wasn't the best of calculated risks, because a moment later, Phil's Glock barked, and glass shattered.

I yanked the door open, keeping my own Glock leveled at the opening, punching it up and out as the door swung open, searching out targets as I pushed in and through the fatal funnel.

The guy in the black polo was on his knees, his hands on his head. The ginger was down and twitching, blood pooling beneath his head, a puckered hole right through the bridge of his crooked nose.

The fat guy still had his hands on Edmonds, having twisted her around in front of him, a knife to her throat.

"This is none of your business. Just turn around and walk away." He was crouched as low behind Edmonds as he could get, but he was a big dude, and she was a petite woman, maybe a hundred thirty soaking wet.

In the movies, I'd probably try to talk him down, being the good guy. This wasn't a movie. He was just trying to buy time, and I saw him tense, getting ready to pull that blade across her neck and open her up to her spine.

I fired, my bullet just missing her ear and punching into his cheekbone just beneath his eye.

It wasn't that difficult a shot, not at that range. We were maybe ten feet apart, and he'd talked just long enough for me to steady my aim. It's still a hair-raising one when you're trying not to hit a hostage. The wrong move at the wrong time and things could go very, very badly.

His head snapped back, and he went limp, though his weight still dragged Edmonds down as his knees let go underneath him. The knife left a red line on her neck as it fell from his fingers, but it was only a scratch.

The guy in the polo shirt must have calculated things at that point, and he didn't come to a great answer. His hands dropped for the SIG at his beltline, and Ken shifted his aim and double tapped him through the skull. He crashed to the floor, spilling gore from what was left of his head.

I moved in. There wasn't time right then to worry about the dead man's poor decision making, though I already suspected that I knew why he'd gambled on that last throw of the dice. They'd been there to commit murder and make it look like a suicide. If we saved the girl, she could testify to it. He'd apparently decided that a long time in prison for attempted murder wasn't preferable to a final showdown.

His decision. I wasn't going to lose any sleep over it.

"Rip, you're with me. Ziggy, make sure she's all right." I was already moving toward the bedrooms. I didn't think there were any more of the bad guys on the place, but we needed to make damned good and sure. Then we could consolidate, take care of Anna Edmonds, and figure out our next move.

That gets a lot more complicated Stateside when there are bodies on the ground, but it wasn't the first time.

Ken fell in behind me as I reached the next door. Behind us, I could hear Phil, his voice calm and gentle as he holstered his Glock. "Anna? It's okay. You're safe now. Your sister told us where to find you. We work for Mr. Romero, and we're here to protect you."

I paused for a heartbeat at the door, my muzzle slightly elevated as I reached down and tested the knob. Pushing it open, I rode it to the stops, clearing the bedroom quickly. It was furnished in pretty classic, rustic outdoor style. The cabin was my kind of place, now that I had a little bit of attention to spare to it.

It took less than two minutes to finish clearing the cabin. Those three had been the only ones.

Phil had Anna Edmonds sitting on the couch, away from the bodies, and he was holding out a handkerchief for her to blot the blood on her neck. She'd already wiped the splatter off from the dude in the black polo. She was clearly shaken, pale and looking more than a little sick. I couldn't blame her. She hadn't signed up for this shit.

Ken looked down at the corpses. The stench in that room was already getting bad. We were going to have to take Edmonds outside before she got sick, especially if we hoped to talk to her at all. "What do we do about these losers?" He looked like he felt like spitting on them. I understood the feeling, though I was still in combat mode, pretty much emotionless.

"Well, the civic-minded thing to do would be to call the sheriff." I looked down at the three dead men as I spoke, wondering just who they were, and if any of the dudes I'd worked with over the years knew them. These weren't MS-13 thugs. "Might keep us ahead of any hot water that might be coming down the pipe from this. The other option would be to get to work, bury them in the back forty, and then clean the hell out of this place. Just make them disappear."

Like they were talking about doing to Edmonds.

I glanced up at her as I said that, and I could see that she'd heard me. For a moment, her eyes shifted to the present, losing that thousand-mile stare, as she looked down at the three bodies with a venom that was simultaneously a little concerning and a good sign. She wasn't all gone. That hopefully meant that we could bring her around and get her talking sooner.

Not that I was going to try to do that while she was still processing the trauma of the last hour or two. That was going to take time, and as urgent as the need for intel was, she was still a human being, and one without the emotional armor that a lot of us had developed over the years.

Ken rubbed his jaw, thinking it over. He glanced at Edmonds. "Ziggy, you might want to take Miss Edmonds outside."

Phil put a hand on her shoulder and spoke, low and calm, to her. She nodded, a little jerkily, and let him escort her out. Before reaching the front porch, he keyed his radio. "Drizzle, Ziggy. Coming out with precious cargo."

"Bring it out. Everything's quiet out here."

I looked at Ken. He was studying the bodies closely, his eyes narrowed, a grimace on his face. I could imagine what he was thinking.

"We don't know how deep this goes." I was thinking out loud. "We get rolled up in an investigation, we could be bogged down for a long time, while the bad guys get free reign to run wild and continue to squeeze Romero and the rest of the company."

"It's possible." Ken wasn't convinced. "However, it's just going to be us three—we can tell Marcos to get out of here, since he didn't fire a shot—and the three of us won't make or break the contract. What *could* is if somebody comes looking for them, finds the bodies, and gets a murder investigation launched." He shook his head. "We had to be sneaky in Mexico for obvious reasons. But we're *based* here in the States. We've got to follow different rules. That's why Goblin's got the lawyers on retainer that he does."

I sighed. I really didn't want to deal with a police investigation, but hopefully Ken was right. It *was* a good shoot, and all the sheriff would have to do would be to listen to Anna Edmonds to see that. Hopefully.

"All right. You call the sheriff. I'll call KG and get the legal beagles moving."

CHAPTER 7

Nick looked at the map and shook his head. "Area familiarization's going to be a bear."

"Particularly without weapons." Casey *really* didn't like this situation, enough so that he was actually being less overbearing than usual. The intel they were getting about San Pedro Sula was making him nervous, and Nick couldn't help but think that was a good thing. "We get rolled up out there empty-handed, and it could be game over real quick."

"Can't disagree." Doug was at the end of the table, leaning back in his chair. He'd seen the map. The no-go zones were all marked in red, mostly delineating neighborhoods controlled by either *Mara Salvatrucha* or *Barrio 18*. There were more than a few overlaps, including places where other gangs, like *Los Olanchanos* or *Vatos Locos* were vying with the big *maras* for dominance, but those two were the big, heavy hitters.

They were also the reason so many Hondurans were braving the long and dangerous trek through Guatemala and Mexico for the United States. Which flow of refugees was conveniently proving a source of income and camouflage for the very human predators they were fleeing from.

"We don't need to prowl the entire damn city." Saul was standing over the table with his arms folded. "Until or unless we get word from Goblin to the contrary, we're not here to run raids and recon. We're here to secure this plant, to keep the Chinese from cementing further control over the supply of industrial chemicals by knocking it down. That means all we really need to be concerned with is the immediate vicinity and the route between the plant and the hotel." He pointed. "Most of the major gang activity is up north, in the thick of the city proper. We can steer clear of those areas easily enough. Especially while we're stuck with pipes and blackjacks for weapons."

"You don't really think that this is going to stay like that?" Casey couldn't *quite* do away with his innate belligerence. "That the mission *isn't* going to expand?"

"Never said that." Saul had always steadfastly refused to let Casey get to him, as obviously irritated as the shorter man might have made him from time to time. He'd never lost his temper, and he wasn't about to start now. "One thing at a time, though. We go haring all over the city, without the right resources, we could potentially get ourselves into an untenable position with no way to get out of it. Better to stay close, get a good feel for our surrounding area and all the routes in and out, and have shorter escape routes if we need them." He took a deep, snorting breath through his nose. "Unless we have no other choice, we're going to have to stay in evasion mode for the time being. Low profile, quiet, heads on a swivel, watch and listen, and get out when it looks like there might be trouble. We've done a good job on the obstacles around the plant here, but we might need to intervene if there's a concerted effort to get into the plant. Otherwise, we stay out of trouble."

"Not sure who named you team leader." Casey wasn't going to let it go.

"Nobody, but he's right." Vern shook his head as he came through the door. "Come on, Casey, you know better than that. This ain't the mil anymore." The unspoken but very loud part of that statement was right there in the open. *So, stop acting like your rank matters a damn.*

Vern came to the end of the table, opposite Doug, who hadn't moved except to roll his head over to look at him. "I'm going to have to interrupt the planning for a minute, though. We've got an appointment for Croak, Thumper, Money, and Whack at La Armeria. Bring all your paperwork and leave any weapons behind." He smiled without humor. "We're going to stick to the main highways, so we *shouldn't* run into any gang activity, but you know how it is. Salt's advice is gonna go double for this trip, at least on the way out. You see anything, we're gonna have to run for it."

***

The drive wasn't that bad, as much as Nick had been dreading going anywhere unarmed. The traffic wasn't all that bad, certainly less dense than some of the places he'd worked, and while the city was comparable to many of the Third World metropolises he'd been in, there was a lot more green than he was used to on contract, so that was nice.

It still wasn't the most peaceful drive he'd ever been on, though. There was a palpable tension in the air in some places, and he could hear gunfire in the distance several times. The gangs ran wild in Honduras, and across San Pedro Sula. These people were living as precarious an existence as those in some of the worst neighborhoods of Baghdad back in the bad days.

Still, they managed to get to the *Instituto de Provisión Militar* without incident. The gate was open, though there were armed guards just inside, and they had to show identification before they even parked.

It was all familiar to Nick. He'd seen it a hundred times, in multiple different countries. The only difference was the language…and the fact that in most of those countries, he'd been on a contract with US government backing, usually working in liaison with the local authorities. This was different. This was a lot sketchier.

All five contractors kept their heads on a swivel as they walked into La Armeria, the official government gun store.

There had been a time when guns had been much less regulated in Honduras, but as per SOP, the government had felt the need to *do something* about the gang violence, so regulating the hell out of firearms ownership and making the government the sole legal supplier had been their answer.

Judging by what he'd heard on the way, Nick doubted the efficacy of the plan, but he was enough of a cynic to know that their plan actually working wasn't the criteria the politicians had been working under.

Vern acted as unconcerned as ever, but that was his way. He walked right up to the counter, put his hands on top, and greeted the middle-aged Honduran woman behind it cheerfully.

The whole process went much more smoothly than Nick had had any business expecting. It still didn't go *quickly*, but that was par for the course. Governments in general are usually not eager to hand out guns to regular people, and even less so to foreigners. Most of the time, anyway. The exceptions to that rule were notable and infuriating.

Finally, though, they walked out with five Glock 19s, three magazines for each, and enough ammunition to fight for about ten minutes. It was less than ideal, but Nick suspected, from some of the things Vern had already said, that there was backup coming, in a somewhat more covert manner, from the States.

He just hoped, as they got into the car to head back to the plant, that they didn't get into too much trouble before that hardware got there. Even if the hardware was just more ammo.

Sure, if they got caught, things could go very, very badly. International arms trafficking was something that just about every government on the planet looked poorly on— provided they weren't the ones doing it—and it could spell the end of Pallas Group Solutions if they got thrown in a Honduran prison for it. But if the alternative was being meat for *Mara Salvatrucha*, Nick was willing to take the risk.

Fortunately, it looked like Goblin was, too.

He looked up just before he got into the car and stopped. Just for a second. Hardly long enough for anyone but Doug to notice. Hopefully his hesitation had been short enough that the men in the low-riding sedan across the street, visible through the open gate, hadn't noticed.

He'd seen that vehicle before. It might be nothing, but he didn't think it was much of a coincidence that it was sitting right there, just outside the compound where the gringo contractors had just picked up their weapons.

From that distance, he couldn't see much of the men inside the vehicle, but he could guess.

"Looks like we might have a tail." He waited until he was inside the car before he spoke. "White sedan, other side of the street. Can't see the plate, but the low-rider thing looks like one I saw behind us on the way here."

"I see it." Doug didn't even seem to be looking that way, but he'd been teaching Nick just how he could let his eyes sort of unfocus, widening his peripheral vision and letting him pick up a lot more of his surroundings. Details still required focus, but the glazed-eyes trick allowed for a lot more awareness than anyone nearby probably suspected.

"Keep an eye on it." Vern put the vehicle in gear and pulled out of the compound and onto the highway. "I don't want to try to interdict if it's our tattooed buddies, not with the self-defense loads we've got."

"This sucks." Josh was sitting in the back, leaning against the headrest, his hand on his Glock. "We've got two of the nastiest transnational criminal organizations in the world right here, and we can't do dick about it."

"Not our job at the moment, any more than it was our job to bring ISIS down, back in the day." Vern was phlegmatic about it. "Stick to the mission at hand. We might still get our crack at those bastards."

Nick did his best to watch the sedan without staring. Sure enough, it started moving as soon as they left the compound. That wasn't a slam dunk, but the correlation of movement was a sign. It quickly fell out of sight, thanks to the way the avenue was built, but he didn't relax.

Sure enough, about a half a mile later, he looked back and spotted that same sedan weaving through traffic behind them.

"They're still on us."

"Roger." Vern was still unruffled. He had good reason. So far, they were just being surveilled. If it escalated to harassment, then they might have to do something. But for the moment, it was just a problem in breaking contact, as subtly and non-violently as possible.

If that car was carrying MS-13 *mareros*, then that might be more easily said than done. That was a problem to tackle when the time came, though.

They had at least enough ammunition to take care of one car of gangbangers. With some left over.

The sedan stuck with them all the way back, but it never closed the distance, never engaged. Nick thought that was a little concerning. He'd come to expect savagery from *mareros*, not this level of subtlety and restraint. That made them less predictable, and therefore even more dangerous.

About the time they turned off 33 Calle, heading south toward the plant, Nick looked back once more. "They just turned off, heading into the hood behind us."

"They probably confirmed that they know where we're going. Only so many gringos in San Pedro Sula these days." Vern still didn't seem to be that bothered. "The first hit will probably come tonight."

Nick checked his Glock again. "So, what *is* company policy on battlefield pickups?"

Vern looked at him in the rear view mirror and grinned. "Whatever it is, it's not written down anywhere to get in the way."

"Noted." Nick glanced at Doug, who had a faint smile on his face as they passed through what would eventually be the main gate.

They had some planning to do.

CHAPTER 8

"So, even after the official declaration that Carr's death was a suicide, you kept digging?" Sheriff Guthrie didn't sound accusatory, but more like he was going over everything to make sure he had it straight.

"It's what we were hired to do." If I sounded tired, it was because this was at least the third time I'd been over the story. Our current attorney, Lydia Monroe, was obviously a little peeved with me, because I was being entirely honest in my after action report to the sheriff. I had the right to remain silent—even though I wasn't technically under arrest yet—but I was talking, describing every step that had led to the triple killing, up to and including what I'd overheard about their intention to murder Anna Edmonds.

"And what made you decide to sneak up through the woods?" That was the potential sticking point, but again, there really wasn't anything adversarial about the sheriff's question. Maybe I was being naïve, but I'd been doing what I could to read the sheriff during the interview. What I'd seen so far was a tired, jaded man who nevertheless was about as hardnosed as they came about law and order. And that included a sense of honor and fair play that couldn't quite stifle his reaction to what those three thugs had been about to do.

I was also pretty certain that he'd spoken to Anna Edmonds first, and we were just corroborating what she'd already told him.

"I can't tell you for sure, Sheriff." I spread my hands. "I got a hunch. I've been in some pretty nasty places, and I learned to trust those hunches a long time ago. I also don't like to just drive right up into the middle of a potentially hostile scene."

I could have sworn that Monroe almost put her head in her hands.

Guthrie just nodded, though, studying me. If he'd been taking notes without looking at me, I might have had reason to start to get nervous, but so far, he'd only looked down at his notes from time to time. Most of the interview, he'd been watching my face and my reactions.

This man was a professional. Far more so than some law enforcement officers I'd met. He was working on reading me as much as I was working on reading him.

"Sounds about right." He put his pencil down. "You ever in Iraq?"

"More times than I care to count." Last I'd figured, I had over four years, cumulative, in that country. Closer to five.

He nodded. "I was all over Sadr City in 2004. I know the feeling." He folded his arms across his chest as I gave him another look. He was a little on the pudgy side, starting to go bald, with a lot of gray in his hair and mustache. The fact that he had to be about my age was a bit of a shock. "Well, Mr. Grant, under the circumstances, with Ms. Edmonds insisting that you saved her life, and every bit of initial evidence that we can see backing up her story—including the cut on her neck and the knife with only..." He looked down at his notes. "Colby Kinkaid's fingerprints on it—I don't think there will be any charges forthcoming."

I frowned, searching my memory for that name. The sheriff noticed, too. "You know him?"

I shook my head. "I don't think so. I wondered, from the weapons and the vehicles, and the fact that they weren't your usual gangbangers or meth heads, if they were contractors. Guys I might have known. I don't recognize the name, though."

"Well, wouldn't be the first contractor to go bad." From his tone, it sounded like the sheriff had some of the disdain for contractors that had been ingrained in a lot of Army and Marine Corps NCOs, and possibly some personal experience.

"Oh, I know, Sheriff. Seen it a few times, myself." I'd known guys who'd gone all the way bad, from drug running, to kidnapping, to murder-for-hire. Those were worse than the poor bastards who had finally had enough and suck-started a gun.

Guthrie studied me a moment longer, then heaved himself to his feet. "Well, thank you for your cooperation, Mr. Grant. You're free to go. I do suggest you stay available for a while, though. There's still going to need to be an investigation into those three. The case is hardly closed."

I figured I knew what the answer to my next question was going to be, but I had to ask, anyway. "Can I get my Glock back?"

He smiled wryly and shook his head. "Afraid the weapons are evidence. They're going to be in our locker for a while." His expression flattened. "I'm serious. We might need to talk to you again. Don't go too far."

I didn't know how much I could promise on that. He might end up regretting letting us go, but there's only so long that we could put our own operations on hold while he wanted witnesses.

The next part he might like even less, so I held my peace altogether as he left the room.

I glanced at Monroe. "You alright?"

"I think you gave me a migraine." She was not amused. "Didn't anyone ever tell you not to talk to cops?"

"Technically, he was a sheriff, not a cop." Yeah, I was being a smartass. I'd had my reasons for being open and honest with Sheriff Guthrie, and she apparently didn't realize it. "Sheriffs are elected. Cops are appointed."

"You realize that anything you said in here *could* have been used against you? Still could be? You could have been looking at some serious time behind bars, not to mention the impact on the company!" She clenched her clasped hands in front of her.

"Relax." I wasn't usually one to be cavalier about the risks, but this was getting ridiculous. "I knew what I was doing. We had to win the sheriff's trust, or else this *would* have gone sideways." I pointed at the door. "You heard him. Sadr City. Let that man figure I was lying to him, and he'd make sure we didn't get out of here this year."

"That's why *I'm* here, or it should be." She still wasn't having it.

I got up and headed for the door. "And I appreciate that. Believe me, I do. But I had to play this my way." Mainly because of the elements to this situation that Monroe *didn't* know about. I'd already determined that Goblin hadn't read her all the way in. *Get my boys out* probably was the extent of her instructions. "Come on, unless you want to hang out in Sheriff Guthrie's interrogation room."

When I came out into the foyer, I found KG waiting for us. "Everybody else out, or am I the first one?"

"You're the first." He inclined his head back toward the door and the vehicles beyond. "Got gear for you in the vic." Meaning guns, meaning he'd already figured out that our Glocks were going to be in the evidence locker for a *long* time.

Good thing they were company weapons, and not our personals.

I looked around. We were about the only people in the foyer except for the desk deputy. "What about Edmonds?"

"They're not telling me." He kept his expression carefully neutral, since we weren't exactly in a private place.

"It looks like we might have to wait for her to make contact." He ran a hand over his face. "Which is less than ideal, if she's worried enough that she didn't want to go home, let alone contact Romero or anyone else at the company."

"She doesn't have many more places to go, though. Unless she goes into witness protection." That had occurred to me just before I said it, and I realized that, while it might be a better option for Edmonds, it would be less optimal for us if we were going to continue our investigation.

"We'll see." KG was pretty blasé about it. What other choice did he have, though? There wasn't much control we had over the situation. If we pushed too hard, we might end up on the sheriff's bad side, and we were already pretty sure we were on somebody's shit list in Nashville. We needed Guthrie as an ally, and that meant treading carefully.

"Head out to the vic. We'll join you shortly." KG didn't want to discuss the plans in the entryway of the sheriff's department, and I couldn't say I blamed him. This needed to be handled somewhere secure.

I just hoped that Edmonds didn't disappear in the meantime. She was the best lead we had. Not necessarily the only one—I already suspected that we'd only need to wait until whoever had tried to strongarm Carr tried it again with either Romero or Carr's nephew—but still the best one. If she'd been a witness that night, she might have some insight as to exactly *why* Carr had been killed.

Or maybe she was just a scared, traumatized young woman who'd witnessed a murder, and they needed to shut her up to maintain the illusion that it had been a suicide.

I just nodded, glanced at the reception desk behind the safety glass, then headed out the front door, down the steps between the columns and glanced around. The street looked like any other downtown American small town street. The vehicle, a white F250, sat at the curb across the street. KG had driven out himself. Marcos, Tom, and Brian had taken care of our vehicles—and our go bags with rifles—as we'd caught a ride with the sheriff's deputies back into Franklin from the cabin.

I felt naked, walking across the street to that truck without a weapon. The lights flashed as KG unlocked it via remote from the front door of the courthouse. I moved quickly to the passenger side, glancing around at the other vehicles on the street as I slipped into the seat and opened up the center console.

The Glock 19 only had one spare mag in a sidecar holster, but it would do for the time being. I got the holster inside my waistband, though I've never been a fan of appendix carry, so it went back just behind my hip. I'd just gotten it situated when KG came out of the courthouse with Phil and Ken.

I kept scanning the street as they got in the truck, looking for anything out of place, anything that might suggest we were being watched by hostile eyes. It was slightly surreal, being in small town USA, everything kind of quiet, sleepy, and still holding onto that Americana that was so comforting, even in days of political and economic upheaval, and still looking around like I was in the Middle East or Mexico. Like I was in a war zone.

I realized that I'd been doing that for a long time, to some extent. It had just been habit before, though. Now, it was in deadly earnest.

You really can't go home again, it seems. Some things are never the same.

We didn't talk much as KG pulled away from the curb and headed back toward Nashville. There'd be time to discuss what had happened and what we'd do next. For the moment, I think we were all pondering much the same thing.

What have we gotten into this time, and how do we finish this?

CHAPTER
9

We'd barely gotten settled in at the team house before the phone rang. KG got it, listened for a moment, replied in a low voice, then hung up and turned to me and Ken. "That was Edmonds. I won't say how she got this number, but she's asking for one of us to pick her up. She's still worried, even though the sheriff and the Franklin police have no leads to suggest that she's still under a direct threat, so she's asking for our help."

Ken frowned. "We take in a stray without getting paid, how's that going to affect our cover for action? We're supposed to be contractors. Not vigilantes."

"If you want to get technical, Romero's paying us to take care of her. He's keeping his distance, just because he doesn't want to spook her. He thinks—and I agree—that she didn't go to anyone in the company because she's afraid someone there is behind Carr's murder. That may or may not be the case, but Romero wants us to protect her and find out if she knows anything. Since you two were there to save her life, you'll be familiar and trusted faces to her. So, you get the detail."

I just nodded. I wasn't going to object. If she really did have a lead, then working protection for Edmonds might put us right at the pointy end of the operation.

There was a part of me that expected that this was going to be boring and go nowhere. There were cartel assholes down south who still needed to be dealt with, and there were still Triad operations in California we could go after. Not necessarily entirely by ourselves, but there was a lot we could accomplish just by intelligence gathering and passing that intel on to people who *could* do something.

But there was something about this contract. It was shadowy and hard to pick out, but I trusted Goblin enough to figure that he'd seen something that wasn't immediately obvious. It was a lucrative contract, sure. That much had been obvious from the bonus that had dropped to my account just after it started. Goblin wasn't one for keeping extra money that he didn't already have earmarked for gear and overhead, so when he got paid extra, he shared it out to the guys on the job. That alone was another sign that PGS was *not* your normal security contracting company.

Ken and I made our way out to the truck, our gear in hand, watching the street for any observers, friendly or otherwise.

I was starting to think that we were going to be doing that for the rest of our lives. When the war comes home, it never really goes away.

***

Edmonds was waiting inside the courthouse when we showed up. That wasn't a surprise. If she was nervous enough that she wanted us to pick her up, she wasn't going to be hanging out on the street corner.

Ken was driving, so I left my weapons in the truck and headed inside. I was even less comfortable with being unarmed under those circumstances, but taking a gun into a courthouse is asking for trouble.

This time, though, as I trotted up the steps toward the front doors, I looked up and could have sworn I'd seen movement in the red brick parking garage next door. Just a momentary flicker, as if someone had been watching me in the opening on the second level, then had faded back into cover as I'd looked up.

My hackles went up, though I didn't stop or stare. Doing that might just alert anyone who was watching that I knew they were there. I'd gotten pretty good at acting oblivious while watching as much of my surroundings as possible as thoroughly as possible, but sometimes it takes effort. This time, not having even so much as a knife on me, it took even more.

Stepping inside the entryway, I pulled out my phone and texted Ken real quick. *Observer on second deck of parking garage. Might be moving fast to get out of here.* I didn't have any illusions that the sheriff's deputies were going to let us out the back or the side, so we might just have to make a run for it.

I didn't think that the bad guys would be so desperate that they'd attempt an assassination in broad daylight in front of a county courthouse. But I wasn't sure enough of that to like the position I was in.

I had to get buzzed in through the second door, though the cheerful female sheriff's deputy on the other end of the intercom didn't give me any trouble about it when I told her I was there to pick up Edmonds.

Anna Edmonds was sitting in a generic office chair in the foyer when I walked in, and she looked up as the door opened. I finally got a pretty good look at her. I'd been a little preoccupied during the fight that had seen the three of us put her would-be murderers in the dirt. She was a petite brunette, about five foot four, and she was currently wearing a jacket about a size too big for her. I didn't think it was hers. It was probably a loaner from one of the female deputies, since I was pretty sure she'd gotten a fair bit of blood spatter on her when I'd killed the man with a knife to her throat.

Colby Kinkaid. I needed to remember that name. There were ways of finding out who he'd been, and who he'd been in contact with.

Then maybe we could work up the kill chain from more than one direction.

"Ms. Edmonds?" I stepped closer but kept my distance, if only to keep from freaking her out. "I'm Chris, with PGS. I'm here to pick you up."

She stood up, then, still pulling the jacket a little more tightly around herself. "I'm ready to go." Her voice was quiet and kind of small, and she didn't really look at me. I could already tell she was poised to run at the slightest threat. She'd been traumatized by what had happened, that was for sure.

That was going to make the next few steps that much more difficult, but I couldn't say it was unexpected. Most people never have to face that kind of violence, especially not when they're aides to the owner of an industrial chemical company. Of course she was going to be messed up, and that was only considering the bloody rescue that had gotten her away from Kinkaid and his cronies. If she'd witnessed Carr's murder, that might only make things worse.

I glanced up at the reception desk, but the deputy behind the glass wasn't paying us any mind. Still, I had to be careful how I worded this next part. I didn't need her to panic.

"The truck's just outside. We should probably get to it as quickly as we can." I hoped I could just leave it at that, instead of getting into the weeds and possibly telling her that I was pretty sure we were being observed, but she just nodded and headed for the door, still clutching that oversized jacket around herself.

I followed her to the vehicle, feeling exposed and helpless with every step. I glanced up at the parking garage as I fell in beside Edmonds, putting myself between her and that vantage point.

That time, I knew that I'd seen someone move. I had to resist the urge to grab Edmonds by the arm and sprint for the truck. Acting normal might buy us a few seconds.

There was a dude up there, all right, and he wasn't hiding this time. He was just leaning against the brick wall, watching. Unfortunately, the way he was situated, he could very easily have a weapon in his hand, just out of sight.

I ushered Edmonds into the back seat of the extended cab pickup. Nothing else had moved. Even the traffic on the street was light. Looking back up at the parking garage, I couldn't see the guy anymore, but I knew he was there. Or, if he wasn't, he'd probably already reported our appearance, the fact that I'd picked Edmonds up from the courthouse, and the make, model, and license plate of the truck.

If he was any sort of pro, he'd have sent that information while I was still inside. And from what I'd seen already, the people behind Carr's murder were hiring pros.

That's not that common. Even those who *should* be pros tended to make stupid mistakes, especially when they turned to crime. I'd known a few who'd gone that route. To have hitters for hire who really *were* competent was rare. And scary.

We would have to be on our toes until this was over, and there was no telling when that might be. We still didn't know who our targets were, or what their backup might be. And the trick about having to be eternally vigilant is that it only takes one slip.

Ken had us moving almost as soon as my door was shut. He took the first right, went around Franklin Public Square, and headed out of town.

"We're only going to have so many options to lose anybody who might be following us." He kept his voice low, his eyes fixed on the road. He didn't want to panic Edmonds any more than I did. "No signs yet, but if they had eyes on, it might only be a matter of time."

"They might not need to follow us, either." I had a few thoughts on how they might corral us, especially since they had a description and presumably a plate number. "If they put a BOLO out, they could just station surveillance teams in likely areas."

Ken didn't respond. He and I hadn't been partners at the time, but we'd all seen what had happened when a cartel had put out a BOLO on the vehicle Drew and I had been driving in Mexicali. Fifteen people had died, fifteen people who hadn't deserved to get snuffed out that day.

Not that I was necessarily expecting that kind of bloodbath in Nashville, Tennessee. The people we were up against were dangerous and utterly without scruples, from what I'd seen, but they still seemed to be trying for plausible deniability. A rash of carjackings and murders might work in a place like Chicago or New York, but not in Tennessee.

That could work to our advantage, but we didn't dare get complacent.

The drive was quiet. I could have started asking Edmonds questions, just in case something happened, but I doubted she wanted to relive anything she might have to tell us about twice. Operationally, I might think that we needed all the information she could give us, as quickly as possible, but I had to take her emotional state into account.

It's something that some guys who come into this business have a hard time wrapping their heads around. Marines, Rangers, SEALs, and an increasing number of Special Forces guys, all tend to be hard-charging action guys. They want to find, close with, and destroy an enemy. They want to kick doors and shoot bad guys in the face. They want things to be as much like it had been while they'd been in uniform, just without all the petty bullshit that has to be dealt with on a day to day basis in the military.

This business, even the relatively high speed side of this business, doesn't work like that. Not only is it a lot quieter and slower, but you often have to deal with people who don't have your level of training, experience, or jaded cynicism and emotional armor plating. Either you learned to be patient and to work around people's foibles, or you got sent home and not asked back out.

So, I glanced back at Edmonds, made an amateur psychological assessment, and decided to leave the questions to KG.

In the meantime, I turned my attention outward, watching the vehicles around us as we hit Highway 31 toward Brentwood and Nashville beyond.

CHAPTER 10

We didn't see anything that looked like surveillance on the way back to the team house, but that didn't make me relax. If anything, it just made me even more certain that the guy in the parking garage had sent a BOLO on us to other teams, scattered around the area.

Presuming that he had actually been looking for us, and hadn't just been some creep waiting for someone with a restraining order against him. It's easy to mistake ordinary, everyday stuff that's just a little off for hostile action, especially in a city. The signal to noise ratio gets skewed pretty fast, especially if there's no active combat going on.

The thing is, when you've got an actual threat on the horizon, you can't afford *not* to notice all those things, and assume that they really are hostile.

By the time we parked, it was entirely too tempting to just relax and figure we'd gotten out of the dragnet. I glanced at Ken, who was still checking the mirrors. He was feeling the same tension I was.

I'd just gotten out, moving to open the back door to let Edmonds out, when an old, beat-up Toyota pickup rolled past. It didn't look that out of place by itself in residential Nashville, but the man in the passenger seat was leaning back from the window, casting his face in shadow, even as he turned to watch us while the truck cruised by.

In downtown Franklin, I was more inclined to take no visible notice. Here, on what was for the moment our turf, I followed the truck with my eyes, my hand just sort of settling close to the butt of my Glock.

The driver didn't waver, but just continued to slow roll past the team house, disappearing around the next corner. If they'd been casing us, they were playing it cool.

Edmonds didn't seem to have noticed. She had somewhat withdrawn into herself on the drive from Franklin. That would be bad if she was on her own, but that was why we were there.

Ken was out of the truck and watching the street, so I ushered Edmonds out onto the sidewalk and into the house.

She looked around as she paused just inside the door. The inside of the team house wasn't exactly that homey. The place was a rental that KG had found, and so it hadn't come with furniture. We'd provided some from the local Goodwill, but then, none of us were staying in the house long-term, so there wasn't much of that. This was a staging area and planning space, not a living space.

I'd have to talk to KG about where we were going to put Edmonds up, but I suspected that he already had an idea on that, if he hadn't already nailed it down.

Almost as if the sound of the door had summoned him, KG stepped out of the bedroom we were using for a planning and briefing room. "Ms. Edmonds. Glad you got here safe. Come on in."

She hesitated, and for a moment it looked almost like she was going to bolt. She'd asked for our help, but the trauma of having been assaulted and restrained by men not unlike us in appearance and mannerisms, who had openly talked in her presence about how they were going to kill her and make it look self-inflicted, had to be messing with her head. That was why I didn't touch her as I held out a hand to usher her toward the back.

Finally, she stepped gingerly toward the briefing room, while KG stepped well away from the door to give her space. He understood where her head was. "Coffee? Tea?"

"I'll take some coffee, please." Her voice was still small and a little hesitant, but she seemed to be getting a little more confident that she wasn't about to be murdered and cut into little pieces. She stepped past KG, not without a tiny bit of a flinch, despite KG's open, friendly face, and into the briefing room.

Compared to the meeting room at Carr & Sons, the former bedroom made for a pretty bare-bones sight. A card table held most of the maps, notes, and radios, with several folding chairs drawn up around it. More maps and bulletin boards were up on the walls, with notations, photos, and notes. Those were pretty spare, still, since we simply didn't have enough information to start building target packages on anyone. Most of what we had was just on the deceased Kinkaid.

Her eyes moved to that photo. I didn't know where we'd gotten it, but Noah Radford, our geeky intel guy who drank energy drinks by the barrel, had a talent for digging stuff up that wouldn't be easily findable.

For a moment, she froze, staring at that photo, the image of the man who'd been about to cut her throat right in front of her eyes. I cursed silently, figuring that we should have covered that up before she came in, but then she seemed to recover, stepping the rest of the way into the room and sinking into one of the folding chairs.

KG came in, cradling a cup of coffee, and set it on the table in front of her. She took it and sipped it, nodding her thanks. She seemed to be getting more of a handle on things. If I'd been through what she had, I might have been a bit more hesitant to accept a cup of coffee from a stranger.

While I leaned against the wall, KG sat down across from her. "You're safe here for now, Ms. Edmonds, though I don't know how long we can let you stay here. Right at the moment, only a couple of *us* are staying here, and the house isn't exactly set up for guests."

Edmonds looked down into her coffee cup. "I don't know where else to go right now."

KG looked up at me. I shrugged. "Find a backwater motel and put her in a room with two of us next door?" It was the best option I could think of. We didn't have the resources for our own version of the Witness Protection Program, but a cheap motel room would be low profile—especially if it wasn't in her name—and wouldn't cost the company that much. Either PGS or Carr & Sons, though I suspected that PGS was going to bill Carr & Sons for this. Romero was already paying us to protect Edmonds, which might or might not be a comfort to her.

KG turned to Edmonds. "I'm going to leave that up to you, Ms. Edmonds, if you're comfortable with it. The men assigned to protect you won't be in the room with you, unless you call them. You'll have it all to yourself."

She thought it over, still staring into her cup. Finally, she nodded, then looked up at him. "I know I asked you to come and protect me, but I have to wonder why you'd go to this length?"

KG glanced at me. I just kept my arms folded and shrugged. That was on him. I was just a gunslinger at that point. He was the team lead.

"We're getting paid." He had taken a minute to think over whether or not to tell her that. It didn't stampede her, though. She just kept watching him, her eyes large and dark, while he continued. "Not only that, but we need some information from you."

He took a moment to let that sink in. From where I stood, I could only see her in profile. She was pretty enough, probably in her early twenties, that even the fear and the stress hadn't taken away from it. If I had been a younger man, and single, I might have even been interested, if I hadn't already seen the alarm flags from what she'd been through.

I'd known guys who would have tried to jump on the bandwagon immediately, never mind the trauma this young woman had endured. They weren't the kind of guys that Goblin hired for Pallas Group Solutions.

Finally, she nodded slightly. "I don't know what I know that you might think is useful."

KG folded his big hands on the table and studied her. He was sizing her up, trying to determine if this was the right time to start asking questions, or if she needed a night's sleep in a motel room, with gunmen next door to keep her safe. After a minute, he leaned forward. "You were at Rodney Carr's residence when he was killed." He didn't beat around the bush or make any equivocations about whether or not he'd committed suicide. We were past that, and I was sure he figured Edmonds was past it, too, after what had happened at her parents' cabin.

She looked down again, but then she nodded, still without lifting her eyes to meet his. "Yes."

KG studied her for a second. "This might be a bit abrupt, but I don't think those three scumbags tried to kill you because you came and went and didn't see anything." He kept his voice low, calm, almost gentle. "Can you tell me what happened that night?"

Her knuckles were white around the coffee cup, which I didn't think would be all that comfortable, considering how hot it had to be. She was quiet for long enough that I was starting to think that KG had pushed a little too hard, and that she'd locked up, but then, in a small, quiet voice, she started to speak. Her tone was flat, even, without inflection.

"Mr. Carr had asked me to come and pick up some files. It wasn't anything urgent, I don't think. He was lonely. He was never anything but professional with me, but he liked to have me around. Sometimes we had dinner together. His wife wouldn't have cared, but I don't think he's talked to her in two years." She was picking her words carefully, trying her best not to impugn the reputation of a dead man. I was sure

85

there were a lot of people these days who wouldn't have cared, at least not in so many words. "I got there just after seven. The front door was open. Not very far, but enough that I could see it was cracked."

She hesitated. She hadn't looked up since she'd started talking. "He never left his door open. It was even locked most of the time. At least, for the last couple of months. There's never been much crime in that neighborhood, but something had made him more cautious. I had a key." Looking up, she glanced at KG and then at me, almost as if she was begging us not to think that her relationship with Carr had been what it sounded like.

"Maybe I shouldn't have gone in. There wasn't anything else out of place. Just that open door. But I went in and called for him." Her face got a little redder. "Then a man came out of the bathroom downstairs and looked at me for a second. I didn't recognize him, but I didn't like the look on his face. I called for R—Mr. Carr again. Then I heard him yell at me to run, then there was a scuffle, and the man who'd come out of the bathroom started to come after me.

"I ran. I don't think I've ever run that fast in my life. I slammed the door behind me, and I think that's what slowed the man down enough that he didn't catch me before I got to my car. I think I might have hit him with the fender when I drove away."

"Could you describe him?" KG had produced a pencil and notepad from somewhere.

She thought about it, then shook her head. "I can't. I'm sorry."

"Was he maybe one of the three who went to the cabin?" I was half hoping that he was, and that we'd killed him, but I knew that was going to leave us back at square one for an actual intelligence investigation.

"I don't think so." She looked up at the picture of Kinkaid, then shook her head with a faint shudder, her hand going to her throat. "It wasn't him."

That meant we still had hitters in the wind, not to my surprise. If we'd cleaned house in the cabin, then there wouldn't have been any reason to suspect that we were being followed from the courthouse in Franklin. Maybe we were just being paranoid, but Edmonds didn't seem to think so.

With a sigh, KG looked down at his brief notes, rubbing a hand across his chin. "If you were close with him…" He hesitated. I could read the question coming, and it could be a sensitive one. "Did he, by any chance, confide in you? Tell you anything that might explain why someone would want to murder him? Or who that someone might be?"

For a second, I thought she was going to bolt. She went very still and very pale. I didn't think that the question itself shocked her so much as it brought to mind the stakes she was up against. Whoever had killed Carr had tried to have her killed, too, and the more she got involved, the worse it was likely to get.

She had some guts, though. "He didn't tell me much, but on the night before he was killed, he did say something to me in the office. It was quiet, and I don't think he wanted anyone else to hear, but he showed me a notebook that he was putting into his safe. He told me that if anything happened to him, what was in that book was probably why."

I glanced at KG, and saw some of the same doubts I was feeling on his face. It seemed a little too pat. How often is there really a final testament for a murdered business magnate, who was probably under pressure from the Red Chinese? That's the kind of thing you see in movies, not in real life intelligence operations.

Though, when I thought about it, the electronic version of somebody's diary got leaked all the damned time. This was just more old-fashioned.

KG was pondering what she'd said, his brow furrowed. "Did you ever get a look at what he put in that notebook?"

"I know he kept notes from all his meetings. He liked to do it the old-fashioned way, with pen and paper." Her eyes dropped to the notepad and pen in KG's hands. "He said it was more secure that way, and that he needed security the way things were going."

"Did he ever say what he meant by, 'the way things were going?'"

"Only vaguely. He said that the Chinese were trying to keep the plant from moving. That if they couldn't do it with money, he was afraid of what they might do." She was tearing up. "He was so serious about the need to bring the company back to the US. He would talk at dinner about what the Chinese were doing to the economy, to the industry, and to the country as a whole. He got passionate about it. He said that we had opened our wrists in the bathtub when we outsourced so much of our chemical processing and manufacturing to China."

That would get some people pissed at him, I would imagine.

"Can you get access to that notebook?" KG was picking his words even more carefully now, knowing full well what he was asking. I wondered if it was worth it. If Romero had access to Carr's office, he could probably get it without subjecting Edmonds to any further fear and stress.

That was, *if* we could trust Romero. He wasn't kin to Carr, that we knew of. He had a stake in the company, but if the bad guys were as keen to use money as they were to use violence, then he might or might not have already been targeted.

I didn't *think* he was compromised. Most people aren't that good at acting. From what I'd seen, he was sincere.

The next twenty-four hours might put that to the test, though.

KG thought it over, studying Edmonds for a moment. "Let's get you somewhere secure and safe, where you can get a change of clothes, a shower, and a meal. We'll talk more about this notebook tomorrow." He stood up. "Kermit! Leprechaun! Got a tasking for you!"

CHAPTER
11

Nick leaned on the rail surrounding the roof of the shorter, northwestern building, looking over the maze of pipes, tanks, and other paraphernalia that made up the chemical plant. He had almost expected to need a respirator up there, but Carr & Sons had taken their safety precautions seriously. There was still some chemical smell on the roof, but it was far from overpowering.

There were a lot of lights around the plant, even though the outer perimeter floods weren't finished yet. Enough that he'd left his night vision in the go bag sitting at his feet, and was scanning the fields around the plant with binoculars.

It wasn't a peaceful night. Despite the drizzle, that had started about an hour before sunset, there was a lot of activity in the Chamelecón neighborhood to the west. He'd heard half a dozen gunshots already, and the night was young.

He scanned carefully. There was a lot of open space out there, and not a lot of cover, but there also wasn't a lot of light. He had several places picked out where the bad guys, be they MS-13, Barrio 18, or some other gang looking for a piece, could approach far too close without being easily seen in the cover of the shadows.

Those were areas he'd already documented and sent descriptions to the men below on the react force. He would put together a comprehensive range card, but he'd only been up there for a few minutes, and was still doing his initial scan. He needed to *see* the terrain and the surrounding neighborhoods before he could build his sector assessment.

He stopped, propping his elbows on the railing, despite the fact that it was low enough that he had to bend almost double to do so, and carefully cradled the binoculars to his eyes, cupping his hands around the ocular lenses to shut out the exterior light from the city around them, and as much from the chemical plant as he could. Something was happening at the soccer field to the southwest.

Steadying the binoculars, he could see that there had been a game in progress, being played under the lights of several parked cars. There weren't a lot of streetlights in Chamelecón. Yet now there were more headlights swinging into the field, and the players had stopped, clustering together as they found themselves backed up against the open fields.

He was the better part of a mile away, so it was difficult to see much detail. He couldn't see just who got out of those new vehicles, or even if they had weapons, but he could tell by the way the small figures in the distance moved against the lights that something very bad was about to go down.

The violence didn't erupt right away. There was definitely some sort of confrontation going on, though it looked like the soccer players were outnumbered, outflanked, and on the defensive.

Then the gunfire flickered across the soccer field, the crackle of the reports reaching him a handful of seconds later. The soccer players dropped like ragdolls, except for two who had dived for the ground and started scrambling away.

Several of the shooters spread out and closed in on them. Some more gunfire rattled across the darkened field, and one of the fleeing figures stumbled.

Then their attackers were all over them, running forward. For a moment, Nick wasn't sure why they didn't just shoot.

Then he remembered who those killers probably were.

He turned aside. He didn't want to watch what came next.

Yet the screams, thin and distant as they were, almost drowned out by the sounds of the city and sporadic gunfire throughout the barrios, still echoed across the field and came to his ears, anyway.

The battles between MS-13 and Barrio 18 continued.

As he turned away from the carnage in the fields, he spotted more headlights moving. This time, they were coming out into the fields along the dirt roads from the north of Chamelecón.

At that time of night, he didn't think there were many reasons they might be coming this way.

"Salt, Croak." He kept his binoculars on the advancing vehicles as he held his radio to his lips. "Got three vehicles coming in from the northwest. Looks like they're turning into the field in Sector Eleven." They'd numbered each of the fields around the plant for easy reference.

"Good copy, Croak." Saul was still every bit as solemn and steady as he always was, even when he got annoyed. Nick had been around him long enough, though, to know that Saul didn't get annoyed when the work was at hand. "Moving."

Nick resumed his vigil, wishing hard that he had a long gun. While he could actually get pretty consistent hits at a hundred yards with a Glock 19, actual disabling hits with a 9mm at that distance were fairly unlikely, and those vehicles were well beyond that range as it was. So, there was nothing he could do but watch and report.

It wasn't a new thing for him, but that didn't make it any less frustrating.

Returning to the binoculars, he focused on the oncoming vehicles. They weren't technicals, but just everyday civilian cars and pickup trucks. This was a warzone, but it wasn't the sort of warzone they'd seen in the Middle East, Africa, or even Mexico. It was more subtle here, in a way, while being every bit as savage, as he'd seen on the soccer field not long before.

The react force didn't speed out across the fields with headlights on, intercepting the oncoming vehicles with a cloud of dust and glaring light. They'd thought about that, but when they considered the nature of the threat, Saul had been one of the first ones to suggest that might be a bad idea, given the numbers and resources they had.

This was going to be as much a psychological fight as a physical one.

Nick steadied the binoculars against the rail as the oncoming headlights came to a halt. Doors opened, the cars' interior lights coming on as men with guns got out and spread out across the field.

His eyes narrowed slightly as he watched them advance. They were moving like they were trying to be stealthy, but they were still mostly backlit by the headlights, even though the vehicles were mostly pointed away from the plant.

Since he wasn't just up there to enjoy the show, Nick keyed his radio. "This is Croak. I count ten foot mobiles with small arms, moving southeast from the vehicles, in a rough skirmish line."

He got two clicks in response. Saul and the others must be close enough that they didn't want to risk making too much noise.

They'd done a lot of work under cover of darkness. There had been no getting around doing some of the obstacle digging in daylight, and therefore exposed to observation from nearby Chamelecón, but the really heavy stuff had been done in the dark, on NVGs.

Those, at least, they'd been able to get into the country without too much trouble, though they hadn't exactly advertised the optics' presence on their way in.

The *mareros* closed in, now barely visible in Nick's binoculars, just movement in the dark vaguely suggestive of human figures creeping across the field. This wasn't anything as open as the hit on the soccer field. They weren't there to send a message, not immediately. They had a different mission in mind.

This wasn't the first time Nick and the B Team had been up against MS-13, presuming that was who these guys were. Sometimes the maras were dedicated to taking control of their target neighborhoods—using their mantra of "Kill, Rape, Control"—but other times they worked as hired guns, as they had in the Southwest against Strand and his clients. He wasn't sure exactly which one was the case here. There was a distinct possibility, based on the intel they'd gotten from Carr & Sons following Rodney Carr's murder, that there was a Chinese paymaster behind this late night assault. On the other hand, it might well be more of a partnership than a client-mercenary relationship.

That was a concern for another time.

"Two hundred yards from the fence." It wasn't as much of a guess as it might have been in the dark. They couldn't put markers out in the neighboring fields, but they'd carefully measured the distance to each border.

Another double click.

For the next few minutes, everything was quiet. The *mareros* continued to advance in a ragged line, moving slowly and quietly. Nick hadn't been generally that impressed with the tactical acumen of the maras from what he'd seen so far, but these guys were disciplined and reasonably stealthy, despite the backlighting when they'd gotten out of their vehicles.

They continued to advance, getting into the outer glow of the floodlights around the perimeter of the plant. They seemed to be getting more confident as they closed in, perhaps because there had been no movement, no reaction to their approach.

Then the first one hit a hole.

It wasn't a full-on punji pit, like Casey, Josh, and a couple others would have liked to dig. There simply hadn't been time. Instead, it was just deep enough and narrow enough to trip someone up and possibly deal out some injury, depending on how hard they hit it, not unlike a gopher hole. Covered over with grass and weeds, the holes were essentially invisible in the dark.

The man who hit the first hole stumbled and fell on his face, triggering a gunshot into the dirt in front of him.

That might as well have been a signal. Half a dozen shots rattled across the field in the dark, muzzle flashes sparking in the dimness. The gunfire was unaimed for the most part, just a reaction more than an actual engagement. That didn't make it any less dangerous, but the react force wasn't in the place where they were shooting.

Nick could hope that there wasn't anyone in the line of fire from the gangsters down there, but the odds that they were going to deal with this problem without taking casualties was probably expecting a bit too much.

That fusillade of gunfire really *was* a signal. Just not for the gangbangers.

The crackle of gunfire suddenly intensified, then went silent. If he hadn't been watching it happen, Nick might have thought that it was all the same burst. The react team, however, had been waiting in a ditch behind several rolls of wire for the incomplete fencing, covered over by a tarp, and as the first shot rang out, they'd come up on the flank of the advancing *mareros*, pistols leveled. The farther group made for longer shots, but in a second, covered by the gangster's own fire, the contractors gunned down all ten of the intruders.

The echoes died away as the bodies hit the dirt. Ideally, they would have been dispatched by single headshots or double taps, at most. Under the circumstances, though, without red dots for the pistols, the PGS react force had needed to essentially mag dump into their targets. From where Nick stood, it looked like it had worked.

The tarp was thrown back, as more of the lights on the perimeter went out. There was a lot of work to do, and they'd need as close to complete darkness as they could get to do it in. The odds of the local cops coming to investigate, this close to Chamelecón—and especially for *yanquis*—were slim, but they still needed to move fast.

There would be ten bullet-riddled corpses in those three vehicles, come sunrise. The cartels and the maras weren't the only ones who could do corpse messaging.

CHAPTER 12

KG had to talk to Goblin about what we were going to do next. Edmonds was clearly scared to trust anyone at the company, but we were working for Romero, not Edmonds.

Unfortunately, I didn't have a solid answer to that question by the time Ken and I had to go switch out with Custus and Rob. Rob had been wounded during the fight for the Bowman Ranch but had recovered enough to rejoin us. He actually put the team slightly over what we'd expected for strength, but KG was working the occasional shift as well as doing the team leader thing, so he was partnered up with Jake.

So, without knowing exactly how much we could say, Ken and I pulled up to the Carr & Sons office at midday.

The street out front was fairly empty for the time of day. Nothing had happened since the killing at the cabin, and that was miles away, but we still pulled up short and scanned the surrounding area carefully before moving in to park out front and head into the office.

It was doubtful that the opposition would attempt anything in broad daylight, and out in public like this, but we still had to be cautious.

Romero was in his office as Ken and I came into the waiting area, where Custus and Rob were sitting, Custus on his phone and Rob reading a magazine. I was vaguely surprised that you could even find paper magazines anymore, though of course, since it was Rob, it was a Maxim. He hadn't gotten the callsign "Bone" for nothing.

"You boys can consider yourselves relieved." Ken found a seat across from the two of them and slumped into it. "Unless you want to stick around, but I don't think there's a bonus for working extra hours."

Rob dropped the magazine on the coffee table and levered himself to his feet. "Nope. I see enough of you guys on the regular as it is." He checked his watch and grimaced. "Of course, it's the middle of the day, and we'll probably be back on shift before the night life really kicks in. I'm getting a little pent up."

"Don't want to hear about it, Bone." Custus got up and stretched. "I really don't."

"Oh, come on." Rob grinned as the two of them headed for the door. "What are you going to do without living vicariously through my debauchery?"

"Plenty." Custus shook his head, his dreads swaying with the movement. "Like go talk to my wife."

Rob snorted. "Boring. Meanwhile I'll be…" He kind of trailed off.

"Yeah, that's what I thought." Custus chuckled as he started outside, though not without pausing near the threshold, still outside of the fatal funnel through the glass, to check both directions. Tired as he had to be after pulling an all-nighter on close protection for Romero, he wasn't getting sloppy. "Come on, Bone. Let's leave Rip and Backwoods in peace."

While it wasn't strictly necessary, we were still using mostly callsigns around the client. It presented a bit of a barrier between us and them, both keeping things professional and reducing the likelihood that we might get burned individually by someone in the company who was on the wrong side.

There was still the non-zero possibility that the *company* as a whole might get burned, but that was something we'd had to live with ever since Drew and I had smoked those MS-13 hitters who'd kicked in the door in that suite in Atlanta.

Ken and I settled in, making sure our Glocks and the various bits of other gear we carried on a regular basis were still concealed, and sat down. I had brought in my go bag, and I fished around inside it and pulled out the old, tattered paperback western I was still working on. I'd probably be done with it well before our shift ended, but that was also why I had another one in there, too.

Got to plan ahead for these sorts of jobs.

While we'd gotten into some pretty good scraps in Pallas Group Solutions—and the company wasn't afraid of them—the reality of close protection work is generally pretty damned boring. And, truth be told, most of the time you want it that way. The day the job becomes un-boring is usually a bad day.

It can also result in you getting benched without pay for a long time, for various and sundry legal reasons, so you hope that things stay nice and quiet and boring for a good, long time, so you can continue to pay your bills.

Fortunately, because Goblin *wasn't* afraid of a scrap when it meant countering and hurting the bad guys, and/or protecting the client, all the benchings we'd had to deal with so far were because of gunshot wounds.

And he had a good enough stable of lawyers to keep us out of trouble even then, too.

Ken had his own book, some obscure true crime story, and we leaned back, reading while still scanning the office and the parking lot outside the glass double doors out front every half a page or so. It's entirely possible to keep yourself occupied and maintain vigilance at the same time, though it takes a certain degree of discipline and practice.

After about an hour, Romero stuck his head out of the door. "Oh. You guys switched out."

I glanced at my watch. "Hybrid and Bone had been on for about six hours. It was time." Most of us had worked eight to twelve hour shifts before, but with the manpower we had in Tennessee, we could just squeak through with six hour shifts—

though that meant there was more to do with the extra time "off."

Romero frowned, looking down at his own timepiece, which wasn't much fancier than some of ours. There were quite a few dudes in the business who sank some *serious* money into watches, some with the excuse that it was "part of their E&E plan." "Oh. I guess you're right. Damn." He looked up. "Well, thanks for coming out. If you need anything, let me or Amanda know." Amanda Byrne was his secretary, and effectively Edmonds' replacement for the time being.

We nodded, and he retreated back into his office. He probably had far too much to do to spend too long shooting the breeze with his protection detail, and we were both fine with that.

I'd been trying to catch up on reading for a while.

Unfortunately, the peace and quiet didn't last much longer.

A large, black SUV pulled up outside the building and parked. Both of us looked up, old habits taking hold as we studied the vehicle, reading matter forgotten as both of us shifted so that we could quickly draw and engage anyone coming through that door.

The group that got out didn't look like a threat, not on the surface. The older man was probably well into his sixties or seventies, in a suit and tie, and the younger, also in a suit, was probably in his late twenties or early thirties. He looked like a stiff breeze could probably blow him away. Skinny and sallow, his hair was immaculately coiffed and looked like there was enough product in it that that same stiff breeze wouldn't move a strand of it.

The woman, probably in her thirties and black-haired, was dressed to the nines, almost more like she was going to a nightclub than visiting an industrial chemical company. I wondered if they were lost, but all three of them looked intent and serious enough that I didn't think they were. They meant to come here.

I hadn't heard about a meeting, though, and Romero hadn't mentioned one. I dropped my novel on the seat, got up, and took two steps to his door. "Mr. Romero? Are you expecting visitors today?"

The door opened, and Romero appeared, a frown on his creased, tanned face. "No." He glanced at the figures approaching as the older man pulled the doors open, and something in his expression went suddenly still. "I guess I can't dodge this one." His eyes flicked to my face. "I'd like at least one of you guys in here with us."

I nodded. I suspected that we both knew who these people were.

The older man led the way inside, glancing at Ken with some distaste, as my partner looked up from his book but didn't move to get to his feet. This was a man used to getting his own way, and having people notice him. Being all but ignored didn't sit well with him. The woman stared at Ken, while the younger man was looking around with a nervousness that was a bit out of place compared to his companions.

Ken, for his part, was far too old—in addition to which, he'd been married for twenty-four years—to be fazed by the woman's stare. He just leaned back in his chair and made a show of returning to his book, even though he was well aware of everything that was happening in the room.

"Mr. Romero." The older man strode forward, holding out his hand. "I'm terribly sorry about your loss." Even as he said it, there was a coolness, a calculation in his eyes and his manner that he couldn't entirely disguise. Maybe it was more obvious to me, a professional paranoiac, but I was pretty sure this guy wasn't at all sorry that Rodney Carr was dead, and he was already looking for an angle on Romero.

Even as Romero shook the man's hand, his own face studiously neutral, I began to suspect that this man, even if he hadn't given the order, was looking at how he could back Romero into a corner and get what he hadn't been able to get from the elder Carr.

"We really should talk. Rodney and I were close to an agreement before his regrettable suicide." The man shook his head, his eyes downcast. It was a textbook performance, and the longer I watched it, the more I was sure it really *was* a performance. I kept watching him and his companions, taking a step back and making sure that I was clear and didn't have Ken in my background. Not that this was going to turn into a gunfight. This was more subtle—and, to my mind, at least, moderately more evil—than that. But old habits die hard.

The man motioned toward Romero's office. My eyes moved to our principal.

Romero's face was a mask, expressionless and giving no clue as to what he was thinking. I knew he had to suspect the same thing I did—that these three were some of the same people that had been pushing Carr prior to his being suicided. Yet, was he going to turn them out, or play along?

I hoped he'd do the former. It would make our job somewhat easier. On the other hand, it might only accelerate things, if these people really were as ruthless as we suspected.

I didn't recognize any of them, but that was no great surprise. For all the intel gathering we did, I didn't have all the big names in business and finance memorized.

To my mild disappointment, Romero turned and held out a hand to usher them inside his office. "Come in. I apologize if things are a little disorganized around here, but losing Rodney was a bit of a shock."

"I'm sure it was. You have my condolences." The older man looked around the office as he walked in, his companions behind him and me looming in the rear. The younger man and the woman gave me looks, since I didn't exactly fit in there, but I just mean mugged them right back. A man was dead and there'd been an attempt to murder his aide—not that we'd made that public—and there was no way I was letting Romero out of my sight.

The older man glanced at me as I took up a chair next to the door. "And you are…?"

"Nobody you need to worry about." I leaned back in the chair with one arm hooked over the back, the other resting on my leg, within easy reach of my Glock.

"Chris is an associate of mine. He's only here to observe." Romero drew attention back to where he'd taken up his seat behind his desk. "Now, what can I do for you?"

"We represent a small group of investors who have been looking at the state of infrastructure and vital industries for a while, and we have concerns. That's why we're reaching out to partner with companies in these major, important industries. We've seen some movement in this particular industry that is of concern, and we'd like to offer our financial partnership. We were discussing the finer details of that partnership with Mr. Carr just before his unfortunate passing." The man was smooth as velvet, his hands folded in front of him as he leaned back in his chair, no longer paying me any mind.

Romero was back in his element, and he leaned back in his chair, his hands on the top of his desk. Despite his apologies for the disorganization, his desk was neat, with only a couple of papers on the surface in addition to his laptop, and the office as a whole was immaculate. "Well, we're a private company. We don't have investors or stockholders."

The older man leaned forward slightly. "We're not talking about a public offering." He shook his head, his tone dropping slightly, becoming friendlier and more confidential. "We're talking about a partnership. We went over some of the moves the company is making with Mr. Carr, and he agreed that there is a *substantial* amount of risk involved. Our partnership will help mitigate those risks."

"What exactly did you have in mind?" Romero wasn't giving anything away, and despite my own desire that he would have sent this trio packing, I had to admire his composure. I wouldn't want to play poker with him.

"Well, we almost had an agreement worked out, for an investment of about a hundred million dollars up front, with arrangements for further integration later on. We would, of course, expect certain dividends, but that would come later. This would primarily be for stabilization in the wake of the facility changes that have currently been undertaken, possibly unwisely, given the current market."

Romero didn't move from his position. "Interesting, considering he never told me anything about any of this, and none of the paperwork that would be needed to even start on such a partnership was in his effects. Or his office."

The accusation was clear as day, but butter wouldn't melt in the older man's mouth. "We had taken the paperwork to get some of the finer legal points ironed out with our legal team. The whole thing needed to stay very confidential, given the sensitive nature of some of the contract terms."

Romero didn't respond immediately, but just studied his visitor. I watched the trio impassively, mentally fuming even as I wore my own poker face. It was plain as day what was going on here, but without concrete proof, we couldn't do anything, and it didn't look like Romero was even going to bring it up.

Of course, he probably couldn't. Again, without that concrete proof, there would probably be a lawsuit filed the next day over any accusation.

These people knew what they were doing, and they had deep pockets. We needed to find out who they were and what, exactly, their game was, but we were going to have to be sneaky about it.

Again, I suspected I knew exactly what their game was. It couldn't be a coincidence that they approached Carr about a "partnership" right after the company started trying to shift its operations from China to the Americas.

No more than it was a coincidence that Carr had "committed suicide" and now they were trying to strongarm Romero into accepting the partnership as a fait accompli.

"Well, since I *am* running the company now, and Rodney is dead, I'm afraid that we're going to have to start all over again." Romero sounded almost bored. "Unfortunately, if he really did think that we needed such a partnership, I can't say that I agree. And, frankly, I'm surprised that he wouldn't have confided in me about it. We ran this company together for twenty years."

"Like I said, matters were quite sensitive." The old man wasn't budging an inch. He was sticking to the lie like it was the truth. "I'm sure he would have told you about it soon, if he hadn't made such an unfortunate decision in the meantime."

I was starting to suspect that the "unfortunate decision" had been telling these people, "No," and from a flicker in Romero's eyes, I figured he was coming to the same conclusion.

"Well, he didn't, and since I'm now the president of the company, at least until Jacob and I agree that he's ready to take the reins, then that puts us back at Square One." He sat up then, putting his hands more firmly on his desktop. "And, due to Rodney's unexpected and tragic departure from this life, I'm afraid that I'm very, very busy." He stood up. "If you have a proposal, I'd ask that you write it up and have it delivered to my secretary. Now, if you'll excuse me, I have a meeting in the next few minutes."

That old guy was a pro. He was as unfazed as ever as he stood up. But when I turned my attention to his companions, I saw that they weren't quite as seasoned. The woman was staring at Romero with barely disguised hostility, and the younger man was looking between Romero and me with a growing nervousness coupled with something else, something akin to the woman's rancor. I'd seen that sort of thing before, usually just before someone did something violent and stupid.

I didn't think this kid was going to pull and start shooting, but there was more going on in the background.

Which was no surprise to me, and probably wouldn't be to Romero, either.

"Well, while I'm disappointed, I understand. We will be in touch." The older man started to turn toward the door, his eyes resting on me as he went. He hesitated, just for a fraction of a second, but I was attuned well enough that I saw it, saw the flicker in his eyes as he sized me up. He didn't think for a second that I was a company associate. What he thought I was, I couldn't say, but he was thinking as he sized me up, and he didn't especially like what he saw.

That was fine with me. I didn't like what I saw when I looked at him, either.

He turned back to look at Romero from the door. "Don't discount what I said about the risks you are taking, either. We are here to help, but if you insist on going it alone, it might not work out well for you."

"Is that a threat?" Romero's eyelids were heavy, and I was momentarily tempted to stand up. I'd loom over all of them in that room. I held my seat, though, watching the older man without blinking, though I had enough peripheral vision to keep his minions in view.

"Only a word of caution. Shifting operations so drastically, particularly now, could have severe long-term consequences, not only for your company, but for the entire world economy. It would be best if you approached this wisely." Without waiting for a reply, he turned and left the office, walking past Ken without looking at him and heading for the exit, his two companions in tow.

Romero let out a long breath and slumped into his chair as they left. "Well, I think we know something of what happened."

"We can guess." Edmonds' fears aside, I figured that the confrontation I'd just witnessed hadn't just been an act. "There are a lot of dots to connect before we can make a real case."

"Yeah." He put his head in his hands. If he did have a meeting—and I was pretty sure he probably did; most of his day was taken up with meetings—it wasn't quite as urgent as he'd made it sound. "It's going to be hard, making a case, when the authorities have already declared his death a suicide."

"Like I said before, cold cases get opened up again all the time." I was being somewhat optimistic, and I knew it. We'd seen just how fast the case surrounding the shootout we'd had in Atlanta had gotten swept under the rug once Strand's lawyers started asking pointed questions. I was under no illusions that we could completely trust the justice system anymore. "But it won't be if all we have is supposition and circumstantial evidence." I leaned back in my chair, since he hadn't asked me to leave yet. "Did you recognize any of them?"

He shook his head. "Never seen any of them before in my life. You notice how they just said they, 'represent a small group of investors?' No names, no fund name, nothing."

I nodded. "This was a very polite strongarm. And I don't think we've seen the last of them, or even the beginning of the actual arm-twisting."

Romero looked at me with a faint smile. "Are you saying I should start watching my back?"

I snorted. "If you weren't already doing that after Rodney Carr ate a shotgun blast, I don't know what to tell you."

There were clients who would react badly to that comment. Even given Romero's candor with us, I was taking a chance making it. But he didn't take it the wrong way.

"If I hadn't been, I wouldn't have expanded your contract." He sighed. "I don't suppose your people would be willing to follow them? Or is it too late to ask that?"

"It might be too late to ask, but I know that we have guys outside, just in case." In this case, it was Phil and Marcos, but as per, I wasn't going to throw names out there unless asked specifically. "Even if they don't follow them, they'll probably get photos. They'll have more pics to look at than we've got eyeballs to go over them."

He nodded. "Those could be useful. If they want to play hard to get, we can still find out who they are." He looked up at me sharply. "That is part of why we brought your company on for security, you know. You guys advertised threat intelligence as well as actual, physical security."

I nodded back. "That's part of the package, yes. We've found that they go hand in hand. If you don't know what the threats are, you can't exactly counter them very well, can you? And that doesn't always mean just watching the news and waiting around." As embarrassingly common as those had been in the really "high speed" security world, overseas, that was a lesson that we'd all learned, sometimes the hard way. Not everyone in the business did learn, whether on the client side or the contract side, but those weren't the sort of people Goblin had recruited.

"Well, keep me in the loop." He motioned toward the laptop on his desk. "In the meantime, while it's virtual, I do have a meeting to get to."

CHAPTER
13

Phil got photos, all right. The analysis part, though, was already proving to be a bear.

"Fat lot of nothing." Radford took another swig of his omnipresent heart attack in a bucket. "Whoever they are, they've got no social media presence at all. I haven't even gotten a match with any corporate websites yet, and believe me, with the facial recognition tools I've got, that's impressive. Most people can't scrub themselves off the internet that thoroughly."

"There have been some who've done it." I was tired, my eyes aching, but Ken and I had come back to the team house as soon as we'd gotten off shift with Romero anyway. I wanted answers.

More than that, I think I wanted targets.

"It takes a lot of money and influence to do that." Radford put his massive travel mug down and shook his head. "Are we looking at something like that Archer business again?"

"Probably." I leaned forward as an alert came up on the computer screen. "We don't mess around with small fry threats in this company."

Radford squirmed in his seat a little as he pulled up the facial recognition program's hit. "Couldn't we do *one* small fry threat? You know, just to mix things up?"

"Take it up with Goblin."

He flinched a little. Radford wasn't a vet. That didn't mean as much to me these days as it might have right out of the Marine Corps, but he had always carried himself with a bit of nervousness around some of us, at least in certain contexts. And questioning Goblin had seemed to be one of the biggest items that would make him twitch.

"Huh." He squinted at the screen, where a social media photo from what looked like a party had come up. Two women were hugging and looking at the camera, cheek to cheek. "The facial recognition thinks the gal on the right is your visitor from this morning."

I peered at the picture. The different lighting and surroundings, not to mention different makeup, hair, and clothing, made it hard to say. She certainly bore some resemblance. But I couldn't be sure.

The smile was what was throwing me, I realized. She hadn't been that attractive when she'd been looking down her nose at us in the office. The more I looked, though, the more I was convinced that it really *was* the same woman.

"So, who is she?"

Radford frowned. "No idea. The photo isn't tagged, and the account belongs to Krystal Davies, the girl on the left. She refers to the woman as Rachel, and they're apparently friends, but it doesn't look like Rachel has any social media accounts. At least not with her photos on them."

"What kind of information can you get on Krystal Davies?" It might not be much of a thread, but it was *a* thread.

Radford laughed. "Give me an hour, and I'll have her phone number, her home address, where she works, and her entire family history."

"Let's not get too carried away. She's a contact, not a suspect." At least, she wasn't a suspect yet. "Just enough information for us to find her and ask about this Rachel person, provided that's her real name. If we can find her, then we might be able to find out who our new friends are."

"On that note." He brought up another window. "I've been looking into that Kinkaid guy you guys smoked. Found a few associates, since he wasn't exactly shy about his tough guy persona on social media. Lots of tacticool photos. Looks like he spent a pretty good amount of time overseas. Iraq, Afghanistan, a few places in Africa." He showed me several pictures of what was undoubtedly Colby Kinkaid, first in ACUs, then in khakis and t-shirts, always with a plate carrier, M4 or similar rifle, though a few photos had him with an AK, and sunglasses on.

"There are about a dozen people he seems to have been in regular contact with. One of them seems to have been Ethan Ulrey, who was the redhead in the cabin." In other words, a dead end. Literally. "Here are some of the others."

I scanned the list, feeling my jaw tighten as I recognized a few of the names. The overseas military/security contracting world is a larger one than most people think, but it's still relatively small. It seems that Kinkaid and I had some mutual acquaintances.

Not that it would surprise me that some of those guys had become accustomed to a certain moral flexibility. There are all kinds in this business, and some joined just for the money and the potential for violence.

I pointed at one of the names. "Brad Jacobs."

"You know him?"

I sighed. "Worked with him a few times. I don't think he'd be in on Kinkaid's gig. Not his style. But he *is* the kind of guy who'd still be friends with Kinkaid—he was friends with everybody—and would keep his ear to the ground and his mouth shut, just in case."

"Will he talk to you?"

I turned toward the door. "Oh, he'll talk to me."

***

Unfortunately, sitting down to a chat with Brad was a bit more easily said than done. That's the problem with the business and the ubiquity of online communications. A lot of

111

us had quite a few friends, but they were scattered all over the country, and we only ever saw or talked to them when we were on the job. That could make finding one of them to have a sit-down a little difficult. Even more so if Brad was still traveling for work.

I had mixed feelings as I searched him out. I still had his contact info, as it turned out, and it matched with what Radford was able to dig up. He lived just outside Chillicothe, Ohio, so while it was a long drive, it wasn't like I had to go all the way across the country to see him.

Brad and I had never been close. We'd worked on the same sites a few times, but never as partners. He'd been friendly enough, and we'd never *not* gotten along, but there was always a certain distance there. Still, he'd come across as a good dude.

I didn't know how he'd react if I came looking for information on Kinkaid. I didn't know their history. That hadn't made it into the social media interaction we'd been able to see. There weren't any downrange pics of the two of them, not that we'd been able to confirm. That didn't mean much; I'd been on a lot of trips where no photos had been taken at all, both through a combination of the client being against it and most of us being less than interested in taking pictures. It still left me in a certain limbo when it came to what Brad's response was going to be.

Looking down at the phone in my hand, I blew out a sigh, hit the call button, and brought it to my ear. I was committed now.

It rang twice, and I was ready for it to go to voicemail, though I wasn't sure about putting this into a recording. Sure, I knew that cell phones were the opposite of secure, even though Brad was using the same encrypted phone app that most of us were running, so even talking about it was a risk, but leaving a voice recording was a step too far.

He answered on the third, ring, though. "Yeah?"

"Brad? It's Chris Grant. Backwoods."

"Holy shit. What's happening, Backwoods?" I could almost hear his grin. "Long time, brother. Where you at?"

"I'm in Nashville, actually. Wondered if we could link up." I was trying to keep my tone casual and friendly, but some of my tension must have come through.

"Nashville's a bit of a hop, but I could get over there." I heard rustling in the background. "When are you thinking?"

"Actually, I was thinking of going up there. You still in Chillicothe?" I didn't know what kind of eyes and ears the bad guys might have around Nashville, and getting out of town was probably a better bet.

"Yeah." More rustling, and then he grunted as if sitting down. "Damn. That's a long drive, broheim. Six hours or so. What's on your mind?"

I hesitated a little. "Not something I want to talk about over the phone." I looked at the map again. "What if we met halfway? Say, in Louisville?"

"Louisville's doable." He'd gotten more serious as soon as I'd said that about not discussing the matter over the phone. "Do I need to come strapped?"

"Probably wise." I wasn't a hundred percent sure that I could trust him all the way on this. It had been too long. But I needed him to trust me, and trying to tell him I was concerned about security and then that I didn't want him to have a weapon weren't the ways to do that.

I sighed. "I need to ask you some questions about somebody. Again, not over the phone. But there's trouble involved." I thought for a second. "Cord sort of trouble."

It took him a second. "Oh, shit." Cord had been the callsign of a man we'd both known on contract. *Everybody* on that program had known about Cord. His name had become something of a byword. He hadn't gone hitman, per se, but he'd been caught offering training to cartel hit squads south of the border. To the best of my knowledge, he was still rotting in a Mexican prison, provided he hadn't already been knifed by one of the rival cartel members in there. "Who is it? No, never mind. Not over the phone. I get it." He sighed, the sound rasping over the circuit. "You want to meet up today? I don't have shit going on at the moment; my next trip isn't for another week." So, he was still contracting. That was important, since it meant he still had a clearance, and that would affect his reactions.

"If you can swing it, yeah." It was getting late, and it would probably be after midnight before I got back to the hotel in Nashville, but we needed this information.

Provided he had it.

"I'll get on the road in the next ten minutes, then. Hit me up when you're getting close to Louisville, and we'll figure out where to meet up."

"Sounds good. See you in a few hours." I hung up and went to get the truck.

CHAPTER
14

Ken had insisted on coming to back me up. I didn't think I'd need the backup. The fact that Brad was still working, and that he'd never quite seemed the type to go for the illegal side of things, made me a little more comfortable about meeting with him. Still, you never knew, so I didn't say anything when Ken threw his go bag in the truck and climbed in.

It was a bit of a long drive, but I took the wheel the whole way. We didn't stop, either. I wanted to get there and get the information, and this wasn't a college road trip.

Neither Ken nor I were particularly talkative at the best of times, but we weren't the sort to just drive in silence for three hours, either. We listened to some Charley Crockett and Colter Wall, talked about almost everything under the sun—as guys in our line of work will do—and passed the time as Tennessee and Kentucky rolled by and the sun went down.

It was just before eleven at night when we pulled into the parking lot of the Chilis just outside Louisville. It wasn't my favorite spot, but it was easy to pick out, and there would be a lot of noise to disappear into.

Sometimes, hiding in plain sight is the best option. If we were alert—and I figured that Brad would be, just as much as Ken and me—we should be able to spot anyone who might be paying us too much attention. Even if we didn't, it would be so loud in there that no one should be able to overhear us.

I knew all too well some of the tricks to overcome that noise—we'd used them several times against enemies foreign and domestic—but sometimes there's only so much you can do.

Brad had beaten us there by a few minutes, and he was sitting in a booth in the back corner of the bar. He spotted us as we walked in and waved.

Standing up as we got to the booth, he shook both of our hands. "Damn, Rip, I didn't know you were coming, too. It's like old home week."

We slid into the booth across from him. Brad had picked it well. None of us had our backs to the door, and we could see almost the entire restaurant and bar area. I scanned the people surrounding us, taking stock. They were all the sort of people you'd expect to see in a suburban Chilis at eleven o'clock at night. Mostly people in their twenties and thirties, none of them paying any attention to us.

If we'd been followed—and I didn't think we had; I'd been watching—then they were either very good at it, or they were still trying to find a parking spot.

The waiter came and took our orders. We waited until he'd delivered our three beers, then Brad took a sip, watching us over the lip of the glass, before putting the drink down and leaning forward on the table. "Okay. Backwoods, I love you, man, but I just drove three hours to a fucking Chilis in Louisville fucking Kentucky. What the hell is going on?"

I set my own glass down. "What do you know about Colby Kinkaid?"

He leaned back with an uncomfortable look on his face, rather like a man waiting for the announcement that his father had just died. "A little too much. What happened?"

"Well, for starters, he's dead."

Brad went very still for a second, then he blinked and leaned back in his seat. "Well, it was going to be either that or prison, the way he was going." He sighed. "How'd it happen?"

Something about the way he was watching Ken and me, still with a bit of coiled spring tension in him, told me that he knew I wasn't just bringing the news of another guy who'd gone down. Too many in our line of work had died early, so it wasn't an uncommon thing. But it's not usually something that you drive three hours out of your way for, and don't talk over the phone about.

"I killed him." I watched his eyes widen a little, though he otherwise stayed composed. "Shot him in the face while he had a knife to a young woman's throat."

The initial shock had already worn off, and Brad just let out a low whistle. "Damn. I mean, I knew he was going down some bad roads, but...damn." He eyed me. "I think you'd better fill me in a little more." His eyes flicked to Ken. "What's going on?"

I glanced at Ken, who shrugged. He was a solid dude, but he'd never aspired to a leadership position, at least not with PGS. I knew he'd held such positions before, and with varying levels of success. I'd never had a problem with him, but I knew guys who had, and he seemed to be trying to get out from under the shadow of those problems.

So, I took the bull by the horns and laid it out for Brad. I didn't go into the full extent of our activities, but stuck with the explanation of our current contract, Carr's murder, and the attempt on Edmonds' life. His frown deepened as he listened.

"So, you were the one guy I knew, that I could trust, who knew him. We don't know who hired him, or how."

Brad leaned back in his seat, looking down at the table while he let out a long, slow breath, toying with the condensation on the outside of his beer glass. "Damn." He took another breath, still not looking at us, obviously thinking it over. Finally, he sat up again, taking a long pull of his beer before leaning his elbows on the table.

"Okay. I knew Colby way back in the day. We were in Pathfinders together. He was always a bit of a wild man, but we had some good times. Lost track of him after the Army, but then we ran into each other on the Triple Canopy contract at Leatherneck." He shook his head. "That was a cluster, and I guess we sort of bonded over it. There were some things we never really saw eye to eye on, but we were friends.

"Now, when I say there were things we didn't see eye to eye on..." He hesitated. He was telling on a friend, even if that friend was dead, and a piece of shit who'd been willing to murder a woman for pay. "You've got to understand. Colby was a friend, but he was always that 'trust me with your life, not your money or your wife' sort of friend. He was always shady. It wasn't about what was right or wrong with Colby, just what you could get away with."

It sounded like a few guys I'd known. There are always a few. Men who'd joined the military for the thrill and the violence and nothing else. Most of them went one of two ways when they got out. They either turned to crime, or they went contract. Sometimes it was both, at least until they got caught at the former.

Believe it or not, despite some of the media coverage of this business, most contracting companies and clients don't like being associated with known criminals. It's a quick way to lose your job and your clearance, as well as your freedom...or your life.

"Did he ever talk about any of it?" In other words, was he so much of a dumbass that he incriminated himself around the others?

That made Brad even more uncomfortable, but he nodded. "He wasn't that good about OPSEC. The only reason, I think, that he didn't lose his clearance, is that he never shot off his mouth around the wrong ears. And that was probably sheer luck." He shook his head again. "He started talking about a new job a couple months ago. He was gloating about it, to be honest. Said he had every bit of flexibility he'd always wanted, great pay, and he could kill anyone he wanted and get away with it." Brad's expression twisted into a pained grimace. "I guess I assumed he was talking about something overseas. Africa, maybe. That place is sketchy enough, and nobody cares what happens there."

"Did he say anything about who he was working for, or how he got the job?" I decided not to rub salt in the wound. He couldn't have *known*, unless he'd asked. He probably should have asked more questions, but that was something that was often frowned upon. The contractor world didn't quite have what you might call a code of *omerta*, but sometimes it got close. Talking out of school was frowned upon, and could get you PNGed.

That meant that it took Brad a long time and about half his beer to come around to answering that question.

"He was trying to get some of us to come on the job. Said it was perfect. The money he was flashing around was sure inviting, too. He never said exactly who it was. There was always that sort of wink and nod thing going on whenever anyone brought up the client. *That* much he couldn't say, but it was always in that way that you knew he was gloating about that, too. That he had an in that was even higher than what we were doing." He glanced at me, and I nodded. We'd both worked for some pretty high-level three-letter agencies, once upon a time.

Some of those agencies would probably have a conniption fit if they knew what PGS was up to.

He pulled out his phone, unlocking it and scrolling through. "He gave me an email address. A place to send a CV, if I was interested in signing up. I really wasn't. I'm doing okay with the program, and, well...like I said, Colby was always shady enough that I don't think any of us really trusted him that far." He looked down at the phone, hesitated a moment, then slid it across to me. "That's all I have. I never sent anything."

I collected the phone and looked at the email address. It was bland and uncommunicative, as most such things were in this business. Just some alphanumerics with a fairly ordinary secure email server attached. Nothing to suggest anything about the reason for its existence.

I copied it down. "It might be useful." I wasn't sure how, exactly, since just about anyone could create such an address, without revealing their location or their business in the process. There would be layers upon layers of insulation between the actual employers and anything we could scrape up about the email itself.

There was one way to exploit it, but that put a twisting feeling in my guts and made me wonder if Goblin would countenance it or not.

That was a question for him, not for me to decide in the bar of a friggin' Chilis.

Brad was looking back and forth between me and Ken with some worry in his eyes. "Guys… I didn't know. I swear I didn't." He gulped. "If you could connect him with me, though, then the Feds might, too. What do I tell them?"

"Just tell them the same thing you told us," Ken said, as I slid his phone back to him and pocketed my own. "Only, it might not be the greatest idea to tell them that you met with us."

That set him back a little. He blinked, then took another swig of his beer, finishing it off and simultaneously waving at the waiter for another one. He probably wasn't going back to Ohio tonight. "You guys aren't going to talk to them?"

I debated briefly and silently on just how much to tell him. "There are some people in very high places implicated in this shit, Brad." I was talking supposition at this point, but past experience suggested very strongly that I was right. "We don't know for sure who we can trust, yet. The shoot was good, we're not being charged with anything, but we need to be very, very careful."

He nodded as the next beer was delivered, and Ken and I finished ours off. He downed half of the new one in one gulp. "Guys." He didn't look at either of us, his eyes fixed on the glass as he put it down on the tabletop. "I wish I could say that I'd be there to help, whatever happens. But..." He swallowed, still not making eye contact. "I've got a good thing going with the program, still. My clearance is good, I just renewed my passports, and I'm going back out in a week. I can't afford to get involved in this, whatever it is."

A part of me wanted to tear into him, but I'd been there. And I hadn't exactly given him enough to prick his conscience far enough that he'd drop everything to come tilt at windmills with PGS. Even assuming that Goblin wanted him. The boss was the final arbiter of who came on and who didn't.

Still, he wasn't even necessarily talking about joining up. He was talking about cooperating—or not—with the law. He wanted nothing more to do with this situation.

I couldn't entirely blame him, but the fury that welled up in my chest had more to do with Kinkaid's crimes, and the lack of interest in making them right. There wasn't much I could do about it, though, and he'd at least given us what little lead he could.

Ken and I stood up. Brad still wasn't looking at us. It was unfortunate, but I was pretty sure that I'd just burned a bridge. If I reached out to him again, he'd think that I was looking for more, trying to entangle him in the trouble that I was dealing with.

Cost of doing business, sometimes.

"Well, we've got a long drive to get back and a lot of work ahead of us, so we'll take off. Take care of yourself, Brad." He just nodded as we turned away.

"Hey, Chris?" His eyes were haunted as I stopped and turned back to look at him. "Stay safe, brother."

I nodded, threw him a two-fingered salute from the corner of my eyebrow, and Ken and I left. We did, indeed, have a long drive ahead.

CHAPTER
15

"Shit." Radford looked at the email address that I'd written out for him. "I don't actually know what to do with this, guys." He was standing at the table in the team house, looking down at the little piece of paper. "I know the email service, and it's a pretty bog-standard privacy-centric service. They're not even based in the US, and even if they were, there's no way they'd give out login information without a warrant. Maybe even with a warrant. And without more info than just the address, I can't even start to socially engineer my way in."

"What about phishing?" KG was sitting at the other end of the table, his chin on his hands. "If these sons of bitches are dumb enough to hire somebody like Kinkaid, maybe they'd be dumb enough to fall for a phishing link."

Radford gave him a look that I could only describe as scathing. "You really want to hang this entire op on that? That *maybe* the bad guys will be stupid? They haven't exactly tripped up enough to tell us who they are, yet."

KG sighed. "No, I guess you're right." He leaned back, dropping his hands to the table, his weight making the chair creak. KG was a *big* dude, even though I stood half a head taller than him. "Damn it. Nobody's airtight. We've got to find *something*."

"What about that chick?" I was tired after getting back to Nashville at almost two thirty in the morning, but the job needed doing. "The one that Radford found on social media, who was being all chummy with the ice queen in Romero's office?"

"Working on that angle, but it's less promising than this, if we can figure out how to exploit that email." He blew a breath out his nose in frustration. "For all we know, that chick might just be an office flunky, with no idea what her boss is really up to. You said yourself that the old guy was dancing around the point like a pro. If he's that evasive with his employees—and he'd be smart to be—then they might not know anything."

"They'd know who the company is, at least." I found it supremely suspicious that there'd been no such introduction made, and no contact information offered. Just a vague *we'll be in touch.*

"And that's why we're not dismissing it altogether, but the C Team is getting on that, especially since the chick saw you and Ken at the office. They get wind that somebody on Romero's detail is sniffing around, and they might just disappear. Or worse, find some way to lawfare us into the ground."

That was another problem that we had to get around. *Lawfare.* It was an unavoidable part of this shadowy, fifth gradient war. Everything was a weapon, and the law most of all.

Money was only slightly more important, and the bad guys appeared to have a *lot* of it.

I studied him for a moment as he brooded. I wasn't entirely sure about this next suggestion, though it was the only way forward I could see, aside from just sitting by Romero and waiting for the next shoe to drop. I also knew that I was probably going to get tapped for it if we *did* end up doing it, and I wasn't sure how I felt about that.

I'd done a lot of clandestine, covert stuff over the years, going back to hiding in a hole or a bush and watching people who didn't know I was there. Recon was a sort of spying, really, though there was a cleanness to it that this sort of skullduggery lacked.

"What if we sent a CV?" The words seemed to echo in the room as I said them, and as much as I didn't really want to, I met KG's eyes as he looked up at me. "They've got three open slots, now."

His eyebrows climbed toward his receding hairline as everyone else in the room got quiet and still. "You know what you're talking about doing?"

"Yeah, I do." I dropped into another camp chair against the wall. None of the furniture in that place was particularly high quality or expensive. We could leave it in a heartbeat and not even worry about losing the company money. "And I can't say that I like it. It could get real nasty, real quick. But I don't see another way to tackle this from where we're sitting. I mean, we *could* rely on the C Team to get to Ice Queen and at least figure out who the funding people are, but in the meantime, what do we do? Sit here and wait to get hit?"

"That is how security *traditionally* works." Custus had just come in from the back room, but he seemed to have heard everything. "We've been hired to protect Romero and the Carr & Sons people, so doing that isn't actually outside of our bailiwick."

I tilted my head to glare at him. "Not my point, Custus."

He grinned, his teeth especially white in his dark face. "I know, but the point needs to be made, anyway." He leaned against the kitchen counter. "The risks involved have to be balanced out by the gains that an op like that would get us. It's up to KG, but I'm not convinced that it wouldn't go sour right off the bat." He waved a hand at the table, indicating the paper with the email on it. "You don't know if that's legit, or if it's entrapment. There could be a Fed on the other end of that email addy, and you show up to a pair of handcuffs and a long, *long* time in the federal pen."

It was a worry. I would be lying if I hadn't thought about it. But I shook my head. "The way we got it doesn't smell right for that. Brad was genuinely shocked when I told him about Kinkaid, and he's scared of losing his clearance and his job. There's too much coincidence to be an FBI setup."

The fact that none of us thought the FBI *wouldn't* do something like that, if they had the foresight and the skill to do it without us noticing, was somewhat telling about our relationship with that particular agency.

It's hard to see "law enforcement" take a report of evidence of wrongdoing and then go after the victim instead of the criminal without developing a hefty bit of paranoid cynicism. And most of us were already cynics from the time we'd spent working for the US government.

"We certainly have to keep the FBI and other law enforcement in mind when we think about this." KG wasn't jumping to any conclusions. "I'm more concerned about what's going to happen if they figure out that their new recruits are PGS contractors. They're ahead of us. They have to already know that PGS is protecting Romero and Carr & Sons. If they figure it out, then any meeting will be an ambush. They'll just remove one more obstacle to either strongarming or smashing Carr & Sons."

I shrugged. "So, we use clean emails, pseudonyms, and fake CVs. There are enough dudes working for the company for a bunch of fake references, if they even care about references. This isn't the government. We can be professional about this."

"We can run recon ahead of time, *if* we get a response and a meeting place, too." Ken was on my side. We'd talked about it a little on the way back from Louisville, though even then we hadn't been all that eager to get into the nitty-gritty details. There were all sorts of nightmare scenarios that I could think of, trying to walk into the lion's den of an undercover op with a paid hit team. I just didn't see any other way to flush them out.

KG tapped his fingers on the table, his lips pursed, as he thought it over. Finally, he shook his head and thumped the table. "This isn't my call to make. We'll maintain our security work with Romero, but I'll send this up the chain to Goblin." Of course, "The Chain" was just a phone call or an email. This wasn't the military with a clear-cut chain of command that had to be consulted on every decision. Team leaders, or even individual contractors, could just hit Goblin up and ask. *If* they could catch him. The man moved around so much that I wondered how he kept the business running when he was popping up wherever there was trouble on the regular.

"Fine with me." Ken got up and headed for the kitchen. "Who else is hungry?"

CHAPTER
16

The gangsters' vehicles were still sitting in the field when Nick, Doug, Saul, and Mike mounted up and got ready to head for the hotel to pick up the day shift. Escorts had been mandated by the client after the first spate of violence aimed at the plant, and the B and D Teams were picking it up quickly, especially after the killing right there at the perimeter around the plant.

"Going to be rough until that fence gets finished." Nick was careful not to uncover the AKM that they'd taken off the attackers in the dark. There hadn't been enough battlefield pickups to equip everyone on the team, but the escorts could at least be a little more heavily armed than just carrying concealed Glock 19s with a couple extra magazines.

"It's just gonna be rough, period." Doug was more somber than usual. "They might have backed off for now, but there's a reason they've left those bodies out there." The silhouettes were barely visible in the vehicles' windows, but they were definitely there, and when the wind was right, the smell of death wafted toward the plant.

Honduras was the tropics. Rot set in fast.

"They'll be back. And it'll be worse next time." He leaned against the van door. "I just hope we get those kits soon."

Nick shrugged as he pulled away from the plant. "If worse comes to worst, we can get some scrap and some shop time and build some Lutys." In the 1990s, Philip Luty had designed and produced a cheap, scrap metal submachine gun in his garage in West Yorkshire, and then published the design in a book entitled *Expedient Homemade Firearms*, mainly as a protest against UK gun laws. He'd gone to jail for it, but his point had been made.

"Eh, I'd rather have something with a rifled barrel and actual sights." Doug didn't say it couldn't be done, probably because just about every man in the business Nick knew had at least one copy of Luty's book. And its sequel.

"There's nothing saying we have to use the *precise* instructions." Nick kept his eyes on the road and the rear-view mirrors, watching for surveillance or a potential ambush. He could feel every nerve seem to quiver as he looked for any sign that the *mareros* were out looking for vengeance for the night's slaughter. He knew enough about MS-13 to know that the killings would never go unanswered. They could hope that they'd put the fear of God into the thugs, but it wouldn't last that long.

He knew less about Barrio 18 but, given the fact that they'd held their own against *Mara Salvatrucha* for so long, they couldn't be any better.

Watching the vehicles piled with corpses as they rolled past, heading north into the city, he continued. "People have been improving on the Luty for years. If we've got enough material, I even know how to make a rifling button."

"So do I." Doug was watching the other side, scanning the line of trees and bushes alongside the canal that bordered the outskirts of the city. "I've been gunsmithing in my garage for years. It's not something I'd be that eager to do when it's time sensitive, though. A lot simpler to just have the parts, a CNC machine, and a block of aluminum."

"Oh, I'm not disputing that. I've built three ARs. They're a lot easier, no doubt." He took the next turn, checking their dispersion with the other van as he went around it. There hadn't been any IED strikes aimed at the plant that he knew of, but it was only a matter of time.

Insurgency was insurgency, he was learning, regardless of the driving force behind it or the environment. He'd started to figure that out when he'd read a book about operations in Vietnam and had been struck by the similarity between some of the descriptions of explosive traps set by the Vietcong and the IEDs built by AQI and other insurgent groups on the roads of Iraq in the early 2000s.

"I'm just talking worst case." He patted the covered AKMS beside him. "We can't rely entirely on battlefield pickups. Besides, those assholes didn't have enough ammo on them."

"We'd need to have the ammo shipped in, too, so why not the parts at the same time?" Doug wasn't letting it go. "We're not going to get a workable amount of ammo for a serious fight from La Armería."

Something had to have gotten to Doug. As a Delta operator, he'd been all over the world in some very dangerous places. He was usually the most laid back and phlegmatic of the team, but something had him fidgety.

That made Nick nervous. Very nervous.

Only a couple minutes later, they entered the city again, hitting 33 Calle and turning east. Traffic was pretty light, as it was still early. Early enough, after the intensity of the night before, that Nick's eyes still ached.

Accelerating down the highway, he kept his eyes out, anyway. The attack the night before had come from Chamelecón, and there were limits to the maras' influence, even in San Pedro Sula. However, while they didn't have much in the way of solid intelligence on the maras' operations, Nick didn't doubt that they had extensive communications and surveillance networks throughout the city, even in neighborhoods they didn't control.

Some of that network was probably formed from members of the gangs. Other parts were probably ordinary people who reported what they saw in order to try to avoid trouble with those same gangs.

That was the way most insurgencies projected power. Terror has a motivation all its own, and the maras were experts at the application of terror.

The drive to the Hotel K-lisma was relatively quick, and while Nick had seen a few things that had raised his hackles on the way, they didn't appear to have been followed. He didn't say as much. He already knew what Doug's response would be. It was the same thing he was thinking.

Just because they hadn't trailed them didn't mean the maras hadn't watched them every inch of the way, cataloging the vehicles, the men inside, the route, and any other detail that might be useful. That was all probably getting passed by cell phone.

The days of *halcones* waving flags or talking on radios were gone. The cell phone, and text messaging, had revolutionized insurgent communications.

Pulling into the hotel, they could relax a bit, since they were effectively inside a walled compound with only one way the gangsters could get at them. Only for a bit, though, as Carlos, the Carr & Sons project manager, came out into the conference room, white as a sheet and wringing his hands.

"What happened?" Nick didn't even wait for him to start. It had been a hell of a night, and now it was looking like it would be a hell of a day to follow.

The gangs weren't going to give them any breathing room. Not that they should have expected them to.

"Adira and Max are missing. No one has seen them since last night. We checked their rooms, too, and they're not in them."

"Hell." Doug looked around. "Who was on security here last night?"

Vern shouldered his way through the crowd of frightened, excited Carr & Sons personnel. "I was, with Abba and Static." Goblin must have sent a couple more bodies south, since Nick hadn't seen those two yet. He didn't know Abba, but he remembered Static, and was slightly surprised that PGS had taken him on. He'd gotten his callsign for one too many times being caught daydreaming, to the point that someone had said there was nothing behind his eyes but static. "One of us was up all night, so we can be pretty sure no one came in."

Doug turned his eyes on Carlos. "Okay, we're going to need some background. Why those two?"

Carlos looked down, a little embarrassed, and shifted his feet. Nick sighed. Some sort of drama was involved, which might even mean that they were wasting their time.

"Were they banging, or what?" Saul asked, and Carlos's flush pretty much confirmed it.

Doug ran a hand over his face and rubbed his eyes. "Okay. So, where did they go to hide?" He muttered under his breath. "Stupid bastards can't just go to their own friggin' hotel rooms…"

"No, that's not what happened." Carlos finally found his voice. "At least, we're pretty sure that's not what happened. They were a couple. Nobody worried about it. They didn't make it a secret, but they didn't shove it in everyone's face, either. They wouldn't have needed to sneak off."

"Unless they wanted to go to the winery down the street without one of us looking over their shoulders." Saul's voice was heavy and disgusted.

Doug closed his eyes, just for a moment. "Of course." He looked at Carlos. "Did they say anything about that?"

The project manager's eyes widened. "I mean, they said something about wanting to go, but Mr. Vern advised against it. They *were* a little exasperated, but I didn't think…"

Nick was already shaking his head. "There's always one." He turned toward the door, the nerves from the night before subsiding into anger. "*Somebody* always thinks they know better. Thinks it's perfectly safe. Until it's not."

Doug was already joining him. "Start at the winery?"

"Only place I can think of. If they didn't make it, then they got snatched off the street."

Shit. On the ground less than two days and we've already had a client kidnapped. Not a great start.

With Doug right beside him, he headed out toward the van. This had just gotten far more complicated than just a trip to the hotel to pick up the client's personnel.

***

"Hell's bells." Doug stood outside the winery, looking up and down the street. It really didn't look like the sort of place that two people could just vanish, but all it took was the wrong time and the right lack of attention.

Talking to the winery's owner had been a chore in and of itself. Nick doubted that the man's Spanish was *that* idiosyncratic. He knew that the Honduran accent was quite a bit different in many ways from the Tex-Mex dialect he'd gotten used to, but that didn't necessarily equate to the sort of communications difficulties they'd run into, especially given the quality of Doug's Spanish, which had surprised him a little. With almost the entire focus of the military having been on the Middle East, Africa, and Central Asia for the last couple of decades, it was a bit of a surprise to have contractors who weren't Hispanic yet were fluent in Spanish. And Doug was fluent.

Which told both of them that the communications problem hadn't been because of the language barrier. It had been because the winery's owner hadn't wanted to get involved.

"Dead end. What now?" Nick realized just how far from home they really were. Even in Mexico, they'd had some idea of where to look, and who to potentially talk to. Here, with only a couple of days on the ground, they were out of their element and at the end of a long line of communications and supply.

It was a lot different from working for the US government, even on contract. Resources were a lot more scarce.

"We might have to talk to the Honduran cops." Doug's tone said the quiet part, but Nick had to respond, anyway.

"From what I understand, that's...not really a good idea."

"Not without the right size bribe, anyway." Doug grimaced. "Get it wrong and you get slapped in jail with the *paisas*."

"I'd rather not go that route, if we can avoid it." Nick wracked his brain as he watched the street. "The cops are going to be almost as much of a threat to us as the maras." He blew out a frustrated breath. "There's got to be *somebody* who'd be willing to talk."

"Why would they? What do we have to offer them?" Doug started toward the hotel, and Nick could only follow. "This is the same as Iraq and Afghanistan. We're not going to be here forever. They'll have to deal with the maras after we've moved on, and they know it."

Nick nodded. He'd been there. Seen it in just about every country he'd deployed to. It was the worst part of any intervention in a foreign insurgency.

The Taliban had had a saying. "The Americans have the watches, but we have the time."

Those two missing Carr & Sons employees didn't have time, though.

There was no good news when they got back to the hotel. "Still nothing. It's like they just walked off the edge of the earth."

Nick noticed that no one rose to the flat earth joke. The situation was just too grim for that.

He'd had an idea on the walk back, but he still held his peace. It wasn't a palatable idea, but he increasingly thought it was a likely one.

So, he wasn't actually that surprised when Carlos's phone rang, and it was Adira's phone.

"Adira. Tell me you're all right." Carlos at least had the presence of mind to put it on speakerphone, which was why the PGS contractors could hear just why his face turned ashen a moment later.

"Adira. So, that's the bitch's name. Good. Listen up, *puto*. You want to see her again, and in one piece, you're going to do exactly what I tell you to do." The voice was harsh and dripping with that sort of gloating malice that Nick had heard from gangbangers before.

He was pretty sure he could hear hysterical sobbing in the background, too. His teeth clenched as he listened.

Carlos looked at Vern, then at Doug, but both men's faces were stony, telling him little until Doug nodded and Vern reached for the phone. With palpable relief, Carlos handed the device over.

"We're listening." Vern's tone was calm and even, but it didn't faze the man on the other end at all.

"Oh, so you're the real boss, huh?" It was a challenge.

"Something like that. What do you want?" Vern wasn't being obsequious or challenging. He was just asking a question.

"You think you can come and set up a factory on our turf without paying the war tax? Nuh uh. Now that we've got your attention, you got to pay." He was getting even more confident, and he hadn't exactly been hesitant before.

"How much?" Vern was being reasonable, but while it had been a while, Nick was pretty sure that reasonableness was only a mask. He was setting the *marero* up to get the wrath.

"You're a big company." The gloating was even more obvious. "We can start at two million dollars." That wasn't a big surprise, given the fact that the "war tax" had driven entire businesses in Honduras out of existence. Extortion was one of the maras' primary means of income.

"Where and when?" Nick's eyes narrowed slightly as he watched Vern. Usually, a negotiator would try to draw things out, tell the hostage taker that it was going to take time to get the money, that they needed proof of life, things like that. Try to take as much time as possible to set things up for the rescue. But Vern was just forging ahead like they were going to pay.

It *was* an option, he realized. As much as it was hardwired into them to never negotiate with terrorists, never pay the ransom, they might not have a choice in this case. Carr & Sons might decide to pay up. That might even already be standing policy, that Vern had been apprised of.

If it was, the other employees didn't know about it. There were a lot of wide eyes and pale faces around the room.

"We'll let you know. Don't turn this phone off." There was a rustle on the other end, the sound of a blow, and a female scream of pain. "Oh, and one other thing. We know everything the police do. You go to them, you call them, and she'll scream a lot, and that's *before* we cut her up into little pieces." The laugh was ugly. "See you soon."

Vern lowered the phone and handed it back to Carlos before turning to Nick, Doug, and the others. "The first shipment of 'special parts' came in last night." He grinned like a skull. "Yeah. Goblin moves fast. We need to get them out to the plant and put together by tonight. I don't think we're going to have a lot of time."

CHAPTER
17

The pre-programmed CNC machines were still milling out the first set of lower receivers when the call came.

"Looks like we might have to do this the hard way. With pistols." Vern beckoned several of the contractors, including Nick and Doug, to join him in the break room, the phone in hand.

He answered it on the third ring, just as Doug gently closed the door behind him. "Are Adira and Max alive?"

"You got some balls, asking questions right away, *pellejo de verga*. You have the money? 'Cause if you don't, there's gonna be blood."

There's gonna be blood anyway, motherfucker.

"Where do we bring it?" Vern didn't *lie*, not exactly. He was good at this.

There was a slight pause, as if the gangster on the other end was taken aback at the cooperation, and wondering what the catch was. Or maybe he was gloating to his homies.

"We can take it at your factory. We'll be there soon." The connection was cut.

Vern dropped the phone on the table. "Okay. Not ideal, but we can make it work. I was hoping that they'd pick a spot out in the hood somewhere, but they want to do it here, so we're actually on somewhat better ground. Those long guns you guys captured last night go up on the roof. The retrieval team will be Salt, Hoop, Croak, Thumper, and me. Concealed pistols. We let them come in, then drop the hammer."

Nick didn't think he'd ever seen Vern so angry or so bloodthirsty. "I take it we don't have two million dollars."

"Fuck no, we don't. And if I asked, Goblin would tell me to nut up and deal with it. That kind of money's not in the cards, and it never was. Instead, we're going to make a different kind of money with this bullshit."

Nick glanced at Doug, but the older man didn't react. Nick decided to hold his peace for the moment, but he wondered about the wisdom of this entire thing. They'd already killed a bunch of *mareros* and left their bodies effectively on display. Now they were declaring open war on yet another clique.

We don't have the firepower for this.

He could see the logic, though. This was prison rules. They had just plunged into a world of vicious street gangs. Gangs that had already targeted them because someone had slipped them the word—and probably some money—to do so. *Mara Salvatrucha* had done mercenary work for the Sinaloa cartel and Los Zetas, though the relationship with Los Zetas had quickly disintegrated due to their mutual savagery.

Tossed right into the middle of that, the only way the PGS shooters were going to stay afloat was to be even meaner than the bloodthirsty killers all around them. They sure couldn't rely on the Honduran police, not given the record that body had in the briefing materials.

If the Honduran cops could do much of anything, there wouldn't be continual turf wars between *Mara Salvatrucha* and *Barrio 18*.

Vern was still thinking things through, though, looking around the room with one eye half squinted. Nick knew the man well enough that he expected him to be smart about it, despite the rage that the kidnapping seemed to have triggered, and a moment later, he was proven right.

"Frog, Gunner. Mount up and head out into the city. Avoid contact but find something to call into the cops. I want them chasing their tails, and if they get into it with the gangs, so much the better." That might be a little cold-blooded, considering the fact that people *were* going to die if that happened, but Nick could understand the reasoning. They couldn't trust the Honduran authorities to side with the gringos. Especially not the sort of gringos that made up PGS. The government might have ostensibly good relations with the US—the current president had extradited her predecessor to the US for drug trafficking—but they were also cozy with the Venezuelans, who were about the epitome of anti-Americanism in Latin America.

So, if they couldn't trust the Hondurans to protect them, they'd get them to run interference.

Casey looked sour, but that was Casey. Manny just nodded and headed for the parking lot.

"Make it as loud as you can," Vern called after them. Manny just held a thumbs up over his head as he and Casey disappeared through the door.

"As for everyone else, here's how I want this set up…"

***

"Two vehicles coming in from 33 Calle." Carl was up on the roof, as high up as he could get, trying to get eyes on the gangsters as they came for their money. "Looks like they came down from the north."

It wasn't much, but if they had to try to backtrack the *mareros*, every bit of information would help.

Nick tried not to fidget as he moved toward his place, just inside the entrance, facing the small parking lot on the north side of the plant. Most of the contractors would stay out of sight as long as they could.

He passed the little break room, where Bob Grayson was frantically sifting through a horror show of MS-13 social media, looking for any evidence of either Adira or Max. The

141

gangsters weren't always the best at OPSEC, especially if they had some intimidation propaganda to wring out of prisoners.

The PGS shooters couldn't afford to assume that the *mareros* would bring the hostages to the plant. There was nothing that any *marero* could say that could be trusted.

He settled in behind the door, out of the fatal funnel but where he could still see through the glass well enough to watch the entire parking lot. Doug was right across from him, while Vern, Josh, and Abaeze walked out into the parking lot, Vern with a duffel bag over his shoulder. It had been stuffed enough to look like it might have money in it, but Nick knew that it just had one of the captured AKM-S rifles, the underfolder stock closed, inside.

This was going to get ugly, one way or another.

The two vehicles were both Fords, which was still a little weird to see in a foreign country. The Escort sedan was in the lead and the Escape SUV pulled in right off its passenger side rear quarter panel. Vern, Josh, and Abaeze lined up facing the two vehicles, far enough apart that one man with a gun couldn't easily take all three of them, at least not before one or another had drawn and shot him dead.

They were still out in the open, but there was only so much they could do. This had to play out.

The doors of the vehicles opened, and four young men in black got out. Two had the extensive facial tattoos that identified them as *Mara Salvatrucha*. The other two didn't, but all four had buzzed heads and were dressed in black. The one with the thin mustache and small patch of beard on his chin, dressed in black jeans and a black wife beater, swaggered forward from the Escort, looking contemptuously at the gringos standing in front of the door.

"Where's our money?" The man didn't have much of an accent. He must have been north of the border at some point, probably for a long period of time. *Mara Salvatrucha* was a truly transnational gang, and they moved back and forth between countries.

"Where are the hostages?" Vern wasn't playing nice anymore. There was a hard edge in his voice that should have warned the gangster, but it didn't.

"You give us the money first, maybe we give you the bitch and her boyfriend." The man grinned, and it was an expression of pure malice. "Or maybe we keep them for a little bit, just to make sure you don't forget to pay again."

Wrong fucking answer.

Doug and Nick were moving almost before the man had finished speaking, yanking the doors open and going out, already reaching for their guns as they went. Vern had let the duffel fall, freeing his hands for his own draw.

The *mareros* were overconfident, but they weren't stupid. Two of them had their guns in their hands already, and they saw the three contractors start their draw strokes. One of them blinked, seemingly shocked that the gringos might actually be mean enough to try to kill them. Most Latino gangsters Nick had encountered figured that white boys were all weak-ass pushovers. They hadn't realized the kind of professional killers they were dealing with.

Two of the gangsters snapped their guns up and immediately started shooting, a bullet shattering the glass door just behind Nick's shoulder as he moved. They weren't really aiming, though, and the contractors were all moving, spreading out even more as guns cleared holsters and cover shirts and came level.

Vern, for his part, was advancing straight on the spokesman, his Glock 19 in both hands and barking. Nick angled off to the right, following Abaeze, trying to get an angle on the last *marero*. One of the tattooed men was already down on the ground, shuddering and spasming in a growing pool of his own blood, but the last one had ducked behind the Escape.

They might have been caught by surprise, but these were men who lived by violence. Abaeze stopped abruptly and threw himself flat as bullets tore through the air over his head, returning fire but only shattering one of the Escape's windows.

Nick dropped at the same time, but he had most of the Escort and the back of the Escape between him and the gunman. Rolling to one side, he searched underneath the vehicles for a target. The Escort was low enough to the pavement that he thought he was going to have to move again, but then he caught a glimpse of movement, put his sights on what he realized was a leg, and squeezed the trigger. The Glock's muzzle blast kicked grit up off the pavement, but the bullet went right where he wanted it to, and the man collapsed, screaming.

Abaeze was up and moving, tracking around the rear of the two vehicles, his weapon leveled. He held his fire, though, as Nick levered himself up off the pavement, already feeling the bruises and scrapes from that abrupt landing, keeping his own pistol leveled, even though the cars were still between him and the target.

Through his peripheral vision, he could see that Vern's target was down. That was enough for now. He had to make sure his own was dealt with first.

Abaeze had circled around farther, but still wasn't shooting. Nick came around the back of the Escort and saw why.

His target lay on the pavement in a puddle of blood, the last of his life pumping out with a sluggishness that belied the spray that had coated the sedan's rear bumper with crimson only seconds before. The gangster's eyes were already glazing over, his face going ashen as he finished bleeding out. Nick had hit him in the femoral artery, by sheer luck.

Rising and turning back toward the building, his weapon lowered and his eyes scanning their surroundings, he saw Vern walk up to the man he'd shot.

The *marero* in the black wife beater had been hit four times in the stomach. Vern stood over him as he held bloodied, quivering hands to his torn abdomen, and kicked the Taurus TH9 away from him.

144

There was nothing but ice in Vern's eyes as he looked down at the dying man. "You tell me where they are, and I'll see about getting you to a hospital. You don't talk, well. I'll just stand here and watch."

The man looked up at him as the other contractors gathered around. The other three gangsters were dead, the quivering one on the pavement next to the Escort's door having gone still with that peculiar finality that no one watching it could mistake for anything but death.

There was a mix of disbelief, hatred, and fear in the man's eyes as he looked up at Vern, shading more toward fear as he saw no sign of anything human in that stare.

"Red…red house." His voice was a mumble, his mouth full of blood. "Red…house…in…Barrio…Medina."

His voice was getting quieter and his movements weaker as he tried to hold in his guts. He'd barely finished getting the name of the neighborhood out when he just…stopped. His last breath rattled out of his lungs with a sigh, and he was still.

"Huh. Must have hit him harder than I thought." Vern turned away. "Get these pieces of shit cleaned up, then we need to find a red house in the middle of a solid MS-13 barrio."

CHAPTER
18

Sirens wailed across San Pedro Sula, accompanied by enough gunfire that the brief shootout at the plant might well have gone unnoticed. Whatever Casey and Manny had stirred up out there had clearly done the trick. It sounded like just about every cop in the city was going north, and the maras were ready for them.

Carlos and the rest of the Carr & Sons employees were clearly shaken, though they'd been well back inside the plant when the shooting had started. They simply hadn't been expecting this level of violence, especially not given the already demonstrated naivete of the kidnapped couple.

"We still don't have the ARs done, so we'll have to take the captured Uzis and AKs." Vern was all business. "We can't spare the whole team, so this is going to be me, Thumper, Croak, Gameshow, and Train. I'd take their Escape, but it got a bullet through a window, so we're all going to have to squeeze into the Escort if we don't want to draw attention. I don't want to take one of our vehicles, for obvious reasons. We'll have to commandeer another one on the target to get the hostages back here, after which, the mara vehicles will be ditched outside of town."

He looked around at his chosen strike force. "Unless there are any questions, gentlemen, we need to get moving. We can hash out the finer details on the way, but those two don't have a whole lot of time left."

Nobody said anything, but just scooped up what gear they could use and the chosen weapons. Nick ended up with one of the two Uzis, and he handled it carefully as he got into the back of the Escort with Carl and Durand. Vern was driving, and Doug was in the front seat.

He hadn't used an Uzi much, but most of a lifetime around firearms meant he got it figured out pretty quickly. Quickly enough that he was able to put the weapon down on the floorboards at his feet, leaning back against the two spare magazines thrust into his belt under his shirt, and watch their surroundings as Vern drove into the lion's den.

They made good time, quickly turning off 33 Calle and onto 3 Avenida SE, only slowing when they reached the outskirts of Barrio Medina. The tension inside the car was palpable as Vern drove into the neighborhood, heads on a swivel as they looked for the red house.

That was where it got complicated. The barrio was practically a small city in and of itself, sprawling across almost a square mile. There were tenements, shopping malls, shops, auto repair establishments, and private homes. They had to find one red house out of all the cinderblock and plaster houses in that multi-block neighborhood.

To make matters worse, it wasn't as if houses in the barrio had yards. They were crammed in on top of each other, tighter than even some of the neighborhoods in Juarez had been.

They'd just have to comb the streets and keep their eyes open.

The signs of *Mara Salvatrucha*'s iron grip on the neighborhood were immediate. Graffiti proclaimed it everywhere, blue gothic lettering spelling out "MS" along with some more gruesome imagery. There was no sign of police presence, either, and the people of the barrio moved around quickly and furtively. There were certain services that the mara did provide, but that came at the cost of constant fear.

The think-tank eggheads called it "parallel governance." What it was, was rule by terror, unchallenged by the law.

"Looky here." Vern leaned back in the driver's seat, one hand draped over the wheel. Nick looked over his shoulder to see what he was talking about, to see two more *mareros*, identifiable by their shaved heads and tattoos, stepped out into the street and waved.

"Can't be that easy." Sure enough, though, there was a red house behind them, and they clearly recognized the car.

"I ain't looking the gift horse in the mouth." Vern started toward the crumbling sidewalk. "Be ready. They're not going to think we're their homies for long."

He stopped the Escort right in front of the house, though still out of the direct line from the front door. The two men in baggy pants and t-shirts sauntered over, one of them with a shiny Beretta in his waistband.

Vern didn't wait around. "On three. One, two, three."

All four doors opened at once and the contractors got out, guns already in their hands. The closer of the two *mareros* took in Vern's long hair and paler skin, and his eyes got wide. These *weren't* his homies. He grabbed for the Beretta and Vern shot him through the throat. The bark of the AKM-S was achingly loud at first, but it was only going to get worse.

Doug had fired a split second ahead of Vern, and his target was down, lying on his back in the street as the rain started, limp as a wet dishrag. Doug's bullet had gone right through the bridge of his nose.

Nick and Durand were already running for the door. They had to move fast and with maximum violence, now.

Nick beat Durand to the door by a split second. He hit it immediately, smashing through the doorjamb with every bit of his two hundred twenty pounds and riding the door to the stops,

149

his Uzi in his shoulder and the sights right below his eye as he cleared the entryway.

Two more gunmen were coming out of the back of the house. The first one was older, gaunt and weathered, with a thin beard, an old, beat-up Hi Power in his hands. The other was almost twice his size, chubby and hairless, with no shirt on and a massive "MS" tattooed across his chest.

Nick gave the older guy a quick three-round burst as he swept his muzzle past him, hitting him in the chest and shoulder. He didn't slow down but drove through the doorway and out of the fatal funnel, hastily clearing his corner—a filthy pile of trash and broken furniture under a barred window—before pivoting back toward his initial target. He could hear—and feel—Durand's shots behind him, but part of working with a team in CQB is trusting your teammates to cover your back.

The grizzled gunman was sagging against the wall, bleeding profusely from what looked like a shattered collarbone and a deep wound in his ribs. Bloody froth was starting to gather around his nose and mouth.

He was still holding his gun, though, trying to bring it up, so Nick shot him with another short burst through the skull, dropping him where he stood, before turning toward the big guy.

Durand had already shot him three times, but he was still on his feet and still coming. He didn't have a gun, Nick realized, but only a bloody machete. And he was suddenly within about six feet of Durand, lifting that edged motif of MS-13 over his head as blood flowed from his mouth, a maniacal grin on his face. Durand was still pumping round after round into his center mass, but he was still coming.

Nick shifted fire and stroked the trigger, putting a single bullet through the fat man's ear. The mass of bloodied flesh stopped mid-lunge, swayed for a second, then crashed to the floor, the gore-crusted machete chipping on the concrete as it hit at a strange angle.

Durand's Glock's slide was locked to the rear, the pistol still pointed at the massive dead man. "What the fuck."

Vern, Doug, and Carl pushed through the door, Carl pivoting to take up security on the street with his captured Beretta M12. Durand, shaking a little, stepped back as the former Delta operator took point, and reloaded.

Vern glanced down at the bodies, but made no comment, riding his AK's sights as he pushed past and deeper into the house. Nick fell in with him and Doug, as Carl and Durand held the front door.

There were two bedrooms plus the kitchen. The first bedroom was piled with trash and a filthy mattress. The kitchen was in even worse shape, with drug paraphernalia intermixed with dirty dishes and what looked like several bricks of cocaine. It took seconds to clear both.

The door to the second bedroom was shut. The stench coming from it was almost enough to knock Nick back on his heels. He had a bad feeling about what they were about to find in there, but they had to get to it. Adira and Max were counting on them. Vern put his back to the wall, got the nod from Doug, who had his own Uzi pointed at the door, and donkey-kicked the door open.

Doug went in fast, Nick right on his heels, digging their corners before pivoting back toward the center of the room.

Neither man lowered his weapon, even though there wasn't anything to shoot. The threat was still every bit as palpable, even though there weren't any *mareros* in the room.

A Halloween skeleton hung from the ceiling, but it was dwarfed by the painted Santa Muerte on the wall. Graffiti covered every inch of the wall, dominated by another gothic "MS" and an equally large "Santa Mu3rt3." The rest of the tags were some variation on them, with several pentagrams and marijuana leaves mixed in.

A small altar was set up below the painted image of Santa Muerte, with candles still burning. Several bottles of booze lay on it, along with a sculpture of a goat's head.

The floor was soaked in blood. Most of it was probably from the two corpses lying in front of the altar.

Max had been beheaded. His face was still frozen in a rictus of agony where his head sat on the floor at the foot of the altar. Whether his head had been cut off before or after one of the *mareros* had cracked his chest open and ripped his heart out was impossible to say.

A woman lay beside him, face down on the floor, naked from the waist down. She'd been stabbed over and over and over again. The sheer amount of blood partially hid her nakedness, not that she had any reason to feel shame at it anymore.

Doug moved into the room, carefully lifting the dead woman's head to see if he could see her face. His own expression was stony as he let her head back down to rest on the floor. "It's her."

Nick glanced at Vern. The team lead was pale, and he appeared to be shaking a little.

Nick didn't think that shake was fear or even sickness at the evil on display.

It was rage.

"What do you want to do, Figaro?" Doug was calm, cool, and collected as he straightened. "We have exactly no time."

Nick was surprised at just how calm he was. He'd known dudes who'd been in ISIS torture rooms and had puked their guts out. He guessed that it was a combination of combat adrenaline and the fact that, on some level, he'd been expecting this. He'd done his research on MS-13.

If ever there was a bunch of monsters who deserved to die, every last one of them, it was this bunch.

"Off the X. We need to get clear before we get dogpiled." Vern's voice was still thick with wrath, but he was keeping it together. They didn't have the guns to fight the entire barrio.

"Coming out!" Doug took the lead, Nick and Vern falling in with him. Durand looked back as they came out, and his face shifted as he took in the fact that they hadn't brought the hostages with them. He scanned their expressions, put two and two together, and his jaw tightened.

"Moving out." Vern took the lead, heading for the front door, but Carl held up a hand.

"We've got movement out there. Two cars just pulled up."

"Fuck 'em. If we try to barricade here, we're never getting out. Move." Vern suited actions to words as he pushed out through the door, his AK at the high ready.

At least half a dozen MS-13 gunmen were already halfway across the street, packing everything from pistols to shotguns to AR rifles. More were getting out of yet another vehicle, and it looked like some were coming from a nearby house.

Vern didn't wait for them, but pivoted as he dashed for the car, hammering half the mag at the closest *mareros*. Most ordinary men would have sprayed bullets across half the street. Nick had seen it even among professionals, never mind some of the Third World militias and militaries he'd trained in Special Forces. Vern, however, only missed twice that Nick could see. The rest of his shots dropped men in the street, and the others scrambled for cover.

Doug leaned out of the doorway and added a long burst from his Uzi to the fire. "Go!"

Nick grabbed Durand, who was looking slightly shell-shocked, and shoved him out the door, right after Carl. The three of them sprinted to the car, Nick dropping to a knee by the rear wheel and dusting three of the MS-13 thugs with a burst of about ten 9mm rounds from the Uzi. One at least was hit, tumbling into the street.

"Get in!" Carl had the door open and was yelling at him, while Durand opened fire from the open rear door on the other side of the car.

Just barely rising to his feet, keeping his head low, he threw himself into the back seat, almost at the same time that Vern threw the Escort into reverse, almost launching Nick face first into the front seat.

Getting the door shut, Nick held on for dear life as Vern backed up to the next corner, almost collided with an oncoming Nissan Frontier as he backed around it at close to full speed, braked, and ripped back around the corner, now heading back the way they'd come.

More bullets chased them down the street, some impacting the body of the car with loud *bang*s. One hit the rear window and shattered it, showering the men in the back seat with broken glass.

Vern stomped on the gas, burning rubber as he slewed around the corner and accelerated down the street. He had to weave between a couple of cars, but he was doing a good eighty miles an hour by the time he hit Avenue Juan Pablo II.

He almost stood the car on two wheels as he went around the corner, and horns blared as wheels screeched while the handful of cars on the street tried desperately to avoid a collision. One Toyota Corolla, the paint peeling off the hood, lost it and went into the median.

Vern was good at this. He slewed around another car, braked just enough to avoid a car going through the intersection just ahead, then raced through, still almost getting the Escort's rear quarter panel clipped by a truck that blared its horn at them.

Then they were on 3 Avenida SE and heading south, still going about as fast as Vern could get the vehicle to move. "Anybody hit?"

A quick check confirmed that, by some miracle, none of them had been. Vern started to slow down as he took another abrupt turn, getting off the straightaway and hopefully breaking any visual contact the bad guys might have had with them. "We need to ditch this vehicle. They'll put a BOLO out for it."

He sighed angrily. "I fucking *knew* we'd never see those two alive again. Not even when they didn't bring them to the meet. As soon as they disappeared. Fucking idiots."

Doug wasn't as outwardly angry, but Nick recognized the cold fury behind his next words, even as he kept his eyes roving over the street and the houses around them. "Now we're committed, though. Before, we were killing mercenaries. Now we're at war with MS-13 on their own turf.

"We'd better be ready to go so hard on them that even those savages think twice about crossing us."

CHAPTER
19

"Well, it's something." KG rubbed his chin as he looked at the screen. He did not appear to be especially thrilled with what he was looking at.

I couldn't say that I was, either.

Phil, Marcos, Ken, and I had submitted CVs to the mysterious email address I'd gotten from Brad. They were all fake, with pseudonyms, falsified histories, and everything. We'd created entirely new email addresses to send them with. The parts that weren't falsified were the references, which were dudes we knew, who were not with Pallas Group Solutions, who would roger up that sure, they knew these guys, and they were good dudes.

Phil and I had gotten responses. They weren't informative, but I hadn't exactly expected them to be.

Unfortunately, they also weren't instructions for a meet. They weren't even instructions for vetting for a job. The emails both consisted of instructions to go to a .onion link.

That was a dark web file suffix. We'd have to use a Tor browser to even find it. That didn't exactly bode well, though it also wasn't all that surprising.

It also wasn't going to be that difficult, either. Radford, to my complete lack of shock, was already set up for Tor browsing at the click of a mouse.

"We doing this?" He might have been set up for it, but Radford was still obviously a little uncomfortable with it. Nobody went into the dark web for good stuff. It was where all the really nasty, illegal stuff could be found, from drugs, to weapons, to human trafficking, to hired murder.

And worse.

Yes, there's worse.

All eyes turned to KG. "I've already talked it over with Goblin." He nodded. "We're doing it. If only to try to get some idea of where these assholes are working. If it's something we can ostensibly do without breaking the law—moral or civil—then we take it. Goblin's words." He looked around at us, as if challenging anyone to object. "We need to know who these sons of bitches are. This is our best shot. Consider it the threat intelligence part of the contract."

"Not sure anyone specified going undercover with a network of hitmen." Phil was more visibly discomfited than I thought I'd ever seen him. "This could get ugly, fast."

"Only one way to be sure." KG turned to Radford. "The Tor browser, VPNs, and everything *should* keep them from figuring out who we are. That's how this sort of thing works to our advantage, too."

Radford still looked a little queasy, but he shrugged. "At least it's a direct .onion link. I don't have to go looking for it. That could get bad." He shuddered. "I hate going into the dark web. Always feel like I need a shower just dipping my toe in it. There's nothing good there."

Despite his complaints, he sat down at the computer, brought up the Tor browser, and put in the link in the encrypted emails.

"Well, well. Looks like it's a vetting and a job at the same time." KG was leaning over Radford's shoulder, reading the screen. "Surveillance. They want to see if you'll deliver, without throwing something out that might make dudes balk." He shook his head. "It's an evaluation and bait at the same time."

"Looks like it." I was reading the same thing over Radford's other shoulder.

Situation: Riley Nyce is a financier living in Richmond, VA. He is 32, works for The Curran Fund. Single. Drives a Rolls Royce Spectre. He lives in The Edison Apartments, downtown. He is believed to have both a drug habit and a taste for expensive escorts.

Mission: Establish surveillance on Mr. Nyce and confirm or deny his drug and sex worker habits. If confirmed, record with photos and/or video, and send to this link.

Execution: Proceed to Richmond and take out a rental vehicle. Preliminary payment of operational funds will be deposited in the linked Bitcoin wallet. Find Nyce and commence surveillance. Daily reporting is expected, to the supplied contact. Final payment will be deposited upon completion of the tasking, at the contact's discretion. First reporting is expected within 48 hours of reading this listing.

Administration and Logistics: All logistics are your responsibility, utilizing the op funds provided.

Command and Signal: All communications will go through the initial contact email.

"This is definitely a vet." KG sounded disgusted. "Who else would use a five paragraph op order format for a private eye gig?"

"Nobody I know." I straightened. There wasn't much more to work with, except that the site included several photos of Nyce as well as his address and some other pertinent information. "Got to be a bit of a try-hard to use it for something like this, though."

"Let's face it." Phil squirted a stream of dip spit into a paper cup. "We all know at least somebody who would. Not everyone in this business is smart, professional, or just not cringe."

"Well, if you've got twenty-four hours, you'd better get moving." KG turned away from the screen. "Radford will get you set up with the comms you need to maintain contact with this guy, and we'll make sure you've got all the documentation you're going to need." He took a deep breath. "You need to be *sterile* on this one, gents. If you get rolled up, you can't be Chris Grant and Phil Tull. That means burner phones, ID in your pseudos, and no contact with anyone unless necessary. Get in there, see what you can find out, and then get clear before reporting in."

"Preaching to the choir, KG." I turned toward the door. "I've already had to kill a couple of these punks, and I know what they were fixing to do. I'm well aware of what's going to happen if we get made."

"It's still gonna be a milk run compared to Juarez."

***

The burner phone in my pocket buzzed and I pulled it out. The caller ID showed nothing but the number. I answered it anyway, since I recognized that number. I just couldn't risk putting it in the phone's contacts.

"Yeah."

"It's me." Goblin and I had known each other for years, going back to the days when we'd been partners on contract, driving up-armored Toyotas through Baghdad, dodging checkpoints manned by both Iraqi Army and Shi'a Militia Groups. "Wanted to touch base before you went off the grid."

"We're just about to the airport." I was a little nervous about that, since all the ID in my wallet was falsified, bearing the name "Walter Callahan." Fake IDs were a little more complicated these days than they had been when I'd been growing up, but they were still doable, especially for a group with the resources that Goblin had put together.

I was sure that some of our former employers would be very interested in some of those resources, but Thad Walker was a canny sort of dude, who had been planning this operation for a very, very long time.

"I've got a guy in Richmond. Used to be part of the Army of Northern Virginia." That was a euphemism I hadn't heard in a *long* time. Most people thought in terms of Robert E.

Lee's Confederate army when they heard it, but within certain circles, "The Army of Northern Virginia" referred to the shadowy network of government agencies and contractors that had mostly been based in Northern Virginia since the beginning of the Global War on Terror. We'd all been a part of it, in one way or another, over the last few years, though the fact that Goblin referred to it specifically told me that this guy had probably been pretty deep. Ground Branch, maybe.

"Don't write the number down but memorize it." He repeated a phone number three times, and I read it back to him. The area code wasn't for the Beltway, either. It was an Alaska area code, if I remembered right. "Good. If you get in trouble, or you just need to E&E, call him, get rendezvous coordinates, ditch everything, and get to him. Walter Callahan and James Kelly will cease to exist. He's a good dude. I'd trust him with my life."

That meant something, coming from Thad. I remembered what Brad had said about Kinkaid, and his "Trust me with your life, not your money or your wife" attitude. I'd known a few guys, both in the military and the contracting world, who'd been like that. Thad never had been. While it had been quite a few years between the last time we'd worked together and my first job with PGS, there'd been a time when we'd stayed at each other's houses between deployments.

"Good copy." I was going to have to end this call soon, and then do what I could to scrub the number from the phone's history. So far, there'd been no mention of a face-to-face meeting with the hitman network, but if we got deep enough, we still needed to be sterile. It was an element of tradecraft that had been sadly lacking in some of the more formally sanctioned operations I'd been involved with.

We'd gotten sloppy over the years. Given the irregular nature of Pallas Group Solutions' operations, we had to tighten things up.

"Hey, Chris. Be safe, all right?" There was a note of genuine worry in Goblin's voice that I hadn't heard in a while.

As the boss, he was generally pretty detached and cool, even when he'd sent us into Mexico to hunt down and do battle with drug cartels. That had been extremely dangerous, especially since we couldn't trust that the Mexican authorities wouldn't come down on our heads just as hard as the cartels. This was different, though.

"We'll be fine, Thad." I was being as reassuring as I could, much like I had been when I'd last talked to Julie. I couldn't tell her where I was going or what the mission was. Most of the time, we'd dismissed a lot of the stringent security measures, especially since the client who'd insisted on them had been *extremely* selective in how thoroughly *they* employed them, but this was one I couldn't talk to her about. Not over the phone, anyway. I'd just told her that I'd be off comms for a while, not to worry, and that if need be, Thad would be in touch.

"I hope so." He wanted to say more. I could hear it in his voice. He was asking us to go into the underworld in a way we hadn't needed to yet. We'd observed from a distance, digging in via computers and watching from follow vehicles and observation posts. This was different.

There was only so much to say about, it though. It was a Rubicon that had to be crossed, and I thought that we'd all sort of understood it as soon as we'd found ourselves fighting *mara* hitters hired through proxies by the son of a sitting Senator. This was a dark, dirty war, fought in the strata underneath the normal world that most Americans knew, and we weren't going to be able to stay out of that strata indefinitely.

Unfortunately, I had some of the same worries that Thad did. First and foremost, that we could get through it with our souls intact.

I'd known some guys who'd worked undercover as cops. They carried invisible scars, moral wounds, that never would go away. We all did, but this was potentially taking us down a road that might dead end in someplace very dark.

"We'll be in touch, Thad. Got to go." The airport was right in front of us. It was time to go.

"Good hunting."

CHAPTER
20

The Edison Apartments were housed in an historic building in downtown Richmond, right in the middle of the business and financial district. It was ideally placed for Nyce to be close to work, and never far from his nightlife haunts, but unfortunately for us, it was considerably less than ideal for purposes of surveillance.

Phil and I had arrived on separate flights, taking out separate rental cars. We weren't going to obviously work as a team, especially since the unknown client had contacted us separately, though with the same target. There'd been no mention in the mission statement of working together. So, we were on our own, though we had each other's burner number, and the encrypted messaging app we were using would delete any record of our conversations within eight hours. Less, if we needed it to.

I walked the streets after checking into my hotel room in the Hilton Richmond Downtown. I wasn't looking for Nyce himself, not yet, nor was I planning on taking too close a look at the Edison Apartments yet. I just wanted to get a feel for the place. Area familiarization. It's a necessary step, no matter what you're doing.

My route ended up taking me past the over-a-century-old building anyway, and I saw just what we were going to be up against.

Ideally, I would have set up in a car on the street, or, more discreetly, in a coffee shop or restaurant across the way from the building. Unfortunately, there weren't many places on either North 7th Street or East Franklin Street where I could do that. The only restaurant that might provide eyes on the building was an Indian place on Franklin, and I shied away from that as anything but a last resort. Indian food and my guts do not agree. There was only so much I was going to risk incapacitation—or even just extreme discomfort—for the sake of this job.

As for parking on the street, the only places to park were metered. Not a good idea when you don't know how long you're going to be there, especially since a man sitting in a car at a parking meter stands out. Nobody just hangs out where it's going to cost them money. It would be a dead giveaway that I was there for some other reason.

Now, I'd had enough experience running surveillance in American cities—which is different from a place like Baghdad or Juarez—to know that the vast majority of Americans are completely clueless about their surroundings. They just don't see what's going on around them. They don't even necessarily need to be glued to their phones, either. They just don't *see*.

That's no reason to get complacent, though. Because the moment you do, that's when you'll find yourself up against someone who *does* actually look around and *does* actually catalog everything they look at, and then you're burned.

I chewed on the problem as I walked around the target building. The easiest thing, really, would be to get Radford digging into Nyce and get me some more information. From the target package that had been included on the dark web listing, the man wasn't exactly shy about his haunts, and had little sense of personal security. He was a playboy, and figured he was too rich for anything to happen to him. He lived in downtown Richmond, for crying out loud, within a quarter mile of the state capitol.

Unfortunately, I didn't have access to Radford and his tools. That meant that I was going to have to do the legwork, myself.

Part of the private investigator training that PGS had paid for us all to go through had included some extensive OSINT—Open Source Intelligence—training. I didn't have *my* laptop in the hotel room, but I had a capable enough, cheap, disposable rig that I'd picked up using the shadow client's op funds before flying out. It had just enough tools on it to do what I needed to do.

I started back toward the hotel, not looking forward to the next few hours.

* * *

Nyce really wasn't shy about his party life. Or any other part of his life, for that matter. Digging up his social media was the matter of a few keystrokes. He put just about everything out on the internet for likes, it looked like. Pictures of his apartment, morning and night, usually with some comment about the beauty of the sunrise or sunset. I came by the callsign "Backwoods" honestly, and didn't see much beauty in a city skyline, but I'm odd that way, these days. Still, it gave me some idea of his schedule. He posted at almost the exact same times, every day. The time stamps were there, and so was the location data.

He probably didn't even think about the location data. A lot of people didn't. I remembered hearing about a forward operating base in Syria that got compromised because the guys working there hadn't thought to turn off their locators and uploads on their FitBits.

From sunrise, and pictures of his breakfast—usually in one of the restaurants within a block or two of the apartment—he proceeded to document all of his business stops during the day. Most of them were of about as little use to me as the street outside the Edison Apartments. They were rarely in the same place, and even those that were tended to present the same degree of difficulty for anyone looking at setting up surveillance.

If I'd had a team, it might have been one thing. With just myself, I had to find a way to get eyes on him throughout the day, without him noticing that he'd suddenly picked up an unknown companion.

It was his routine after work that got more promising. He had a handful of bars that seemed to be his favorites, and those I could map out pretty well. Bars are actually good starting places for surveillance, since the crowd, the dimness, and the noise make for good camouflage. There's still a significant risk of losing the target, because of those same factors, but if you know what you're looking for, unless the target is aware and using those factors to his advantage, it can be awfully hard to shake a determined tail once he's spotted you.

I looked through his posts, looking for a pattern. It stood out soon enough. While many of his work stops were relatively random, Nyce had an almost religious schedule for his bar hopping. It was weird, but it was going to work to my advantage, so I was going to use it.

I'd see him at the Capital Alehouse that night.

***

I was armed when I walked in, but I had a permit that Virginia recognized—though that was under a fake name, too; this could get ugly if I had to pull and got caught—and the pistol inside my waistband had started its life as an 80 percent polymer receiver. It had no serial number, as such, and it definitely wasn't a Pallas Group Solutions company gun, so there would be no connection there. I hoped not to have to use it, but I was still carrying it, just in case.

From the looks of the interior of the Capital Alehouse, if I had to use the gun, it wasn't going to be here.

The place was almost more of a diner than a bar. Brick and plaster walls offset each other, and the furniture was all dark wood, along with a lot of the accents. Pictures were up on all the walls, above the booths, as well as several large TVs that were currently showing at least three different football games. There were families there as well as single people.

I found a spot in the corner, out of the way, but with a good view of the bar and the rest of the establishment. I was hungry, though I knew that I might have to leave the food and follow if Nyce got up to leave, but I hadn't spotted him as I'd come in, so I figured I had some time. I also would need to be careful not to drink, both for the purposes of alertness and the fact that I was carrying a gun.

Some laws are more prudently followed, especially on this sort of a job. I knew some people in the business who insisted that a surveillance asset should always be unarmed, but that wasn't the way I worked. Too many years in warzones.

My burger had just showed up when Nyce walked through the door.

He was probably in his mid-thirties, of thoroughly average height and build, though his hair was immaculate, and the slacks, polo shirt, and shoes he was wearing probably cost almost as much as my gun.

He was a lot less impressive in person, and I hadn't been especially impressed with him when I'd been looking over the target package.

Not that what I thought about him mattered. He was nothing to me, only a means to an end. I'd watch him, document his movements, if possible, get the blackmail material on him, and then pass it on, hopefully bringing us a bit closer to the sons of bitches who had murdered Carr and tried to murder Edmonds.

It did bother me a little bit that that was what I was involved in. This was a blackmail op, there was no doubt in my mind. There was no other reason for some anonymous hitman network on the dark web to be looking for evidence of drug and sex trafficking. If this were a legit PI job, then it would have come through much more legit channels.

But, I reasoned with myself as I sipped my water and watched Nyce out of the corner of my eye, we'd use it to come down on the blackmailers like a ton of bricks. That was my justification.

I still didn't like it.

Nyce had a couple of beers, since it was happy hour, which seemed to be his routine. The bartender obviously knew him. They chatted a little, though Nyce was constantly fidgeting with his phone. I noticed that he tended to hide the screen whenever the bartender or anyone else came close enough to see it. That was a tell.

It was possible that he was just being private, but if the target package was on point, then I suspected it was stuff that he *really* didn't want anyone seeing, lest they talk to the cops.

He dawdled over his last beer, then suddenly got very interested in his phone. His eyes lit up, and there was something about the expression that I didn't like. Even less so when he suddenly looked around, hiding his phone again, as if making sure that no one had seen his reaction or what was on the screen.

I was sure *that* was aboveboard.

Finally, he tapped out one more message, gulped down the last of his beer, paid his tab, and headed out. Fortunately, I'd finished up and paid my own tab, and was lingering over my water, making a show of scanning through my phone. There wasn't a lot there, since "Walter Callahan" wasn't a real person and therefore had no real friends, but it kept me from being obvious that I was watching him.

Since I'd paid, it didn't necessarily stand out when I gave him a minute after he'd gone out the front, then stood up and left. I picked him up as he got into his car, parked just down the street, as I climbed into my rental car.

I could have sworn I'd seen Phil in there, but if he was doing his job, he was blending in well enough that I couldn't be sure.

Keeping my distance on the streets of Richmond wasn't easy, but I'd been trained, and I'd had a good deal of practice. Again, it would have been a lot easier if we'd been able to work as a team, allowing us to stay a lot closer and switch out, so that he didn't notice the same car in his rear-view mirror for an extended period of time.

Nothing for it, though. I was stuck working solo, so that was what I'd do.

He headed south, across the James River, and into Old Town Manchester. The buildings got more industrial, and the overall feel of the place got a lot sketchier than up north. And that was considering that his apartment and my hotel were right smack dab in the middle of the financial district, right next to the state capitol, which was full of politicians.

His first stop was a large public parking lot. I pulled over across the street, which put me next to another, identical lot on that side, but also put me beneath a tree and in the shadows, as I killed the lights.

I might have seen another car behind me make the same maneuver. I'd be somewhat surprised if I hadn't. It wasn't as if Phil had a different target.

I wanted to hit him up via text message, but I also needed to keep eyes on Nyce. If he was doing what I thought he was doing, then this could be the first report that the shadow client wanted.

Sure enough, I watched Nyce pull up next to a sedan almost as nice as his Rolls Royce, and I got photos of the exchange of cash for a paper bag between the two vehicles. Then I put the phone down as Nyce circled around the parking lot and kept going the same direction he'd been driving. I waited, watching the drug dealer's car, but he pulled out almost at the same time, and I still had eyes on Nyce's car as he turned the corner up ahead.

He continued on through the neighborhood as I followed, taking turn after turn, finally parking in front of a small, white house set a step up from a crumbling, weed-choked sidewalk. I pulled over about a block away, keeping my headlights off, wishing I had a blackout switch, and settled in to watch.

Something prompted me to start recording, just in case. I set the phone up on the dash and started the video.

For a few minutes, nothing happened. Nyce didn't get out of his vehicle, which was noticeably out of place in that neighborhood. Nobody else on that street was driving a Rolls Royce Spectre, or even anything within a mile of its price tag.

No, that wasn't right. There was a Mercedes parked outside that house. It was out of place, too.

After about half an hour, a man came out of the house, looking around the street with a faintly furtive sort of motion, then stepped down, crossed the street, got into a Volt, and drove away. I hadn't quite seen that vehicle before, because of the angle I had on the street, but while it wasn't as expensive or flashy as Nyce's Rolls or the Mercedes, it was still newer and more expensive than most of the other vehicles around there.

Almost as soon as the man in the Volt had driven away, Nyce got out of his Rolls and walked up onto the porch. I zoomed in, silently cursing the quality of the phone camera video, and saw him greeted at the door by a young woman in a negligee. He handed her the paper bag and she ushered him inside.

I didn't need to have it spelled out, and neither would anyone else with any common sense who watched the video.

It was conceivable that the client might want something juicier, but while I might have made a living running surveillance, there was some stuff I didn't want to touch. What was going on in that house was one of those things.

So, I just stayed where I was, maintaining the video surveillance of the front of the house and Nyce's car. He was in there for about an hour, during which time yet another expensive car pulled up and parked just down the street, the driver staying in the vehicle for the time being.

After that hour, Nyce came out and went to his car. The guy in the Lexus wasn't as patient or discreet as Nyce, as he got out immediately and passed Nyce on the way in.

I waited until Nyce had driven away to follow, slowly rolling past the small house. I was glad that the curtains were drawn.

I sincerely hoped that what I'd captured would be enough for the client.

CHAPTER
21

Nyce took a pretty direct route back to the Edison Apartments. Something about the way he drove was a little off, and it took me an embarrassingly long time to figure out that he was probably high, and therefore he was driving excruciatingly slowly to avoid getting pulled over. I'd seen that before.

He still made it to the building and pulled into the parking garage as I slowly rolled past, heading for my own hotel. It was getting close to one in the morning, and I was tired. There wasn't any good way I could maintain surveillance once he was in the Edison, so I peeled off and headed for bed.

It only took a few minutes to get the laptop up, get the Tor browser going, and send the night's take to the shadow client. I kind of felt dirty, doing it, but once again told myself that he really was a scumbag, and we were going to burn down the people looking for leverage on him, anyway.

Without waiting for a reply, I crashed. I wasn't getting paid to stay up for twenty-four hours for this crap.

***

I'd set the chat deletion feature short enough that if Phil had tried to message me during the night, I hadn't seen it. As I was scarfing down breakfast, the phone buzzed, and a message from him popped up. Like the call from Goblin, there was no name on the number, but I recognized it, anyway.

You should check the news this morning.

I knew Phil well enough to know that if I asked, he wasn't going to tell me. So, I turned on the TV in the room and flipped to the local news station.

There it was, plain as day. Flashing blue and red lights around the very same house that I'd been watching the night before. I was reasonably sure that Phil had been, too. The marquee at the bottom of the screen told the story, even without turning the sound up.

Prostitution ring broken up in early morning raid.

I looked down at the phone again. *They sure moved fast, didn't they?*

Almost as if they're on a timeline. Did you look into this guy Nyce's finance dealings?

I frowned a little. *Nothing past the target package, no. I was trying to find him.*

He's been involved in several nasty short sale fights on the stock market lately. Same sort of stuff that our boy in Atlanta was getting into. Even with the encryption on the app and the destruction of all messages after a relatively brief time, Phil was being careful not to mention Strand.

Heading off some of our mutual friends' acquisitions?
Looks like it.

It explained why he'd been targeted. Possibly. There were any number of other possibilities, that might be even more unsavory, and this could just be a coincidence. It was unlikely that an underworld network of hitters would be working exclusively for just one client.

I hated to think about just how far this depraved rabbit hole might go.

My phone buzzed with the encrypted email's message notification. A moment later, I got another text from Phil. *And I've just been called off. Looks like they got what they wanted.*

I checked the encrypted email. Sure enough, another message from our shadow employer was right there. *Reporting received. Most excellent. Payment will arrive in the next twenty-four hours. You may extract now. We will be in touch if we require your services again.*

With a grimace, I switched back to the messenger. *Same here. Except we didn't exactly get what we wanted.*

He didn't reply right away. *Contact the boss?* It was unlikely that even if anyone could crack the encryption, that they'd recognize Goblin's callsign, but we were still being extra cautious.

May as well. I think we should maintain surveillance on Nyce. I didn't see anything that appeared to be surveillance on us. We should be able to get and keep eyes on him and see if anything changes. It might tell us something.

The three little dots that indicated Phil was typing stayed there for a long time. Phil wasn't the wordiest of men, so I figured he was rewording. I didn't know why he was bothering. I wasn't the type who'd get butthurt because he disagreed with me.

There's an Indian restaurant across the street. I'll go there as soon as they open. Phil was notorious for liking any food that registered roughly on the same heat level as a volcano. Thai was his favorite, but he wouldn't turn down Indian food if he had a chance at it. I would take a pass on that, plus it would still be best for our cover if this was about as close as we got.

Of course, while the Indian restaurant was across the street from the Edison Apartments, it didn't have eyes on the front door. There wasn't really a good place that did, since even the breakfast and lunch place on the south side of Franklin was set far enough back that it would be difficult to keep eyes on the door from there.

That limited our options, but I had an idea all of a sudden. We knew which apartment was Nyce's. I brought up the Edison Apartments' website and started looking.

Within a few minutes I had requested a showing of the open apartment three doors down from Nyce's. It wasn't ideal, which would be right across the hall, but it was something.

You still there? My silence must have unnerved Phil a little.

Yeah. I outlined my plan. *I requested an early showing—got to get to work—so that hopefully I can get on him before he leaves for whatever office he's going to tomorrow.*

Sounds like a plan. I'll be in touch.

* * *

Fortunately, the manager wanted a renter for that apartment. I didn't know if the middle-aged woman in the pencil skirt and white blouse who met me at the door was the manager or just someone who worked for her, but she greeted me at the door with a dazzling smile, which was wasted on me. I hadn't slept all that well the night before, probably because I was stress-bombing about the situation I found myself in, and I hadn't had more than one cup of coffee yet.

I was thinking somewhat nostalgically about the unhealthy wide awake cocktails we'd put together in Iraq in the Marine Corps, mixing energy drinks with metabolism booster supplements.

"Mr. Callahan?" She held out a manicured hand. "I'm Rose Wagner. I'll be happy to show you the apartment. I'm so glad you're considering renting with us."

If I was serious, I wouldn't be considering renting here. Not when a studio apartment cost almost two grand a month. But that wasn't the point of being up this early, much less getting her out of bed this early, so I bit my tongue and shook her hand. "I've heard some great things, and the location's fantastic." I was dressed in business casual, already entirely too warm for the day, even though my slacks and light blue shirt should be light enough. I was a Westerner born and bred, and I don't like humidity. The dark blue blazer that hid the polymer pistol on the back side of my hip wasn't helping anything, but it contributed to the appearance of being another high-energy finance guy.

178

I supposed the coffee in my hand helped, too, even though it was closer to burnt hair than what I'd call good coffee. And I don't even consider myself that much of a coffee snob.

"Well, let's head up, shall we?" With a beckoning wave, she led the way toward the elevators.

She chattered on about all the amenities and the nearness to the Capitol and the business and financial districts, all things that I already knew. She seemed to think they were great selling points, and to people like Nyce, they probably were. I was just doing my damnedest to watch every opening and corner, cataloging everything I saw while trying not to make it obvious that was what I was doing.

We got to the tenth floor and started down the hall. I was only half listening to Wagner as she chattered on, occasionally inserting a monosyllable where it seemed necessary. She wasn't paying any mind to my apparent disconnect. She was probably a great saleslady.

Starting down the hall, I glanced over as the door to the stairwell at the far end of the hall opened.

I immediately became much more interested in what Wagner was saying. If only to make sure that the younger man from the trio who had tried to strongarm Romero didn't notice me as he walked into the hallway, flanked by two others, one of whom might have been armed security, and went straight to what looked like Nyce's door.

They knocked, and Nyce answered. I was trying to listen and watch out of the corner of my eye, wishing I could get to my phone and alert Phil, but I had to smile and nod as Wagner chattered on, following her into the apartment.

She showed me around, and I took a few pictures, taking advantage of the time on my phone to send Phil the message, pretending I was taking notes. *Person of Interest Number Three from the office in Nashville just knocked on Nyce's door. Currently occupied and can't maintain contact. Get eyes on the door and get on him as soon as he walks out.*

Rgr. If we needed any confirmation of the link between the shadow client and the parties that were trying to strongarm Carr & Sons, we sure had it. Unfortunately, the two of us were on our own, and couldn't openly work together.

I had to suffer through the rest of Wagner's presentation, finally leaving her with the hurried assurance that I'd consider it, talk to my girlfriend, and that I had to get to work.

As I came out into the hall, I glanced toward Nyce's door. It was shut, and there was no sign of him or his guests. From the look I'd seen on his face when he'd opened the door, he hadn't been happy to see them, either.

I kept my eyes open as I headed back down. By the time I walked out onto the street and got back in my rental car to go to my nonexistent work, I had the beginnings of a plan.

I didn't think that Person of Interest Three was there to kill Nyce. That would have made the blackmail irrelevant, and that guy hadn't seemed the type. Too high-strung, too nervous. So, unless Nyce got so scared that he committed suicide or tried to leave town, he should be there that night. I doubted he'd venture out to his usual watering holes again.

I had a house call to make that night.

CHAPTER 22

Getting back into the Edison in the middle of the night was a problem. There was a parking garage on the alley behind it, but that was a public parking garage, and not connected to the Edison Apartments. The alley itself, which might have given me access to a back door, was under video surveillance, and I didn't want that kind of attention.

I had most of the day to think over my approach, and by the time the sun was going down, I was pretty sure how I was going to have to tackle the problem. It wasn't ideal, and there were a lot of ways it could go wrong, but it was probably my best bet.

I'd hung around Franklin for the most part for most of the day, keeping eyes on the building. I hadn't seen Nyce leave. That was interesting. Even more so when I followed up a couple of times and got eyes on his Rolls. It hadn't moved since the night before.

Every indicator told me that they wouldn't have killed him. Whatever had happened in that apartment, though, he wasn't sticking his head out. I even checked his social media on my phone as I moved around the area, from restaurant to coffee shop. He finally posted something around lunchtime. Predictably, it was a photo of his lunch. He was probably trying not to let out that anything was amiss, but it had the effect of letting me know that he was alive, at least.

Phil was giving me quick but necessarily vague situation reports. He was still following our person of interest, who appeared to make a couple more stops before going into the Commonwealth Hotel. I was glad I was staying in the Hilton. Less chance of getting spotted and potentially recognized.

Finally, it was time to move in.

If I'd been really high-speed, I would have picked the lock on a back door and slipped inside. Unfortunately, that potentially meant getting spotted and recorded on CCTV. There were signs all over that back alley declaring that it was under video surveillance. While I was pretty sure that Nyce wouldn't call the cops after the discussion that needed to happen, that didn't mean that the building's management wouldn't.

So, it was time for some social engineering. Not as sleek or sexy, but when it works, it works.

I waited until I spotted a middle-aged woman walking toward the front doors, a paper shopping bag in her hand. As she turned toward the doors, I was apparently on my phone, though there was no open call.

"Hey, man, somebody just came up. I'll be up in a sec." I waited until she opened the door and grabbed it to hold it for her. She glanced at me, and for a second I wondered if I'd invited a diatribe about how she could hold her own doors, but she just nodded her thanks and pushed on inside.

I didn't take the same route to the tenth floor that I had with Wagner. I was dressed differently, having changed back into my usual jeans, boots, and an untucked, collared shirt, but that didn't mean I wouldn't be recognized, if anyone was paying attention.

The skilled predator in this environment takes full advantage of people's general lack of attention, but never entirely relies on it.

So, as soon as I was out of sight of the woman who had unwittingly let me in, I headed for the stairs.

It was a long climb, but I'd been keeping up on the PT for a reason. It had already proved worth every hour of pain down in Mexico, when we'd had to get old school on the recon, and now it was proving to be a good call again. I was still breathing a little hard by the time I got to the tenth floor, but it could be a lot worse.

The hallway was empty as I stepped out into it, but I still made a show of nonchalance, my phone to my ear, acting as if I was supposed to be there.

Believe me, that gets a lot more nerve-wracking than it sounds, when you're trying to infiltrate a place where you really *don't* belong, and all without backup.

Still, no one appeared in the hallway by the time I reached Nyce's door. I hesitated. I had the tools in my pocket to let myself in. A pocket knife and a paperclip would suffice for a tensioner and pick, but they took some time to use, and there was a good chance, even given the relatively late hour, that someone would come out in the hall and see me picking the lock. Better to play this cool.

So, I knocked on the door.

If I'd done my job right, Nyce shouldn't have seen me at all during the previous day and night that I'd been following him. I should just be a stranger knocking on his door.

That might or might not go well, given the visit he'd gotten that morning, and his apparent reaction.

I was about to knock on the door again when it was cracked open. Nyce looked considerably less polished than he had before. He'd made an effort to style his hair, so he wasn't the Hollywood picture of depression and anxiety, but there was definitely something off.

He didn't just slam the door in my face, though. His eyes widened, but he still stayed in the doorway. "What do you want?"

"I just want to talk, Riley. It could have a great deal of impact on your future prospects."

I didn't know how that was going to go over. He might panic and slam the door. He might panic and try to fight or run.

Instead, he just stared at me for a few seconds. "Look, I'm already doing what you asked."

That certainly explained that the visit he'd gotten that morning was exactly what I'd figured it was, but I needed more. "Shall we have a sit-down, or are we really going to have this conversation in the hallway?"

He looked around, then, as if suddenly noticing that I *was* standing in the hallway, and therefore we were within earshot of every one of his neighbors. He stepped back and ushered me inside the apartment, looking past me into the hallway one more time before closing the door.

I noticed he didn't lock it. Maybe he just wasn't paranoid enough. Maybe he didn't want to be locked inside his apartment with me.

That was probably the wisest decision he'd made yet.

He stood in his living room for a moment, keeping his distance but still facing me. He was sort of fidgeting, and after a moment I began to suspect that much of the fidgeting was drug related. Especially when I glanced at the kitchen table and saw the plastic bag there. It wasn't dead certain to be a drug bag, but knowing what I knew about him, it wasn't a stretch.

Without an invitation, I sat down on his couch. It was something of a calculated move, establishing that I was perfectly comfortable, and that I was in control here, even though it was his apartment. It also put me in a position where I *could* draw quickly if I needed to, but it didn't look like it, hopefully putting him somewhat more at east.

From what I'd seen on surveillance, I didn't know how at ease I really wanted him to be, but for the sake of the information I needed, I couldn't afford to panic him.

"You had a visit from some people my associates and I are very interested in, this morning, Riley." A part of me had always wanted to use that turn of phrase: "My associates and I."

That threw him for a loop. He must have thought that I was with those people, so when I clearly wasn't, he didn't know what to think. He blinked at me, his mouth opening and closing.

I kept my cool. "I need you to tell me everything that happened this morning, Riley. Who they were, what they wanted, and what they told you to do." I tilted my head to one side. "Or should I hand the recordings I possess of your entry and exit from that illegal brothel I saw got raided this morning over to the Richmond PD? I'm sure they'd be interested."

He looked away then, and tried to take a step toward the kitchen, but his knees buckled. He caught himself, dragging himself into the armchair set at a ninety-degree angle to the couch, and sinking into it. "What do you want to know?"

He was definitely high. I'd just asked him that. I still held onto my patience and repeated myself. "Who were the people who came to this apartment this morning, and what did they want?"

He blinked again, then leaned forward a little bit. "Look, I told you. I already did everything that Todd told me to do. I dumped the stocks he wanted me to dump, and I bought the ones he wanted me to buy. The funding's going where TC wants it to go. What more do you want from me?"

The drugs were making him confused, but that might end up working to my advantage. I wasn't a huge believer in *in vino veritas*, but sometimes it worked out that way. At least I already had a couple of names, though I needed more.

"TC? And who's Todd?"

"Talbot Consulting, man." He looked at me as if I was behind the power curve. "Oh, they're not on the Stock Exchange or anything, but everybody who's anybody knows them. They're *huge* movers and shakers. They're, like, *the* network for these sorts of things. Nobody crosses them." He seemed to fold in on himself a little bit. "I hadn't really worked in the same circles, but I heard about them. They're almost the boogeyman."

185

He seemed to be shutting down a little. I had something to go on, but if Talbot Consulting was anything like Archer-Lin Investments, I'd need a bit more. "Who's Todd?"

"Todd Linemann is one of the few partners I know about in Talbot. It's a small company, such as it is, but their reach is enormous. They manage things for a few LLCs that are really anonymous front companies, most of them based in Panama or the Bahamas. I don't think anyone knows who all they work with."

Todd Linemann. We had a company and a name. We could track both. "Why would they want you to move stocks around, and why would they feel the need to blackmail you to make sure you cooperated?"

"Man, I don't know." Nyce looked like he was about to cry. Any sympathy I might have felt was tempered by the fact that I was pretty sure he was guilty of drug and human trafficking. "They didn't tell me. I don't think they tell anybody. You do what they want, or they crush your nuts." He did start to cry, then.

I watched him for a few more moments, considering whether or not I was going to get anything else out of him. The drugs were definitely taking hold, and I wasn't sure he would be conscious for too much longer. I wondered if I should take steps to make sure I left no evidence of my presence in the apartment, in case he overdosed. It was probably far too late for that, but then, I hadn't touched any of the drug paraphernalia, nor had I forced my way in, so there was nothing that would link me to his death if that happened.

"What stocks did they want you to move?" I didn't know if it would be useful, but I cataloged the list he rattled off, with an increasingly slurred voice.

Finally, I stood up. From the looks of things, I didn't think Nyce was able to stand up. I still loomed over him, and he rolled his eyes to look up at me. "Just so we're clear, Riley, this conversation never happened." I hoped that he'd only have blurred and indistinct memories of it, thanks to his chemical enhancement, but it paid to be sure. "If anyone hears about it, then some people you don't want to might find out about what you do on a Thursday night."

He flinched at that, shrinking in on himself in the chair. Drugged or not, he understood what I'd just said.

I left him in his stupor, careful to wipe the doorknob off with the tail of my shirt before I pulled the door closed. It probably wouldn't change anything, but it might pay to be careful.

CHAPTER 23

"Ten o'clock."

"I see it." Nick was riding in the passenger seat this time, while Doug drove. It was almost the same route, the same trip, that they'd taken for the last several days, moving the client personnel back and forth between the hotel and the plant. They varied which streets they took as much as possible, but the unfortunate truth about the two fixed positions where they were tasked with security was that there were only so many ways they *could* vary the route.

And the bad guys had noticed.

The PGS contractors had cataloged at least half a dozen obvious surveillance units over the last few days. Mostly stationary cars, but there had been knots of young men just hanging out, watching traffic. That wasn't all *that* strange, in and of itself, but there were indicators that the experienced special operations contractors could pick up on that wouldn't necessarily be all that obvious to other people.

Sometimes, survival in a combat zone was as much a matter of a finely tuned gut instinct as it was precise intelligence and training.

This time, the indicator was another car, a battered Ford Focus with three young men sitting inside, staring at the two vans as they went by. One of them was on a phone.

Nick took a pair of discreet photos from just over the lip of his window as the vans drove past the car and sent them up to the TOC that Vern had set up in the plant.

They couldn't just move all the contractors to the plant, as much as the extra site security was needed. The client was still staying in the hotel, and especially after what had happened to Max and Adira, there was no way they could leave the hotel unsecured.

So, they were split up and spread thin, but at least they were a bit better equipped, now.

Nick still hoped that they didn't get stopped by the Honduran cops. The duffel bags at his feet and behind Doug's seat were sure to get them slapped in jail, probably right alongside the very same *mareros* they were fighting. The Hondurans weren't likely to be enthusiastic about a bunch of *yanquis* driving around with body armor, helmets, night vision, short-barrel AR carbines without serial numbers, completely off the La Armeria registry, and a whole ton of ammunition.

Nick had no idea just how much pressure Goblin had put on Carr & Sons to get them to agree to help smuggle the parts and the ammunition in. Entire barrels of what were labeled industrial chemicals had been full of 5.56 and 9mm ammunition, already loaded in a whole lot of magazines. That was leaving aside all the gun parts.

They probably *could* have gotten full rifles in, if that was the way things were going to go, but he could see the wisdom in going with the machined, unserialized lowers. There was no way to trace any of them, if the Hondurans got their hands on one and got their shit together enough to try to do forensics.

It still felt good to have a proper full loadout again, especially considering the war they found themselves in the middle of.

Hunkering down in his seat, he peered through the rearview mirror, watching the Focus as they drove away. It didn't follow them, this time. Some of the MS-13 elements had.

Straightening back up, he resumed his scans of their surroundings. Never a good idea to get so focused on one threat that you lose track of all the others.

They spotted three more observation posts on the way to the plant. He couldn't tell which clique they were attached to. That was a problem when dealing with these sorts of decentralized and irregular forces, but he'd spent his entire adult life in some form of conflict with organizations like that. It was just par for the course.

The fence was well on the way to completed, overwatched by gunmen on the roof with their two scratchbuilt AR-10s. They'd used mostly Aero Precision parts but machined close approximations of the M5E1 lower receivers.

The two vans pulled through the gate, watched by two more guards with pistols openly carried on their belts, their own rifles and gear well out of sight. Carl waved, and Doug returned the gesture as he drove through the gap in the fence.

Parking in the lot outside the plant office, they let the client personnel head inside while they gathered their duffels and secured the vans. The fence was a help, but there were certain habits that died hard, and needed to be maintained.

They stepped out at the same time, their duffels slung over their shoulders, unzipped so that they could easily reach the rifles as they scanned the fields beyond the fence. It was one more habit that was getting hard-wired in.

If he was being honest, Nick had to admit that they were habits built from years in active warzones, that were coming back to the surface in this hellscape of gang violence.

With a glance up at the roof, Nick confirmed that the guy on overwatch had them covered before turning toward the office. Doug was right beside him.

Neither man spoke as they walked through the foyer and into the TOC. Vern was sitting back in a chair, looking over the photos that Nick had sent.

"They're getting thicker." He tapped the table with a pen. "They're gearing up for something."

"Sucker bet that they're going to try to ambush the motorcade." Nick let his duffel down to the floor. "They got their asses handed to them when they tried to assault the plant."

"That probably just pissed them off even more." Vern shook his head, his eyes still fixed on the screen. "These guys don't *do* pragmatism. They were on the savagery arms race long before even the cartels up north were." He sighed and dug his thumb and forefinger into his eyes. Who knew how long he'd been sitting there, watching the feeds. "The fact that they haven't made a move for the last few days tells me they've got something special in mind."

In fact, there hadn't been much movement since the PGS contractors had hit the "destroyer house" in Barrio Medina. Nick agreed with Vern, though. That quiet wasn't actually a good sign.

"How's the drone recon going?" Doug asked.

"Slow." Vern leaned back farther in the chair and stretched, reaching for his coffee. "There's a lot going on, and it isn't as if these guys wear ID. We do think we've identified two more destroyer houses in Barrio Medina and at least one in Chamelecón. They'll be first on our hit list when the time comes. However, it does look like there's something brewing."

Straitening up in the chair, he brought up a video window and hit "Play." Nick and Doug leaned in to watch.

"They're staging, all right." The video showed a group of *mareros* parking a vehicle close to one of the intersections they hadn't been able to avoid and leaving it. It wasn't necessarily a car bomb, but it could be. "This is only one of the caches we've watched, and then there's this." He switched videos again, and this time it was even more obvious.

Six gangsters converged on a house that Nick recognized from having passed it about a dozen times over the last week. The drone's angle wasn't such that they could see much of the interplay between the gangbangers and the homeowner, but the general body language of the men gathered around the front door was pretty unmistakable. They were there to get something, and when the young woman and her kids fled out the door and down the street, followed by gestures that were at best obscene, then it became even more obvious what they were after.

"That place needs to get some love." Nick glanced at Vern. "You want to hit it?" The *mara* was setting up an ambush position. They'd done something similar before, forcing families out of their homes to create buffer zones with Barrio 18.

"Tempting, but I think we need to try something else. We've been getting some attention from the Hondurans since the hit we pulled in Barrio Medina. They can't prove anything, and it seems like there are a few on the force—even highly placed officers—who see our presence and capability as an opportunity, rather than a burden."

"They think that we can clean out some of their opposition, without them having to get their hands dirty." Doug sounded more disgusted by that than normal, until Nick figured out that he was probably thinking about the corruption that plagued just about every Latin American police force.

Hell, it plagues just about every Third World law enforcement agency on the face of the planet. Nick had seen enough of the same sort of "pay to play" model throughout the Middle East, Central Asia, and Africa. It wasn't new. In fact, honest cops were the exception, worldwide, rather than the rule.

Some of that was because of tribalism. Some of it was simple, human greed.

"And I'm fine with that." Vern had always been somewhat pragmatic about some of the shadier elements of the profession. Sometimes, when they'd worked together, Nick had wondered a little if the only thing keeping the other man from getting into some of the underworld activities that a few of their compatriots had been killed or gone to jail for was the fact that he was too smart for it and didn't think the juice was worth the squeeze. "If it gets us more information and lets us kill these fucks more efficiently, I'm all about it."

He swiveled around in the chair. "I know you guys just did a run, but we've got a little something in the works. You up for it?"

Doug snorted. "It was a twenty-minute drive, Vern. Don't church it up. What have you got?"

"How'd you like to clear out some of these animals we've been watching?"

Doug grinned like a skull. "Sounds groovy. Only one thing."

He sat down on one of the ratty couches they'd pulled into the break room they'd turned into a tactical operations center. "I know a lot of animals that are way better than any of those fucks out there."

CHAPTER
24

The sun was starting to go down when the vans pulled out of the plant and started back toward the hotel.

They weren't moving that fast. Nor were they creeping, but just going the speed of traffic. There was nothing in their outward appearance or movement to suggest that this was anything but the plant personnel heading back to the hotel at the end of the workday.

The contractors usually did two runs, though more and more of the actual workforce was made up of native Hondurans. They were part of the reason that Carr & Sons had built the plant in the first place, since their labor was considerably cheaper than Americans'. However, while that might have chafed on a few of the Pallas Group Solutions security contractors, there was an added benefit. Some of those Honduran workers were excellent sources of intel on the local area and the atmospherics.

Those workers had confirmed some of the suspicions that Vern had developed, watching the reporting from the transport convoys and the drone sweeps. That had determined where things were going to go down.

About a block short of where the drone had documented the *mareros* taking over a house, the lead van seemed to stutter, then pulled over to the side of the road, just outside a truck accessories store called *Truck Chrome*. It seemed to die, then, and the driver got out, cussing, and lifted the hood.

For a few minutes, as the second van pulled up next to it, nothing seemed to happen. The men in the vans could feel eyes on them, but no one moved.

Josh, leaning over the engine compartment, muttered into his radio. "Would be a lot more convincing if we had some steam or something coming out of here."

"Clear the net." Vern didn't sound amused, and Josh subsided, though he kept glancing around to his flanks as he pretended to fiddle with a malfunctioning engine.

Inside the trail van, Nick found he was sweating. It *was* Honduras, so of course he was sweating, but there was more than just the local heat and humidity at work here. If the bad guys didn't oblige the contractors, this could get ugly, fast. It could turn into a massacre that would effectively end both the Carr & Sons and PGS operations in Honduras.

"Contact. Three military age males, armed. South side, coming up the street."

"Four more MAMs coming along 33 Calle, toward us from the east."

Nick flexed his hands around the AR between his knees, the suppressed muzzle pointed up at the ceiling. That was another old habit. Muzzle down, an accidental discharge could put a bullet through something vital in a vehicle. Muzzle up in a vehicle, muzzle down in a helicopter.

"Only seven?" Casey sounded downright insulted. "What a waste."

"Give it time. As soon as these seven get dumped, a lot more are going to come out of the woodwork." Saul was in the zone. Otherwise, he wouldn't have been nearly so polite with Casey. He'd run out of patience with their retired sergeant major sometime back in California.

"Any more visible?" Vern didn't want to spring the trap prematurely, but Josh was getting a little nervous, hanging his ass out in the breeze.

"Not yet, but if we don't go now, these fuckers are going to try to skin me alive." Josh sounded more than a little keyed up. No wonder, really. He had his body armor on under his shirt, and his Glock 19 in his waistband, but his rifle, helmet, and chest rig were still inside the vehicle.

Vern was in the right seat of the rear van. He craned his neck a little, though from where Nick sat, he could see that the hitters were still alone. "Stand by, Money. We're not going to let them scalp you. Let them provoke things, though."

"I mean, it's an okay plan, except for the fact that they've already got their weapons out, and I'd have to draw." Josh was getting *really* uncomfortable. "That reaction gap is real, Figaro."

"Just hang in there, Money." Vern was as in the zone as Saul. His tone was almost soothing as his eyes flicked from one angle to another, his face otherwise utterly still. Nick could almost see the wheels turning in his head as he calculated the best time to spring the trap.

Nick was right at the sliding side door, twisted around in his seat, one hand on his rifle and the other on the door handle, just waiting for the word. The vans didn't have side windows, but he could see the oncoming group of *mareros* well enough through the windshield to be able to calculate where everyone was.

They were getting closer to Josh, coming up behind him. One of them lifted the pistol in his hand, calling out, though Nick couldn't hear the words through the body of the van.

"Now."

Nick yanked the door open and launched himself into the street, snatching his rifle up in an arc that terminated with his support hand forward on the handguard, pulling the buttstock back into his collarbone as he caught hold of the firing control with his other hand and dropped the red dot level with the oncoming *mareros*, his finger tightening on the trigger as his thumb swept the selector to "Fire" and he identified hostile act and hostile intent.

There'd been no question of what they'd do once Vern gave the word. They were there to kill thugs, and that was what they were going to do.

He rode the trigger as he raked the oncoming group of MS-13 hitters, moving forward and away from the door as he did so, clearing the way for Doug, Saul, Mike, Manny, and Casey. They came out fast, hitting the ground moving, spreading out in a "V" from the vehicle, each man opening fire as soon as he was clear of the man in front of him and had targets. Nick felt a bullet *snap* past his ear as Doug took advantage of the first opening that presented itself.

The oncoming killers didn't really have time to register shock at the sight of men in helmets, plate carriers, and chest rigs full of ammo, spilling out of the van with suppressed rifles. They were cut down in seconds, bullets ripping through unarmored torsos to blow ragged holes in hearts and lungs.

In the time that it had taken Nick to go from the door to a position just off the front quarter panel of the van, all four were down in the street, already dead or very quickly headed that way, blood seeping out onto the pavement.

The contractors didn't get back in the vehicle, though, even as Nick heard Josh report from the front, "All clear." They were there to spring the ambush that had been in the offing for the last couple of days, but they were also out to do more damage than that.

They spread out in pairs, taking up covered positions on the corners of the nearest buildings, eyes and muzzles trained down every approach toward the two parked vans. Neither vehicle had been hit in the brief storm of gunfire, probably because it had all been going one way.

"Time starts now." Vern's voice was flat, clipped, and businesslike over the radio, as if he neither knew nor cared that they'd just ended seven lives in less time than it took to describe it. Nick wasn't bothered by that. He was in the zone, himself, and he doubted he'd ever find himself in the position where he gave half a fraction of a fuck about dead MS-13 murderers.

Especially not after what they'd found in that destroyer house.

What had been done to Max and Adira.

The timing was going to be tricky, though. None of them wanted to get into a firefight with the San Pedro Sula police. They'd have to be gone before they showed up, and this wasn't quite one of the *mara*'s usual barrios.

The only advantage was that it also wasn't one of the parts of the city the cops were that interested in patrolling. Not too many rich people there.

For a few seconds, they held their position, waiting for the inevitable reinforcements. The idea was to let the *mareros* dogpile them, slaughter the gangsters as they came, then get out.

But as the seconds ticked by, there were no reinforcements. As if those seven men currently lying dead in the streets were all that MS-13 had sent.

That didn't seem like them, and worse, it didn't work for the plan. But that was why they'd developed contingency plans.

"Alpha Element, moving on the target house." That was Carl, taking charge up front, leading the way as the four assaulters pushed through the vegetation behind the Truck Chrome shop and toward the house they'd identified as an MS-13 staging area.

Nick was starting to think that those guys—Josh, Carl, Durand, and Abaeze—were probably going to get most of the action. Presuming that the house they'd targeted was the primary staging point for the ambush.

He should have considered response times. The gangsters hadn't been prepared for the stiff resistance they'd gotten, so the seven dead men had apparently decided to handle it themselves. The word had gotten out, though.

Suppressed gunfire crackled behind him. It took years of discipline to keep his eyes and his muzzle fixed on the street in front of him, trusting the others to cover that direction until they called for support. This was his sector.

It was a good thing he and Doug stayed on task, too.

The Nissan Frontier that came around the corner at the far end of the long block was almost overflowing with young men, most of them with short hair and baggy clothes, and all of them armed. It said something about police presence in this part of San Pedro Sula when, even though it wasn't technically a mara neighborhood, they could roll around with that kind of firepower openly displayed.

Doug opened fire first, having identified the threat immediately. Nick cursed silently as he followed suit, feeling once again like his partner was two steps ahead of him.

He wasn't sure which of the two of them hit the driver, though he was pretty sure it was Doug. Glass shattered, red sprayed across a window, and the truck slewed to the side as the dead man behind the wheel dragged it over, crashing into a parked Subaru on the side of the street. The avenue was narrow enough that there really wasn't a whole lot of space for the out-of-control truck to go.

Several of the gunmen in the back had been thrown clear in the impact, and the rest were hurting, but they were starting to get themselves together, one of them lifting a Draco and ripping off a burst up the street. The rounds went high, and Nick didn't even flinch as he heard them crackle overhead. He just laid his sights on the gunman and dropped him with a controlled pair, even as Doug got up and started to advance down the narrow street, keeping between the cars and the walls of the houses on either side, his weapon up, still pumping bullets at anything with a weapon. Nick heaved himself to his feet and followed, though he knew he wasn't going to risk a shot on the move until he was a lot closer.

Three more of the gunmen went down with six shots. More gunfire was starting to rattle down the street, bullets smacking into plaster walls, shattering glass, and going winging off over rooftops to hit somewhere else. Nick brought his own rifle up and returned fire, further shattering more of the Nissan's window glass, knowing he wasn't going to be nearly as accurate as Doug, but just hoping to force the *mareros'* heads down.

A long, ripping burst of fire spat bits of pavement into the air and chewed into the wall in front of him. He threw himself flat. There weren't as many cars on the street as there would be even in a place like Baghdad or Juarez, so there was less cover.

Going prone in the little bit of a ditch there was on the side of the road, as choked with stagnant water as it was, actually put him in a better position.

Setting the rifle on the magazine, he clamped his off hand over the top of the handguard, leaned into the gun, and dumped the rest of the magazine at just about mid-calf height.

It wasn't quite the same as running a machinegun at knee level, but it had much the same effect. He chopped the legs out from under four more of the gunmen, even as he blew out three of the Nissan's tires, and when the gangsters fell into the street, he quickly finished them off as he raked his fire right and left. The incoming fire almost ceased altogether, and Doug suddenly sprinted forward, coming out from behind the only other parked car on the street, slowing only slightly as he came closer, his carbine rotating like a tank's main gun as he brought it to bear on the remaining *mareros.*

The shooting that followed, while it was technically a gunfight, since the gangsters were still trying to bring their weapons to bear on him, was more like an execution. Doug's weapon crackled in a continuous, tearing roar, as he dragged the muzzle across the clumped group of gang gunmen. The tempo of his fire didn't even slow while his muzzle moved smoothly from one side to another. He still got at least two rounds into each man's vitals as he pulled the weapon from left to right.

He stopped shooting as soon as the last one was done, though he continued to move around the back of the wrecked pickup, checking the dead space just to be sure. Nick had reloaded, and was now back up on a knee, even as the radio call came from the vehicles. "This is Figaro. Collapse on the vics. Time now."

Nick held his position as Doug rolled back across the street from the stricken Frontier and sprinted past him, heading back toward the vans. Only when he heard, "Turn and go!" did he get up and move, himself.

In less than fifteen seconds, they were pulling the doors shut as the drivers started them moving away from the scene of carnage. Sirens whooped in the distance, but it was far too late for the nearly two dozen tattooed killers lying dead in their own blood on the street.

CHAPTER
25

If not for the action that the B and D Teams were getting into down in Honduras, I would start to get worried that the client might decide that they didn't need the extra security anymore.

Phil and I had gotten back from Richmond and gone right into another six-hour shift of protection duties for Romero. We had to keep things low-key, since we hadn't exactly told Romero what we'd been up to. He had to have noticed that the two of us were gone for a couple of days, but if he did, he didn't comment on it.

Of course, from the reports we were getting from Figaro down in San Pedro Sula, I could imagine that Romero was a little preoccupied.

Most of the time, so far, he'd taken time out to chat with his detail. He didn't this time, though I didn't get the impression that it had anything to do with our absence. He was deep in thought most of the time we saw him, and thoroughly absorbed in his work. When we got him home, he thanked us, then headed upstairs and we didn't see him again before we switched out with Tom and Brian.

I was tired, but I still needed to check in with KG. We hadn't really had a chance to do a thorough hot wash of the op in Richmond.

When I walked into the team house, he was sitting in the kitchen, in front of a laptop, a look on his face that didn't bode well. He wasn't mad, but he was looking down at the screen with his eyes a little wide, his eyebrows raised, with an expression that told me he hadn't expected what he'd found, and that it made things only more complicated.

I dropped my go bag inside the door, grabbed another chair, flipped it around, and sat down, leaning on the chair back. "I don't like that look."

He took a deep breath and lifted his eyes to meet mine. "There's not much to like." He swiveled the laptop around so I could see the screen.

There were multiple windows open, but the first one was a website for Talbot Consulting. There wasn't much there, just a couple of testimonials and a contact page. The design was slick, and it looked like someone had sunk a pretty penny into it, but there simply wasn't much information.

"Turns out that Talbot Consulting isn't a fund, per se, but a financial consulting firm. There's not a whole lot of information about them out there, at least not that's readily available over normal channels. I've got a couple buddies who are deep in the stock market I've reached out to, in case they've heard something." Most of us knew a few guys like that. There's usually a good deal of time to kill when you're working contract overseas, and that could be filled with school, TV shows, side businesses that could be managed remotely, video games, trying to find the end of the internet, or investing. A fair number of the guys I'd worked with had gone with several of those options.

"What we *have* been able to find, thanks to that name, Todd Linemann, isn't encouraging." He tapped a command to switch windows. What came up was a photo of Todd Linemann, arm in arm with a major public billionaire, who also happened to be a big-time campaign donor for half a dozen senators and representatives. The next photo was worse. Linemann, the older guy, and a few others were gathered around the House Minority Leader from a few years ago. They all looked quite friendly, presuming the photo hadn't been posed. Yet another showed him with Senator Archer, the father of the man we'd smoked in New Mexico for trying to get the Bowmans murdered, since they wouldn't sell out to his Chinese cronies.

"Oh, that's just *awesome*. Another politically connected bunch of scumbags, hiring out blackmail and intimidation squads to get what they want." *And hitmen. Don't forget hitmen. The kind of guys who will blow a man's face off with a shotgun and make it look self-inflicted. And then kidnap a young woman in her twenties and get ready to do the same thing to her.*

You know, the same bastards you're currently trying to blend in with.

I shook off the thought. I was already uncomfortable enough with this whole undercover op, and the part I'd already played in it. The only hope I had of redeeming those days I'd spent in Richmond was that we'd get to the sons of bitches who had set all this in motion.

"That's what these people do. It's the nature of the beast." KG turned the laptop back toward himself. "This is the war we're in. Fought with money and influence at least as much as it is with actual violence and physical destruction." He looked at me from beneath one raised eyebrow. "I *know* you've read *Unrestricted Warfare*."

"Guilty." I had a bit of a rep. My semi-Luddite ways, country drawl, and intense dislike of cities—despite and because of all the time I'd spent working in them—might have earned me my callsign, "Backwoods," but I also had a rep for being the war and history nerd who read voraciously.

Like I said, you needed to have *something* to do to kill time downrange.

"Elite capture's part of it. The economic and commercial aspects are another." He pointed at the screen. "That's what this is all about. Keep the US dependent on China for vital industrial chemicals. If that means killing some people, siccing a bunch of MS-13 savages on the plant down in Honduras, and forcing money around with blackmail, then that's what it means. These people have the morals of a sewer rat, you know that."

I shook my head. I was tired. "So, what's the next move?"

That drew his eyes back to the screen, a frown creasing his forehead. "That's the thing. I don't know for sure. We've got the name, we've got your testimony that you saw him meet with Nyce after you'd run surveillance that revealed some shady shit. The questions as to who hired you to do that and why *will* come up, though. We don't exactly have an airtight case to take to the law, even presuming that they'd listen to us for a heartbeat, anyway." The FBI turning on Strand when he'd gone to them about the attacks on his operation was still a source of bitterness and a considerable amount of caution in Pallas Group Solutions.

The silence stretched out a bit after that. I knew I wasn't the only one who was chafing a bit at sitting there waiting and guarding Romero and his managers, while the B Team got to stack bodies down in Honduras. A lot of us had learned how to get along in the quieter life of private security, as well as how to navigate the twisted skullduggery that went along with covert action and financial warfare, but that didn't mean we weren't still meat eaters who, deep down, wished that we could just shoot some bad guys in the face and fix the whole problem that way.

That is, sadly, not the way it works in the real world.

He looked up. "Have you checked Walter Callahan's email since you got back?"

I tried not to grimace. I hadn't. I'd already felt dirty enough running a blackmail op on a finance guy. I didn't know what they had in mind next, and I wasn't sure I wanted to know.

I still went to the back, pulled out the Faraday bag with the burner phone in it, and picked up my go bag. "I'll be back." I didn't want to start that phone up inside our team house. There was no guarantee that they were tracking it, but there was no guarantee that they *weren't*, either.

I headed out to the truck.

***

It was a long drive to get out in the sticks, but somewhere where I still had decent cell signal. I finally settled on a trailhead in Percy Warner Park, pulled into a parking spot, even though there weren't many other cars there at that time of night, killed the engine and the lights, and started up the phone.

There was an email waiting for me. With some reluctance, I opened it.

Mr. Callahan,

We were quite impressed with your performance in Richmond. Most excellent. If you are interested, we have another job for you. The listing is on the same site. The job is somewhat time sensitive, so we will expect your response within forty-eight hours, or else we will have to offer it to another contractor.

I sat there in the truck, looking down at the phone, and sighed again. I realized that I'd hoped that identifying Linemann might have given us the thread to pull on that I could cut away from this operation. The anger at their crimes that had led me to suggest this course of action had cooled, and now I really wanted to find another way to tackle this.

It's one thing to think about how risky and cool it would be to work undercover. It's something else when you're faced with what you might have to do to maintain that cover.

It wasn't that I didn't think I could kill my way out if I got burned. I was pretty sure I could. I was just increasingly disgusted at being associated with these people, even if it was only for the purpose of bringing them down.

With a deep sense of reluctance, I sent the brief acknowledgement, powered down the phone, returned it to the

Faraday bag, and started the truck. I'd have to go back, get with Radford to get onto the dark web site, and find out what they wanted me to do this time.

And whether I could stomach it.

***

"That's not a lot of information." I was getting a nasty feeling in my guts as I looked over Radford's shoulder at the .onion site.

"No, it's not." KG was on the other side, scanning the screen. When he looked over at me, there was concern and uncertainty in his eyes. "If they don't even want to put the mission on the dark web..."

"It could be that they don't think a simple surveillance tasking was quite enough of a vetting process." I straightened and rubbed a thumb along my jaw, thinking. "Maybe they're still feeling us out." Phil had gotten the same message, and a link to the same listing. "This could be the next step. Maybe it's not so much a job as it is a vetting course of some kind. We delivered on the surveillance, so now we get a face to face for further evaluation."

"It's a long shot. And I don't know that we've got anyone in St. Louis. Goblin had backup in Virginia, but *I* don't know anybody in Missouri. And we can't spare anyone else from the team. We're getting spread thin as it is." KG was not comfortable with this, and I couldn't blame him, even though it was my hide on the line, and I was even more uncomfortable than he was.

"We've got two days." The listing only gave a gear list, a rendezvous point in St. Louis, and a timeframe, three days away. I was assuming a day for travel, since I was planning on driving. Unlike the Richmond job, there were no travel instructions, so I'd rent a car as "Walter Callahan" and drive there. Less visibility that way. "I'll talk to Goblin."

***

He'd actually flown out, somewhat to my surprise. I knew it wasn't just because of our St. Louis op. The man had a *lot* on his plate, and given the lengths he'd already gone to, and been willing to let us go to, I suspected that there were dimensions to this operation that we would probably never see. I'd never have imagined, all those years before, driving around Baghdad with him, that Thad Walker would get to be such a schemer, but so it had played out.

When I'd called him, he just told me to sit tight. He was half an hour out from the team house.

It struck me how haggard he was looking. Waging a guerrilla war against the kind of powers we were up against was not calculated to keep a man looking young and fresh, and all of us had already had some miles on the odometer before we'd started with PGS.

With a wave at KG, he started toward the back room, where we kept some extra gear and a couple of cots where watchstanders could crash. "Chris, Phil, let's talk."

We followed him back, Phil closing the door behind us as Goblin sank down onto one of the cots, his hands on his knees. "Talk to me."

I laid out what was going on as succinctly as I could, along with some of my own concerns and fears. "I want to burn these guys down, Thad. I really do. But I don't know if I'm willing to sell my soul to the Devil to do it."

"I'm right there with you, brother." He looked at Phil, who was sitting on the other cot while I leaned against the wall. "You feeling the same way, Phil?"

"Maybe not as strongly as Chris, but yeah." He was leaning forward a bit, his hands on the edge of the cot, his legs crossed in front of him. "I don't really want to do something that'll get me fifty to life in the pen, just to get to whoever's pushing this. We don't exactly have qualified immunity."

That was a big factor. Pallas Group Solutions had an excellent group of lawyers, but they were only able to help us if we were ostensibly doing what we were doing in accordance with the law, which mainly meant in defense of persons or property. The B Team's actions down in Honduras were in a bit more of a gray area, as had been our mission in Mexico. But this was looking more at doing what could be considered felonies on American soil, which was a whole different animal.

Goblin nodded, looking down at the floor for a moment while he chewed his lip. While a lot of us sported facial hair of some form or another—Phil was currently enjoying the reactions he got from one of the dirtiest-looking mustaches I'd seen in a while—Goblin had been clean shaven for a long time.

When he looked up, it was with a faint, thoughtful squint. "I'm not going to tell either of you that you *have* to do this. If I didn't make that clear before, I apologize, because I should have. Yeah, we're at war, but it's not the kind of war where I'm going to draft a man to violate his conscience in order to win. I don't think that kind of war really ever exists in the first place, and I know you don't either, Chris." When he didn't mention Phil's feelings, Phil just shrugged. He was a little bit more morally flexible than I was. "I can ask you only this much: go to the rendezvous and see what there is to see. If you get a bad feeling, get out. Listen to your gut, do your advance recon work, and step carefully. If we can get the information we need to nail these cocksuckers, then let's do it. If it's going to cost too much…then fade and we'll come at it a different way."

He looked back and forth between us. "Fair enough?"

I glanced at Phil, who shrugged. Phil probably had fewer second thoughts about blackmailing a scumbag like Nyce than I'd had, though he still had lines he wouldn't cross, and those were a lot farther back and less flexible than some dudes I'd known in this profession. "Fair enough, Thad."

Goblin stood up. "Good. I suggest you boys get prepped and get moving soon. Better to get into the area and get some familiarity and groundwork laid before they show up. In the meantime, I've got some stuff to go over with Kevin."

He moved to the door and opened it, pausing to glance back at the two of us. "Stay safe, and good hunting, boys.

There's something really rotten going on here, and the sooner we can get to the bottom of it and excise it, the better."

CHAPTER
26

The meeting place was in a three-story industrial building in central St. Louis. It didn't actually look all that different from some of the nondescript commercial spaces that I'd seen more than a few contracting companies and covert operations organizations work out of, though those were usually staged somewhere in northern Virginia. At least, the entrance looked the same. We'd been given a passcode, since there was no receptionist, and I let myself in, following the short hallway past the water fountain and the restrooms, toward the back.

The place was a warehouse, and the shadow client hadn't made any real effort to improve it or furnish it. It was just a big, empty, concrete and brick room in an L-shape, with rollup doors at one end.

I'd beaten Phil there, but not the other two. One was standing next to a small plastic table, looking at a tablet, while the other was going through a plastic storm case on the floor nearby when I walked in.

I didn't recognize either of them, which was a good thing, and something that we'd been worried about. The contracting world is bigger than some people think—I don't know *everyone* that worked even on some of the smaller programs that I did—but it's still pretty small. If someone who knew Chris Grant saw "Walter Callahan" walk in, things could get very uncomfortable.

Both of these guys were strangers, though. The one with the tablet looked like he had some Asian ancestry, though his hair was brown. The other guy, a mountain of muscle with a brow like a Neanderthal, wore his blond hair a little long, almost like a surfer. His shirt was about a size and a half too small for him, but given the size of his muscles, I suspected that was deliberate.

It sure wasn't because he was too poor to get a new shirt, judging by the watch on his wrist.

They both looked up as I walked in. The blond guy stood up, sizing me up. He seemed friendly enough, despite his size and the fact that he was here on what was almost certain to be a very illegal contract. The other guy, his hair close-cropped and a pencil mustache over his lip, watched me coldly. This guy trusted nobody, and I had to expect that he'd turn on me in a heartbeat if he felt the need. That was an attitude that I would have expected in an operation like this.

"You Number Three?" The blond guy didn't come forward or hold his hand out, but his voice was as friendly as his expression.

"Looks like it." I didn't offer my hand, either. This didn't seem like the right place or time, and neither of the two of them moved to close the distance. I had my unserialized, 3D printed Glock clone in my waistband, and I was pretty sure they were similarly armed.

No honor or trust among thieves. Or hitmen.

"We're waiting on one more." The half Asian guy turned his attention back to the tablet in his hand, though I noticed that he never got so absorbed in it that he couldn't simultaneously watch me or the blond mountain. Which meant neither of these two knew each other, either.

Since there wasn't a whole lot of conversation going on, though the blond guy kept glancing between us, looking like he kind of wanted to talk, I found another one of the storm cases and started going through it. Neither one of them objected.

What I saw wasn't encouraging. Most of it was electronics, but there were a lot of metal containers that looked like industrial chemicals. Flammable ones.

If this was a car bombing, I was going to have to do something.

As I thought it over, keeping an eye on my two taciturn companions, the door opened. "Anybody here?" It was Phil.

"That must be Number Four." The half Asian guy didn't seem to have any doubts about that, as he put the tablet down. Probably because the four of us were supposed to be the only ones with the code for the cipher lock out front.

There were any number of problems with that assumption, but I wasn't going to volunteer anything.

Phil came around the corner and took a look around. He did a good job of masking any recognition when he looked at me, though I thought I saw a flicker when he looked at the blond guy. That could be bad. The blond guy didn't react, though, so maybe he just looked like somebody Phil knew. I hoped so.

"Okay, now that everybody's here, let's get down to business." The half-Asian guy seemed to want to get things done and go away. He sounded slightly angry, but that was often the way guys in our line of work came across. "The target is an industrial chemical plant, belonging to Alton Chemical. The mission is to put it out of commission, preferably for a minimum of six months."

I resisted the urge to glance at Phil. This was confirmation, if anything, that the movers and shakers in this operation were looking to corner at least some part of the industrial chemical market. The more they could put their rivals out of business, the better.

I still strongly suspected the Chinese. The fact that Carr & Sons was inshoring from China pointed to that, but we still didn't have a smoking gun. I didn't think this particular job was going to give us that smoking gun, either, but it was another piece in the puzzle.

"Now, the client doesn't really care just *how* we accomplish this. They just want it done. They've provided some materials that we can use, but if we can pull it off with some judicious vandalism, they're fine with that. A full-blown arson investigation might work against us." His jaw tightened, ever so slightly. "I'm also not convinced they won't throw us under the bus in a heartbeat if it comes to that. So, if we can pull it off without burning the plant down, I'm down."

I just nodded, listening and taking stock. So did Phil.

The blond guy, though, was going to be the gregarious one. "So, what's the immediate plan? Recon and surveillance? Maybe see if we can get someone inside?"

"Recon, yeah." The other guy, who seemed to be the default Number One, looked faintly disgusted. "As for infiltration, no way. Trying to get one of us hired would be risky and would take too damned much time. Are any of you chemical engineers?" When everyone shook their heads, he nodded, looking like he felt like spitting on the floor. "Didn't think so. We'd have to start as janitors, or something, and, like I said, it would take too long. I have no intention of sitting here for half a year building a cover. We need to identify infiltration and exfiltration routes, get inside where we can, do our damage, and get out. And it has to be in the next week. Three days is better."

I stifled a snort. A week just for the recon was probably asking too much. This was already shaping up to be far too hasty and slapped together. Even if we let it go through, it was going to be a mess.

While I didn't know about Phil, I had no intention of letting this happen. It put me in a tough spot, since intercepting this sabotage mission was going to risk compromise, but I was right there with Number One. Not only did I not want to potentially face charges, but the fact was that letting another

216

chemical plant get put out of commission was only going to play into the bad guys' hands.

I didn't play this intel community game of letting bad shit go down just because there *might* be a chance to stop some hypothetical worse shit in the future. I'd seen that far too often, seen far too many murderers let go, just because of a fantasy that some intel weenie or overly ambitious officer had of "catching the bigger fish." It was the same logic that had ostensibly led to the ATF's "Fast and Furious" op, that had funneled thousands of weapons directly to Mexican cartels, supposedly so they could be tracked, though no tracking had actually happened.

"So, here's the play." Number One must have done this a time or two, since he was assuming the leadership role. "Two and Three, you'll run our recon. Four and I will prep what devices we might need here. I want us to be ready to go by midnight tomorrow night. It doesn't give us a huge amount of time, but the longer this takes, the more likely we'll get spotted. The lease on this place is for a month, but I'll be damned if I'm going to hang out here that long." He sneered. "I've done my time sleeping on cots."

I'd seen the four mil spec cots lined up against the wall and couldn't say I was all that eager to spend a night on one of them, either. They're moderately more comfortable than sleeping on the floor, but only moderately.

"Have we got a vehicle, or are we going to have to use the ones we brought?" I kept my arms folded. "Because I can see that becoming a security issue, too."

"There's a car in the parking lot. It's a bit of a beater, but it's got a clean title, registration, and insurance, though the insurance expires in a month. And no, I don't know where it came from, nor am I going to ask."

Par for the course, I thought. I just nodded.

"We've got cameras, some magnified optics, and a tablet for recording and reporting." The blond guy was already pulling surveillance gear out of the storm case. It was pretty high-end stuff, too. The sort of stuff I'd seen while working contract for the government.

That didn't mean this was a government op, of course. Just that whoever had laid it on had money to burn.

"Where are the keys?" I really didn't want to hang out here longer than necessary, though our reconnaissance would probably go better after dark, and close to a shift change. That might be a little dicey, but I assumed—I hoped—that there was that degree of intel provided, at least.

"In the car already." The blond guy motioned me over to the table. "Come on. I'll show you what we've got."

CHAPTER
27

Alton Chemical's St. Louis plant was fenced, but it wasn't exactly fortified. There weren't checkpoints at the entrances, which were divided up into main, employee, and truck entrances, but I didn't see any security guards, armed or otherwise. That was a surprise, given the sheer degree of violent crime in St. Louis. I heard sirens almost continually, and red and blue flashers were pretty common sights.

"I wonder why they're having us do this instead of some rando street thug." The blond guy, who had introduced himself as Nathan once we'd gotten away from Number One, was a lot chattier in the car than he had been back in the warehouse. "I mean, don't get me wrong, I'm fine with the paycheck, but in a place like St. Louis, it seems like they could hire it out a lot cheaper."

"The problem with hiring street thugs for your wet work is keeping them quiet." I'd done some advance work, looking into the area, before I'd even driven out from Nashville. "The thugs around here are the bragging type. They'd sing like canaries as soon as one of them got rolled up. Even if they *didn't* get rolled up, they'd still start bragging about what they'd done. Word would get around." I watched the plant go past as we continued around the next turn. "No, this way they're a lot more certain that nobody's going to talk out of school."

Nathan snorted. "I've known a few guys with some serious security clearances who talked out of school. Of course, nothing happened to them."

"That's the difference between that world and this one." I was liking this less and less. Not because Nathan was a bad guy, but because he didn't come across that way. He was friendly, outgoing, and we clearly had some common background. His approach to the recon and the intel dump prior had been entirely professional, and he clearly knew what he was doing. In different circumstances, he might have made a good candidate for PGS.

That he was working for whatever network of psychos Kinkaid had worked for made the whole thing depressing. I was probably going to have to kill the guy at some point, and despite knowing what I knew, I didn't *want* to.

"Yeah." Something in his voice brought me to glance at him. He wasn't looking at me, or even at the plant. For a second, he was staring over the wheel at the road, a look on his face that suggested he was thinking back to the chain of decisions that had brought him here, and that he was regretting it.

Too late now, buddy.

We had photos of pretty much the entire exterior of the plant by now. That was the easy part. Finding a vulnerability that would shut the plant down without committing an act of arson that would poison half the city for the next six months would be the hard part.

I was sure that the only reason Number One didn't want to go the mass destruction route was because he didn't want to become the subject of an investigation. That one didn't seem to have a conscience at all. I was pretty sure, just from the last couple hours with him, that Nathan had shut his down by rationalization to protect himself.

How long are you going to let this go on? I wondered. The alternatives were getting narrower and more unpalatable.

The fact was, unless we wanted no more than just the intel that Carr & Sons weren't the only target, we had to figure something out that didn't burn us. If we were going to get to the heart of this operation, we still had to appear to be useful.

Not necessarily trustworthy, because the kind of guys who went in for this didn't believe *anyone* was trustworthy. And within this circle, they were probably right.

"We could try to get interviewed for a job." Nathan was still thinking about the mission, having apparently brushed aside whatever had been bugging him. "It's getting late in the day, but if we tried first thing in the morning, we might be able to get a good look around before we've got to get down to real mission planning."

"Have you got the creds to make that believable?" I turned toward him. "Because it's been a *long* time since high school chemistry, and I can't say that's been one of my hobbies. Janitorial probably won't show us what we need to see."

He grimaced. "No." He gripped the wheel. "There's got to be *some* way to get in there!"

He was getting more worked up than the situation called for. "There's always the clipboard gambit."

He frowned. "The what?"

"Come on. Tell me you didn't learn about that in the E4 Mafia." Where I came from, it was the Lance Corporal Underground, but "Callahan" had been Army. "Doesn't matter where you go, if you carry a clipboard and look like you belong there, most people are going to assume that you do."

"Oh, yeah." He nodded, then his frown deepened again. "You really think that's going to work here?"

"It might." The fact was, I had no idea if it would or not. It might be worth a try, but I was starting to think along different lines.

The on-the-ground infiltration might work, but it also might go disastrously badly. On the other hand, it was potentially the only way to derail this thing, because if Number

One thought of what I was starting to consider, then there wouldn't be any other way, short of violence. A plan was starting to come together in my head, but I needed to talk to Phil about it. The trick there was doing that without alerting Nathan or Number One.

"I've got an idea." Nathan turned away from the plant and started to head north, toward I-55. "We need to get to an electronics store."

I felt a combination of relief and dread as he said that. He'd just thought of what I'd been considering, but it was going to make this a lot harder.

***

Fortunately, Nathan knew exactly what he wanted to get, so he left me with the vehicle while he went inside. That gave me an opening. I just hoped that Phil had the same opportunity.

Bringing up the encrypted messaging app, double checking that it was still set to erase the messages after thirty minutes, I contacted him. *Looks like we're going the drone route. That's going to make this harder. I'm not going to sit by and be a part of this, but we have to make it look good.*

I had no idea if I was even going to get a reply or not. If Phil was smart, he had his phone set not to even vibrate when he was around Number One. That guy was suspicious enough without giving him a reason to wonder if the two of us knew each other, and why we might both be there.

So, I was a little surprised when I got a response almost immediately. *Things are shaping up the same here. Number One's been doing research on how to take out an installation like this, and he's found reports about a drone swarm that penetrated the Palo Verde Nuclear Generation Station a few years ago. It's given him an idea.*

I glanced up to make sure Nathan wasn't already coming out of the Schiller's Camera store with the drone. I didn't have a whole lot of time.

Drones are going to make this harder. We can't just call the cops about a break-in.

There was another pause, though the little triple bubble down below showed me that Phil was typing. I glanced up again, to see Nathan coming out with a box under his arm. I was out of time.

Fortunately, I had just enough time to look down at the screen. *I already sent Goblin the heads up. We'll need to make it look good, but this is going down tonight.*

Then Nathan was at the car, and I shifted into the driver's seat while he stowed the drone in the back. There was no time to answer Phil, and I had to hope that he'd figure that was what had happened.

Also, that he wouldn't give the "go" signal before I could figure out what the hell we were doing.

I drove back to the warehouse, taking a different route, careful to avoid the really high-crime areas. Nathan and I were both armed, so I wasn't that worried about a carjacking, except for the elevated profile that would come from having to kill some stupid gangbangers who tried to carjack the two big dudes in a rental Civic.

Still, while I heard more sirens, and once had to pull over to get out of another cop car's way, we stayed out of trouble until we got to the warehouse. It was starting to get dark by then, though there were still plenty of streetlights bathing the streets and the parking lot in an orange glow. We still got out and scanned the area carefully before Nathan retrieved the drone box and hustled inside.

I dawdled while I secured the car. Nobody left car doors unlocked in St. Louis, not unless they lived in one of the suburbs, and we were a long way from any of those places. It also gave me a moment to check my phone, hoping that Number One wasn't watching from just inside the door.

Phil had sent another message, a considerably longer one.

Goblin's going to call in an anonymous tip to the cops around 0230, saying that he saw what looked like drugs and bomb making materials being brought into this warehouse. Our job is going to be to get clear with our compatriots. I've already got an escape route planned, and Goblin thinks that he can make sure we're covered. He's got an old friend who's a St. Louis city cop. We'll have to make it look good, like we're covering their escape, and then break contact and link up with him. I've got coordinates.

I could think of a dozen ways that could go wrong, but I didn't have a better plan. I shoved the phone into my pocket and headed inside.

***

The rest of the evening went slowly. Not because we weren't busy. We were. Number One went out and got another drone, while we prepped the first one for recon and started it moving toward the plant.

We were still watching the feed as we circled around the plant, looking for some critical vulnerability that we could hit with a drone carrying a roughly ten pound charge.

"I think we might have to fall back on arson." Nathan rubbed his jaw as he stared at the screen. "I don't see any other way to do enough damage to put it out of commission." He pointed to the overhead image in another window. "If we set it here, in this tank farm, then it shouldn't hurt too many people."

Except for everybody downwind for miles.

It was weird, watching the mental gymnastics Nathan was going through. He seemed to genuinely not want to be a bad guy, but he must have really needed the money. Or something. It didn't take away from the fact that he was still here, still plotting an attack that would not only probably hurt a lot of people, but would give the enemies of his country even more of an advantage than they already had.

"I'm less worried about the arson angle if none of us are going to be anywhere near the place." Number One was back. "Give me a hand getting this set up." He put the box down and opened it, pulling out drone components. It was a different model from the one Nathan had picked up, bigger and with six rotors instead of four. It looked like it could probably carry a bigger payload, which meant Number One already had the arson idea in mind. "The drone should be completely destroyed in the strike, and unless someone's tracking all drone traffic in St. Louis—and I know they're not—then there won't be any slam-dunk evidence to trace it back to us." He grinned, and there wasn't much human feeling in the expression. "Got to love some standoff for this sort of thing."

Phil and I had been carefully avoiding eye contact, knowing that we were at about the most dangerous part of the op. Depending on timing, this could get really bad. Goblin was going to call the cops somewhere around 0230, but that didn't guarantee that Number One wouldn't have launched the strike before then. If that happened, then cover or not, we were going to have to step in.

At least, that was the way I was thinking. Phil and I hadn't discussed it. That was a problem, too. Phil might think that we needed to let this play out, in order to get to the spider in the web. I'd worked with Phil enough that I figured he'd follow my lead if I made a move, but it would still be more ad hoc than I would have liked.

Of course, it was probably going to be a gunfight here in the warehouse. If we got the drop on the two of them, then it would be over very quickly. Number One had relaxed a little, but he was still looking up at random times. He didn't trust anyone or anything. Getting the drop on him was going to be difficult.

I was resigning myself to the idea that I was just going to have to kill him. Nathan we might be able to capture and interrogate, since he wasn't paying as much attention to us, being absorbed in the drone reconnaissance. Nathan still seemed like the kind of guy who figured that if we were there, we were all in, and that there was some sort of brotherhood at play.

I wondered where he'd come from, and what had led him into working this sort of a job.

Surreptitiously, I checked my watch, and silently cursed. It wasn't even close to midnight yet. If Number One had decided to go with the mass destruction angle, then he was going to be ready to go in the next hour, if not sooner. That meant there was no way the call was going to go down in time for the cops to break this up before the drone launched.

I risked a look at Phil. He felt my eyes on him and turned to meet my gaze. We communicated without words for a second, as I moved my eyes from him to Number One, and back. He nodded, ever so slightly. He got it, and while he *might* have thought that we were burning the whole op, he was going to follow my lead.

He knew what was at stake. We might be making it more difficult to track down the center of this network, but if we let this go down, not only were people going to die—industrial chemical fires are nasty things—but the bad guys were going to get more of what they wanted, putting them a little bit farther along the road to winning.

I looked at Number One, who was finishing up the drone prep. He'd clearly done this before, as he had the charge put together, along with the remote detonator, in record time. Of course, with guys finding work all over the world as the GWOT had wound down, some going to Ukraine to volunteer in the war there, there were still all sorts of new skillsets to learn and plenty of places to learn them.

It also meant we were about out of time.

"All right, let's kick this pig." Number One started up the controller, and the drone hummed to life. He checked it over, then, looked over at Nathan. "Go ahead and open that door onto the courtyard. It'll be more discreet to launch it from there." The drone was small enough he could probably just fly it through the door, without risking exposure to anyone who might be outside watching.

Of course, that courtyard was fenced in and had several trees growing in it, so there wouldn't be much to see, anyway. He'd thought this through.

While Number One was absorbed in the drone controls, we had our opening. Nathan had his back to all of us, walking over to the door. I locked eyes with Phil, got the nod, and turned to Number One.

He was wired tight, that was for sure. He sensed something wrong and looked up from the controls for a second. He saw me looking at him, and recognition flared in his eyes. He dropped his hand to his waistband.

I was a fraction of a second faster. Sweeping the shirt tail out of the way, I grabbed my Glock clone, pulling and rotating it as it cleared the holster, my finger already tightening on the trigger as it came level and I moved, stepping around to his left, forcing him to turn to face me.

I punched the gun out as his pistol cleared its holster and shot him center mass from about ten feet away, before I'd even picked up the sights. He jerked as the bullet tore through his upper abdomen, but then I was on sights and coming down from recoil. I dumped three more 9mm rounds into his chest before a fourth went through his head.

He was already falling by the time the fourth round left the barrel, and it went through his forehead, punching out the top of his skull with a spray of blood and bone fragments.

"Whoa, whoa, *whoa!*" Nathan had turned at the sound of gunfire and had his hands up, his eyes wide, while Phil covered him. "What the *fuck* just happened?"

I moved to Number One's body, kicking the Shadow Systems CR920 pistol away from his hand. The dude had been awfully sure he wasn't going to get made, if he'd brought a gun like that on an op like this. Nobody I knew would be willing to toss a Shadow Systems if things went south.

Neither one of us had said anything, though I was already cursing in my head. This had gone sideways six ways from Sunday, and now we had a live one on our hands who could identify us. But he'd thrown his hands up, and Phil hadn't shot him, so we *might* have a detainee to interrogate. Maybe.

Making sure that Number One was good and dead, I went through his pockets. In the meantime, Nathan was freaking out.

"Fuck, fuck, fuck, *fuck*." He was staring at Number One's body as I pulled a wallet full of cash, prepaid credit cards, and an ID out of his pocket. The rest of his pocket litter was about what I'd expect of a guy in this business. Two knives, spare mags, a lockpick kit, about twenty feet of paracord, a small med kit, several more tools on his keychain, and two phones. Phil still had Nathan dead to rights.

While he was still hyperventilating, when I looked up at Nathan, my own gun still in my hand, I saw that he was calming down a little, the wheels turning behind his wide eyes. There was something about his expression that told me he'd gotten past the shock and now was calculating just how far past fucked this whole operation was.

"Who are you guys with?" He'd made that jump, anyway. He must have realized that the reason I'd gunned Number One down was because we couldn't just sit there and let an act of terrorism go down. There wasn't much other reason I could have done it.

I glanced at Phil, but my partner in crime wasn't feeling talkative. I stood up and faced Nathan, my pistol still in my hand, but not quite pointed at him.

"Okay, guys. Let's all stay real cool, here." The shock was definitely wearing off, but there was something weird about this. "I'm going to take my gun out and put it on the floor. Don't shoot me, okay?" He waited until Phil nodded, then, keeping one hand high and visible, he very slowly and carefully reached under his shirt, pulling a Glock out of an inside the waistband holster with his thumb and forefinger, slowly and gingerly squatting down to lay it on the concrete floor. "Now, I'm going to reach into my back pocket. I'm not reaching for a gun, or a bomb trigger, or anything. I just have something to show you."

That was when it clicked. From the sigh, Phil figured it out at the same moment.

Fuck.

With exaggerated slowness, Nathan reached into his back pocket and came out with a flip-open badge holder. "I'm an FBI agent. I've been tracking this guy for a while, but I didn't think I had any backup here. So, who are you guys with?"

"Motherfucker!" Phil lowered his own weapon and turned aside in frustration, as I maintained my position facing Nathan. He fumed for a moment, then turned back on the Fed like a striking snake. "Were you just going to let him blow up a fucking chemical plant in the middle of a fucking city? Why? The 'bigger fish' out there somewhere?"

"Was he a Fed, too, I wonder?" There was more of an edge to my voice than I'd intended, and Nathan flinched just a little. "Is this like the Aryan Nation meeting a while back, where it turned out the cell was all FBI, ATF, and DEA?"

"I'm pretty sure he wasn't." Nathan was getting defensive. "Like I said, I've been tracking him for two months. This was the first time I was able to get close enough. Except you guys smoked him before I could find anything more."

"We can't tell you who we're with." I was starting to get a plan together, messy and off the cuff though it was. "The fact that you weren't told about us should tell you that much. We're not after him, though. We're after the guy giving the orders."

"That was the next step." Nathan wasn't standing down, even though neither of us had a gun on him at the moment.

"That's why you were just going to let him launch that fucking drone?" Phil was still pissed. I was just as angry, but I seemed to be doing a better job of keeping it quiet.

"I needed a reason to arrest him." It was weak, and we all knew it. "Look, this guy's been implicated in several kidnappings, a bank robbery, and even a murder, but he hasn't left evidence that we could really pin him down with. We *needed* a smoking gun. I didn't intend to let him get it all the way to the target, but I had to let him launch it." He was starting to sound as frustrated as the two of us were angry. "Now that's fucked."

I'd taken a look at the control tablet as I'd searched Number One's corpse. "You're actually in luck, Nathan. If you'd let him launch that drone, there would have been no way to recall it." I pointed to the tablet. "That was a fire-and-forget strike. He'd programmed the whole flight plan, complete with a timed detonator."

I saw the color drain from his face as I spoke. He started to take a step forward, then hesitated, looking at Phil. From the set of his jaw, I could tell that Phil *wanted* to point his weapon at the Fed, but he restrained himself. Nathan stepped past his sidearm and walked past me, keeping his distance to avoid giving me any reason to think he was going to make a grab for my handgun, and picked up the tablet. "Oh, *fuck*."

When he looked up at me, the horror in his eyes was palpable. He still didn't know who we were, but we'd just saved him from letting a major terror attack go down.

At least, that was what he wanted us to think. In his case, I thought it was genuine. A lot of Feds were assholes, and the less said about their leadership, the better, but there were still some decent dudes in there. Probably not as many as you might hope, but even so.

"Well, there was no other way to stop this, but now all of our covers are blown." I had decided to push on with my plan, though I hadn't had a chance to run it past Phil. I holstered my Glock clone. "Unfortunately, we still have a whole network to ferret out, but if they think that we're Feds, then they're going to disappear."

Unless they came after us, but that would be difficult if they were looking for Walter Callahan and James Kelly, who weren't real people.

Nathan was pretty quick on his feet, though. While I might not have a very high opinion of a lot of G-men, he was a thinker, and apparently something of an outside the box thinker.

"Well, somebody's cover is blown, that's clear enough, but it doesn't necessarily have to be everyone's." He looked down at Number One's corpse. "There might be a way to salvage this."

I folded my arms. "I'm listening." The fact that he hadn't pushed on who we were was looking promising. I couldn't say I'd ever bluffed a Fed before.

"My mission was this guy, Bob Williams. I had to fight tooth and nail to follow up on him, too, because the evidence was so thin. With him down, my tasking is technically over." He looked back and forth between us. "If I take credit for killing Williams, and report that there were two more who got away, then you might be able to maintain your cover with his network. Then you can continue your operation."

It was too good to be true. "How are they going to take your word for it when your weapon wasn't fired, and the bullets in Williams don't match?"

He snorted. "That whole bullet matching thing is TV bullshit that the Bureau actually got in trouble for a few years ago. It's not a thing. As for my weapon being fired, well… I'll put a few more rounds in the wall and the window around that door after you leave. Say that was the way you escaped." He pointed to the opposite wall, above the table where the prep had been done. "If you guys want to shoot that wall a few times, then that will back up the story that we shot at each other while you broke contact."

That choice of words was interesting. I'd never heard a Fed use it, but I'd heard a lot of former infantry and SOF guys use it. It was an infantry term.

231

I glanced at Phil, and he shrugged. He didn't have a better idea, and I sure couldn't think of a better cover than having an actual Fed—an agent of the bureau that had tried to burn us for sending them evidence of criminal wrongdoing by a Senator's son—cover for us.

"All right. But make sure that it gets around that there were two who got away. We'll report it to the contact, but you know how cover stories go."

"I do, indeed." He sighed and put his fingers in his ears. "Probably sooner is better than later."

Phil and I each dumped a mag into the cinder block wall, then vanished out through the door into the courtyard.

I might have reloaded and made sure I was well out of the fatal funnel and moving away at an angle before I turned my back. Nathan had seemed like a decent dude, but you never know.

We heard the gunshots as he finished out the rest of the cover story as we went over the wall and disappeared into the night.

CHAPTER
28

It was almost 0200. Most of the city was quiet. Chamelecón, however, was still restless.

There were two targets in the barrio that night, and Nick was glad that the D Team was on security on the plant. The entire B Team, with Vern, was closing in on the barrio.

They weren't coming from the plant. That would have been too obvious and easily interdicted. There was zero doubt that the bad guys had every inch of the open fields between the plant and the barrios watched. So, instead, they'd gone around to the south, circling around the oblong suburb of San Pedro Sula until they reached a wild stretch of road on the banks of the Rio Chamelecón, where they'd piled out of the vans and headed into the brush.

There would be no disguising themselves as regular, everyday Westerners in Honduras that night. Every man was in camouflage utilities, boots, plate carriers, and helmets, with NVGs down and unserialized rifles in their hands. This wasn't a security detail or a reconnaissance element. This was a hit squad, and they were closing in on their enemies in the dark.

It had been a long and arduous movement, up and over the spur of the Merendon mountains that stood between the bow of the river and the city beyond. The jungle wasn't nearly as thick as it might have been, and there wasn't anyone out and about in the mountains that they'd seen and heard, but the terrain was steep, and the growth was still dense enough to slow them down.

Now, NVGs down and rifles at the ready, the eleven of them crept through the last few dozen yards of vegetation toward the Zona Industrial Chamelecón.

Only a few lights were on down there. Electricity was a little spotty on the outskirts of San Pedro Sula lately, which was unusual for Honduras as a whole. Nick could only assume that the constant fighting between Barrio 18 and MS-13 was degrading things in the southern part of the city.

He was on point at the moment, moving from tree to tree as he picked his way down the hillside toward the large building that, if his land nav was on point, was the GASPRO Honduras building. Gunfire rattled through the night, and he froze, scanning carefully around him, though he hadn't heard the telltale *snap* that would have told him that the bullets had been aimed in their direction.

Sweat soaked his cammies and was dripping into his eyes from under his helmet. The fights so far had been fast, furious, and short, and they'd been able to go back into the air conditioning in the vehicles or the plant afterward. This was back to the old days of hiking through the bush, advancing to contact.

He had to admit that he'd missed it.

The PS-31s cast the landscape around him in shades of bluish gray. He'd trained and fought for years with the green phosphor NVGs, and the white phosphor had taken a bit of getting used to, but he liked them. They were a little bit clearer, and they still allowed a good sight picture through his rifle's red dot, unlike the four-tube pano goggles that he'd tried before.

The rest of the team was grouped more tightly than he would have generally liked, but the jungle on the mountain was just dense enough that they had to stay close to avoid losing contact with one another. He saw Doug lower himself to a knee about two yards behind him and to his left, then Vern did the same on his right.

From where they had stopped, just off a road that had been cut in a sharp switchback up the mountain, terminating at a gazebo that overlooked the entire city, they could see a lot of the industrial zone and the barrio beyond it. This was the time to take stock and see if the plan needed any last minute adjustments.

First things first, though. Resting his rifle on his knee, Nick slowed his breathing and went as still as he could, despite the sweat, the bugs, and the chafing, and just watched and listened.

There was a lot to see and hear. Despite the hour, there were vehicles starting up and headlights lighting up the streets of the barrio below. He frowned as he watched, as several cars and pickups started to move around the southern part of Chamelecón. That gunfire hadn't just been random. Something had just happened.

Fortunately, the lights all seemed to be some distance away from their target. He couldn't see the house they'd fingered as another MS-13 destroyer house but there weren't a lot of lights around it, so they should be able to get in close, provided they worked their way around to the north of the industrial zone.

They still had to get across the six-lane Boulevard Del Sur, but it was early enough in the morning that there wasn't much traffic.

It just needed to stay that way for the next hour. If they were still in there by 0300, things would have gone very, very badly.

Vern finally moved, shifting to the center of the tight perimeter they'd formed in the trees and bushes on the side of the mountain. "Okay." His voice was low, though not quite a whisper. Whispers can actually travel farther in the night than a low murmur. "Plan remains the same. Down to the industrial section, stay out of the light, hold up just behind the Super 7 until we are clear to cross the highway. Two by two, scrolls to the road. Rest of the plan remains as is."

Under different circumstances, they might have conducted a quick recon of the objective before committing, but there was too much risk of compromise, even if they'd brought a drone. There *was* a drone overhead, but they'd only hear what it saw if something came up that looked like a potential mission-ender. There was too much going on for a constant flow of radio traffic.

Besides, there was also another factor they had to take into consideration. While they might not have had a very high opinion of the Honduran forces around them, but there was probably *somebody* on the ground associated with the PLA. This entire op stank of Chinese proxy war, and if the Chinese were the ones who had sicced the maras on Carr & Sons—which seemed likely—then they might have technical assets that could at least pick up on the fact that there was more radio traffic on the air that night than normal.

Maybe that was paranoid. Nick had served and worked in a few places where the fears of technical intercept had turned out to be little more than paranoid fantasy, mostly allowing certain people to pretend they were James Bond or Jason Bourne. With the Chinese, though, they couldn't discount anything.

Pallas Group Solutions had managed to stay in the shadows so far, even as they'd stacked bodies like cordwood in a few places. They had to step carefully if they were going to keep it that way.

With the plan confirmed, Nick rose to his feet and started down the hill.

They moved like ghosts, though there was still some sound that was impossible to avoid. Branches brushed against utilities, gear, and helmets. The PS-31s allowed for some more depth perception than the old PVS-14 monoculars, but their focus was still limited, and the branches were blurry up close. Nick heard a muttered curse behind him as someone smacked his NVGs into a limb and had to duck lower to get underneath it.

They were getting out of the jungle and into the industrial buildings. And Nick was starting to hear more noise that concerned him.

More vehicles were moving, and another burst of gunfire sounded through the night, echoing across the barrio. Somewhere, what sounded like a voice rose over a megaphone, shouting in Spanish. It was too distorted, and his Spanish was sketchy enough, to make out what was said, but it was answered a moment later by even more gunfire.

Something was brewing in Chamelecón in the dark hours of the morning.

The vegetation provided shadow and concealment right up to the Super 7 convenience store, which faced the Boulevard Del Sur. More trees loomed on the median, and a few headlights were visible, mostly turning into or out of the barrio to north or south.

Nick took a knee beneath the last tree before the highway, scanning the road and the buildings nearby. More gunfire sounded, and he heard engines and several car horns. That made him hunker down a little bit lower, scanning the highway and the industrial buildings around it, looking for movement. Something was going down. The question was whether they could take advantage of the chaos or needed to scratch the mission and get out.

Vern moved up next to him, just as a quintet of vehicles came roaring out onto the Boulevard Del Sur, headlights blazing overhead as the PGS contractors ducked low to avoid being spotted amidst the vegetation alongside the road.

Those three pickups and two beat-up SUVs got about even with the PGS position before a storm of muzzle flashes erupted up north, and bullets tore through the air overhead with a rapid series of *crack*s that drove the contractors even lower. Glass shattered as one round struck an oncoming vehicle and smashed a windshield.

The vehicles screeched to a halt, one of them swerving sharply and crossing two lanes to bounce onto the median. They hadn't exactly been advancing slowly and cautiously. More gunfire erupted as *mareros* piled out of the vehicles and ran for cover at the edges of the road, spraying bullets back toward their attackers.

Nick thought he knew exactly what was going on here. There was no one gang that held full sway over Chamelecón. It was a battleground between MS-13 and Barrio 18. And apparently, that ongoing conflict had just erupted again, right in front of them, at zero dark thirty in the morning.

Vern must have reached the same conclusion, and he was thinking fast. He was suddenly at Nick's ear. "We're going to thin the herd a bit. You, Thumper, Salt, Gameshow, and Train will hold here. I'm taking the rest north, to hit that bunch up there. Hold your fire until we open up, unless you have to." Nick nodded, and Vern gave his shoulder a squeeze, then he was gone.

Getting lower in the veg, Nick glanced around, needing to crane his neck a bit more than usual to see through his NVGs' twin tubes. Doug was on a low knee behind the tree that stood just behind the Super 7, with Saul covering his six. Carl and Durand were on a knee behind the warehouse next to him. Meanwhile, Vern, Casey, Michael, Abaeze, Josh, and Manny, keeping low, dashed in long bounds toward the north, through the parking lot behind the Super 7 and toward the recycling center to the north. They were dim shadows in the uneven lighting, and hopefully would go unnoticed in the crazy lightshow of muzzle flashes and headlights on the highway.

More of the *mareros*—it was impossible to tell, in the dark, which gang was which, though the bad guys presumably could with some ease—were trying to take cover behind the vehicles, which had halted at various angles across all three lanes of the highway. There was no other traffic out there, mainly because of the hour, but also due to the fact that there was an active gunfight going on. Anyone else who might have been on the road had hastily found another route.

The dark figures of the gangsters were popping up over hoods and beds, ripping off long bursts of AR or AK fire, then ducking back down again. They were wasting a lot of ammunition, but that was about what Nick would have expected from irregular forces like this.

Then three of them peeled off across the median, dashing for the Super 7, clearly intending to flank their rivals.

They were coming right toward the PGS shooters.

It wasn't a difficult decision to make. It didn't sound like Vern and the others were in position yet, but Nick and Doug, without even doing much more than trading a look and a nod, leveled their rifles and opened fire.

The other *mareros* didn't even notice as the harsh *snaps* of suppressed gunfire ripped through their fellows as they ran across the road. The suppressors, handmade in the plant's machine shop as they were, were still quite good, and showed next to no flash. The unsuppressed gunfire flying up and down the Boulevard drowned out the muffled gunshots, so the only indicator was the three figures suddenly falling to the pavement. The first two simply stiffened and dropped, while the third was knocked halfway around and almost yelled before the follow-up shots ripped through throat and brain, and he collapsed.

Carl and Durand moved up as Nick pushed out, dropping prone in the grass and tucking in behind his rifle, looking for targets. One of the *mareros* looked over and must have seen the dark shapes slumped on the roadway, and let out a yell, just as Nick shot him through the chest. He fell on his ass, somehow looking shocked even as not much more than a dark silhouette in the white phosphor image of Nick's NVGs, just before the next round dropped him onto his side.

Then all five were shooting, Saul and Doug adopting the same high/low stance as Carl and Durand. Bullets tore through the gang shooters as the five Pallas Group Solutions contractors rode their resets, dumping nearly a mag apiece into the dark figures around the vehicles. The first six or seven gangsters went down almost immediately, one triggering one last burst as he fell that shattered more glass and hit one of his compatriots in the head.

The rest realized quickly what was going on. They'd been living with and by violence all their short lives, and they reacted almost as quickly, skirting around the nearest vehicles and getting to cover as best they could. Unfortunately for at least one, while he crouched behind the engine block of one of the pickups, Nick had a shot on him underneath the vehicle, from where he was lying in the prone. Two shots dropped him to the pavement and a third silenced him.

Return fire was starting to smack into the walls of the Super 7 and the warehouse, but it was still inaccurate and wild, and each time a *marero* fired, at least two suppressed weapons zeroed in on his muzzle flash. One went over backward, three rounds taking him in the skull at the same moment, spilling him onto the asphalt.

The gunfire to the north seemed to stutter a little, then erupted with renewed intensity a moment later. If Nick hadn't had electronic earpro on, he might not have been able to discern the crackling storm of suppressed gunfire over the full volume shots, but a moment later, those suppressed rifles had put the rest down.

That was all in a sort of peripheral awareness for Nick. His focus had to be on the fight in front of them, because there were still at least two hostile shooters on the far side of the boulevard.

"Standing." With Carl and Durand on a knee and standing just to his right and behind him, he really didn't want to accidentally invite a bullet in the back of the head. He got a knee under himself and pushed himself up to his feet. "Moving."

"With you." Doug was pushing up along the wall of the Super 7, his rifle up as he glided toward the front of the store. Nick, for his part, sprinted toward the corner of the warehouse.

They all had body armor on, but he'd learned a long time ago that body armor only helped if you were being smart. Acting like they were on the flat range was only going to get somebody shot who didn't need to be.

He reached the corner and dropped to a low knee, just as one of the *mareros* stuck his head and his weapon out and sprayed rounds across the street. He couldn't see much, since Nick was still in the shadows, but all it would take would be one lucky round. Bullets smacked into plaster and metal over his head, and he got as low as he could, returning fire with a fast trio of shots that shattered glass and struck sheet metal with loud *bang*s that were just audible across the street.

Then Doug was sprinting past him, muzzle high, streaking across the closer three lanes and throwing himself prone in the median, taking up the fire with a string of shots that flattened several tires and had one of the *mareros* screaming, though only for a moment before Doug's follow up shot canoed his head.

Nick was already up and moving, taking full advantage of the momentary lull in the fire as his own shots and Doug's forced the survivors to rethink their position. He fully expected the *mareros* to resume shooting at them soon, but he pushed out to the nearest vehicle, dropping to another low knee behind a large tire, then bending over to almost put his helmet on the ground, finding his red dot with some difficulty in his NVGs as he craned his neck to try to spot his quarry.

For a moment, he couldn't see anything. He shifted so that he could see better, but then he spotted the man who'd been shooting at him.

The hard-core, Santa Muerte worshiping gangbanger had taken to his heels, and Nick just got a glimpse of him as he went over the gate leading into the San Pedro Productos distribution center.

"This is Figaro. Mission is scrubbed. Fall back to last rally point."

Nick straightened up, scanned his surroundings, and then looked back toward the warehouse. Carl was there at the corner, covering down the length of the boulevard.

Getting to his feet, he pivoted back the way they'd come and ran for the shadows beneath the warehouse, passing Doug as his partner stayed in the median covering his own movement.

They might not have gotten to the destroyer house, but they'd definitely put the hurt on the maras in Chamelecón that night. That was something.

CHAPTER
29

Romero looked even older and more careworn than he had a week before. I didn't imagine I looked much better. The strain was getting to me.

It was hard to imagine. I'd been in firefights all over the world, and once took a wrong turn into a Sadrist neighborhood in Baghdad, when it had just been Goblin and me in the car. Here I was Stateside, with plenty of backup nearby, doing a six to eight hour shift and going back to a hotel to call my wife and kids, then go to sleep.

Except that I was still waiting to see what the fallout from St. Louis was going to be.

It was possible that Nathan was on the up and up. The fact that we hadn't already had the FBI knocking on our doors suggested that even if he wasn't, they didn't have any prints or other forensics they could use against us, so they were looking for two dudes who weren't real.

But at the moment, the Feds were almost the least of my worries.

There had been nothing from the nondescript email or the dark web network since things had gone down and I'd smoked Williams, if that was really his name. We'd sent our respective reports, just different enough that it wouldn't seem like we'd rehearsed a cover story, but essentially getting the gist across—there'd been a Fed on the team, and he'd thrown the entire op in the shitter.

That was backed up by the public reports, which lauded Agent Nathan Patten for quick thinking and heroic risk to his own life in stopping a terrorist bombing in St. Louis. Who the bad guys had been—one had been killed, though the FBI was neither confirming nor denying that there had been any others—was still uncertain, though half the internet was already pointing fingers at the Russians. They were the convenient boogeyman, especially given what they were doing in Ukraine at the moment, not to mention the almost daily threats coming from the Kremlin.

We knew better, but none of us were going to say anything.

As for Romero, the source of his harried, hangdog look was almost as bad. There hadn't been any more attempts on him, not so far, though Jake and Clint had reported surveillance at least twice. No, the stress was based on the constant reports of violence coming from the Honduras operation, not to mention the financial cost that violence was inflicting on the company.

He wasn't being particularly talkative with us anymore, and Ken had muttered about being worried that sooner or later, Romero was going to decide that having a bunch of shooters on the payroll, who might or might not be exacerbating the situation in Honduras, wasn't worth the squeeze. I doubted it, but there were people who thought that way, and I was sure there were a few of them at Carr & Sons, putting a bug in Romero's ear.

Some people just can't wrap their heads around the concept that once the first shot has been fired, there's no going back until the reason for the killing is gone. And we hadn't fired the first shot.

Still, for us it was pretty boring, which only allowed me to get too deep into speculation and contingency planning surrounding the clandestine operation we were running in the background. And I was stress-bombing about it.

So, it was almost a relief when I got an email on "Walter Callahan's" email. It had been almost a week.

The cluster in St. Louis was unfortunate. It was definitely not "most excellent." However, that was apparently on our vetting, not your performance. Furthermore, we are reasonably confident that you have not been exposed. We have contacts that would inform us if you were.

There is another job coming up. Time sensitive, but it is close to you. We'd created the legend that Callahan and Kelly both lived in Nashville. It made things simpler. *It's easy money, primarily just a standby position in case the operation needs you to step in. Details are on the listing. Pay is less, but considering there will be no pay for completion of the St. Louis job, that shouldn't be too much of an issue.*

The pay was the least of my worries. There was a fair bit of crypto in the digital wallet that was "Callahan's," but I couldn't really spend any of it, not without giving things away. Sure, crypto was supposed to be untraceable, but that wasn't a chance I wanted to take.

Especially not if this asshole had sources within the Bureau that could tell him whether or not Nathan had fingered either of us. Tracing someone who wasn't "Walter Callahan" spending crypto from the "Callahan" wallet was iffy, but it was still *possible*, so I was staying away from it.

No, the issues went with finding out who was behind all this. So far, all we'd accomplished was being involved in a couple of extremely sketchy ops, meeting one of the actual operators working for this network, and killing him. We were no closer to the spider in the web than we had been when I'd blown Kinkaid's brains out.

I'd checked the email on the burner phone, while Ken drove on an extended, serpentine surveillance detection route back to the team house. I was VPNed up like nobody's business, and the encrypted email service itself was supposed to be secure from anywhere, but with the kind of people we were up against, I didn't think there was such a thing as "too paranoid."

For all we knew, this was being driven by somebody within the highest levels of federal law enforcement or the intelligence community. We'd seen plenty of that sort of corruption, lately.

By the time we got to the team house, I'd calmed down a bit. Not that I'd been freaking out, but the stress levels had me tense, and probably weren't doing anything good for my blood pressure, either.

Our past operations had certainly been risky. We'd had the FBI sniffing around after us, and nobody goes up against Mexican cartels without knowing full well that it could end badly. Combat didn't bother me so much. Hell, even a lot of the clandestine stuff was just a matter of caution and a degree of paranoia that had become second nature over the course of a relatively long career of military and contract service.

This was different. This was far, far more precarious. I didn't have a team of hardassed shooters at my back when I went into this world. It was just me, and sometimes Phil, in the lion's den. And I knew the sort of guys in that den, and knew that one on one, I was a lot more evenly matched with any of them than I was with your average *sicario*.

Sicarios and *mareros* are savages, but these guys had degrees of training and skill that none but a tiny handful of those animals could claim. These were the dark side of the same coin we were on.

There were those who would consider Pallas Group Solutions no different. I can't speak to those people. There's a context that they can't see. Or won't see.

As soon as we got back to the team house, I found Radford in his hole. He'd taken over most of the TOC, squirreled away in one of the two bedrooms, and had at least three monitors up as he worked his cyber magic. The ever-present bucket of energy drinks was on the desk next to his computer, and the box of empty cans on the floor was overflowing.

He looked up as I came in. "Another listing?"

I nodded. He took another gulp of his liquid heart attack and turned to his Tor browser.

The email had said, "Close" but the rendezvous wasn't in Nashville. Maybe whoever was coordinating this had a flexible idea of what constituted "close," or maybe he figured that anywhere we could drive to in less than half a day was close enough. There didn't seem to be much point to flying to Indianapolis, at least not to me.

The instructions were, as usual, vague. *Get a room in any of the below hotels. You have two days to conduct area familiarization and link up with the rest of your team in Room 534 of the Embassy Suites Downtown. Make sure you have primary, secondary, and tertiary escape routes. Your target will be in The Conrad on the 7th. You will need to conduct a thorough reconnaissance of The Conrad, determining all entrance and exit points, and develop a plan to cover them. Surveillance on the entrances will be required on the 7th, along with comms watch.*

You are not the main effort on this. You are the backup plan. You will receive a target package at the rendezvous. Be prepared to interdict the target, should the primary plan fail.

Operational funds will be in your crypto wallet within twenty-four hours.

"Well, that's interesting." Something was nagging at me about it, something in addition to the fact that I was being asked to be ready to interdict someone in the middle of downtown Indianapolis. The number of ways *that* could go wrong would form a list as long as my arm.

Radford got it first, though. "Oh, shit. You know who they want you to interdict?"

"The President?" I was being flippant, because I was tired, the stress was starting to reassert itself, and I really didn't have any idea what he was talking about. Without that target package, we had nothing. Just an area and a timeframe.

Radford, though, wasn't just a computer geek. He twisted his head around to squint up at me. "Dude. Romero and Carr have a meeting at The Conrad in Indianapolis on the 7th. They got an invite from Thomas Zhang, the billionaire."

There it was. It wasn't the same as a smoking gun for the hitman network, but it explained some of the weight that had been brought to bear on Carr & Sons.

Thomas Zhang was half Chinese, half German. He was one of those transnational billionaires who flew around with politicians, captains of industry, tech CEOs, actors, and everybody else with money and influence. Nobody knew exactly how much he was worth, but it was a lot.

He was also one of those "citizen of the world" types. He'd been to Davos more times than I knew, and while he wasn't nearly the big name that some other financial and political movers and shakers that went there were, he was always talking about the need to "adapt to a new global paradigm."

To the best of anyone's knowledge, he had never lived in China, but he had plenty of business connections there. Whether or not he was entirely in Beijing's pocket was an unknown, but it seemed likely.

Even more likely, if he was ramrodding the attempt to put Carr & Sons in an untenable position.

It was possible that he was just a prop. That the real movers and shakers behind Talbot Consulting had wooed him along to lend some legitimacy to the proceedings, whatever they were supposed to be. Whatever was going on, it had apparently seemed legit to Romero.

Either that, or he felt so backed into a corner that he didn't figure he could beg off.

I went looking for KG.

We all had hotel rooms, but I didn't think KG had budged from the team house since we'd gotten there, except when he was taking a shift on Romero's or Carr's details. Right at the moment, he was crashed out on the couch that had come from someone's Craigslist ad in the living room.

I hesitated. This might wait until morning. The man was exhausted. I could see that day by day.

With a grimace, I shook my head and reached down to shake his shoulder. I knew KG. I might have wondered about him at first, since we'd never worked together downrange, and a lot of times the middle management that these companies picked was less than stellar, but the dude was solid.

A regular contract middle manager wouldn't have fireman's carried my best friend's body out of a firefight outside of Mazatlán, only refusing to let me do it because as the team leader, he figured it was his responsibility.

He grunted as I shook him, and reached up to run a hand over his face without opening his eyes. I might still have started awake, but KG was apparently too tired. He blinked up at me. "When'd you get back, Chris?"

"Not too long ago. Got another job from the network." I could speak freely in the team house, but there was still something a little off about saying, "*I got another job from the hitman network that's trying to kill our client.*"

He heaved himself up to a sitting position as I stepped back, running both hands over his face. "Yeah? What have we got this time?"

"Backup for another op. Possibly interdicting someone in or around The Conrad in Indianapolis."

He might have been tired and sleepy, but he wasn't so out of it that he missed that. He froze, just for a moment, then looked up at me. "No shit?"

"No shit. The target package wasn't with the listing, but it's supposed to be there for the team in Indianapolis." I sighed. "I seriously doubt it's a coincidence."

"Oh, I'm sure it's not." He got up and looked at his watch. "Shit. It's getting late. Still, we'd better head over to

Romero's house. Forewarned is forearmed, as they say." He glanced at me. "You just get off shift?"

"I did, but if I'm going to be covering his would-be kidnappers or murderers, I think I'd better be there to tell him." I'd anticipated KG's decision. This wasn't something you wanted to talk about on an open cell connection. Romero, to the best of my knowledge, didn't have the encrypted apps that we used for communications. "I already grabbed the keys."

CHAPTER
30

This is a switch.

Surveillance wasn't exactly a new thing for anyone in Pallas Group Solutions, and it certainly wasn't new in San Pedro Sula, either. So far, though, the B Team had been primarily concerned with surveillance and countersurveillance against MS-13 or Barrio 18, with some attention paid to the Honduran police on the side, to make sure they stayed out of trouble.

This was different. This was surveillance on a target that wasn't necessarily going to try to cut their hearts out, but still might call down all sorts of destruction if they got wind of the fact they were being watched and panicked.

The name Talbot Consulting had come from the A Team, up in Nashville. There hadn't been a lot of information about sources and methods, but Nick figured that there was some skullduggery involved in finding that name. He'd never heard of them, and he was involved enough in the finance world—he had long been one of those contractors who spent a good deal of his spare time and extra money investing—that the fact he'd never heard of them, yet they were trying to get Carr & Sons in a financial chokehold, was an indicator. Whoever Talbot Consulting was, they wanted to stay in the shadows.

They also had an office in San Pedro Sula.

Research hadn't turned up much. Incorporated in Panama, they were an international financial consulting firm, and that was about it. No public lists of who worked for or with them. A bland, thoroughly uninformative website. Contact forms that seemed to go nowhere. If you were going to work with Talbot Consulting, you had to already be in the circle, or so it seemed.

That was why Nick and Doug were currently in one of the less violent parts of San Pedro Sula, watching the nondescript little commercial property where they had located the office. There was no signage, but even someone with the sort of connections and secrecy of Talbot Consulting couldn't *quite* keep their rental of a place like this a complete secret.

The office was in a second-floor property above the Plaza Numa shopping mall. That made things both simpler and more difficult, at the same time.

Being up in the Mackey District, in the north of the city, they were in a much more affluent part of San Pedro Sula. That meant both less crime and violence, and more security. They needed more of a reason to be there besides just hanging out.

Unfortunately, there wasn't much of one, except for actually going to the mall. That could create a problem, since this wasn't an area where two grown men would just go and hang out at a mall. Part of surveillance involves observing and adapting to the atmospherics of the area of operations, and this wasn't what either man would consider a permissive environment.

Still, they needed to get eyes on the office, and most importantly, the personnel. Once they had Talbot Consulting's operatives in San Pedro Sula identified, they might have a little more breathing room.

Without eyes on the ground, they hadn't really been able to determine the best course of action, so they'd driven past the place the day before, getting just enough of a look to determine some of the atmospherics, and whether or not there were CCTV cameras.

Both were surprised when they didn't see any cameras. It didn't necessarily mean they weren't there—the hardware was getting smaller and more streamlined every year—but the cameras in the Middle East had usually been relatively easy to spot. Maybe the locals who ran the mall figured that they were more secure in Mackey, so they didn't bother.

After some deliberation, they'd still decided to be careful. So, they'd parked in a corner of the parking lot, underneath a tree, and Doug had gone in first. As per, they were using phones for most communications. Everyone seemed to have one, and it was therefore a lot less conspicuous than trying to talk on a radio.

Not getting any real attention. Doug had been inside for the last ten minutes, while Nick stayed in the vehicle and watched the parking lot and the windows upstairs. *This place is swank. I don't think any of these people give much thought to what's going on down south.*

That much had already been somewhat obvious, judging by the quality of the landscaping, not to mention how new and clean the whole mall looked. The Mackey District might as well have been a whole different world from the gang-ravaged barrios down south.

Nick sent his acknowledgement, then pocketed the phone and stepped out of the car. Time to really get close.

He still kept his eyes open as he crossed the parking lot, but he was acting as blasé and casual as he could, just sort of letting his gaze wander curiously, trying not to look like he was staring at anything in particular. It took practice to catalog everything he saw that way, but he'd had quite a bit of training and experience.

Walking past Doug, where the man was lounging at one of the tables in the little courtyard inside the arms of the "U" of the building, Nick headed upstairs. There wasn't a central, inside area, which actually simplified matters. There was no security checkpoint with a metal detector to get past, like a number of malls both of them had been to in the Middle East.

He walked past a couple of boutiques and small cafés. The office had once been another boutique, and the darkened glass was decidedly out of place amid the colorful and affluent stores and eateries in the Plaza. Nick wondered who had made that decision. There had to be less obtrusive places to put the office, but maybe someone in TC had simply liked the place, or the nearness to one or another café. Either way, it put him in a decent spot to walk past the office on his way to find a seat in the outdoor seating on the porch of the café across the corner.

The food looked and smelled great, so he ordered, still fiddling with his phone like any tourist, facing the Talbot Consulting office. To any casual observer—and everyone around him at least appeared to be a casual observer, when they looked up at all—he was just one more guy, having lunch, uninterested in much of anything but what he could read on his phone.

His food came, and he dug in. It wasn't quite what he was used to, even after weeks in Honduras, but it was good. What wasn't so good was the fact that he'd been sitting there for over half an hour, and there hadn't been any movement from the Talbot Consulting office. He was dawdling over his food, but there was only so long he could do that.

It wouldn't be the end of the world if he didn't get a hit that day. They could rotate most of both teams through the Plaza over the next week or two, until they *did* get a target. He just hoped they could get something sooner rather than later.

If Talbot Consulting really was behind the attacks on Carr & Sons and their employees, then Nick was hoping to get a line on them sooner, rather than later.

It was impossible to hear the gunfire from up north in Mackey, but the war between Barrio 18 and MS-13 in Chamelecón had intensified since the PGS shooters had massacred their fighters two nights before. It was taking some of the heat off the plant, but only some. Several of the other cliques in San Pedro Sula had intensified their own attention, but they hadn't made another major attack, though there'd been some harassment.

There was no guarantee that taking Talbot Consulting out of the picture would remove the threat of the maras, but it was certainly worth a try. At the very least, they might get a better idea of what was behind the violence.

He was about to give up, ask for the check, and head out, when the door to the office opened.

The man who came out wasn't a local. He was chubby and pasty, though he dressed a little like a local. Not that that said much, in Mackey, where everyone seemed to dress like every other Westerner Nick had ever seen.

He had some Asian in his background, but something about him told Nick he was an American. He'd been around Chinese, Japanese, Thais, and numerous others, and there was something about Americans that stood out, even if they were technically full blooded Asian. This kid probably wasn't. And his attitude was entirely American.

The younger man went straight to the café where Nick was sitting, and Nick got some pretty good photographs on the way, all without looking up at him. He sent them to Doug. *Looks like one of our boys. Came out of the office.*

There was a pause before his partner replied. *Got it. How long can you maintain contact?*

Not long. Just finishing up lunch right now.

Another pause, probably while Doug thought over contingencies. *Finish up and head down to the car. There are a couple other people hanging out. We can hold what we've got for a little while.* The former Delta operator probably was hoping much the same thing that Nick was. Hoping that they could push the mission a little farther that day.

There's something to be said for a steady paycheck, and security in a high-threat environment provides that well enough, but every man who worked for Pallas Group Solutions tended to be a mission-oriented sort of individual. They would all rather take the fight to the bad guys, end the threat, and get on to the next job.

Nick acknowledged, then finished up his food, while Chubby sat down at an adjoining table and ordered. The waiter took his time bringing the check, so he had some time to observe his quarry before he had to leave.

The guy wasn't really paying any attention to his surroundings at all. He was glued to his phone, and from where Nick was sitting, he thought he could see some sort of game on it. Even as Nick paid his check and got up to leave, the man didn't twitch or look up once.

He headed downstairs and into the parking lot, heading for the car in the far corner. He walked past Doug, who gave no sign that he even noticed him.

Once in the car, he leaned back in the shadows and settled in to wait.

***

Doug rejoined him after about half an hour. "He went back inside." Of course, with the courtyard designed the way it was, it had been easy enough for his partner to spot Chubby once he'd been pointed out. "I took a stroll around, and it doesn't look like there's a back door. He's going to have to come this way when he goes home."

"You thinking of grabbing him here?" Nick wasn't sure about that; for one thing, they didn't have the go from Vern. If they snatched Chubby before there was a place to take him, this could get interesting.

"I'm thinking of following him until he gets to somewhere more conducive, or we can pinpoint where he lives. Do a little B&E." Doug was watching the plaza with one eye while he tapped out another SITREP to Vern. "I've already coordinated both courses with Vern."

Of course you did. Nick tried not to get frustrated at how far ahead of him his partner was. Doug had been doing this sort of thing a lot longer than he had, and he'd been doing it for a while.

It wasn't that Nick was bad at it. Doug was just better. Nor did he think that his partner was trying to one-up him. He'd known guys who were like that. Doug wasn't one of them. He was just very focused and put the mission above any possible hurt feelings.

Nick despised people who put their feelings above the mission, too, which made the fact that Doug's actions bothered him just piss him off even more.

Doug leaned back in the seat. "We'll have to see how late these weirdos work.

***

As it turned out, not very late at all.

The sun was still pretty high in the sky when Chubby and an even larger woman came out of the office and headed down into the parking lot.

They had an ID on Chubby by then. Daniel Foy wasn't exactly all that shy on social media, and that had led to a few other things, including his Harvard class. The guy was considered something of a genius for financial shenanigans, though he'd never been caught *actually* breaking finance laws.

Having a name meant that they also had an address. It seemed that Talbot Consulting, as secretive as they were, saw no reason to hide their personnel anywhere but in plain sight. Foy had a house not far away, where he'd probably have an apartment in a big city up north. Here in Honduras, the US dollar went a *long* way, and so small fry financiers could afford full houses that somebody like Nick would struggle to pay for Stateside.

With Nick driving, they pulled out behind Foy's Audi, careful to maintain their distance. With an address, they didn't necessarily need to follow him, but it would help to confirm that he was going home, and not to a bar or nightclub. Nick hadn't thought that Foy looked like the type, but he'd been around enough that he knew that the look of a nerd didn't mean that their quarry wouldn't try to indulge in the nightlife, anyway.

Sure enough, though, Foy went straight home. "Astounding. They're down here doing dirty and hiring mara thugs to try to burn the plant down, but they act like they're in any city back in the States, with nothing at all to worry about." Nick shook his head.

"They're pretty confident in the precautions they've already taken, that's for sure," Doug agreed. "Let's not let his sloppiness rub off on us, though. Complacency kills, brother."

They rolled past the house after Foy had pulled in, Doug watching the dumpy-looking financier go from his car to his door, not even looking up as the PGS car went by. A moment later, as the door shut behind Foy, they rounded the corner and lost sight of the house.

"Okay." Doug checked his watch. "Let's give it a few hours."

CHAPTER
31

There were a lot more lights in Mackey than there had been in Chamelecón. There was more money in this neighborhood, and therefore the need for security was considered more acute. The people who lived there weren't content to live in squalor and darkness.

That made the approach to Foy's house a little trickier. There weren't a whole lot of lawns to cut across, and many of those were walled. The lights on the street were few and far between, but almost every house had plenty of lights out front, and from the faint rumbles that sounded through the night, most of them probably had backup generators in case the power went out.

There'd been some back and forth about the best way to come at the target. The final solution had been to just do it the old fashioned way.

So, the two vehicles rolled right up in front and the hit team got out.

There was a balance to be struck. There were definitely cameras in that neighborhood, though they seemed to be almost all privately owned and operated. That didn't mean that the Honduran cops couldn't access them, but it would take longer.

Hopefully, this would all be over by the time they were actually able to trace anything, and all four PGS operators that walked up to Foy's door were wearing hats pulled low that would make it difficult—not impossible, but difficult—for face recognition software to do its thing.

Doug was in the lead, his Glock 19 concealed and a bump key in his pocket. They weren't sure that Foy didn't have a burglar alarm system, so they were hoping not to have to actually break in. The lower key they could keep this, the better.

So, while it seemed a little counterintuitive, given what they were doing, Doug stepped up to the door and knocked.

For a long few seconds, it seemed like it wasn't going to work. Foy's social media showed that he wasn't shy about substance abuse, either, so it was entirely possible that he was passed out drunk or drugged out of his mind.

They waited, trying to look casual, though every one of them had a Glock 19 concealed under a shirt or in a waistband. This was nothing like the hit in Chamelecón the other night. They were doing what they could to look as little like paramilitaries as possible.

Doug was about to use the bump key when the door unlocked and cracked open, Daniel Foy in his boxers, squinting out into the light on his porch. "What? We weren't supposed to meet until the morning."

Doug shoved him inside, Nick right on his heels, while Saul and Manny pushed in behind them, shut the door, and set security on the front of the house and the parked vehicles.

Foy was completely confused. He stumbled and fell, his feet scrambling on the tile floor as Doug reached down, grabbed him under the armpit, and hauled him to his feet. "What? What's going on? I was going to be there!"

Nick had no idea what he was squawking about, but it might turn out to be some valuable information. "Our employer doesn't think you're being entirely aboveboard." He caught a glance from Doug, but none of the other contractors said a word. He was winging it, but in this case, winging it might get them some more of what they were looking for, especially if he capitalized on Foy's confusion.

The man stank of tequila, too, which might make things easier. It accounted for his unsteadiness as Doug propelled him backward toward his couch.

If they were really lucky, and he was drunk enough, he might just black out and forget this entire encounter had ever happened when it was over. Nick doubted it, but he could hope.

"What?" That seemed to be Foy's default reaction, and Nick had to suddenly wrestle with the whimsical temptation to yell a movie quote about it in the man's face. Not the time, nor the place, and they had a limited amount of time to wring Foy dry of everything he knew about MS-13 and the attempt to shut down the Carr & Sons plant.

"Don't give me that shit, Daniel. You know full well 'what.'" *Don't let me screw this up.* He had to think fast to figure out what to say next. "You're down here for one reason, and that doesn't seem to be working out. Why is that plant still standing?"

He barely managed to avoid flinching. That was a hell of a gamble, and he knew it. He felt Doug's eyes on him, but a moment later, Foy blinked stupidly and gaped at him. "I...I didn't have anything to do with that, not after the initial contacts! That wasn't my job!"

"Like hell." Nick decided to push. He was committed, now, and hopefully Foy's drunken terror would keep him from figuring out that this was a fishing expedition. "You were the one who was supposed to coordinate things. That was the deal. This was supposed to be small and quiet, and yet there's gunfire and bloodshed all over the city."

"That wasn't my fault! Yeah, I was supposed to make some of the initial contacts, but I wasn't talking to the...the...*contractors!*"

Something about the way he'd said "contractors" told Nick that he knew exactly what he'd been hiring, but he was still, even drunk, trying to hide from it. Foy might have been shady, but he wasn't quite as sociopathic as some of the people they'd been dealing with. He was still trying to protect himself, even interiorly.

"Don't give me that crap. You had one job."

"I had a lot more than one job!" He was getting indignant. That might be a good or a bad thing. "And this was hardly as clear cut as calling your bunch for this!"

Nick hoped that Doug or Saul had remembered to start the audio recorder. This was turning out a bit more of a seat of the pants interrogation than they'd planned, but they were barely needing to turn the screws.

"We had to find a local contact first, and then we found out that we had to get into the *prison*! And if you think that's easy, I've got some bad news for you! We had to get a journalist in to make all the main contacts, because what would a finance guy be doing in the *Reclusorio*? Then we found out that just talking to the government wouldn't get us in; we had to get word to the *prisoners!*" He took a deep breath. "You haven't been in there! It's a nightmare! They've got *guns!* The *prisoners* have *guns!*"

Nick had heard that about the mara wings of Honduran prisons. It had been in the intel dump before they'd headed south.

"It was all we could do to get to the First Word and pass him the message. I didn't even know if he'd care, or if he'd have us killed right there for having the gall to give him a job! Do you *really* think that I could tell *him* how to do it?" He shuddered. Drunk or not, he was already having waking nightmares about meeting the First Word, the gang leader that most of the local clique leadership looked to. "We passed the message, the journalist got his story, and we got out. If the client wanted more of a sure thing, they should have just called you guys."

Nick was starting to gather that Foy thought they were contracting for whoever had put Talbot Consulting up to bringing Carr & Sons down. Which told him a few things. For one, it was damning. If they could ever find a way to make a drunken confession given in a foreign country to home invaders stick in court, it would—potentially—bring Talbot Consulting down in a heartbeat and put a lot of people behind bars.

Except that this wasn't exactly going to be admissible, and Talbot Consulting wasn't technically an American company.

Which complicated things a bit.

"Well, the client's not happy about how slowly this is going." He may as well continue to play the role. It was getting them what they wanted, and they didn't even need to break any of Foy's fingers. "We're going to be taking over from here. Who is this 'First Word?'" That was something they could *probably* find out from open sources, but it was worth getting as much intel from Foy as possible.

"Carlos Ramirez. He's like the top dog First Word in San Pedro Sula. All the other MS-13 clique leaders listen to him. Well, from what my sources say, except for Luis Arias. I don't know what's going on with him, but I'd guess he wants to take over."

That wasn't relevant to their current needs for information. "Where is this Ramirez?" If he was in prison, that was going to make things even more complicated.

"He's in the MS-13 wing of the *Reclusorio de Menores*. You're not going to get in there easily, though." He shuddered, his eyes staring at nothing. "The guards won't let you in without the prisoner's approval, and the prisoners are armed to the teeth. The *prisoners!*" Foy was definitely drunk. He was repeating himself.

Nick glanced at Doug, who had an eyebrow raised despite himself. This had been too easy, but they had what they needed. Offing the First Word might not stop things, but it could take some of the heat off of them. He turned back to Foy, who was looking a little more glazed over. His initial terror was giving way to the stupefaction of however much booze he'd put down that night, assuming there weren't any pills in the mix. "You're a smart man, Daniel. Stay that way. We were never here, and this conversation never happened. You understand me?"

For a moment, he thought that maybe Foy was just too far gone. But he got a limp-necked nod after a few seconds. "Of course. Don't want any trouble." Despite the man's obvious intoxication, the fear had just sobered him up just a little. "I don't even want to *remember* this conversation, much less talk about it." He started to look around, ignoring the men looming over him, presumably looking for a bottle.

"Let's go." Doug was already moving toward the door, and Nick followed, though not without turning back to check on Foy, just to be sure. If the drunkenness had been an act, things might get a little sporty.

Foy, however, appeared to have passed out. The four PGS operators slipped out the door, down the walk, and into their vehicles, disappearing into the night.

There was a raid on a Honduran prison to plan.

CHAPTER
32

The new "team" in Indianapolis was made up of about the kind of guys I would have expected. If I was being honest, these operations with the shadow network were making me appreciate Pallas Group Solutions all the more. Goblin had screened his applicants *very* carefully. Much more carefully than the individual or individuals on the other end of that nondescript, encrypted email.

Once again, like St. Louis, everyone was going by numbers. Number One was an older guy, skinnier than anyone else, clean shaven and short haired, with a prominent Adam's apple and a scar alongside his head. He didn't have much to say, but then, there really wasn't any small talk going down in that bunch to begin with.

Number Two looked like he'd either been undercover or actually been in a motorcycle gang. Big, barrel-chested, and shaggy, his hair was almost as long as his beard, and the tattoos crawling all over his arms were a combination of old military crests and newer, darker motifs. No swastikas that I saw, but the dude had clearly had some connection with the Mongols. He hadn't said a word, just listened to the brief, nodded, and gone to prep his gear.

Number Three was Phil. I was Number Four. Number Five didn't quite look like he belonged there, being easily ten years younger than the youngest dude in the room, baby faced

265

except for a thin mustache. He wore his hair high and tight, and looked like he was at least partially Hispanic.

The guys we'd killed down in Mexico would have had him for lunch, if looks were anything to go by. It was entirely possible that they weren't, and I'd been around long enough that I wasn't going to discount the kid. I'd known some thoroughly harmless-looking bastards who'd cut someone's heart out like it was nothing.

Number Six was the one I was really keeping my eye on, though. Because I knew him.

I didn't think he remembered me. Given the substance abuse that had gotten him fired from that contract, I would be quite surprised if he did. Skyler Pertman had clearly hit the roids hard, as he was massive, easily thirty pounds heavier than he had been the last time I'd seen him. He'd shaved his head and his beard, too, so he was now a hairless Mr. Clean, all the way down to the too-small white t-shirt.

He hadn't showed any sign of recognition, and from what I remembered, that was a pretty good sign that he didn't remember me. Even if he did, he didn't seem inclined to reminisce. Just as well; we'd never gotten along back in the day, anyway. Still, I needed to watch him carefully.

Since this was a backup team, there wasn't a whole lot to do once we'd established our area familiarization, which we'd all done on our own prior to the rendezvous. The fact that Number One hadn't done more than ask whether everyone had done it told me more about the level of professionalism at work here.

Not that these guys weren't good at their jobs. Pertman, despite his character flaws, was *very* good at his job. I knew that from personal experience. But there's always the risk, when you're that experienced and well-practiced, that you start to figure that you're on top of things, and you get lazy. I suspected there was some of that going on here, especially since it appeared that none of these guys had worked much with each other before.

Phil and I were still playing at not knowing each other.

I'd wondered just how we were supposed to monitor whether or not we were supposed to intervene from the parking garage, where we were currently sitting in a pair of vans, especially since none of us had apparently been tasked with getting into the conference room and bugging it. There was quite a bit of audiovisual equipment in the vans, wirelessly connected to *somewhere*, but it was all dark at the moment.

The meeting was supposed to start in the next hour. We'd moved into the parking garage—there wasn't anywhere else to stage, not right in the middle of downtown Indianapolis—just as the sun had started going down, at about 1800. Phil and I were both in the second van with Number Two, which wasn't ideal. I would have preferred to have one of us in each vehicle, but without direct comms to coordinate, that would present its own problems.

Number Two was chewing on a Power Bar. I hadn't seen him eat anything else for the last six hours I'd been around him, and if I'd been the more squeamish sort, I think that the sight of the damned things would have made me nauseous by then. Especially since the big man ate *constantly*. There's an old saying in Recon, that "chow is continuous," but this guy took it to new heights.

Phil was being less unobtrusive about his disgust than I was. He glanced over his shoulder from his place in the driver's seat with barely concealed disdain as Number Two chewed, then squirted a blob of dip spit into a paper cup. It was funny that the guy dipping thought the other guy who was turning into a Power Bar processing machine was gross, but that's the way it is, sometimes.

The screen lit up, and both Number Two and I raised our heads to look at it. For a moment, it just showed a test pattern, then the video cleared, to what looked like a body cam.

I realized a moment later that that was what it was, only smaller. It was a button camera on somebody's jacket or shirt.

Then another window opened, showing a similar view, but of a different part of the conference room. I could see the hotel's service staff wheeling in carts of drinks and food, and the music was already getting started. Several more nondescript young men who looked like security were spread out around the room, while a knot of people in the middle talked in low voices, too low for the cameras to pick up.

I recognized Todd Linemann and the older Talbot Consulting "investor." Several more of the men and women gathered around the two of them had much the same look. These were people with a lot of money and ideas about how to use it.

More windows opened, until we had six different views of the conference room and one of the hallway outside. So, that was how we were supposed to trigger. They had the entire shindig under surveillance, and from the looks of things, as Linemann walked over to one of the security guys with a wire on, looked into the camera, and nodded before speaking, that was all part of the plan.

"*Mr. Zhang's supposed to be here in the next fifteen minutes or so, and we're expecting the other guests about twenty minutes after that. Make sure that the doors are secured once they get here. We don't want them to rush out. If they want to leave, we need to slow them down as best we can.*" He clapped the man on the shoulder. "*Lot of money riding on this one. Don't want to let the golden goose get away, huh?*"

I decided I hated his laugh. I looked forward to the day I could silence it.

That was an interesting thought. We were operating farther and farther afield, and while we'd been willing to include at least the local law in our operations before, we were increasingly getting into uncharted legal territory. Where *was* the line we couldn't cross? Or wouldn't?

Sitting there, undercover, without any legal sanction to do so, amid hitmen and kidnappers, I had a lot to wonder about, and no solid answers that I could find.

Thomas Zhang showed up, as predicted, almost exactly fifteen minutes later. He ignored the security men, walking right past them without even glancing toward any of the cameras, and went to greet the older Talbot Consulting guy.

I'd seen a few videos of Zhang at various public appearances, and he came across as warm, engaging, shaking hands and smiling, always pushing generosity and "doing the most good for the most people."

That wasn't the version of Zhang I saw through candid body camera. His face was a blank, grim, cold mask as he shook the older man's hand. "You're sure this is going to work?"

"Am I sure? Sir, nothing in this business is 'sure.' You know that." The older man was apologetic but firm, probably firmer than most functionaries would be when facing a demand from one of the richest men on the planet. "It's got a good chance. Carr & Sons has taken a lot of losses, and they're struggling. A scandal will be one of the last things they can handle. They'll listen if that's what they're facing."

Zhang didn't look all that convinced. He was probably under a lot of pressure from whoever was pulling *his* strings. I was pretty sure whoever that was wore black suits and lived in the Forbidden City. The older guy spread his hands, though it was more a gesture of conciliation than helplessness. "Besides, sir, if this *doesn't* work, we have a contingency plan in place. It's considerably less elegant and a *lot* more risky, but if your bosses want Carr & Sons, then they'll have them by the end of the night. One way or another."

That was why we were there. I wanted to glance at Phil, but he was listening without watching, his eyes roving across the inside of the parking garage, his spitter still in his off hand, his gun hand resting close to his Glock clone and the CZ Scorpion EVO resting beside his seat.

Number Two didn't look at either of us, but just watched the screen with a blank expression on his face and chewed his Power Bar.

Zhang still didn't seem to be satisfied, but he drifted away and scooped up a drink off one of the nearest carts. He wasn't happy, but between our efforts and the violence that the B and D Teams had wrought on the MS-13 thugs they'd sicced on the Carr & Sons operation in Honduras, their effort to stop a vital bit of chemical processing from transferring out of Chinese control was hurting. Things must be getting desperate. Not that they *couldn't* afford to back off, from a purely financial point of view, but they had to be getting pressure from the powers that wanted that control.

I glanced at Number Two, again, then at the taser, CS gas grenades, and zip cuffs that were for use on Romero and his entourage, if the plan up in the conference room didn't play out. We *could* use them on our "compatriots," provided we moved fast enough. I was seriously considering doing just that, right now, before things got interesting. It would blow our cover in the long run. There was no way that we'd be able to walk away after quietly disabling the rest of the team, and *not* have the network figure it out. We'd gotten lucky in St. Louis. That luck wouldn't apply here.

But the whole reason we'd embarked on this undercover op was, at least in the near term, to protect our client. Participating in the kidnapping of that same client, just to maintain our cover, wasn't going to work.

Especially since we hadn't filled Romero in on what we were doing.

I couldn't exactly coordinate with Phil, not with Number Two sitting there chewing. If I was going to make a move, I was going to have to do it on my own.

Still, I glanced up and caught Phil watching me in the rear-view mirror. He nodded, ever so slightly. He was thinking the same thing.

I sighed as silently as I could. This wasn't something I was looking forward to, because it was probably going to get messy. The only sure way through this was to kill everyone who wasn't PGS in the two vans, but doing that without raising the alarm—and getting the cops on our backs—was going to be tough.

Not that subduing them without gunfire would be easy. I was developing a plan, though. I just hoped that Number Two wasn't so big that he could shrug off a taser hit.

Scooping up the device, I shot the leads into his back while he peeled another Power Bar. He stiffened as the power crackled through the wires, gritting his teeth, but he still tried to turn on me.

I'd known that might happen. Contrary to movies and expectations, a taser usually doesn't knock someone out. I was on top of him almost immediately.

I might have tried to choke him out, but he was a *big* dude, and there was no way I could have done that without making the van rock so violently that everyone in the second vehicle would have noticed. Phil was doing an admirable job of looking bored as Number Two tried to curse at me through the grinding in his jaw.

I let go of the taser, mainly so I didn't get a shock myself, and hit him in the base of the skull with a clenched fist.

That wasn't a guarantee, either, but there was a reason that we'd called that spot the "reset button." I'd been knocked out in training that way. It's almost better than a direct shot to the chin on somebody with a glass jaw. Given the amount of hair and the man's sheer size, I didn't hold back, and hit him as hard as I could.

The impact sloshed his brain back and forth in his skull, and he went out like a light.

From there, it was a matter of a few seconds to zip-tie him, adding some paracord to make sure he couldn't get his hands and feet into a position where he could snap the zip-ties. He started to move and make noise after a few seconds, but fortunately, he was positioned where I didn't need to move very far to hit him in the base of the skull again.

Then I was gathering up the CS grenades, more of the zip ties and paracord, and pulling on one of the gas masks that had come with the rest of the gear that the network had supplied. Our guns were all purchased with op funds. Or, I should say, the parts had been purchased with op funds. The guns themselves were mostly machined or 3D printed.

"It might give them a couple seconds warning, but I don't know that I can do this by myself, brother." I wasn't nearly as confident that I could neutralize the second vehicle without shooting, but I had to try.

"With you." Phil didn't even hesitate. He'd hardly looked back as I'd taken care of Number Two, but he'd done that to cover us in case the other three were watching the van. Neither of the vehicles had windows except in front and in back, but there had been some movement. Number Two was a *big* old boy, and taking him down had definitely rocked the van.

I stepped out the side door, which was, fortunately, facing away from the second vehicle. It took a second to scan the parking garage and see that I wasn't about to pull on a gas mask while a soccer mom and her rugrats stared at me. There was no one else on that level that I could see, so I pulled the mask on, pressed my palm against the filter, blew out, then sucked in to get a good seal. Contrary to every NCO I'd ever had in the Marine Corps, I *could* get a seal, even with my beard.

Then I was moving, the zip ties and paracord in my back pocket, the CS grenade in my hand.

Phil was going to get some of the CS, but he was approaching the passenger side door, and if he'd walked up with a gas mask on, it would have given away the game. He knocked on the window, asked some innocuous, bullshit question when it was rolled down, then started back toward our van while the window went back up behind him.

For a second, I thought he'd chickened out on me, but then I realized that he'd bought me time to get close to the back doors unnoticed, prepping the grenade as I went. He'd backed off because we needed the windows up for the full impact of the gas to hit them hard enough.

I hesitated, looking around once more. If the wrong person saw this—we were outside of the CCTV coverage, at least the coverage that was still working—then we'd have flashing red and blue lights and sirens down around our ears in the next few minutes.

Then I popped the grenade, reaching up to the door handle as it began to hiss and spew white smoke. I yanked the door open—the doors had all been left unlocked for rapid deployment if the game upstairs didn't work—and tossed the grenade inside. I'd given it just enough time that it was spewing CS in thick clouds by the time it clattered to the floor of the van.

I hit the lock and slammed the door shut, just to let the concentration of CS inside the van build and the confusion intensify, then I moved to the sliding door.

It came open and Pertman stumbled out, his eyes and nose streaming tears and snot, coughing uncontrollably. I was on him in seconds, wrapping him up in a choke, and he unconsciously tapped for a brief second before he went limp.

Phil had been slightly more prepared than I'd given him credit for, and he'd pulled on his own gas mask as I'd opened the back door. He was on Number Five in a heartbeat, sweeping his legs out from under him as he stumbled out of the van. As the baby-faced kid fell on his hands and knees on the concrete, Phil kicked him savagely in the head. He'd wound up pretty good for it, and the kid went out like a light.

If he was lucky, he'd wake up with a hell of a headache. I knew of at least one dude who'd never awakened from a hit like that, though.

Fortunes of war. Not that our enemies, or the cops, would necessarily see it that way.

I was already in the van, kicking the still hissing CS grenade into the front, while Number One struggled with the lock, coughing and choking. I'd landed the grenade right behind the center console, so he'd already gotten enough of a dose that he really couldn't see. I wrapped him up and hauled him halfway across the console, locking my left arm around his neck and bearing down on the back of his head with my right. Then I squeezed, as he choked and gurgled in my grasp.

It only took a few seconds for him to go limp. I held on longer, continuing to choke off the blood supply to his brain, until I was good and sure he was out, and would be for a while.

Phil already had Pertman zipped up, and was levering him back into the van. Number Five was lying on his side on the concrete, not moving. Phil checked him real quick, as I secured Number One, then zip tied him and shoved him back into the van, on top of Pertman. He was still breathing, anyway.

There was definitely a non-zero possibility that one or more of the four of them weren't going to wake up again. That's the risk you run. I didn't have much sympathy.

There wasn't much more we could do at the moment. We *might* have been spotted, but so far I hadn't heard any alarms, and the vans had police scanners, anyway. After taking close-up photos for facial recognition and taking their phones and other comms, I took the keys, locked the doors, and left them to marinate in the remaining CS as Phil and I fell back to our van.

Both of us kept the gas masks on as we got in. Number Two hadn't moved, but he was still breathing, and his heart rate felt right. We left the gas masks on for the moment, since there was now CS in our clothes. I could feel the sting on my ears and the back of my neck.

"What now?" Phil looked down at Number Two where he was having his unwilling nap. "Should we stay in place?"

"At least until Romero's clear." Looking up at the screen, I could see that our principal and his entourage, including Tom, Brian, Clint, and Patrick, had arrived. "We don't want to disappear and then have these assholes wake up and push forward with the mission. This would have been a waste of time."

"Might still be." He sounded a little skeptical. "We can't be sure that somebody didn't notice something and call the cops. I don't know about you, but I really don't want to get arrested with these assholes because we waited around."

I reached over and turned up the scanner. "No cops yet. And Romero's here. Let's play it by ear. We should have some warning, even if somebody catches a whiff of the CS."

If nobody had called the cops yet, that was probably the most likely way we'd get compromised. CS isn't a pleasant smell, and the closer you get to it, the nastier the effects get. Somebody without experience with the stuff might well call the utilities company, thinking there was a leak somewhere, and that could blow our cover, too.

But we needed to make sure Romero got clear without interference, so we settled in to watch and wait.

CHAPTER
33

Thomas Zhang was all the way into his friendly, affable, public persona, though Romero wasn't receptive to his arm-around-the-shoulder conviviality. From the moment that Phil and I resumed our monitoring of the surveillance footage—well, I'd resumed it; Phil was back in the front seat where he could watch the other van, just in case—I'd seen Romero refuse at least two drinks.

That was smart. If they were trying to drum up a scandal, a roofied drink would be one of the quickest ways to get it.

Rohypnol or Ketamine would do the trick, if they could get it into him. Fortunately, Romero had come alone, leaving Jacob Carr back to run the business. Zhang was doing a good job of disguising his emotions, based on what I'd seen so far, but there seemed to be a stiffness, a frustration, that he couldn't entirely hide.

Maybe that was just me. It was hard to say through the grainy button cam footage. Maybe I just *wanted* him to be frustrated.

After all, this guy wasn't an amateur. If we were reading the intel right, he'd wooed his way through governments and multi-billion-dollar transnational corporations and NGOs to build his influence. That takes smarts and skill. We underestimated Thomas Zhang at our peril.

Of course, it also took ruthlessness, which was why we were sitting there in a van with the unconscious body of a hitter who'd been hired to kidnap his competition.

"I know that things have been rough for you lately, Gage." Zhang had given up trying to put his arm around Romero's shoulders and was standing there next to him with a drink in his hand. "Losing Rodney that way was tragic, and the financial problems since then…" He sipped his drink, his eyes on the bottle of water in Romero's hand. I suspected that Romero, or at least Tom, who was standing just behind him, had made damned good and sure that that bottle had been properly sealed before it had been opened. "I don't know how he felt, but I counted Rodney a friend. It wouldn't seem right if I didn't try to help his nephew and his best friend out."

"I've told you already, Thomas." Romero shook his head, though his tone sounded cordial enough. "We've got things in hand. I wouldn't want to burden you."

Zhang actually laughed. "Burden *me*? Gage! This is business, not a burden."

"Okay." Romero didn't share in Zhang's mirth. "So, let me rephrase. I don't want to burden *our* company with new debt. We've got enough on our plate as it is."

"We're hardly talking about the kind of crippling debt that you're worried about, Gage." Zhang took another sip, apparently relishing the cocktail. Probably a slightly ham-fisted attempt to tempt Romero into a drink of his own. "This would be more of a partnership." He shook his head. "I can understand your company's desire to remain independent, and it would be admirable under different circumstances. But this is bigger than just wanting to keep the company in the family. The market share of these chemicals that your company owns is significant. We don't want to see the sort of economic impact that losing that capability might inflict, if you miscalculate and go under."

That was a threat, if ever I heard one, and while I couldn't see Romero's face clearly enough to be sure, I suspected that he heard the threat as well. He still didn't even blink an eye.

"Well, you're right about the need to keep the company in the family, Thomas." He sipped water again. "Far too many family owned American companies have gone corporate over the last few decades. Rodney was determined to avoid that, and we owe it to his memory to follow through on those wishes."

"You owe it to his memory to keep his company afloat, and make sure that his employees remain gainfully employed, Gage." Zhang sounded reasonable enough. He sighed. "This is a poor way to start a party, though. The real meeting isn't until tomorrow, anyway. Are you *sure* you won't have a drink?" He lifted his cocktail. "This is simply exquisite."

Romero shook his head. "Not feeling up to drinking tonight."

Again, the cell phone quality of the button cameras didn't give a whole lot of detail, but I could have sworn I saw a flicker of dissatisfaction cross Zhang's face in one of the windows. This wasn't going according to plan. Romero wasn't drinking, was staying aloof, and wasn't accepting anything that might be drugged. Tom hadn't said a word so far, but he was staying right in Romero's shadow, just in case.

"Well, at least have some hors d'oeurves." Zhang swept a hand toward one of the tables. "This is a night for networking and socializing." He shook his head in turn. "I must apologize for getting right to business immediately. I get passionate about these things sometimes."

Romero seemed to sort of brush off the comment, and while he allowed himself to be drawn into the growing crowd, he still kept himself aloof, sticking to his bottled water and steering clear of any of the food unless he'd seen one of the other guests partake.

Old boy was getting mighty paranoid. I felt so proud.

Things got quiet and boring after that. The small talk continued, though Zhang and the Talbot Consulting people seemed to cluster around Romero as much as they could. More drinks were offered, to Romero, his aides, and to our guys, but were politely declined. Romero was making it clear that he was there for business, not to play around and get drunk.

He *was* good at keeping his cool, but I still imagined I could see the steam gathering under Zhang's collar. This was *not* going according to plan.

The button cameras were mostly following Romero, but I could still see when Zhang slipped aside to the corner and pulled out a cell phone. He was much too far away, and the ambient noise of meaningless chitchat was too loud, for me to hear what he was saying, but he was clearly somewhat urgent, though whatever was said, he wasn't terribly happy about it.

Finally, he put the phone back in his pocket, put his game face back on, dazzling smile lighting up the room, and rejoined the party, such as it was.

Several of his people were clearly enjoying the open bar, which had been wheeled into the corner of the room. The main Talbot Consulting people, and Zhang himself, were still stone cold sober. It was a game, now, albeit a tense and increasingly hostile one.

I was pretty sure that Zhang had just flipped over the table with that phone call. I just wasn't sure how.

When the doors opened again, I saw just what the game was. If he couldn't get to Romero and his people with drugs and alcohol, he'd try something a bit more primal.

The four young women who walked in would have been stunning, if it wasn't quite so obvious what they were. Zhang might not have cheaped out on the escorts, but young women in skintight dresses, some of which barely reached their thighs, don't just join business parties.

Romero had his back to the door—we still had a *few* things to work on as far as cultivating his paranoia—but when Tom looked over his shoulder and nudged him, he turned to look.

One of the security men with a button camera was standing right next to the door that the women had entered through. I was pretty sure the man himself was ogling the ladies, but his button was pointed toward Romero.

Our client took in the sight of the scantily clad women as they looked around, scanning the room for their prey. Zhang, standing just behind Romero, nodded toward him, and the honeypots proceeded to close in.

Romero's face had gone blank at first, but now, as the women filled the view, I saw his expression shift into cold rage. He turned toward Zhang, but not without a nod to Tom, who interjected himself between the women and Romero.

"So, this is the game, is it?" Romero's voice was thick with wrath. "It's not enough that you try to get me to drink, to weaken my inhibitions while you push me to sell out my best friend's family company. Hell, it wouldn't surprise me if there was a bit more than alcohol in those drinks. You know, just to be sure. But that didn't work, so now you bring in the hookers." There were some protesting noises from the women, but Tom just glared—he's good at that, almost as good as me—and they suddenly shut up. Maybe they'd just picked up on the fact that there was a very dangerous game going on here, one that could even erupt into violence at any second. Several of the security men had moved closer.

"I shouldn't have come here. I knew it was probably a trap, but I thought I owed you at least a chance. It seems I should have taken a hard line from the beginning."

That was somewhat rehearsed, I knew. Zhang and his people thought that they'd been the only ones playing the game, but Tom and the others all had wires on, too. Not to mention the fact that I intended to pull the electronic storage here in the van before we left. This was another step in a very dangerous, very subtle form of war.

What came next was the question. We'd heard Linemann tell their security not to let Romero leave. Things could get sporty in the next couple of minutes, and I could see, even in the faintly blurry and occasionally rebuffering button cam footage that all four of our guys were getting ready to draw and go to work.

As they say, forewarned is forearmed, and we'd expected this to go pear-shaped.

Tom and Brian had closed in on Romero and his aide, and while both men might have appeared to be still relaxed and casual, I could see the faint tension and the way that both of them were positioned, facing the nearest security men, their hands at their sides, where each could quickly sweep cover shirts aside and draw.

The security saw it, too. At least one of them did. I saw him hold out a hand to forestall one of his compatriots from stepping forward. There was trouble in that room, and he could feel it. Even over the surveillance footage, pixelated though it might be, I could almost *feel* the tension. The escorts had shrunk back near the wall, looking around with wide, frightened eyes, huddled together as if they were cold.

With a final glare at Zhang and his Talbot Consulting cronies, Romero turned toward the door.

I already had my hand on my own Scorpion. If this was about to turn into a hostage rescue, we would have to move fast. That conference room was quite a few floors up, and we weren't going to be able to take the elevators.

For a moment, in one of the video windows, I could see Zhang's face. His expression was blank, though there wasn't enough detail in the video to see the look in his eyes. I wondered just what he was going to decide, until Romero made his decision for him. "Don, call the cops. At the very least it looks like we've got human trafficking going on here. Possibly drug distribution, too." He was staring right at Zhang as he spoke, and he got the reaction he was probably looking for.

"Gage, there's no call for that. You're overreacting." Zhang was clearly trying to be conciliatory, but there was a note of desperation in his voice that I could hear even through the faintly distorted audio. "The girls aren't what you think. They're just here to liven things up a bit." He held out a hand toward Romero's aide. "We don't need to waste the police's time. I'd hoped to handle this in a friendly way, but you don't seem to be receptive." He shook his head, as if disappointed. "I won't try to keep you. I tried to help, because I think that your company is valuable, and I don't want to see the devastation to come if you go under. But let it be on your head." He spread his hands, and the gesture seemed to be something of a signal. The security men seemed to all take a step or two back, opening things up and hopefully dispelling some of the tension.

There was a long moment of silence, as Romero stared daggers at Zhang, who was still playing the affable, misjudged, and hurt host. The wheels had to be turning. These people had managed to get the Nashville authorities to close the case of Rodney Carr's murder as a suicide, so what kind of backstopping did they have in Indianapolis, farther away from Carr & Sons' home ground?

Would calling the cops blow this open, or just make it worse?

Finally, Romero seemed to come to a decision. "Let's go."

Two of the Talbot Consulting security guys started to move, apparently still operating on their earlier instructions to keep Romero from leaving easily, but a sudden, sharp motion from another one of them made them subside. I saw Brian bow up, just a little, on one of them, just enough of a confrontation to let the guy know that he'd seen it and knew what the game was.

We didn't call Brian "Scrappy" for nothing.

As soon as the doors shut behind Clint and Patrick, Linemann went to one of the security men and looked straight into the button camera. From the looks of a few of the other agents, they were okay with wearing the wires, but they were more than a little confused about this behavior, which told me that they hadn't been read in on the whole plan. Good for them.

"They're coming out. Fix this." Linemann turned away.

"Guess that's our cue." I started pulling the SD cards from the monitors. There had been a chance that these wouldn't record, but this was a blackmail operation, and the shadow contractors were the ones charged with it, so it made some sense that they'd have the recordings right there in the vans, instead of taking the risk of having yet another receiver somewhere. It also gave us what we needed.

We were going to ram this right down Zhang's throat.

Phil was already out of the vehicle, bringing the keys with him. Number Two was starting to stir, finally coming out of the near-coma I'd put him into, though I was sure he was still concussed. I'd hit him pretty hard.

Again, I had zero sympathy. If it were a just world, I could have shot him and left him to rot.

I got out of the back before he came all the way back to consciousness, hauling the side door shut as Phil locked the doors. I'd brought my Scorpion with me, but it went under a jacket, the pistol brace folded. Tucking my hands into the jacket's pockets to make sure it stayed closed, one fist wrapped around the SD cards, I followed Phil away from the two vans.

We had our separate rental cars several blocks away, and neither of us looked at the other as we headed for them. We needed to get out of town with a quickness, and then "Walter Callahan" and "James Kelly" would cease to exist, for good. We were as burned as we could get.

We hadn't gotten as deep as we'd hoped, but we had biometrics and phones for several of the shadow network's hitters. It was a start.

It was far from the end, though.

CHAPTER
34

"Well, well, well." Goblin lifted his spitter to his lips as he watched the videos. "This little infiltration might not have gotten us the head of the guy running Dark Web Hitmen R Us, but it just gave us one hell of a weapon."

I scratched my beard. I'd just trimmed it, in case the cameras had caught us leaving the vans, though it was of some interest to me that there hadn't been any police reports about four dudes tied up and concussed in a pair of vans outfitted with surveillance equipment and stinking of CS. Either Number One or one of the others had managed to come to, free themselves, and get out, Talbot Consulting had cleaned up quickly, or the bad guys really did have someone in the local police force, well positioned to sweep these sorts of things under the rug.

"How exactly are we going to handle this, though?" It wouldn't be the first time we'd leaked information to push a reaction or gain an advantage, but this was a little different. "The case could be made that this was all a setup—on our part—and that this video footage isn't showing what we say it is."

Goblin turned to look at me, his eye crinkling with a faint smile. "It's all in the presentation, Chris. We won't leak it ourselves, not exactly. I happen to know a good investigative journalist who can massage the right parts of it, work the context in, and make it sensational as all fuck." His grin got wider and more wolfish. "Sure, there will be skeptics—and fans of Zhang's—who will do everything they can to tear it apart, and they'll probably be able to. The fact that Romero *didn't* allow things to go very far works against us, but the simple fact that it was being recorded clandestinely, by the security personnel—and those instructions Linemann gave are fucking *dynamite*—all points toward exactly what we say— what we *know*—it is."

"So, we're relying more on perception than what's actually in the videos?" I wasn't all that happy with the idea.

"Of course, but that's exactly what they were going to do to Romero." Goblin grabbed my shoulder and squeezed. "Trust me on this, Chris. I had to learn a lot of this information and messaging stuff. To a lot of people, perception *is* reality, and the fact of the matter is, we've got reality on our side as much as perception. Even if they manage to obfuscate things in the aftermath, even get it taken down—though the internet is forever, and too few people understand that—for the majority of the population, the initial story is the one that sticks. That's why so many government officials and media weirdos just throw out whatever they *want* the story to be, then quietly issue the retraction six months later. By then, only a handful of people are still paying attention. The rest, who largely let others spoon-feed their worldview to them, have taken the first premise, accepted it, and moved on, with that lie now part of their knowledge of how the world works. We're just going to take advantage of that fact."

His eyes flashed as he turned back to the screen. "And while it might appear on the surface that Zhang's got enough money and connections to wriggle out of anything, part of his usefulness comes from his public image. He'll have a lot of the usual suspects covering for him, of course, but this is going to hurt him. Bad." He spat into the plastic bottle again. "Now, the only thing to see is what he'll do. The tree has been shook, and shook hard. Now we've got to wait and look for whatever rotten fruit falls out of it."

***

While Goblin hadn't said who his investigative journalist friend was, I wondered if maybe it wasn't Ella Brolin, the danger-haired independent journalist we'd rescued in Atlanta. She didn't really like us much, despite the fact that we'd saved her bacon a couple of times. We went against a lot of what she believed in. She didn't like the very idea of our existence, let alone the somewhat outlaw way we operated.

She had integrity, though, and she'd report the truth if we gave it to her. It wouldn't stop her from digging in deep, to try to prove that we were wrong, but that could be an advantage in and of itself.

It wasn't her, though. At least on the surface, Lauren Pearl was the diametric opposite of Ella Brolin. When she showed up on the screen—she had her own social media video channels, on just about every platform there was, and apparently had pretty large followings—she could have been a supermodel. Hair and makeup were perfect. In fact, her face was so flawless that I seriously suspected she was using a filter.

She stared out of the screen with a practiced expression of seriousness and outrage. "Welcome to tonight's Digging Deep with Lauren Pearl." She peered into the camera for a long moment and sighed ever so slightly. "You all know that I've covered a lot of the corruption and the misuse of money and power in the highest circles of this country for a while now, ever since I started to really see what was going on. Most of what I've shown you, though, has been based on interviews, data from forensic accountants, and that sort of thing." She stared hard into the camera. "Tonight, however, I have something more. I have video of an international financial titan trying to blackmail an American business owner. On the surface, it might not appear to be much, but there's a lot going on in the background. I'm going to show you all the footage,

287

and then I'm going to point out what's going on. Tonight, on Digging Deep with Lauren Pearl."

Of course the sponsorship segment came next. Segments, I should say. There was about five minutes of advertising before she got to the meat of the story. Not that I was surprised, but I was sacrificing time on the phone with my wife to watch this.

She went through the usual breathless outrage again before she actually showed the video. It was a compilation of several of the surveillance streams, edited together to show the highlights, usually from the best angle possible. She—or her team—had put a lot of work into this. The strange part, though, was that the parts where Linemann had issued instructions hadn't been included. I started to wonder just how much this woman was really on our side.

Pearl reappeared on the screen. "That's not all of the footage, but every individual recording, from at least six hidden cameras, will be up on the channel by midnight tonight. Then you can look over all of them and see just what is going on behind closed doors."

She steepled her manicured fingers in front of her as a window came up next to her head, displaying a still of Zhang from one of the surveillance videos. "This is Thomas Zhang, international financier. No one knows for sure how much he's worth, but estimates put it well into the billions. He was an honored guest at the White House just last month, and at Buckingham Palace two weeks before that. He has had private meetings with the president of Russia and the President of the People's Republic of China. He has business interests all over the world, and he has the ear of every major world leader.

"So, why is he involved in trying to get the CEO of a chemical company into a compromising situation, while recording it?" She leaned forward. "In case you think this isn't showing what it's showing, ask yourself this. *Why* would there be covert body cameras all over the room, if this was simply an ordinary business dinner? Even if you accept that maybe the women who showed up near the end were just exotic dancers, and not the sex workers that Mr. Romero accused them of being, can you really tell me that it's a coincidence that they were there, after Thomas Zhang was on the phone, while the entire thing was being recorded?"

Her eyes narrowed, and I realized just why she'd left out the parts with Linemann. She knew her audience. "The worst is yet to come, friends. I'll show you the part that wasn't included in that compilation, after this quick word from our sponsor."

She knew how to work the algorithms, too.

Unfortunately, this was a live stream, so we couldn't skip her pre-recorded segments, flogging gold IRAs and VPNs. Neither of which I was necessarily against, but neither of which I wanted to hear about right then.

When the ads were finished, she looked even more serious. "What I'm going to show you next, though, is the smoking gun. No, it isn't Thomas Zhang himself in the following segments, but it is someone he has worked closely with, and you'll see in the second clip that he is right there, apparently approving of everything that is said."

"*Mr. Zhang's supposed to be here in the next fifteen minutes or so, and we're expecting the other guests about twenty minutes after that. Make sure that the doors are secured once they get here. We don't want them to rush out. If they want to leave, we need to slow them down as best we can.*" Linemann wasn't looking at the camera for that one, but she'd found just the right clip, with him right in front of the button cam. When it faded out, she was looking at the camera, her eyebrows raised.

"And that's not all." She pointed up toward the corner of the screen. "Watch this."

The next one was of Linemann looking directly into the camera, telling Number One and the other hitters to, "Fix this."

"Now, I wasn't able to find out exactly who Todd Linemann was talking to in that clip, but given the fact that it was someone on the other end of what was apparently supposed to be a blackmail video, I can only imagine. Sources have told me that there might have been a plan to *kidnap* Mr. Romero. I haven't been able to corroborate that with any other sources, but it sure doesn't look good, does it?"

She leaned forward on her desk, looking into the camera as if she was making eye contact with her audience. "It is long past time that these so-called elites are held accountable for their actions. Mr. Zhang has made all sorts of powerful friends with his money, but apparently that's not enough for him. This rich and powerful friend of the rich, powerful, and connected will stoop to blackmail, and possibly even kidnapping, just for another bit of market share!

"Is this the sort of person invited to the White House?" She flashed several photos of Zhang with the President, the Vice President, and quite a few important members of Congress. "Have we fallen so far as a country, as a society, that gangsters like this are free to come and go and take what they want, all without scrutiny or punishment?"

She kept going, but I tuned it out. The framing was there. The evidence was damning. Not that any of us expected an investigation to be started. Not as connected as Zhang was. Still, there was hope that it might shake something loose, especially given the fact that Linemann and the older guy were now in the open.

***

"I don't believe it." KG stared at the news story on the screen.

I couldn't quite wrap my head around it, either. Not after what we'd seen since working for Strand. The FBI had opened an investigation into *Strand* after Strand's organization had presented them with evidence that Devon Archer had been involved in several attempts on Strand's life. They operated in accord with the interests of the powerful, not the equal application of the law.

At least, that was what we'd come to assume. Still needed to, despite what we were looking at.

Federal Investigation Opened Into Thomas Zhang

It looked like Zhang wasn't quite as connected as he thought he was. Either that, or he *was*, but whoever was backing him figured that he'd just raised his profile a little too high, and in the wrong way, so he was being thrown to the wolves.

In a world where a former President of the People's Republic of China could be marched off while the current President didn't even look at him, I doubted that a man like Thomas Zhang would be considered untouchable, at least at a high enough level.

"That's only part of it." Radford switched to another window, with a bunch of data on it that I couldn't make out. It looked like flight tracking, only more complicated. "He's already left the country. The investigation might be aimed at him, but it wasn't a surprise. He flew out way early this morning, only about an hour after Lauren's show."

"Where?" Goblin's voice was hard.

"Looks like Panama." Radford brought up some more flight schedules, then some property records and photos. "He's got a major operation down there, with the Open World Institute. That conveniently comes with a pretty considerable secure compound, just outside the Canal Zone, within an easy drive of the UN Development Program. He's got a lot of friends down there."

"Especially since the Chinese practically run Panama, now." KG rubbed his jaw. "Started when they took over the Canal Zone back in the early 2000s."

I looked at Goblin. "What's the play? We shook the tree, and the rotten fruit turned into a bird and flew away."

Goblin turned faintly amused eyes on me. "We've got guys down in Honduras wrecking house. What makes you think Zhang's out of our reach because he's in Panama?"

"Is Zhang the target? What about Talbot Consulting?" The last few months had made it abundantly clear to all of us that we weren't going to be able to just "cut the head off the snake" and be left alone. The fact that Zhang had fled told me, at least, that there were bigger puppet masters pulling strings, and Zhang was just another one of the pawns, as big as he seemed to be.

"We're in luck." Radford turned around in his chair and grinned. "Guess where Talbot Consulting is incorporated?"

"Fucking Panama. Just like Mossfon and all those other anonymous companies." I sighed. "Do we have a contract as a cover for action?"

"Don't worry about it." Goblin clapped me on the shoulder. "You get packing, and we'll have a contract by the time you're ready to fly south."

CHAPTER
35

"We're gonna get burned if we stay this close." Nick was getting decidedly nervous as they circled around the *Reclusorio de Menores*, the largest prison in San Pedro Sula and where they were supposed to be able to find Carlos Ramirez, the First Word of *Mara Salvatrucha* in the city. "Even if the guards aren't interested, they're probably going to tell the gangsters something. At least one of them is. All it takes is one dude on the take."

"I'm right there with you, brother, but it's a risk we've got to take." Doug was as cool as ever. "If Saul and Manny get in trouble in there, we can't afford to drive five miles to go get them."

Nick took a deep breath as he tried very hard to emulate Doug's calm. The two of them had been partners for quite a while now, ever since Matt Patric had been badly wounded during the fight for the Bowman Ranch in New Mexico. He *should* have picked up on some of the way the other man could just roll with the punches and never seem to worry, but he was starting to suspect that the attitude had less to do with Doug's Special Mission Unit background, and more to do with his personality. He was just wired that way.

They took another turn onto Calle Hacia Aldea el Carmen, rolling toward the Mormon temple for the fourth time. The nearness of the Mormons, plus the Catholic church just up the road, lent an eerie sort of familiarity to the scene. It didn't seem to Nick, who'd spent most of his operational career in Africa, the Middle East, and Central Asia, as if a place with normal churches instead of mosques should be the kind of war zone that those countries had been.

It was an illusion, and he knew it. He'd seen savagery in this nominally Christian city that made the jihadi atrocities he'd witness pale in comparison. The jihadis were vicious because they thought God wanted them to be, to punish the infidels. The *mareros* hated God and took it to a whole new level.

He'd had nightmares about that destroyer house ever since the raid. Not every night, fortunately, but enough.

They rolled past the blue-roofed Mormon temple, Nick still scanning every nook and cranny around them for an ambush, an IED, anything. IEDs were supposed to be GWOT weapons, but the maras had used them, too.

The idea that makeshift bombs were something new in 2003 was ludicrous on its face, he knew. They were as old as explosives themselves. The "bomb thrower" went back at least to the anarchist movements of the 1800s, and roadside and car bombs were old hat by the time the mob, the IRA, and a dozen other Communist and Arab nationalist terrorist movements had used them. Even the VC had used artillery shell IEDs in Vietnam.

It was a symptom of the short memories that had become par for the course in the military. It was part of why Nick had gotten out. As soon as a conflict was seen to be "done," then everything was brain dumped, ostensibly to get ready for the next war, except that it never really seemed to work out that way.

He'd watched it happen in multiple organizations. He had his theories as to why it happened, mostly revolving around egos, but there was a reason he was with Pallas Group, and not getting ready to retire from Special Forces.

The radio crackled. "This is Salt. We're out. No sign of pursuit yet. Heading for the barn."

Doug blew out a long breath. Maybe he had been more worried than he'd let on. "Okay. One more turn around, then we head back."

Nick leaned back in his seat, though not without his hand straying to the rifle under a shirt at his side. Extract was always the most dangerous part of a mission, and if the *mareros* inside the prison hadn't bought the idea that Saul, six foot two, built like Schwarzenegger, and with long, black Conan the Barbarian hair, was a journalist, then they could expect trouble at any moment.

Still, if there hadn't been trouble inside the prison, maybe it had worked. That place was *their* turf, after all.

That didn't help him relax at all, as Doug drove around the outside of the prison again before turning away and heading back toward the plant and their team room.

***

"Well, I don't know how many journalists these guys have met, but they seemed to buy it." Saul ran a hand through his hair, letting it drop to his shoulders. "Maybe all the vetbros who've gone reporter worked to our advantage."

"They still figured that just two of us were easy prey, though." Manny wasn't a talkative sort of guy at the best of times, but he seemed to feel the need to temper everyone's expectations. "Most of the guys in the MS-13 block are hard core. They're also armed to the teeth. They saw our visit as a means to brag and increase their influence. Nothing more."

"Manny's right." Saul leaned back on the couch. "I don't want you guys to think I'm downplaying it. If anything, the way they talked to us and looked at us was out of sheer contempt. We walked into *their* house, and they let us go unmolested because they *could*, not because they were scared of us."

"Did you identify Ramirez?" Vern wasn't being impatient. He was taking in everything that the two of them said.

"We did. Actually sat down and talked to him." Saul shook his head. "Dude gives me the creeps. I've met a couple of former *mareros*, but this guy, as old as he is—I mean, he's probably only about thirty-five, but for a gangbanger, that's old—well, there's nothing *former* about this dude. He's a shark. Dead eyes." Saul, as normally unflappable as he was, actually shuddered. "I gotta tell you, fellas. If I'd had a hope in hell of getting out of there in one piece afterward, I'd have killed him right then and there. That guy's not human."

Before Vern could prompt him any further, he pulled out a piece of paper and started to sketch. Saul had been with the Ranger Recon Detachment back in the day, and a good reconnaissance man was always taking in as many details as possible and should be able to draw as well as he could take a photo. Nick wasn't sure how much that was still being taught these days, but Saul had always stuck with it. He was old school.

"There are three main sections to the prison. The Barrio 18 assholes are here, the MS-13 types here, and the rest of these buildings are the scrubs, the *paisas*. They're mostly unarmed, and from what we saw, they just try to stay out of the *maras'* way, but they could still end up being a factor, especially if somebody panics, or tries to curry favor with one of the *maras* by helping them out.

"Now, here's the main way in. Guard posts are here, here, and here…"

***

The debrief rapidly rolled into a planning session. There wouldn't be a whole lot of time for rehearsal, even if they could find a facility that would suffice to be enough like the prison, and was far enough away from prying eyes, particularly those that reported to the *maras*, never mind the Honduran police.

Furthermore, there just wasn't time. This was going to have to happen during their down time. The full-scale assaults on the plant had stopped, for the moment, but that wasn't keeping the bad guys from taking random potshots at the plant or the vehicles in the parking lot. The *maras* had taken a hit when Nick and the rest of the team had torn through them in Chamelecón, but they hadn't been put out of the game.

That meant that they still had to conduct their regular security duties, both site security and close protection, until they had a break from the D Team, and could go into action.

The planning session went well into the night, which was the D Team's shift at the moment. That had been deliberate on Vern's part. The B Team was his wrecking crew, to some of the D Team's chagrin, so they had been moved to day shifts so that they could work off the clock in hours of darkness. That had meant that the D Team had gotten to deal with most of the attempted break ins and sabotage operations.

It also meant that the longer they stayed up planning, the less sleep they were going to get.

Nick set his alarm with a groan, knowing that he'd have to be up in about four hours, and crashed, the walk-through, talk-through of the plan for the next night still on loop in his head as he closed his eyes.

CHAPTER
36

I couldn't quite believe the contract Goblin had gotten us in Panama. I wasn't alone, either.

"Unbelievable." Ken shook his head. "Don't get me wrong, I've done work with some shady people. But this is just weird."

"Not that weird." I hefted my duffel. It had a lot more than just the clothing and toiletries that it was supposed to, which was why it was heavy as hell. Fortunately, our client had certain privileges that had gotten the hardware through Panamanian Customs.

Sometimes you can make the corruption work for you, not against you.

The fact that Goblin had gotten us a high-risk security contract with the Corrine Foundation, one of the newest and biggest up-and-coming humanitarian NGOs working on the human trafficking problem in the Darien Gap, pointed to just how ruthless and talented the man was. I didn't think I could have kept a straight face, selling Pallas Group Solutions to that bunch of professional bleeding hearts, but he'd done it.

The Corrine Foundation had been named after a young woman who had died of exposure trying to get from Venezuela to the United States. At least, that was the story. I didn't exactly buy it, and nor did most of the rest of us. It was a little too pat, and the odds that any of these rich New Yorkers and

Beltway Bandits had ever actually found out about some nameless, human-trafficked woman who'd been killed in the Darien Gap when the cartel facilitating her travel—probably for sex slavery, if we were being honest—were pretty close to astronomical.

One thing we'd all seen over the years, being around both government agencies and NGOs, was that while the government might be corrupt, it had nothing on the NGOs.

Still, while they were probably skimming donations like crazy, and unlikely to do much of anything to help the people they pledged to be down there to help, they were putting us where we needed to go, so we weren't going to look a gift horse in the mouth.

"You don't think it's weird that a bunch of professional humanitarians have hired a bunch of former SOF killers, *and* brought all their hardware into the country, complete with greasing the appropriate Panamanian palms, no questions asked?"

I had to laugh as the elevator doors opened, and we stepped out onto our floor in the Hotel El Panamá. "No, I don't. Show me one rich gun-grabber who *doesn't* have half a dozen security guards with Glocks, minimum, around them at all times. With *very* few exceptions, these people's 'high moral fiber' is all an act, and always has been." I looked up and down the hall, but it was mostly empty, which was unsurprising, given the hour. "Of *course* they want all the firepower to defend themselves. They might not want to *see* it, but they still want it to be there. Especially since the US Army isn't down here anymore." I found my hotel room and paused. My phone, which had an international plan, fortunately, had just buzzed in my pocket.

The message was from KG. *Team meeting, with gear, in my room. 2100.*

Ken had gotten the same message. "Looks like we're hitting the ground running."

"Wouldn't expect anything else." I unlocked my door. "We're not down here just to make money."

Ken grinned as he started toward his own room. "Speak for yourself, brother. I'm always here to make money."

I shook my head as I stepped into my room and let the door shut behind me. I had a little bit of time to get settled—though given the situation, I was going to stick to my Recon roots and keep packed and ready to move the entire time I was in Panama—and call Julie.

I hadn't had a lot of time to talk to my wife and my two sons since we'd started work with Carr & Sons. The undercover operation on the side had made that even worse. She understood, but it was still rough. Especially since there was even more that I couldn't talk about this time, as compared to when we'd been guarding Strand and working down in Juarez, on the hunt for the Mendez faction of the Sinaloa Cartel. This was simply too dicey.

I couldn't exactly tell my wife, even over encrypted comms, that I had been infiltrating a covert, dark web network of hitmen, some of whom I knew from the military and contracting. It wasn't so much that I couldn't trust her, or that I was afraid that she'd think less of me for it. It was just that I couldn't trust the encryption *that* far.

The truth was, we were still sort of feeling this out. I'd worked contract for the US government for years, spending far more time overseas on those jobs than I ever had in the Marine Corps. When I'd finally quit, we'd had a chance to be a closer family again, and Julie had been glad of it.

When I'd gone to work for Pallas Group Solutions, ostensibly for financial reasons—I was going broke working for $18 an hour—it was going back to a work model that we'd thought we'd put behind us. Sure, I had more free time when I was home, but I was gone a lot again, and there was considerable risk involved. That had become obvious as soon as those MS-13 thugs had opened the door in that hotel room in

Atlanta, heralding the fact that we weren't just on some boring, time-burning close protection gig anymore.

I checked the time once again and dialed my wife. Time to check in and be a family man, even from three thousand miles away.

***

"Okay, gents, here's the game plan." KG had his laptop set up, but he wasn't using it for this brief. "We've got a pretty easy contract here. The Corrine Foundation people are worried about the crime level—and they've got good reason to be—but most of them are staying right here in Panama City and the Canal Zone, so we don't actually have that much to do. That's by design. If things were different, they probably wouldn't even have bit on the contract, but there was a fact finding mission down in the Darien only a few weeks ago, that almost went sideways on them. One of their people went off by herself and got assaulted. Like everyone in the Corrine Foundation, she was connected, so there was a mass freakout, and so we're here. The timing couldn't have been better.

"The requirements were for a max of four guys, since they really are pretty much staying in their offices across from the UNDP. However, because they're all freaked out, Goblin was able to talk them into the whole team, saying we came as a package. We've also got some reinforcements, new hires that Goblin just brought on. Since they're still relatively wet behind the ears, and not entirely read in yet, they're going to be covering the actual contract, while we do what we came here to do."

"I'm still a *little* hazy on that, to be honest, KG." Tom had his arms folded. "It *sounded* like we were coming down here to do a little extrajudicial dirt-planting. But that would be crossing one hell of a line, wouldn't it?"

"Line we should have crossed years ago," Brian snorted.

Tom turned a long suffering eye on him. "Sure. Just get us on *everyone*'s hit list, why don't we?" He shook his head. "We can't do that."

"Of course we can." Brian folded his arms as he leaned against the wall. "The people we've been up against haven't exactly been nonviolent. Why is it okay to kill the hitters they've sent after us, but not kill the people sending the hitters?"

"It's not about..." Tom started to get exasperated, while the rest of us just watched. There was a reason those two were always partnered up, and their callsigns were "Scooby" and "Scrappy."

"We *can*." KG interrupted before the entertainment could really get going. We must be on the clock. "Whether or not it's *advisable* is another question. We've pulled off what we have so far because we've been under the radar, and we've covered our tracks. If we get too overt, it all comes crashing down on our heads, and those of us who survive get put *under* Leavenworth. You want that?"

Brian subsided. "No."

"Good. Can we quit the grabass and get down to what we're here for?" KG had to be stressed. He was usually a lot more easygoing than this.

"We're listening, KG." I decided to try to defuse things a little. "What's the plan?"

"Zhang's compound is almost due north of here. We want to get eyes on it, but the immediate target isn't Zhang. It's Talbot Consulting." He pulled out a map. "Finding their main offices was a bear, but Radford pulled it off. I didn't think they'd actually have an office here but apparently they do, not far from the Fondaro & Company headquarters. Fondaro & Company apparently helped them get incorporated. They've got a record for doing that sort of thing. We don't know for sure if they're just the regular, run of the mill tax evasion scheme, or if they're in bed with the Chinese, too. Could be both.

"Now, we could go Scrappy's way, and go full kinetic on them, burn their office down, shoot anyone in there. You know, scorched earth." The sarcasm was so thick you could cut it with a knife. I frowned, studying KG. He was strung out, that was clear. More strung out than I'd ever seen him. "However, that wouldn't do what we want, since they almost certainly have everything scattered across multiple operations, and we *know* they have a presence in the States. We can't bank on their Panama office being it.

"So, here's the plan. We set surveillance on the office, find the right time, break in, scrape their hard drives—I mean scoop up *everything*—and then get out." He took a deep breath, then let a faint grin lift the corner of his mouth. "We're going to do a repeat of the Panama Papers, only weaponized."

Clint was nodding, even before it clicked for me. "We're going to get a good look at their portfolio, and then burn *that* down."

"Got it in one, Kermit. That's the plan." He ran a hand over his jaw. "We might still need to find a way to neutralize Zhang, but it's possible that the investigation was enough. As near as we've been able to tell, he's holed up in his compound and hasn't budged from there since he got down here. He's been hugely useful to his friends, but we all know that once that usefulness wears off, these people find that they don't really have any friends anymore. We'll keep an eye on that situation.

"In the meantime, here's how we're going to approach getting into the Talbot Consulting offices…"

CHAPTER
37

Finding the Fondaro & Company offices wasn't the hard part. This was Panama. They had nothing to fear here—aside from maybe some of the organized criminal groups they did business with deciding they wanted a bigger cut—certainly not from the US, even though they weren't all that far from the US Embassy. That was part of why outfits like them incorporated in Panama in the first place.

Getting in, that was the hard part.

The office was on the sixth floor of a business center in the financial district. There was a *lot* of security around there, a lot of cameras, and a lot of eyes. It was obvious in the first five minutes that a break in was going to be difficult, if not impossible.

Ken and I sat in the La Vespa Ristorante and Cocktail Bar, downstairs from the office, and tried to brainstorm what needed to happen. "We're not going to be able to brute force this." We hadn't even been able to get upstairs without a keycard, and there were cameras on every corner and every stairwell. "This is going to require some social engineering. Either that, or Radford needs to do some of his cyber magic."

"I don't know if he can do that much." Ken sipped his drink. "There's a *lot* here, and the financial district is going to be a lot tighter on cybersecurity than, say, some of the places the B Team penetrated up in California." He shook his head.

"This is a whole different beast from getting into a triad front company. These bastards know what they're doing."

"That's the problem, yeah." I shook my head, looking down at the table. In actuality, I was scanning my peripheral vision, but people tend not to think that you're watching them when you appear to be absorbed with what's right in front of your face. Unfortunately, I couldn't see anything that might help. The clientele were mostly wealthy, mostly completely absorbed with their own affairs. No threats were apparent, and neither were any clues as to how to proceed. "Terrorists, narcos...those are easy threats to identify and counter, relatively speaking. These bastards have perfected that Chinese 'non-martial warfare.' They sit in plain sight, slowly strangling you while appearing entirely innocent and aboveboard."

"Oh, it's not always that slow." Ken leaned back in his chair. "Look at what they've been doing so far. It's just a networked version of old Pablo Escobar. '*Plata o plomo.*' They could take his silver, or his lead. They offer their targets a partnership. When they get turned down, then it gets violent. Same old, same old, just harder to put the pieces together unless you're willing to do some skullduggery of your own." He grinned behind that salt-and-pepper beard. "Which we are."

I didn't reply, turning my attention back to the only spot I could see that led inside and upstairs. How the hell were we going to get in there?

Plans and ideas flitted through my head, as quickly discarded as they came up. We simply didn't have the infrastructure in country to do this quickly. We'd have to get more hardware in, some of it of questionable legality, and map out every inch of the electronic landscape around the financial district. We'd have to get into every wi-fi network, figure out where every camera was, and work out the right way to disable the right ones in such a way that it didn't raise any red flags. We'd have to spend enough time in that part of town to build a pattern of life, both for us and for all the other people working in the area. That way, we could plan for the time when there were the least number of people in the vicinity of the office to make our move.

This could take weeks. And during that time, any number of things could happen to throw a wrench in the gears. That's the problem with actually being patient and developing operations the right way. Sometimes the conditions change abruptly, rendering all your preparations moot.

And that happened in the next hour.

***

"Well, *something* has to have happened to get us yanked without a relief." I admit I was a little frustrated. Generally speaking, KG had been pretty good about pushing the word out to the individual contractors. That seemed to be Pallas Group Solutions SOP as a whole. This time, though, we'd just gotten a message to drop everything and get back to the Hotel El. No other information, just instructions to get back ASAP.

"More than one thing, actually." KG looked a little more harried than usual, like he was trying to keep up with about half a dozen different tasks at a time. Ordinarily, he was pretty good at that, but it seemed to be wearing on him. "Radford called in some favors, so now we don't really need Talbot Consulting's records anymore."

I raised an eyebrow, looking around the room and seeing much the same expression mirrored among the other teammates. "Can we be sure that whoever gave this favor is trustworthy?"

"So far, yes." The shadow of a wry smile crossed his face. "Come on, Chris, you've got to know by now that Noah doesn't take *anything* in the information sphere at face value. He's been digging hard ever since he got the package. Most of it has checked out."

"Most of it?" Custus sounded a little skeptical.

KG sighed. "This is a tangled web, gents. Smoke and mirrors, front companies, entities that exist as a handful of alphanumerics incorporated on some Caribbean island somewhere. Tracing all of it is going to take time."

"So, if it's going to take time, why were we yanked?" I was still putting pieces together. Sure, the new intel might be useful, but that didn't usually mean we abandoned a surveillance mission.

"Because we've got something more pressing at the moment." He pivoted the laptop on the desk around so we could see the screen. "Clint and Patrick have been surveilling Zhang's compound. Take a look at who just showed up."

Ken let out a low whistle. Todd Linemann was easily identifiable, as was the older guy whom we'd never gotten an ID on. The four men around them were obviously security, though something about them looked a little off. I couldn't tell from the photos, but something told me they weren't Americans.

The group behind them was even more off.

Four more security contractors walked about ten yards behind Linemann and his boss, surrounding a fifth man in a diamond formation. That was pretty standard operating procedure for a protective detail, but the man was carrying himself differently, his head down and his arms held close to his body. There was every reason, from his body language, to think that he was a hostage.

"That guy in the second group, behind Linemann, appears to be Simon Rutledge, Rodney Carr's other nephew. He's apparently wanted nothing to do with the business, but he's maintained a familial bond with the Carrs, particularly Jacob.

"Jacob hadn't heard from him in a while, though that wasn't entirely unknown, but he apparently tried to call him recently, and it went straight to voicemail. It's done that for two days now, and here he is in Panama, being escorted into Zhang's compound in the company of the Talbot Consulting people."

"Hostage taking is one hell of a line in the sand to cross." Tom rubbed a thumb along his jaw. "Unless they just got to him, and he's cooperating willingly? That's been known to happen."

"That's what we need to find out. Unfortunately, we can't trust the Panamanian authorities to even look into it, for two reasons. One, they're going to want to know how we know that Rutledge is in there, and we can't very well explain that we had two dudes in the weeds spying on a transnational billionaire's compound. Furthermore, with the Chinese influence here in Panama City growing by the day, we can't be sure that the Panamanian authorities might intervene to *protect* Zhang and Talbot, assuming that they're Chinese assets. So, we're on our own."

"What's the plan, then?" Marcos was eyeing the photos of the compound. It looked formidable enough, with a low wall surrounding about half a dozen beige-plastered buildings with red tile roofs. There might have been barbed wire along the top of the wall. Not insurmountable, but if Zhang's security had sensors or cameras watching it, getting over might be damned difficult.

And that was assuming an assault, not an infiltration to try to determine whether or not an assault was needed or warranted.

"We've got some surveillance equipment and a couple of small drones that—provided we're careful—we can use to get audio and video inside the compound. It's going to mean some jungle work, but if Rutledge really *is* a hostage, we need to know sooner rather than later."

Fortunately, we'd come prepared for that eventuality. I suspected that the Corrine Foundation people would have a collective stroke if they had any idea of the gear that they'd helped us get past Panamanian Customs.

I glanced at Ken, and he shrugged. "Ken and I will handle that part, KG."

KG nodded. "I suggest you get your stuff together, then. We'll drive you out to the jungle, and you can jock up in the van." He grinned. "I doubt that any of our fellow guests will be all that thrilled if you walk out of here in camouflage, paint, and full battle rattle."

"Probably not." I turned toward the door. "I'll be downstairs in five."

CHAPTER
38

The jungle was thicker than it had been around Mazatlán. After a career that had mostly taken me to the desert, I was spending an awful lot of time in the jungle lately, and I couldn't say that I liked it. The desert is miserable, but nothing like the jungle.

The desert's not trying to eat you while your skin rots off. And that was just what it felt like an hour after insert.

The van had dropped us outside the Altaplaza Mall, at the entrance to the trail that led to the Capilla La Palangana ruins. With our gear stowed in large, commercial hiking packs, which were almost certainly a lot heavier than most of those that were usually seen on the trail, we headed up the hill.

It took some careful timing to find a spot where we could get into the weeds without being watched. The plan to jock up in the van had been discarded once we'd really looked at the terrain and where we were going to have to get off. If this had been a regular warzone, it would have been relatively easy, but it wasn't. We needed to blend in, if only to make sure that Zhang and his cronies didn't get advance warning we were coming. There might be people in camouflage on the trail, but we didn't have any way to know for sure, so we'd opted to go with regular civilian outdoor gear, our camouflage utilities, chest rigs, weapons, and all the other gear we'd need stuffed into the bulging rucks.

As it turned out, there hadn't been anyone else on the trail, at least not at that time of day. We got past the housing development and over the Corredor Norte, then immediately turned off the trail and into the jungle.

Pushing a hundred yards in took almost half an hour. We were already dripping and tired by the time we halted, pulling our broken down Recce 16s out of our rucks, putting them back together and loading up before I held security so Ken could get changed.

Getting geared up didn't take long, even though we were effectively changing clothes in the middle of the jungle. Our civilian hiking trousers were green or brown, so we just changed shirts, painted up, put on our chest rigs, and then rucked up again before moving out. The time we'd spent changing had given us the chance to make sure no one was following us, and despite the sound of traffic not that far away, and the various noises of the jungle, I was pretty sure we were alone in the woods.

Then we stepped it out.

We had less than a mile to cover to get to our drone launch point. However, as anyone who has ever done any work in the jungle can tell you, three quarters of a mile in that terrain can get rough. Not only is the vegetation constantly resisting you every step of the way, but navigation is a bear. Without being able to see far enough to properly terrain associate, you have to rely on dead reckoning. We had GPS as a backup, though both of us were leery of using it where the light might show. The shadows under the canopy were dark enough that I expected the light of the screen to travel a decent distance, especially as the clouds rolled in and the sunlight that did make it through the trees got even dimmer.

There was also the fact that neither of us entirely trusted it, especially after some of the reports in recent years of Chinese and Russian GPS jamming. There wasn't any particular reason either power would have to deploy that jamming here, but it was still a good reason to rely on the old tried and true.

I'm honestly not sure we were any slower, running on azimuths and pace counts, than we would have been with a GPS in front of our faces. We just had to pause fairly often to make sure we were still on azimuth.

Once we finally got to our designated spot, the sun was almost down, and it was getting awfully dark. We both already had our PS-31s down in front of our faces, though the images were already getting grainy. Even the fancy NVGs need ambient light to work.

The drones were small, so they didn't have a lot of range, but they were unobtrusive and dead quiet, which was useful. They'd apparently started as cheap civilian knockoffs of the military's Black Hornet drones, but somebody Goblin knew had ripped out most of the innards and redone everything. They had better range—still not great, but better than the out-of-the-box fifteen minutes' flight time—better cameras, and they were also linked together into a drone swarm that gave us a capability that I wouldn't have imagined a few years ago.

We launched them, the tiny helicopters whirring aloft through the canopy, automatically adjusting their dispersion according to the program. I sweated the next part a little bit, because they only had the forward facing cameras, and detecting branches and other obstacles that might take one out was probably going to be a little sketchy. We did lose two to branches, their separate windows either showing the one tumbling out of control, its rotor broken, or the other just going dark.

The rest glided just above the canopy toward Zhang's compound.

I had control, while Ken held security. Right at the moment, from what we'd seen on the movement, I was a bit more worried about snakes, centipedes, and the like than I was about enemy gunmen, but good tactical habits are good tactical habits. I couldn't exactly keep an eye on things, anyway, since

I was underneath a light blocking cover, watching the screen and with headphones on so that I could hear what the tiny microphones were picking up.

I'm no code geek, so I couldn't imagine what kind of programming legerdemain had been needed to pull this off, but the swarm was feeding all its data to a program that created a 3D model of the observed area. It would also record all sounds within that area and locate them in the 3D model. It was a hell of a useful tool for this sort of reconnaissance.

The compound resolved itself on the screen, and the faint hum of the rotors and the noises of the jungle began to be overtaken by the sounds of life inside the walls.

There were still limits to the drones' capabilities, and while they were able to create a pretty good model of the compound's buildings, and even the trees, vehicles, and a few personnel walking around inside, it was still fuzzy, and the audio was indistinct. I'd have to do this one building at a time.

The first was a shed or some other form of storage. Maybe a garage. It was dark and quiet. Nothing to see or hear. With limited battery life remaining, I quickly moved on to the next, a smaller outbuilding next to the main house.

I was sweating under the cover, since there was zero ventilation, but I was also sweating the drones' range. At this rate, I was going to have to recall them in the next few minutes so we could swap batteries out. Which was going to take almost as much time as the actual flight.

There was movement in that building, and I closed the swarm in a little. I had to be careful. They were quiet, but they weren't *silent*. Get too close, or knock a drone into something, and we'd be made.

Voices. They were indistinct at first, but the program started to clean up the audio a little. I dipped the drones closer, and got a look in the window.

The group of security contractors who'd brought up the rear in the photos were gathered around Rutledge, while

Linemann, the older guy, and Zhang watched. The young man was on his knees on the floor, facing a camera.

"…and if you do not reply within seventy-two hours, maybe we send you a little gift?" The voice was accented. Not a Spanish accent, either. Russian? That would explain the feeling I'd gotten that these guys weren't Americans, though they were Caucasians in the Western Hemisphere. If this was the kind of operation that I thought it was—and given recent history I had no reason to think otherwise—then the Chinese and their organized crime pals were going the extra mile for deniability, even though they were at least partly burned already.

The spokesman took hold of Rutledge's hand, wrenching it around when the young man resisted. Pulling a knife out of his pocket, he flicked it open and held the blade against Rutledge's little finger. That got the younger man to stop moving, real quick.

"We start with a finger. Then we get bigger, until you are ready to listen, no?"

I'd seen enough, and the drones were about out of juice. I recalled them as I started to prep the data package to send it back to KG.

We were going to have to move fast.

CHAPTER
39

Linkup went just after midnight. Ken and I had switched out, swapping batteries on the drones repeatedly as we maintained what watch we could over the objective.

We'd run out of batteries about half an hour before. The drones didn't take big batteries, so we'd been able to bring a lot of them, but they still burned through them fast. Fortunately, as of the last flyover, everything was still quiet, and it didn't look like they'd done anything more to Rutledge.

Hopefully it stayed that way.

The rest of the team filtered into our little position after KG and I exchanged IR flashes. The others took up security in a rough but tight perimeter, while KG joined Ken and me in the middle.

"Anything new?" His voice was pitched low, not quite a whisper, more of a murmur.

"Not so far. Most of them seem to have gone to sleep. They're not worried." There wasn't much reason why they should be. Presuming that the message had been for Carr & Sons, they'd sent it from a different country, and presumably over a VPN. If it wasn't for the fact that we'd already followed Zhang down to Panama, we'd never know where to look.

KG shook his head. He and the others had helmets on, while Ken and I were still running the skullcap mounts we'd brought in our rucks. "Seems like hostage taking is the new hotness for this kind of bullshit." We'd run into the same trick when we'd been contracted to defend the Bowman Ranch. The cartel *sicarios* who'd besieged the place had taken Ariana Bowman hostage when she'd slipped away to go see her boyfriend, and we'd had to go into a cartel stash house to get her. Now here we were again, lining up for yet another hostage rescue to remove the bad guys' leverage on our client.

In a just world, we wouldn't *have* to do this. We'd be able to speak to the proper authorities, and either the Panamanians, the US Marines, Delta, or even the SEALs would take care of it. But it wasn't a just world, we couldn't expect not to get hammered for just knowing what was going on, and we also couldn't trust that the people we contacted weren't in an alliance with the bad guys.

So, I accepted my helmet from KG—I'd already broken down the whole drone and comm setup, and had it packed in my ruck again—and got ready to move.

Ken took point, with KG and I right behind him. We had only about four hundred yards to go, most of it downhill, but that was still going to take about an hour.

We had to hope that they'd been serious about that seventy-two-hour timeline.

***

The wall was about eight feet tall, and it did have barbed wire along the top, angled outward. Nothing that Ken or I had managed to spot with the drones suggested that they had pressure sensors anywhere along it, and even the wire didn't seem to be hooked up to anything in particular. That made this a *little* bit easier.

Ken still had to stand on my legs while I braced my back against the wall so that he could reach up and cut the barbed wire. He was one of the smallest of us, but it's still not that easy to hold a man up when you're doing the electric chair against a plastered concrete wall.

Fortunately, it took him only seconds, then he dropped back down again. "Got a bit of a look over. Got two guards out at the gate, but everything else is quiet as the grave. Not even any lights on except at the gate and the front of the main house.

That was interesting. Apparently, our opposition didn't feel like partying that night.

"Okay. Hybrid, Bone, you're up first. Ziggy and Drizzle are gonna be their stepping stools." KG's whisper was harsh in the damp, humid night. "Let's get everyone over before anybody opens the ball."

Phil and Marcos set their backs to the wall, and Custus and Rob swarmed over, pausing right at the top to sweep the immediate area with their muzzles. Then they dropped lightly to the ground, and Tom and Brian took over as stepping stools.

It took only a couple of minutes to get the whole team over. We spread out inside the wall, staying low and in the shadows of the palm trees that grew around the outside of the manicured lawn which looked extremely odd, even through NVGs, after that movement through the jungle, past ancient ruins left over by Mesoamericans in ages past.

The closest building was that storage area that I'd scanned first with the drone swarm. We moved to it quickly but quietly, KG and I in the lead. I'd gotten the best look at the target, even though I'd sent the full recording, so I was jumping to the front of the stack.

Stateside, we'd gone unsuppressed, mainly for appearances' sake. Legally, it would be difficult for any of us to use company suppressors across state lines. It was doable, but Goblin was presenting a certain face to the public.

Here, though, we all had cans on the rifles. It made them a little longer, but they were stubby suppressors, off the books, machined in a company shop somewhere I wasn't going to ask about.

KG paused at the corner, and I moved up next to him, reaching out with my muzzle high to give his shoulder a squeeze. We both went around the building quickly but smoothly, scanning our surroundings over our sights as we went. Then we were moving toward the target house.

Muzzles tracked toward the window as we moved on the front door, while Custus and Rob moved into position behind some of the landscaping, covering the gate and the main house. We stacked up on the door, as I tested the doorknob.

It was locked. That was somewhat surprising, but if they figured Rutledge was secure enough if he was locked in the house, maybe that would make this easier.

I felt a pang as I reached for the entry tools in my chest rig. Drew had been better with locks than me. But Drew was gone.

It took a couple seconds to get the door open. I pulled it open and stepped out of KG's way as he flowed in with Jake, Tom, and Brian on his heels. Ken and I fell in behind them, while Clint and Patrick moved to cover the back.

The entryway was dark and empty, opening up on the living room to the right, where we'd seen Rutledge's hostage video being taken, a kitchen to the left, and what looked like a couple of bedrooms straight back.

KG, Jake, Tom, and Brian were in the living room. Ken and I swept past the kitchen, careful to pie it off with our muzzles as we went, and moved on the first bedroom.

We were still staying soft. No white lights, no unnecessary slamming of doors or banging around. If the bad guys had just locked Rutledge in the house and left, we might be able to get him out without being detected.

Unfortunately, they weren't quite *that* complacent.

"*Shto vy?*" The shape of a man loomed in the hallway, a flashlight in his hand.

I mentally filed the Russian question away in the back of my head as I lifted my rifle. I couldn't see much of him, as his light was whiting out my NVGs, but he started as he realized there were men in jungle camouflage, plate carriers, and helmets pointing guns at him.

He shouted as I lit him up with my weapon's light. I wasn't going to shoot at shadows, especially not with Rutledge in the house. Squinting against the glare, he turned and ducked around the corner. *Fuck.* I hadn't seen a weapon, so I hadn't shot him. I pushed ahead to the corner, pieing around it, my thumb on my light's tape switch. It was vital for target identification, but it could also give him something to shoot at.

Someone upstairs must have been looking out for me. I don't know why I didn't just pop the corner, but for some reason I "ran the rabbit," pushing across the short hallway to the far wall, flicking my light on as I moved. The Russian's shotgun blast missed me by a hair, blowing plaster off the wall behind me. I might have heard Ken grunt, but then my weapon light blinded the Russian even as my red dot settled on his upper chest, and I stroked the trigger.

I shot him five times, riding the reset until he went down. The suppressor was good, but the *clap*s of the shots were still painful in that hallway. He crumpled as my bullets ripped through his black t-shirt, and his shotgun slipped from nerveless fingers just before he hit the wall and slid down it to the floor, leaving a red smear on the plaster.

That tore it. There was no way the entire compound hadn't heard that shotgun blast. We were going to have everybody on us in a few moments.

Ken joined me. I glanced at him quickly, taking my eyes off the hallway to check. His sleeve was dark and wet. "You good?"

"Got trimmed, that's it. Let's push." He still had his eyes and his muzzle on the hallway. Behind us, I could hear Tom and Brian making entry into the bedroom alongside the kitchen. We moved on the next door.

There was a quick decision that needed to be made, there. The Russian was lying next to the far bedroom, and that door was open. However, the closer door was also open, we didn't know where Rutledge was, and so that was where we went first, hoping that he wasn't in that far room, getting his throat slit.

I didn't hear any screaming, so hopefully we were right.

I hooked through the door, Ken right at my elbow as I passed the threshold. There were still no lights on, and I'd twisted my PS-31's tubes up out of the way as I strobed my weapon light into likely target areas. Nothing. The room was fully furnished, but there was no one in there.

"Jackpot!" That call came over the radio from Tom. They had Rutledge. We flowed back out into the hallway and headed for the last room, anyway, even as gunfire erupted outside.

That clear took seconds. The Russian I'd killed must have been there on his own. The room was a wreck, but it was otherwise unoccupied. We flowed back out into the hallway.

More gunfire rattled from the front of the building. Even as I came around the corner, facing the entryway, Custus and Rob rushed in, their heads down and muzzles high. Tom and Brian were shooting from shattered windows in the living room and kitchen.

"Friendlies coming in!" Custus roared out the deconfliction almost at the same time he reached the threshold. Bullets chased them, smacking into the walls, one going right over Custus's shoulder to miss my ear by inches.

Ken and I got out of that hallway fast. I went sideways, into the living room, while he fell back into the back, to cover the rear door. Facing the front door like that was an extended fatal funnel, and a good way to get shot.

"We've got four from the gate and a bunch more coming from the main house." KG and Jake were in the kitchen. "That shotgun blast sure stirred up the hornet's nest."

Keeping low, I moved up next to Tom. Rutledge was flat on the floor next to him, his hands over his head, trying to stay out of the line of fire. I rose up behind my rifle just far enough that I could see out the window and shoot if I had a target.

The storm of cover fire that had torn through the night while Custus and Rob had run for the house had driven most of Zhang's security to ground. There was at least one body out there, sprawled on its face in the grass, but the rest had hunkered down behind buildings, trees, and bullet-pocked concrete planters.

"We can't stay here." Sooner or later, either they were going to move on us, or, worse, they were going to get the Panamanians involved. It might shake out that they'd been holding a hostage, working with Russian gangsters—or PMCs; I wasn't sure which, and at the moment I didn't care—but that wouldn't do us much good if we were already dead or in a Panamanian prison for arms smuggling and conducting an unsanctioned assault in their country.

"There's a garage between here and the main house." KG shifted his position to see more of the angle toward that main house. "If we can get to it and commandeer one of Zhang's vehicles, we can drive out of here."

There was going to be a little more to it than that, but we were all professionals. We shouldn't need it to be spelled out.

He keyed his radio. "Kermit, Leprechaun, we're going to need some cover fire."

"Stand by."

I looked around the room and started to move toward the door. Custus was already there, on his feet, just inside the threshold, aimed out through the opening. "With you." I reached up and squeezed his massive shoulder.

"I'm moving to that shed." Custus had already looked at the angles and figured out that Clint and Patrick weren't going to be able to cover the front of the main building, not while giving the rest of us a corridor to run to the garage. "On three. One, two, three."

We burst out the door, Custus firing a fast three shots at a shape that was moving through the landscaping toward our position. The man had been deftly slipping from planter to tree to planter again, but Custus caught him with at least one round as he dashed toward the shed. It was a wild trio of shots, but a moment later, I'd thrown myself onto a knee behind the palm tree that loomed above the little guest house where they'd been keeping Rutledge and put two more, better aimed, rounds into the man as he tried to get up.

Then, as Custus, Clint, and Patrick proceeded to mag-dump at the main house and anyone moving in the courtyard in front of it, Ken, Jake, and KG came out fast, Tom, Rob, and Brian trailing behind them with Rutledge in tow. Brian had the hostage bent almost double, his own rifle slung and his Glock in his hand, so that he could still engage if he needed to.

I joined them as they sprinted toward the garage. Two sports cars were parked outside, but neither one of them would fit all of us. We needed something bigger than the Ferraris.

Glass shattered, plaster was pulverized to dust, and bits of concrete and vegetation flew through the air as a couple hundred bullets smacked into every bit of cover available, driving Zhang's security back even farther behind cover. It wouldn't buy us that much time, because there were only so many rounds in a mag, but we only needed a little.

Custus and Tom had sped to the front. KG could sprint as hard as he needed to, but he was a powerlifter, not a runner. He was sucking wind by the time we reached the garage, Jake pivoting to donkey-kick the side door open.

He rolled out of the way as Ken and I moved on the door, slowing down just enough that we could go through ready to shoot. I hooked right, Ken went left, which didn't leave him much space, as he came up against the rollup door, but then all hell broke loose.

I had cleared my immediate area of responsibility, and turned back toward the four big, expensive SUVs that took up most of the garage, when the door from the main house opened and four of the Russian security guys poured in, all armed with what looked like Draco 9mms.

Moving along the wall, I momentarily lost sight of the Russians and the figures behind them behind the vehicles, but it took me seconds to reach the corner and start to move along it, even as Ken opened fire over the hood of one of the nearest SUVs, dropping one of them before any could return fire.

A storm of 9mm rounds shattered more window glass and punched holes in the rollup doors as a voice was raised, cursing in Russian. Ken hit the floor, and a detached, clinical part of my mind—about the only part that was working at that point—hoped and prayed that he hadn't gotten hit.

I was working my way around the backs of the vehicles, Jake on my heels, and was already pointed at the far corner as two of the Russians, in a half crouch, their Dracos held muzzle high, moved around behind the biggest vehicle. One of them spotted me immediately, and his eyes got wide, but I had slightly less distance to move my muzzle.

Jake had his own rifle leveled past my shoulder, and we both opened up at the same moment, dumping the two security guards with half a dozen rounds each.

We'd trained for controlled pairs or failure drills, but bitter experience had taught us all that sometimes you just had to keep shooting them until they stopped moving.

The one in front jerked, stiffened, and dropped onto his face. The second one fell backward, sitting down hard on the concrete, looking a little shocked as his shirt front turned red and he slumped over, spasming slightly as his life leaked out.

More gunfire thundered in the garage, and the screams redoubled. "Get in those first two vics!" The longer we stayed in place, the worse this was going to get.

I kept pushing forward, as Ken kept shooting from the front, Jake still right there with me. As long as there was a threat, we had to continue to attack. Especially in a garage, giving them a static target was a good way to get dead.

We stepped over the two Russians, kicking the 9mm Kalashnikovs out of the way. The late model Hummer was big enough that I couldn't see the door on the other side of it except through the shattered window glass. Someone on the other side was freaking out, dumping 9mm rounds through the opening, so Jake and I got low, almost duck walking around the rear bumper.

There must only be one shooter. The fire suddenly stopped as he ran out of ammunition, and I surged to my feet, my muzzle already pointed at the door as I moved toward it.

I pied off the opening, all too aware that I had no idea how many bad guys were in the house and that I could be sticking my head out into an opening that had multiple gun barrels pointed at it.

The guy with the Draco was still crouched in the hallway, hastily reloading, as I eased out around the doorjamb and covered him with my red dot. He looked up, the magazine just seated, and I shot him through the cheekbone. Blood and brain matter spattered across the wall behind him, and then the rollup door rattled up into the ceiling to my left.

Someone in the main house behind the guy I'd just shot freaked out. I heard more gunfire, but only a single shot went through the door, hitting the side of the Hummer behind me with a *bang*. Who knew what had gotten hit inside, but as long as we weren't getting shot to shit, I wasn't going to worry about it.

The first two SUVs were pulling out of the garage. "*Get in!*" Ken roared.

I took a deep breath, then plunged across the doorway, keeping my weapon pointed as I moved. Someone started to lean out into the fatal funnel, and I saw just enough of a weapon to prompt me to dump three rounds at him. I didn't know if I hit him or not, but I sure hit *something*, as there was a gush of flame and a yell.

Then I was sprinting for the two big Escalades out front, Jake right behind me. Ken was at the bumper, most of the bulk of the vehicle between him and the house, dumping a few more rounds at the doorway to dissuade anyone who might want to follow.

I threw myself in, almost crushing Rutledge in the process, then Jake and Ken were in and Custus was stomping on the gas, sending us careening toward the gate.

"Uh, Custus? The gate's still closed, buddy." KG was in the passenger seat, apparently ready to get out and open the gate, but Custus was accelerating.

"You worried about getting pulled over with a crumpled bumper?" Custus wasn't slowing down. "I think that's the least of our worries at the moment."

"Yeah, actually I am." KG was bracing himself for impact. That gate looked pretty solid. "We've got extract laid on, but if we can't get there because you wrecked us against the gate, that's not going to go over very well. With Goblin, or the rest of the team."

"Fine." Custus braked, hard, almost throwing me into the seat in front of me, bringing the big vehicle to a stop just in time for KG to jump out, get the gate open—there was a simple button in the bullet-riddled guard shack, and jump back in. I'd cracked the door open as soon as he'd gotten out, twisting around in my seat and clamping my rifle against the doorframe, just in case, but the bad guys all seemed to be absorbed with the fire that was currently engulfing part of the main house. Lambent flames flickered in the windows.

Then the gate was open, KG was slamming his door shut, and we were roaring out down the private road leading to the compound, leaving flames, bullet holes, and bodies behind us.

CHAPTER
40

At almost the same time that the A Team was hitting Zhang's compound, Nick, Doug, Saul, Vern, Carl, and Durand approached the west wall of the *Reclusorio de Menores* in one of the vans.

They'd looked at trying to infiltrate on foot, through the Mormon church grounds. It wasn't the best route they'd been able to think of, but it was the only one with a moderate amount of concealment and almost guaranteed to be abandoned at that time of night. The rest of the prison's surroundings were all residential areas, and all of the PGS contractors had experience with trying to maintain a low profile in a residential neighborhood, especially one in a high-crime city.

Outsiders get spotted quickly. Outsiders in combat gear, who intended to go into what amounted to a gang-run prison to kill a gangster warlord, were going to be spotted and reported to *somebody* who didn't need to know about their presence, as soon as they tried to slip through some local's backyard.

So, if they were going to move in on foot, they would have had to use the Mormons' property, and hope they forgave them if they ever found out. Fortunately, they had another plan in mind.

What I wouldn't give for a couple of Little Birds right now. It would be awfully high profile, swooping in on AH-6s and jumping off in the middle of the courtyard, guns blazing, but it wasn't like this was going to be subtle once things really kicked off. It felt like there would be a lot fewer things that could go wrong that way, though.

Breaching that gate would be rough. Not that it was impossible, but even if they'd had the explosives, they would have needed to deal with the Honduran prison guards before they could even get to the prisoners, and that didn't bode well. So far, they'd managed to stay out of the Honduran police's way. It prevented more than just adding one more enemy to a laundry list that was already there, but it also kept the client happy. Carr & Sons understood, to some extent, that they were involved in a war—even though the PGS contractors had mostly managed to keep the particularly savage parts of this war out of their sight—but that didn't mean they'd be happy with dead cops, even corrupt Honduran cops.

Fortunately, in this case, that corruption was going to work to their advantage. In a manner of speaking.

Saul and Manny hadn't gone straight in to talk to Ramirez when they'd gone into the prison. As "reporters," they'd wanted *all* the human interest, so they'd chatted with the guards first, before working their way deeper into the prison. While neither man was particularly gregarious at the best of times, they still knew how to engage people, and Saul was pretty sure he'd spotted a weak point in one of the guards. A man with a family, who was perpetually bitter that he was paid as little as he was, while these *mareros* were allowed to run roughshod. He'd lost a friend in the last prison riot, but he was stuck.

Saul had gotten his contact information, saying he wanted to tell his story, in addition to the story on the prison and the First Word. From there, they'd worked on the man, until he was willing to open the gate for them at the last minute for a follow-up interview.

Saul was on the phone at that moment, making contact. He spoke briefly, then hung up and nodded. "He's waiting."

Officer Hernandez wasn't aware that the full team of Pallas Group hitters was coming in. Fortunately, he wasn't expecting to meet Saul at the gate, but just to let the vehicle in and then meet him at the main office. That was a relatively fortified building just inside the gate. It was supposed to be a regular government center, but the signs of hardening against the inmates were pretty obvious, from the bars on the windows and doors to the barbed wire around it.

The van pulled up outside, and Hernandez, a short, slightly pudgy man in blue came out. Saul paused, then took his helmet off and unclipped his sling, leaving his shirt on over his plate carrier and chest rig, before getting out and shaking Hernandez's hand.

The side door slid open, and the rest of the shooters piled out, as Saul tightened his grip on Hernandez's hand. "Take it easy, *compa*. We're not here for you." He started to steer his new friend toward the door. "Keep calm, keep your head down, and you can keep yourself and all your *compas* alive and safe, and only the assholes who deserve it are going to get smoked tonight."

Nick and Doug were already moving toward the door. The second van had caught up quickly and had ridden the rear bumper of the lead vehicle into the compound, without Hernandez noticing right away. The rest of the team spilled out, spreading out and taking up security while Nick, Doug, Vern, and Manny prepared to make entry, in case Hernandez decided not to cooperate.

The Honduran cop, however, was considering his options, even as his hand was caught in Saul's big mitt, and he was steered toward the door. Everything was still quiet, and it looked like the guards were being as low-key as the prisoners were at the moment. It was late at night, though not yet so late that they really could expect that *everyone* was dead asleep.

That would change quickly.

Hernandez, however, seemed to have decided that his bitterness over how much control the prisoners were given overrode any objections he might have to being effectively taken hostage. "You're here for Ramirez?"

Saul might have held that back, but he apparently figured that the rapport was worth the OPSEC risk. "That's right. He's been giving the orders to have us killed, so we're going to return the favor."

Hernandez nodded, his decision made, and turned to reach for the door. "I'll tell them that you held me at gunpoint, and that I didn't know who you were." His voice got bitter and vicious. "Make that *culero* suffer."

Saul didn't comment, as Hernandez opened the door and ushered the team inside. Weapons were still leveled, corners and doorways quickly cleared, just in case. The entryway was empty and mostly dark, though, as it was well after hours, and the only ones there were the prison guards, and none of them were in the reception area because Hernandez had arranged to meet Saul there.

"Manny. Lights." Vern took charge, as Hernandez moved toward the reception desk with Mike keeping a close eye on him. Saul was busy putting his helmet on and retrieving his rifle.

Manny had noted the main breakers on their first visit, and quickly moved to shut off all the lights on the compound. In moments, everything was dark, the contractors watching their exits through grayscale NVGs. Hernandez, for his part, was almost blind, but he was going to play his part to the hilt, even though he hadn't been prompted. He reached for his radio, and when a suppressed rifle muzzle tilted up toward him, he held up his hands. "I'll tell them that there's a riot, and that we have to lock down. No one is going to try to interfere, not at the beginning. Too dangerous. We are outnumbered, and they have more guns. The Army will be here eventually, but it will take a little while."

Vern nodded. "Hoop, Whack, you guys stay with him. Make sure he doesn't get froggy, and cover our exit. The rest, with me." He paused just short of the door, looking back at the whole team. "Anyone with a weapon dies." That had already been established during the planning, but he felt it needed to be reinforced. They were eight men going into a prison packed with hundreds of armed gangsters with a streak of savagery that made some of the jihadi throat-cutters they'd fought in the Middle East, Africa, and Central Asia pale by comparison. Violence was going to be the only way they'd survive the next ten minutes, let alone the next hour.

Then he was going through the door, Doug on his heels, and the team flowed out into the courtyard.

There was no moon, so the shadows were even darker, and their PS-31s' images were relatively grainy. The wider, shorter building to the left housed most of the Barrio 18 gangsters, while the longer, narrower one to the right was mostly the *paisa* wing. The three H-shaped buildings across the far side of the courtyard were their targets.

All the lights on the compound were out, though the glow of streetlights and home security lighting still lit the low clouds overhead beyond the wall. It was enough to provide some illum for their NVGs, but hardly enough for the gangsters to be able to see, as Vern and Doug led the way along the *paisa* wing, keeping at least one muzzle and set of eyes on the Barrio 18 wing as they went.

Nick, right behind Doug, was mostly focused on that wing, though he still pied his way across any of the windows of the *paisa* wing as he passed. This was a hell of a dangerous situation, and while the *paisas*—many of whom were effectively political prisoners—weren't likely to side with either of the maras, they could still panic and make things much more complicated.

Furthermore, there was a non-zero chance that the Barrio 18 *mareros* would get involved as soon as things clacked off. They weren't there for Barrio 18, but that didn't mean they'd hesitate to put some more gangsters in the dirt.

They reached the end of the wing, and while Carl, Durand, Casey, and Manny took up exterior security, Saul, Doug, Nick, and Vern stacked up on the first door.

In an American prison, they'd expect the door to be locked. Here in a Honduran prison, effectively run by the inmates, it wasn't. It still squealed loudly as Vern pushed it open, Doug's muzzle dropping level over the team leader's shoulder to cover the opening.

A sleepy, irritated curse in Spanish floated down the hallway from one of the cells. Somebody'd heard them, but they weren't quite made yet.

Two by two, the contractors flowed into the hallway, little more than black shapes faintly lit by the glow of their NVGs, weapons up and fingers hovering near triggers.

Carl and Durand stayed at the door, holding the exit open. The rest continued in deeper. Casey, Saul, and Manny took up the cross-building hallway at the center of the H, while the others moved toward the end of the hall, where the First Word and his entourage had their cells.

They had pied off every cell as they'd passed it, knowing that at least one of the prisoners had heard the door creak open, and that they were deep in the belly of the beast. Every cell held more than one savage killer, and all of those killers were armed.

Even as Vern and Doug neared Ramirez's cell, one of those killers nearer to the door came fully awake. Maybe he could see just enough out the open door to spot either Carl or Durand silhouetted against the slightly less dark courtyard. Maybe he was just paranoid about the lights being out and the door open. He started yelling in Spanish, and a moment later, the whole wing was awake.

CHAPTER
41

Nick didn't need to be prompted. None of them did. They surged forward, taking full advantage of the darkness, and they were at Ramirez's cell in a handful of strides.

The four men in the cell were already up, on their feet, weapons in their hands, peering at the darkness in the hallway. Nick caught up with Doug, overtaking Vern for a second, as the two of them pied off the cell door, fingers already tightening on triggers.

There had never been a question of taking Ramirez prisoner, or even trying to coerce him into reversing the attack orders aimed at the Carr & Sons plant. That was unlikely to work, and getting him out of the prison wasn't just going to put them on the maras' target deck.

No, this was a targeted killing. Given the crimes he knew that Ramirez was guilty of, and what he'd already directed from that cell, Nick considered this a long-overdue execution.

One of the *mareros* had a flashlight, and he suddenly triggered it, the cone of bright white illumination stabbing out into the hallway just ahead of the Pallas Group contractors.

Nick blasted the man with the flashlight with a quick trio of shots, raking his muzzle back toward the figure who'd just been lit up enough to identify him as Ramirez. The flashlight went tumbling wildly, the circle of white light spinning crazily in the cell, shining right into the eyes of a heavily tattooed, bald man who positively rippled with muscle, a short submachinegun in his fist.

In that split second flash of light, Doug shot Ramirez and the big guy about four times each. Blood splashed against the dingy wall behind them, and Ramirez crumpled while the big man fell back against his cot, clutching a hand to a neck that had just started spurting crimson. There was a look on his face as he started to spasm that was nothing short of pure terror, as the violence he had visited on other people came back to him.

Nick took one more step out, even as gunfire erupted up and down the cell block, and shot the last man through the skull. That one had been crouched behind the cots, but he still had a gun in his hand, and was looking for a target in the faint backsplash of the flashlight on the floor. That made him a target, as much as it felt like shooting fish in a barrel.

More suppressed gunfire raked the cells from the central hall. Screams were punctuated by gunshots, and Nick realized that they had a gauntlet to run to get back to the door.

Carl or Durand was shooting in through the door, engaging several of the *mareros* in the cells closest to the exit. One of the shooters in the central corridor was mag-dumping into the cells along the hallway, while it sounded like another was doing the same down that central connecting hall.

There were two ways to do this. They could pie off each cell, engaging each and every gangster as they went. It would be bloody, but they'd expected to reap a lot more than just Ramirez in there that night.

The drawback would be that it would also be slow, and they couldn't guarantee that they wouldn't end up facing a few too many bad guys at a time.

The other option was just to run for it, spraying down the cells with gunfire as they passed, in the hopes that they got a few and at least drove the rest back for cover.

Doug and Vern opted for the second course of action.

They sprinted toward the exit, both men dumping rounds into cells as they went. If it had been anyone else— Nick included himself—then most of that gunfire would have been spray-and-pray, probably most shots wasted. As it was, Doug at least was dropping an armed man with every hammer pair. Vern might have been a little looser, but only a little.

Nick caught up with the two of them about at the central corridor.

Casey was lying prone on the floor while Manny raked the near cells with gunfire and Saul held security on the rest of the hallway. Even in the limited illum, Nick could see the bodies piled in the cell at the far end. Saul was saving his rounds, even as they heard the rattle of cell doors starting to open. The dogpile was about to begin.

From the size of the dark puddle underneath Casey, it was clear he was dead. They couldn't leave him there, though. Nick had never gotten along with him—none of them had, really—but he was one of theirs.

The gunfire had died down a little bit, but that was mainly because those who had a shot on them were already corpses, or else had been forced back by the imminent death invited by taking a shot in the dark.

That was not going to last.

Nick grabbed Casey's body, heaved him up into a fireman's carry, and adjusted the weight. "Up."

"Move." Vern tapped Manny, and they started to run for the door, as Carl shifted his position and started raking the cells with fire, bullets sparking off metal bars as the rest of the team sprinted for the exit.

They came out into the courtyard and faced yet another fight.

The Barrio 18 wing was awake and starting to break out to get at the MS-13 *mareros*. Durand had already dumped a full mag at the nearest door to keep them back. Not so much to keep them away from the *Mara Salvatrucha*, but to avoid getting the team caught in the crossfire as much as possible.

With Manny and Doug in the lead, they started to sprint past the *paisa* wing, heading back toward the exit and the vehicles.

Bullets spat mud around their feet, and Nick felt a few of them go entirely too close to his head with painful *snaps*, smacking plaster off the wall of the *paisa* wing as he ran, Casey's dead weight threatening to drag him down and make him stumble. He'd dragged dead men before, but carrying one in a fireman's carry was a new experience, and not one he'd recommend. It was one thing to carry a man on his shoulders who could lend at least a hand to stabilize himself, but Casey's corpse was threatening to slide off and make him fall over at any moment.

He reached the door they'd come out through and plunged through, even as Manny rolled out of the opening and barricaded himself on the threshold to cover for them.

Nick stumbled a little, especially as he found that he was now essentially the number one man, and he only had one hand free. He let his rifle hang and drew his Glock, getting out of the fatal funnel and covering down on the reception area, just in case.

His heart was pounding, his throat ached it was so dry, and Casey's weight felt like it was fusing his vertebrae. Manny was shooting, though he couldn't see at what. He could hear bullets hitting the side of the building, though, and he knew that shit was getting bad.

The rest plunged through the door as Manny ceased fire to avoid a blue-on-blue. Nick heard a grunt and a body hitting the floor. "Fuck!" Carl's blurted curse was laden with pain.

Then Doug was at Nick's elbow. "With you." They needed to get the hell off the X as fast as they could, and Doug was telling him that they had everyone.

Living, or dead.

Nick moved past the reception desk, where Hernandez was hunkered down with his hands on the desktop, just to make sure there were no misunderstandings. Abaeze was right inside, watching him, while Mike was outside, still maintaining visual contact with his partner. As Nick staggered out the door under Casey's weight, Mike pushed out with him, even as sirens erupted elsewhere in the city. There wasn't much time.

Mike started the second van while Nick got Casey's body into the back of the first. Only then was he able to turn and see that Saul was carrying a body, too.

It took only seconds to take stock and see who'd gotten hit.

Vern was limp and motionless as Saul loaded him into the second van.

It took seconds to get everyone in. Manny and Mike held on to the last, covering down on the open door while the rest got in the vehicles.

Meanwhile, the volume of gunfire inside the prison escalated. If they were lucky, the maras would think that it had been one of their rivals that had started this.

The two vans had been combat parked, facing the gate. This was where things could get unfortunate, if Hernandez decided to double cross them, but the gate swung open as they approached. Sirens whooped in the distance. The response to the violence was on its way.

The vans weren't exactly race cars, but they could still move faster than the up-armored jobs that Nick had gotten used to on contract elsewhere. They roared out of the gate and turned sharply north, making sure to take a different route out than they had taken in.

That was when their luck ran out.

Two trucks full of young men with guns came roaring up the road behind them, clearly heading for the prison. One of them turned into the gate, which was still open, but the other kept going, apparently following the vans.

"We've got company!" Manny was looking out the back, over Casey's body.

"Brake check 'em." Saul was in the front seat, and it just seemed natural that Saul was the one to make the call. "Get 'em off us."

Mike braked, and Manny threw the back door open, while Nick twisted around in his seat and leveled his rifle. The two of them mag-dumped into the front of the oncoming vehicle, shattering glass and punching holes into the hood with showers of sparks. The driver was hit first, as both of them were aiming at that part of the windshield as best they could. The vehicle started to drift to the side of the road, slowing as the driver slumped at the wheel, and soon it was dwindling behind them, even as more muzzle flashes flickered from behind it as the *mareros* shot back at them.

Soon, they rounded a corner and left the gangsters' vehicle behind, and Manny reached out, Nick holding onto his gear, to pull the door shut.

They sped into the dark, heading for the hills before circling back toward the plant.

Nick looked back at Casey's body, moving limply as the van rocked down the road. They'd gotten their target, but they'd paid a hell of a price for it.

Only time would tell if it was worth it.

As it turned out, they had less time than they thought.

CHAPTER
42

Trouble was already brewing when they pulled into the plant. There was extra security at the gate, and it looked like the entire D Team was up and on watch.

Saul was already halfway out of the passenger door before the van had even stopped moving. "What happened?"

Alex, the team lead for the D Team, loomed next to the vehicle, in full gear. "Had a vehicle try to run the gate about twenty minutes ago. We chased it off, but we've been seeing a lot of movement in Chamelecón and Residencial Brisas Del Merendon. I think that they might be getting ready for a big push." He paused. "We heard that the A Team's got Talbot Consulting on the run. Got them with a sting in Indianpolis, and they ran for Panama. Those boys just pulled a hit down there, and while we didn't get much in the way of details, I think somebody's not too happy about it."

"Shit." Saul looked back out the gate, toward the lights of the nearby neighborhoods. There were definitely headlights moving around, more than they'd seen most nights since they'd set up in San Pedro Sula. "Gonna be a long night, boys."

Nick was already out and pulling Casey's body from the back of the van. They'd have to do something with the corpses. They couldn't very well bury them with full honors in a Honduran cemetery.

He hoped that it wouldn't boil down to burning them with thermate grenades in an abandoned car in the jungle somewhere, but they'd all known that it might come to that, when they'd accepted that they'd be working extralegally. They might be doing the right thing, but that didn't make them any less outlaws to some people.

Manny helped him with Casey. Doug and Carl were pulling Vern out of the other one. Alex looked over at what they were doing, and his shoulders fell, just a little. "Oh, fuck."

"Let's get them somewhere out of the way, where the client won't see them, then we need to get ready to get hit." Saul was all business. He had to be hurting after losing Vern. They'd known each other a long time. There were a lot of relationships like that in Pallas Group. Goblin seemed to have drawn from a relatively small pool, mostly men who'd worked a fairly small number of highly classified contracts around the world since the middle of the GWOT.

Saul and Casey had gotten along like oil and water, but Casey still had been one of theirs. Saul might not mourn him deeply—Nick knew he probably wouldn't—but there was still going to be some hurt.

There just wasn't time to process it.

"Over this way. The secondary storage shed." One of the other D Team guys, a hulking redhead named Dave, whom Nick vaguely remembered from a trip to Libya, led the way. He was carrying one of the M5 marksman rifles instead of an AR-15, but he was big enough that the difference was hardly noticeable.

They carried the dead men over to the shed, laying them out and covering them over with some of the industrial tarps stored in there, though not before taking their weapons and ammunition. It might be needed, especially since they'd expended quite a few rounds inside the prison.

Nick took a deep breath as he laid the tarp over Casey's face, or what was left of it. He'd died quickly, at least.

Then there was no time to mourn or reflect. There were security positions to man, and so they turned and left their dead teammates behind.

There had only been so much they could do to harden the plant's defenses, at least without it appearing to be a firebase. The client wasn't comfortable with that, and it had appeared, from those few interactions they'd had with the Honduran authorities, that the Hondurans weren't either.

So, there weren't any proper fighting positions, dug in and with overlapping fields of fire. There were just sandbagged points in several of the outbuildings—preferably with as few volatile chemicals as possible nearby—where they could set up. Mostly with windows or doors facing the outside, though since the plant had been built as a chemical processing plant and not a fortress, those positions still left large swathes of the surrounding fields occluded. Which was why they had marksmen on the roofs.

His and Doug's position was in a small shed on the northeast corner that actually *had* been put there for just that purpose. It didn't look out of place, but there was nothing in it except sandbags, water, and extra ammo.

Currently, two of the D Team boys, a skinny guy named Glenn who looked about twelve to Nick's eyes, and a wiry, quiet man named Bill, were holding security in the shed.

"What up, fellas?" Glenn's voice was deeper than his boyish face would have suggested. Nick didn't really know him, but he knew enough of Goblin's hiring philosophy that he didn't figure the guy was quite the kid he looked like. "Thinkin' things are about to get sporty." He had already turned back to the window, which faced the northern field and the roads approaching the front gate. He spat a stream of brown liquid from the massive dip in his lip into a cup. "Last time I was in a FOB where somebody tried to run the gate like that, it was a *long* night."

That certainly established that Glenn *wasn't* some wet-behind-the-ears wannabe, even if Goblin had been likely to hire such a man. "Where was that?" Nick leaned against the wall and peered out into the night. The lights were all on, so his NVGs weren't quite as useful as they might have been, but he could still see more of the darker areas, and the dark shapes moving through the fields, with them on instead of off.

"Syria." Another squirt of dip spit. "Not too far outside of Green Village."

Nick kept watching the outside. Headlights were moving and getting more numerous, and he thought he could see the shapes of people moving around on foot near those headlights. If he wasn't mistaken, it looked like a mob was forming.

Well, *Mara Salvatrucha* wasn't stupid. They were savage and ruthless, but not stupid. If they really wanted to hem up the plant and its security, they could get close if they approached in a mob, without showing weapons. They knew that no American company would be willing to risk having their security shoot into an unarmed crowd. Maybe some would, but the sort of people that made up MS-13 tended to assume that their gringo enemies were weak and cowardly.

The jihadis had assumed the same thing and had often been proved more or less right. Nick had seen the same tactic used before.

The radio crackled. "Croak, Thumper, this is Salt. Need you guys back at the TOC if you can be spared from your position."

Glenn keyed his own radio. "Salt, this is Sky Shark. I'm here with Armadillo. We're good." He glanced at Doug. "No offense, boys."

"None taken." Doug keyed his own radio. "This is Thumper. Be there in two mikes."

Nick picked up his go bag and glanced back at Glenn. "Sky Shark?"

The younger man snorted. "Had a bad jump, my first out of Airborne School. Stole my squad leader's air, and he wouldn't stop calling me 'Sky Shark' for months. I finally resigned myself to it."

Nick nodded. He'd known a lot of callsigns that had started that way. "Good luck, gents." He got a wave from both men as he followed Doug out the door and back toward their TOC.

Saul and Alex didn't look happy, and neither did Carlos, who was standing back in the corner of the room as if he was afraid of the reaction that his mere presence might provoke. "What is it?" Doug's eyes narrowed as he took in the scene.

Saul sighed. "We're getting called off."

Nick frowned. "What do you mean, 'called off?'" He glanced at Carlos. "We're just supposed to leave these people to their own devices?"

Alex shook his head. "Not exactly. The fighting down here has Carr & Sons worried, especially after what went down in Indianapolis and Panama, in addition to the intel we got from the Talbot Consulting office here in San Pedro Sula. They've decided to temporarily evacuate the San Pedro Sula operation until things calm down."

Doug glanced toward the door, by implication taking in the perimeter and the fields outside. "With all this movement, that might be more easily said than done."

Saul nodded. "That's why we needed you guys. Neither Alex nor I think that we can get everybody out on the ground. Which means we're going to need somebody to run the gauntlet, get the handful in the hotel back here, and then we'll set up an LZ in the fields south of the plant."

"Have we got helos coming?" That was news to Nick.

"We will. That's still getting sorted, but right now we need everyone in one place." Saul looked each of them in the eye. "Like you said, things are fixing to get rough tonight, so we need most everybody here to hold the plant. We won't do anyone any good if the place gets burned down before the birds can get here. That means we can't spare more than four or five guys to go in and get the rest."

Doug and Nick shared a glance, communicating with that short look. "We're on it. Who else?"

"Mike and Abaeze are already at the vans." Saul looked over at Carlos. "There should still be about ten people there. Most of the rest of the plant personnel are locals, so we've got a total of about thirty engineers and management to get out."

That was going to be a pretty tall order, depending on the helicopters available. Between the security personnel and the Carr & Sons management, they were looking at close to fifty people. Depending on the helicopters that were available—provided they could even get into Honduran airspace—that could mean as many as five trips.

It really was going to be a long night, provided they got through the run to the hotel and back in one piece.

"We're on our way." Doug slung his go bag and led the way out.

CHAPTER
43

We might have set land speed records for the roads in Panama, getting to the north coast. Ordinarily it would have taken about an hour, but we made it in almost forty-five minutes. Not bad when you considered the very real possibility that Zhang's people might have called the cops on us. Not that I expected they'd say anything about the fact that we'd rescued a hostage and killed our way out, but they'd probably at least call in the vehicles as stolen, if only to slow us down.

So, it was with more than a little surprise that we were able to skirt around Rainbow City without being stopped or even getting more than what appeared to be a passing glance from anyone out on the road—and it was getting late enough that there weren't that many other cars on the streets and highways.

KG pulled out onto a narrow gravel road leading out into the coastal marshes, somewhat inland from the shore itself, and turned off the headlights. We did the same, dropping NVG tubes back in front of our eyes. It got dark quickly, despite the glow from Rainbow City to the north.

The lead vehicle stopped at the end of the road, opening up onto a clearing in the bush. The brake lights went dark, and then we were piling out, quickly establishing a perimeter, guns up and looking for targets. Panama might not technically be a hostile country, but after that night, it was hostile until we could get out and make the gear and weapons disappear.

KG was on comms for a few minutes, then went around to the rest of the team. "Bird is inbound. Five mikes. We need to get on fast as soon as it's down. Time is *very* limited."

I could bet. The timeline probably precluded filing a flight plan, not to mention the unlikelihood that any Panamanian flight controllers were going to okay a flight plan that terminated in an open bit of marsh.

We waited, quiet and in the dark. Even Rutledge, who was about as far out of his element as could be, kept his mouth shut, though when I glanced over at him, I could see that he was crouched low and shaking. The shock of what had happened over the last day or so, not to mention the killing he'd witnessed in Zhang's compound, was finally setting in.

I heard the bird after about two minutes. Scanning the horizon didn't reveal anything, which started to make me wonder. Goblin had produced resources—put together either through careful investment or extensive networking—that I'd never suspected, but I seriously doubted that invisible helicopters were among them.

Regular helicopters with pilots who were entirely comfortable flying a hand's breadth above the treetops was something else.

A blacked-out AW169 roared overhead and circled the clearing, as KG cracked an IR chemlight and tossed it just in front of our position. It wasn't the most orthodox LZ marking, but I'd marked landing zones with a single IR strobe before. As long as the pilots knew what they were looking at, it would work.

After one circle, the helo came in fast, flaring and kicking up bits of vegetation in a whirlwind of rotor wash. The pilot was good, setting the bird down with almost no bump at all, but I should have expected as much from anyone Goblin recruited.

"Let's go." KG was already up and moving. He'd hold on the ground just long enough to make sure that everybody was aboard, but the message was pretty clear. There was no time to dawdle.

Brian still had Rutledge with him, though he'd instructed the man to grab hold of his gear, freeing his hands so that he could use his rifle. He and Tom started for the bird first, with the rest of us forming a rough V behind them, shielding them as best we could from anyone who might come at us from the flanks.

We didn't think we'd been followed, but caution was definitely called for.

The side doors were open, and I could have sworn that the man in helmet and combat gear just inside was Goblin. Tom and Brian were already propelling Rutledge into the bird, while Ken, Custus, Rob, and I formed a rough perimeter around the tail.

It was going to be crowded, but the AW169 was a good-sized helicopter. It would accommodate all of us, just barely.

I stayed on a knee until the last moment. Getting jumped, whether by Russians, *mareros*, Zhang's hired hitters, or even just the Panamanian police, would be catastrophic at that moment. I held my position until I felt a hand on my shoulder, and KG yelled in my ear, "Last man!"

I turned and launched myself up into the bird, Goblin grabbing my arm and helping me the rest of the way in as he pulled the door shut. I had barely gotten my balance when I was almost driven to the floor as the helicopter surged up off the ground and into the air, the pilot dipping the nose and sending us hurtling toward the shore.

In seconds, as I got myself into a seat, we were out over the water, the lights of Panama receding behind us. We were clear.

For the moment.

***

The flight was a long one, after a brief stop at what looked like a small, hasty FARP in a clearing only a few miles away to refuel. Almost three hours. I dozed off and on for most of that time. It was late, it had been a long day already, and something told me that I'd need the rest.

Besides, catching a few Zs whenever possible had become something of an SOP, one that I'd readopted since Pallas Group's operations had become less close protection and more special operations.

So, while I wasn't exactly what I'd call rested when we flared and came in to land on the back deck of what looked like a superyacht, though one that was about the size of a naval destroyer, I wasn't as worn out as I might have been.

Which was going to be a good thing.

KG and Goblin led the way forward, until we were out of earshot of the still-turning rotors. The compartment where Goblin stopped and faced us looked like it was once a ballroom, or something like that. It was currently stacked with equipment cases, comm gear, and maps.

"I wish I could tell you job well done, gents, but we're not finished yet. As soon as that bird gets restocked and refueled, we're going to be heading right back out. Fortunately, I came prepared, so we've got relief pilots."

He pointed to one of the maps. "It's going to be another long flight, but we're already sailing north to close some of the distance. Romero and Carr have decided to evacuate the plant in Honduras, and we're going to facilitate. We've got another ship in the area—well, a friend who owes me a favor does—so we'll have a second bird. But it's going to be a *long* night, fellas, especially since I just got word that it looks like the bad guys might be massing for some revenge. The B Team took out one of their warlords tonight, and things are fixing to get *nasty*. So, reload if you need to, grab some chow, and get ready to get back on the bird in fifteen minutes."

I looked at Ken, we both shrugged, and then we headed for the pile of chow boxes against the bulkhead. Probably nothing nearly as fancy as that yacht was used to, but it was what it was.

It *was* going to be a long night.

CHAPTER
44

Nick was behind the wheel as they roared out of the gate, partially illuminated by the headlights of the growing crowd of vehicles moving down from the north. They weren't moving fast, but were spreading out across the fields. That looked ominous, especially considering what time it was.

Unfortunately, things were going to get worse before they got better, since they were going to have to drive closer to Chamelecón than Nick would have liked, but it was the only way to get to a major road that would get them across the canal to the northwest, at least without driving right *through* that ragged line of vehicles coming south from 33 Calle.

Nick was eyeing the lights in Chamelecón as they drove away from the floods that illuminated the immediate area around the plant. Doug seemed to be able to read his mind.

"Speed is security, brother."

Nick nodded, took a deep breath, and floored it.

The road wasn't the best, since it was Honduras, which was hardly even a moderately wealthy country. The van bounced and groaned as he stomped on the gas, but they were going fast enough by the time they passed the barrio that the nearest buildings flashed by, and while he was pretty sure somebody took a potshot at them, it was wild and went wide.

Then they were past the immediate threat and turning onto Cañeras road, accelerating once more. Nick wasn't so much worried about the risks of the drive—though they weren't inconsiderable—but he didn't want to spend so long getting to the hotel and back that they ended up cut off.

It took only minutes from there to get to CA13, take a right, then a hard U-turn and race north, toward the hotel. When they made the turn, though, Doug looked back.

"I think they sent somebody after us."

Nick took a look, but if there was another vehicle trailing them, he couldn't see it. There wasn't time to worry about trying to lose it, either, even if that had been an option, given how little traffic there was on the street.

He continued to accelerate, until he was getting awfully close to losing control of the van. With its high center of gravity, the vehicle wasn't exactly intended for fast driving. He only braked when it was time to get off on 33 Calle, though, heading toward the hotel.

That was a short run, and he blew out a deep breath he hadn't realized he'd been holding when they pulled up in front and he didn't see truckloads of thugs already laying siege to the client's accommodations. They were in the clear, at least for now.

He was still jocked up and armed to the teeth as he and Doug piled out and headed inside. Things had gone much too far for anything else.

Alex had provided them with a list of room numbers. Unfortunately, they weren't all in the same place.

"I'll hold the door." Doug stood just behind the van, where he could watch the entrance into the little sheltered parking lot in the courtyard. That would leave Nick to herd cats, but if they didn't keep their exit open, they could find themselves in an even worse position.

He didn't bother to grumble. He just ran for the door.

The first was right on the ground floor, fortunately, and he pounded on it, hard. When he didn't get an answer, he pounded again. This time, the door opened a little bit, and he saw one wide eye on the other side of the security chain. "What is it?"

"Didn't you get the word? We're leaving, tonight. You need to grab what you can take on a helicopter and get in the van, now."

The eye widened even further. "Oh. Uh... That's now?"

Nick bit back an exasperated curse. "Yes. Now. Right now. Grab your shit and get to the van."

Almost as if to punctuate his words, his radio crackled. "We just had a vic go past, and we got mean mugged. Time's wasting."

Nick turned back to the still-open door. "I've got to get the rest. You've got about two minutes. Move." Without waiting for an acknowledgement, he turned and headed for the next room.

***

Nick was surprised as hell, given how long it took to get everyone moving, that they hadn't been hit yet by the time he got back down to the vans. What didn't especially surprise him, though it did make him mad, was that not everyone was at the vans yet.

"Who are we missing?" His carefully cultivated civility was close to cracking. "We don't have time for this shit."

"Cora and Mike aren't down here yet." The voice was that of the older man who had answered the first door.

"Shit." Nick checked the list again. At least the shooting hadn't started yet. He turned to head back upstairs, just as a middle-aged woman, her face red and her breath coming in puffing gasps, rushed out of the hallway and toward the vans.

"That's Cora," the older man said. "That just leaves Mike."

Nick was already moving. He took the steps two at a time, heading up to the second floor where Mike's room was.

The door was open, and Nick shoved through unceremoniously, having neither the time nor the patience for this. He found Mike, a man in probably his fifties, and at least that number of pounds overweight, trying to stuff a bunch of things in a suitcase.

"No time, no room. Come on. We have to go, now." He grabbed a day pack, which was already full. "What's in here?"

"Just a few things, my meds, stuff like that." Mike had stopped packing, blinking at Nick. Nick grabbed him by the arm, shoved the pack into his hands, and propelled him, not gently, toward the door.

"We're leaving on helicopters, and there isn't room for suitcases. Sorry, but you're just going to have to replace that stuff later." He tightened his grip on the flab on the back of Mike's arm when the fat man tried to turn back. "Trust me, it's not worth your life."

That seemed to finally get through, and the Carr & Sons technical consultant assented to be propelled the rest of the way to the vehicles.

Doug already had everyone in by the time they reached the vans. "Got a suspicious looking vehicle parked across the street. This could get a little ugly."

Nick slammed the door as he swung into driver's seat. "Especially since we've got to go back the way we came." He grimaced as he put the van in gear. "Speed is security?"

Doug made a show of fastening his seatbelt. "Speed is security. Let's keep an eye out for impromptu barricades or IEDs, though."

"Way ahead of you." He pulled out, taking an immediate sharp turn to the left, and accelerated.

He saw the vehicle that Doug had been talking about right away. The beat-up old sedan might not have looked especially out of place, except for the man in the driver's seat, sticking his shaved head out of the window and watching the hotel intently.

The gangster started as the vans came speeding out of the parking lot, and ducked back inside the car. As they roared past, an arm and what looked like a Mac-10 came out of the window, and sprayed bullets at the rear van.

"Hoop, Thumper, you good?" Doug craned his neck to look back at the other vehicle.

"We're good. Couple more holes, but nobody got hit," Mike replied. "Keep pushing."

The sedan surged away from the curb, coming after them, but Mike must have twisted around in his seat and cracked the passenger door, bracing his weapon in the gap. He opened fire, and the sedan suddenly swerved wildly, either because the driver was hit, or else had panicked and was trying not to get hit.

Then they were back on the 33 Calle, heading back the way they'd come, toward the Boulevard Del Este, and their shadow disappeared around the corner. They were clear, for the moment.

Now they just had to get back to the plant.

CHAPTER 45

"Oh, shit." Nick hadn't intended to say that out loud. But the situation had clearly deteriorated during the trip to evacuate the hotel.

The plant was surrounded. Dozens, possibly hundreds of people were gathered around the fence though, so far, nobody seemed to be shooting. It wasn't quite the mob that Nick had been expecting, though he was pretty sure, just going by the numbers they could see from where they'd halted just outside an orchard, that there were a good number of unwilling conscripts dragged out of the barrios by the *mareros*. There was some yelling going on, with laser pointers flickering over the sides of the plant and a few fires in the fields, but nothing seemed to be cohesive, as if they were trying to stage it as a protest.

Of course, a couple of the riots that Nick had been around in the Middle East hadn't bothered with that sort of obfuscation, either. When they'd wanted to go wreck someplace, they just went to wreck it. It looked like the Honduran gangsters were following the same playbook.

"Salt, Thumper. We're to the southeast, but it doesn't look like we're going to make it back in. I'm seeing easily a hundred bodies approaching the fence with a good dozen vehicles backing them up. No heavy weapons in evidence, yet, but we're probably not going to be able to get through without a bloodbath."

"Good copy." Saul sounded unruffled. In fact, he sounded calmer than he had before they'd left, which probably wasn't a good sign. "If you can, go ahead and set up an LZ out there. The first bird is inbound, and will make contact on this freq." There was a pause. "We're trying to hold things off as long as we can, but I'm shifting as many personnel to the south fence as possible. We might have to break out and come to you. This isn't looking too good."

Nick glanced over his shoulder. The radios were inputting to their headsets, not a speaker box, so the client personnel hadn't heard that, which was probably good. The last thing they needed was to have the people they were trying to protect freak out.

Unfortunately, there was no way to keep them from noticing the encirclement of the plant, or the fact that the vans weren't getting any closer.

"What's going on? Why are we stopping here?" The voice from the back was already starting to rise, the fear palpable.

"We're here to wait for the rest." Doug kept his voice low, sounding almost bored. "The helicopters are coming here, so there's no reason to go all the way in."

It might not be the most solid excuse, but it was enough for the moment. Nick grabbed his rifle and stepped out, quickly sweeping the area around the vehicles. The fields were empty, and they'd killed their lights soon enough that they didn't appear to have attracted the crowd's attention.

They hadn't quite lost their tail, though.

As he finished his scan, he saw the dark shape of a sedan with its lights out creeping along Cañeras. "Whack. Seven o'clock."

"I see them." Abaeze was moving away from the van, into the orchard toward the road. "Looks like they didn't get the message back at the hotel."

"No, they didn't." Nick had joined him, leaving Doug and Mike to secure the vehicles. Two guns against the sheer numbers to the north wasn't going to do much, but if they got jumped from behind, they were screwed, anyway.

The two of them spread out, moving quickly from tree to tree, NVGs down again as the blacked-out car came closer. They could probably have engaged already, but Nick wanted to get close enough to make sure.

That it was the same car, he had no doubt. The bullet holes in the windshield made that evident. It wasn't positive identification that made him want to get close.

No, he wanted to make sure they killed the *mareros* before they had a chance to get a shot off. Since Abaeze hadn't started shooting yet, he was evidently thinking the same way.

They still could only let the bad guys advance so far. They had to already have eyes on the vans through the trees, though less clearly than the contractors could see them. Finally, they hit the point that Nick decided had to be the drop dead line.

He leveled his AR, picking up the red dot in his PS-31s, and opened fire.

The suppressor spat, the rounds still making harsh *hiss-cracks* in the night, and his first pair went right through the windshield, punching into the driver's chest and jaw. Meanwhile, Abaeze dumped more rounds into the passenger seat and the back.

They kept advancing on the vehicle as it started to slide off the road, the driver dead or dying, continuing to fire, their suppressors masking the flash and blast of the shots, though there was no completely silencing gunfire. They continued to rip bullets through sheet metal, fiberglass, flesh, and bone, until, in Nick's case, the bolt locked back. He transitioned to his Glock as he continued to advance on the car, slinging the rifle to his side as the pistol came out.

He held his fire, though, shifting around toward the hood, the handgun leveled.

The three *mareros* in the car were all slumped over, their blood painting the inside of the vehicle, dark in the grayscale of the PS-31's tubes. One of their weapons had fallen out of the shattered window onto the road.

Without another word, they held for a moment while Nick holstered his Glock and got his rifle back up. Then they headed back toward the vans.

They had an LZ to set up.

***

Things were getting spicy around the plant. The crowd was closing in on the fence, and the yelling was getting louder. Even as the contractors knelt near the IR chemlight that marked the LZ, the first Molotov arced, glowing and sputtering, over the fence.

It exploded with a splash of fire near one of the tanks on the south side. Fortunately, much of that part of the plant was still under construction, so there wasn't anything volatile stored there that could catch fire. It was only a matter of time, though.

Of course, having a helicopter land twelve hundred yards away was going to draw some attention. Fortunately, there was a canal between them and the mob, but that wouldn't hold them off forever.

Nick swallowed as he thought he could hear the growl of rotors in the distance. This was about to get really, *really* hairy, and not just for the four of them.

Because the PGS contractors couldn't go out on the bird. They had to get the client people on it and then hold the LZ for the next trip.

And they didn't have a whole lot of cover to hold off that mob if it came for them.

Of course, that wasn't the only issue. He hadn't heard any gunshots yet, but that was probably only because Saul and the rest were maintaining a hardassed enough presence that the mob didn't want to risk getting mowed down to rush the gate.

But they were going to have to come out of there, eventually, and then it was going to get ugly.

Then the bird was coming in, and the whole dynamic changed.

A few gunshots rattled in the night, answered by more *hiss-crack* suppressed fire, as the helicopter soared in, circling around to the south and then flaring and coming to a hover above the field where the marking chemlight glowed in IR. Rotor wash beat at the surrounding vegetation, the vans, and the people gathered around them. Then the helo was on the ground, the tips of the rotors glowing with static discharge in Nick's NVGs.

"Get them in!" Doug's roar was still barely audible over the thunder of the helicopter's rotors. Mike was already hauling the van doors open and propelling the Carr & Sons people toward the aircraft. Fortunately, they didn't need much urging, not after the violence they'd already seen that night. They all ran, mostly bent almost double for fear of the rotor blades, toward the doors.

Doug was at the side door, having a shouted conversation with the crew chief. Nick was out at the front of the lead van, watching the crowd. They'd gotten some attention, that was for sure. A few gunshots were coming their way, but at twelve hundred yards, it would take some phenomenal luck—or lack thereof—to get hit.

The rotor wash redoubled in intensity as the bird pitched its rotors to take off and surged into the sky. The pilot was good. He'd barely gotten airborne when he banked, skimming the top of the orchard's fruit trees on the way out, avoiding going right over the mob. A few desultory shots followed the helicopter, but they were too far away to be effective.

The first load was out. Nick and the others hunkered down, mostly getting into the prone, watching the road and the fields, waiting for the next shoe to drop.

Nick didn't know when the bird would be back, and it could be a very long time, regardless of how many minutes it took.

CHAPTER 46

"Feet dry! Ten minutes!"

It had been a hell of a long time in the helicopter. We'd flown from Panama to the yacht, then from the yacht to the ship belonging to whoever owed Goblin a "favor." That was *another* superyacht, with an even bigger helipad on the fantail, which could probably hold two AW169s, though it would be tight.

We stayed aboard that ship just long enough to refuel the bird, and then we were heading for San Pedro Sula. It was getting awfully late, though we'd gained an hour going back to Honduras from Panama. It sure didn't *feel* that way, but we at least had a bit more darkness to work with.

The bird that had been stationed aboard the yacht had already made one trip, but it had run into a problem on the return. Namely, that the PGS contractors and their charges were shut up in the plant and hadn't been able to get out, as the crowd pressed in on the fence, throwing rocks and Molotov cocktails when they weren't shooting.

It hadn't turned into a bloodbath yet, but as soon as the Honduran Army showed up—and we'd gotten reports aboard the second yacht that they were mobilizing—it was going to turn into one.

We had to get in there and get our people out before that happened.

The lights of San Pedro Sula flickered ahead, visible through the windscreen as I looked forward. I glanced at KG and the rest of the team. This was going to get rough.

Mainly because we weren't going back out on the bird. Not immediately. There wasn't room. We had to fight our way in, link up with Saul and the others, get them out to the LZ, load as many Carr & Sons people as we could up on the helos—the secondary bird was ten minutes behind us on this run—and then hold what we had until the birds could come back for us.

That was not going to be fun. Especially not when sunrise was less than two hours away.

The bird banked to the south, aiming to come in the same way the first one had on its initial run. It was the clearest lane, though it sounded like the Honduran authorities were already screaming bloody murder over the radio as we passed the airport. If there had been more to the Honduran Air Force, I think we probably would have been shot down as we'd gotten within twenty miles of the city.

The fact that we were flying about six feet above treetop level, having to actually pop up to go over power lines, probably had something to do with it, too.

Flames were already visible inside plant's fence as we came in on the IR chemlight that Nick and a couple of the other B Team guys had set out as an LZ marker. Things were getting bad already.

I could hear chatter over the radio as I piled out with the rest. "…eyes on a combined column of Humvees and Saladins on 33 Calle."

"Good copy. Frog has eyes on the bird touching down again. Five mikes to move. We're still getting loaded up." That sounded like Saul.

We spread out around the helicopter, and four figures in plate carriers and helmets came out of the dark near two big vans. I thought I recognized Nick and Abaeze. It was too dark and there was too much crap flying around from the rotor wash to make out the other two.

"Good to see you boys." That would be Doug. I'd met him once or twice. "As I think you can see, the situation is deteriorating fast. Salt is getting everybody still on the compound loaded up into a couple of old pickups and a box truck that delivered parts yesterday. They're going to try to break out of the south fence, since the Army's coming from the north."

"But they need somebody to draw that crowd away." KG finished the thought.

"That they do." Doug jerked a thumb toward the vans. "We can get closer with these, though they're probably going to get shot to shit. We'll have to go around that canal right over there." He pointed north and west. "The terrain's not good. If we try to draw them off to the west, we run right into Chamelecón, which is solidly bad guy land. That canal's going to hem us in on the east. But we've got to get that mob diverted and spread out so that Saul can get the rest of them out. It's going to be tough enough, busting through that fence."

"You're the man on the ground, Thumper." KG wasn't going to play the billet card. "Lead the way."

It took only a few moments to load up in the vans, though the side doors were left open. This was going to get hairy.

The helo stayed on the ground for the moment, the rotors still turning. I had a feeling that crew was at full pucker, and I didn't blame them.

With the lights off, the vans rumbled up the road, rounding the turn at the canal crossing and heading north along the bank. We held on as best we could while keeping our weapons ready.

The noise got louder as we got closer. Shouts, gunshots, small explosions. There were quite a few gangsters and their minions out there, and as we got closer and unassed the vehicles, I could see that they were already trying to get over the fence.

Or trying to push it over.

The flames were getting higher. It looked like they'd finally hit something volatile with the Molotovs, and a growing fire was engulfing the southwest corner of the plant. The "temporary" evacuation was looking like it was going to be more permanent by the minute.

We stopped about five hundred yards from the fence, and then, with a deep breath, Doug turned on the headlights.

He was feeling a bit more humanitarian than I was. I would have been fine with opening fire on the assholes throwing flaming bottles of gasoline into a compound full of volatile chemicals with our people in it.

At first, the headlights didn't seem to do jack. They were too far away to light up the crowd much, and they were so focused on the plant that they didn't even seem to notice.

"This is Salt. Going to need a bit more than headlights." Saul apparently was thinking along the same lines.

"Stand by." We were already spreading out, moving up along the canal. We hadn't gotten far, though, when somebody in the crowd noticed something.

Maybe it was the headlights. Maybe it was the helicopter sitting in the field to the south. They'd apparently already shot at the first one, but with it gone, they'd shifted their attention back to the plant. Now, however, somebody with a megaphone started yelling in Spanish, and a chunk of the mob broke off and started toward the south.

As they moved away from the flames, I got a better look. A lot of those guys were armed.

Perfect.

I couldn't say who opened the ball. But with a ripping crackle, we all opened up on the armed *mareros* who were hustling toward the helicopter.

These guys were gangsters. They had more training than most street gangs, and there were plenty of examples of the maras executing full-blown paramilitary operations. But in the early hours of the morning, and on familiar ground, even some of the best can get sloppy, and these fuckers weren't the best. Half a dozen of them dropped immediately, and they weren't diving for cover.

Then all hell broke loose.

Realizing they had another threat on their flank, even as the Honduran Army opened fire on the mob to the north with medium and heavy machineguns, the crowd started to waver. More gunfire rattled from within the crowd, as the *mareros* who really wanted blood started to shoot the locals they'd drafted into the mob who looked like they were going to run. Or maybe they were trying to shoot at us, and just didn't give a shit who they hit.

As if all that wasn't enough, Saul chose that moment to make their breakout.

Engines roared, and a box truck came speeding out of the unfinished part of the plant, accelerating toward the fence. Two battered pickups came after, and gunmen in the beds were already laying down cover fire, punching more of the mob off their feet and scattering still more as panic set in.

The box truck hit the fence hard, tearing the cyclone wire aside and cracking the windshield in the process. It went over the remnant of the wire and kept going, knocking a few of the crowd aside as it kept moving, the two pickups coming through behind it.

Fortunately, they just kept moving, going right past us and heading straight for the turn around the canal and the LZ beyond.

Nobody in their right mind wanted to stay there and try to slug it out with a couple hundred *mareros*, especially not when they were being driven our way by the Honduran Army. Tom and Brian started the retrograde, bounding down the line of the canal before turning and laying down cover fire.

Unfortunately, the flat field on the outside meant we had to either run across open ground as the dawn started to lighten the sky in the east, or we'd have to wade, which would be entirely too slow.

We ran.

It became less of a bound and more of a bump, as we stayed close to the canal and the vegetation that at least gave us a backstop to blend in with. As soon as the next pair met Tom and Brian, they got up and sprinted down another twenty yards or so.

We kept up the cover fire for a few hundred yards, until it became apparent that the mob had lost all cohesion and was scattering, most of them running for Chamelecón. Some were still shooting in our general direction, but it was getting light enough that it was hard to see with NVGs, let alone naked eyes. We ceased fire after a couple more bumps, and then we splashed across the canal, forced our way through the veg on the other side, and ran for it.

The vehicles were already at the LZ, and Saul and Alex were overseeing the process of getting the Carr & Sons personnel onto the helicopters. The second bird had landed, close enough to the first that there couldn't be more than a few feet between their rotor discs.

Again, Goblin looks for the best when he goes recruiting.

We were about halfway back when the first bird lifted into the air, rotating toward the northeast and dipping its nose to send itself hurtling through the early morning twilight toward the coast and the yacht beyond. The second wasn't that far away.

Then we pushed into the orchard and met up with the rest of the B and D Teams, while the helicopters' noise faded into the distance and the plant burned fiercely, sending up orange flame and black smoke into the sky and cutting us off from the Honduran Army column that now sounded like it was just shooting at anything that moved.

As we gathered into a perimeter in some Honduran farmer's orchard, KG checked his watch. "It'll be about half an hour before the birds can get back. Think we can stay holed up in here that long?"

"Maybe." Saul sounded a little doubtful. "There are going to be some of those *mareros* out for blood. We killed their First Word last night, and they must have figured out where the vans came from."

"I figured this was a contracted hit." Clint sounded a little surprised.

"I doubt it. This was revenge. We got followed a short way from the prison where old boy got schwacked, and they must have compared notes on the vehicles." He sighed angrily. "If we'd had more time, we might have set something else up."

"Well, that describes too many of these ops." Alex just sounded tired. "Let's hunker down and see if we can lose ourselves in the shadows for another thirty minutes."

***

Unfortunately, while we might have stayed hidden until the birds got there, there was no way to hide the helicopters themselves.

It was getting lighter and lighter. Sunrise was still a good twenty minutes away, but I'd already flipped up my NVGs because the contrast was shot. The gray predawn twilight was giving way to dawn itself, and colors were starting to get more obvious.

That orchard looked like a lot less concealment in that light than it had in the dark.

It would have been lighter if not for the ugly black cloud still billowing into the sky from the burning chemical plant. That wasn't going to be good for the health of the people of San Pedro Sula, but we hadn't exactly started that fire, so I wasn't that concerned about it. I *was* glad that the wind was blowing it away from us.

The bad part was that it was blowing it away in such a way that we didn't see the two pickups come out of Chamelecón until they were almost on top of us, even as I picked up the snarl of helicopter rotors coming back in from the northeast.

Humvees and Saladin armored cars had spread out around the plant, largely holding security for the fire trucks that were trying to fight the fire, but the smoke and the distance had disguised the oncoming vehicles from the Army. I didn't doubt they'd be on their way as soon as the helicopters set down again, but for the moment, those two pickups were our biggest concern.

Ken and I moved up next to a tree, off to the left from Nick and Doug. I wished I had an LPVO on my rifle, but we'd stuck with red dots for a while, since the majority of our work involved closer quarters than was practical for magnified optics. So, I had to make do.

I was pretty sure those trucks were full of bad guys, though.

When the helicopters came into view behind me, and they skidded to a stop, men in black and carrying guns jumping out of the backs, then I knew it.

We didn't hesitate. We were fewer than twenty men in a city almost wholly owned by vicious gangsters, and our ride out was almost there. Let these assholes hit the birds with a stray bullet, and we'd be in a world of hurt.

I shot the first one through the throat. I'd been aiming for his chest but got a little high. I shifted right as Ken blasted the man in the driver's seat of the lead pickup, and then a ripping fusillade of suppressed gunfire tore out from the orchard and dropped most of the rest.

Most. One had dropped as soon as the shooting had started, and now he got up and ran, shooting wildly back at us as he tried for the ditch off the side of the road.

Ken and I both shot him at the same time, sending him tumbling into the dirt with a spray of red.

The helos were right over us, then. "KG, KG, this is Gray Goose. Is…is the LZ cold?"

For a second, I felt a flash of dread that he was going to turn around and leave us. It was a long way to the coast on foot, and the yacht was fifteen nautical miles offshore, in international waters. That would not be a good several days.

"It's as cold as it's going to get." KG had lifted his head to peer at the helicopters, then back toward the nearest Honduran Army vehicles. Two of the Humvees and three of the Saladins were starting to come our way. "We have no time."

"Roger." If the pilot was considering leaving us, he must have had second thoughts. He dropped toward the ground, the rotors swirling the smoke around us as he landed. The second helicopter came in without hesitation, setting down a couple dozen yards over.

We didn't wait. We ran for the birds.

KG took one, Alex took the other. It was going to be a tight fit, and possibly slightly overloading the birds, but we piled on, the two team leaders counting men on, even as the Army vehicles trundled across the field toward us, and I had no doubt that some Honduran was screaming at them over the radio.

I felt my guts drop as the bird clawed for the sky. Would some trigger-happy gunner try to shoot us down? We weren't *that* far from the Saladins. And one of those armored cars did take a shot, muzzle flash bright in the smoke and the early morning light.

The round missed, and then we were streaking out over the jungle and the villages south of San Pedro Sula, heading for the coast and extract.

Behind us, the plant, and Carr & Sons' Honduran operation, burned.

EPILOGUE

It had been a couple weeks, but Romero still looked shell-shocked. None of us talked much around him, even as we went about our duties, wondering how long they were really going to last. Ken and I were both surprised we were still employed. Romero had made the appropriate noises about his gratitude that we'd gotten their people out, which was the important thing, but Carr & Sons had lost *millions* with the destruction of the San Pedro Sula plant.

It looked like we'd failed, despite the fact that we'd effectively dismantled Talbot Consulting. Even Thomas Zhang was dead. The news said he'd committed suicide in his mansion in Panama, but I didn't really buy it. I thought he'd probably gotten caught in the crossfire when we'd fought his Russian bodyguards.

But if the goal had been to safeguard Carr & Sons' operation to inshore from China, well. That didn't look like it had gone well at all.

Ken and I were back on the close protection detail. Romero hadn't said a word on the drive into the Nashville office. He looked like a man on his way to an execution, not to work.

To my surprise, however, Goblin was waiting in Romero's office when we walked in. "Mr. Romero." He stuck out his hand. "I'm sorry I couldn't come see you sooner, but there were a number of arrangements to be made."

Given the favors Goblin had called in during our operations in Central America, I wondered how much of those arrangements involved finding backups for those resources.

He had another surprise up his sleeve, though.

Romero sighed as he sat down at his desk. He didn't look up at Goblin at first. Finally, resting his elbows on the desk, he met the boss's gaze. "I want you to understand, Mr. Walker, that neither Jacob Carr nor myself consider your men at all responsible for the losses we've taken. I mean that. I've heard a couple of them muttering about 'mission failure,' but we hired you to keep our people safe, and you accomplished that. I've seen some of the footage from the fighting down at the plant, and I don't see how you could possibly have kept that from happening.

"However, it is true that, while the financial dismemberment of Talbot Consulting may be well underway, they still won. We can't afford to close the China plant, now." He looked down at the desk again.

Goblin, however, seemed unfazed. "Eh. It was a loss, certainly. But not defeat. Not yet." At the tone of his voice, Romero looked up with a frown.

The door opened behind us. "Mr. Romero, I'd like to introduce you to a man who is very interested in your company...for the opposite reason the Chinese were. Gage Romero, meet Merritt Strand."

***

Ken and I retreated. We weren't needed in there, and if there was anyone who could talk Romero into a partnership— that would probably result in an actual American plant, not a Honduran one—it was Strand. If anything, he'd gotten even more hard core since the fight for the Bowman Ranch. He'd recognized the war for what it was, and he was all in.

Goblin came out and softly closed the door behind him. "How are you boys doing? Recuperated from Panama and Honduras?"

Something about the way he said that made me study him narrowly. "Mostly. We ain't exactly young bucks anymore, but it's been a couple weeks. What's up?"

"Nothing immediate." He ushered us into a conference room and shut the door. "I was going over some of the emails you got from the shadow network, Chris. And I think I might have picked up on something.

"Just about every one of them used the phrase, 'Most excellent.' I've only ever known one man who used that phrase consistently, even in emails."

I raised an eyebrow. "You know who the spider is?"

"Maybe. And knowing who he is won't necessarily get us any closer to finding him. But if you boys are up to it..."

"Find us the cover and we'll do it, boss."

AUTHOR'S NOTE

Thank you for reading *Silver or Lead*. This one was slightly more speculative in many ways than the two preceding volumes, for a couple of reasons. One, there are no *documented* news stories I was able to find about this degree of criminal pressure aimed at a company trying to inshore from China. However, the fact of the matter is that there is a *lot* of money and influence that has been aimed at keeping the Western world dependent on China for any number of vital industries, including chemicals. Coupled with other examples of Chinese proxy warfare using organized crime, it seemed logical.

The other part lies in the situation in Honduras. That country is indeed a warzone between maras, and a large part of the influx of migrants coming north from Central America are refugees trying to get away from the gang wars. There is very little reliable imagery or information to be found online about those wars, however, so I had to do some filling in the blanks.

I hope you enjoyed this foray into the dark corners of modern warfare. As Goblin said at the end, it's far from over.

To keep up to date, I hope that you'll sign up for my newsletter—you get a free American Praetorians novella, *Drawing the Line*, when you do.

If you've enjoyed this novel, I hope that you'll go leave a review on Amazon or Goodreads. Reviews matter a lot to independent authors, so I appreciate the effort.

If you'd like to connect, I have a Facebook page at https://www.facebook.com/PeteNealenAuthor. You can also contact me, or just read my musings and occasional samples on the blog, at https://www.americanpraetorians.com. I look forward to hearing from you.

Also By Peter Nealen

Brave New Disorder (Pallas Group Solutions Thrillers)
Gray War
The Dragon and the Skull
Silver or Lead
Frontiers of Chaos

The Brannigan's Blackhearts Universe
Kill Yuan
The Colonel Has A Plan (Online Short)
Fury in the Gulf
Burmese Crossfire
Enemy Unidentified
Frozen Conflict
High Desert Vengeance
Doctors of Death
Kill or Capture
Enemy of My Enemy
War to the Knife
Blood Debt
Marque and Reprisal
Concrete Jungle

The Maelstrom Rising Series
Escalation
Holding Action
Crimson Star
Strategic Assets
Fortress Doctrine
Thunder Run
Area Denial
Power Vacuum
Option Zulu
SPOTREPS – A Maelstrom Rising Anthology

The Lost Series
Ice and Monsters
Shadows and Crows

Darkness and Stone
Swords Against the Night
The Alchemy of Treason
The Rock of Battle

The Unity Wars Series
The Fall of Valdek
The Defense of Provenia
The Alliance Rises

The American Praetorians Series
Drawing the Line: An American Praetorians Story (Novella)
Task Force Desperate
Hunting in the Shadows
Alone and Unafraid
The Devil You Don't Know
Lex Talionis

The Jed Horn Supernatural Thriller Series
Nightmares
A Silver Cross and a Winchester
The Walker on the Hills
The Canyon of the Lost (Novelette)
Older and Fouler Things

CPSIA information can be obtained
at www.ICGtesting.com
Printed in the USA
LVHW041512090723
751940LV00016B/855/J